I0576922

Charles McKew donor Parr, George Shaw-Lefevre Eversley

English Commons and Forests

Charles McKew donor Parr, George Shaw-Lefevre Eversley

English Commons and Forests

ISBN/EAN: 9783337329686

Printed in Europe, USA, Canada, Australia, Japan

Cover: Foto ©Andreas Hilbeck / pixelio.de

More available books at **www.hansebooks.com**

ENGLISH
COMMONS AND FORESTS.

ENGLISH

COMMONS AND FORESTS:

THE STORY OF

THE BATTLE DURING THE LAST THIRTY YEARS FOR
PUBLIC RIGHTS OVER THE COMMONS AND
FORESTS OF ENGLAND AND WALES.

BY

Rt. Hon. G. SHAW LEFEVRE, M.P.

CASSELL AND COMPANY, Limited:

LONDON, PARIS & MELBOURNE.

1894.

[ALL RIGHTS RESERVED.]

PREFACE.

I HAD some time ago collected the materials for, and had written, the greater part of this work, with the object of giving an account of the battle, since 1864, for the preservation of the Common lands and Forests of England and Wales. I delayed, however, completing and publishing it in the hope that a more favourable occasion might arise for claiming that the main object of the movement had been accomplished, either by the completion of the long series of lawsuits, which had for so many years been running their course in the law courts for the prevention of inclosures under the Statute of Merton, or by the adoption of legislation, which would render such litigation unnecessary in the future.

That occasion has now offered itself. During the past year, 1893, two most important results have been achieved. In the first place, Parliament has passed a measure for the virtual repeal of the Statute of Merton, under the assumed sanction of which, all the attempted inclosures of Commons, during the period referred to, were made. In the second place, after a struggle in the law courts of thirteen years, for the saving of Banstead Commons, in what it is hoped will be the last of the great Commons suits, Parliament, in spite of most

determined opposition before Select Committees of both
Houses, has sanctioned a scheme for the regulation of
these Commons, under which they will be placed under
the control and management of a body of Conservators
elected by the ratepayers of the district. It has
therefore decided that a Common may be practically
taken out of the control and management of the Lord of
the Manor and placed under that of an elective body
in the interest of the district.

These two important measures may be considered as
having virtually effected a legal revolution in the relation of Lords of Manors and their Commoners to
the public with respect to Commons. The fitting
occasion, therefore, has arisen for putting on record
the history of the movement, and for describing in
detail the course of litigation which has had so large
a part in forming public opinion and in rendering
possible this legislation.

I should have preferred that some other person
than myself should have undertaken this task. But,
in fact, of those who were concerned in the initiation
of the movement, I find that I am the only survivor,
who has continuously taken an active part in directing
the policy of the Society for the Preservation of Commons, and who is conversant with all its proceedings.
I must claim excuse, therefore, if I have occasionally
lapsed into a narrative in the first person, and have
referred to my own action.

I have to render special thanks to Sir Robert Hunter
and Mr. Percival Birkett, who were professionally

engaged in so many of the great law suits referred to, for the aid they have rendered in supplying me with information, and in assisting me in revising and completing this work. The account of the Banstead Commons litigation is mainly derived from a pamphlet by Sir Robert Hunter, whose able pen and wise counsel have contributed so largely to the success of the cause.

I am also indebted to Mr. P. H. Lawrence, who took so large a part in the initiation of the movement; and I desire to acknowledge the kind assistance of Mr. James Hole and Mr. Fithian, who almost from the commencement of the Commons Society have been its Honorary and Acting Secretary.

Some of the paragraphs in the opening chapter on the origin and history of Commons are taken from an account I published a few years ago of the then position of the movement for their preservation. The stories of some of the Commons cases, and especially of Epping Forest, may be partially known to the public, or may be found to some extent in the law reports, but they have not, I think, before been fully told, or collected together, with the object of giving a succinct history of the movement, and of explaining the process by which the Courts of Law, Parliament and the public have been gradually and fully convinced of the necessity of preserving our Commons and Forests, and have been instructed how to accomplish this object.

G. S. L.

January 12*th*, 1894.

CONTENTS.

CHAPTER IX.

ASHDOWN FOREST AND MALVERN HILLS.

CHAPTER X.

COULSDON, DARTFORD, AND WIGLEY COMMONS.

CHAPTER XI.

BANSTEAD COMMONS.

CHAPTER XII.

TOLLARD FARNHAM COMMON AND ROWLEY GREEN.

CHAPTER XIII.

THE NEW FOREST AND THE FOREST OF DEAN.

CHAPTER XIV.

BURNHAM BEECHES.

CHAPTER XV.

RURAL COMMONS.

CHAPTER XVI.

ROAD-SIDE WASTES.

CHAPTER XVII.

VILLAGE GREENS.

CHAPTER XVIII.

REGULATION OF COMMONS.

CHAPTER XIX.

ATTACKS BY RAILWAY COMPANIES.

CHAPTER XX.

THE REPEAL OF THE STATUTE OF MERTON.

MAPS.

ENGLISH
COMMONS AND FORESTS.

— ◆ —

CHAPTER I.

ORIGIN AND HISTORY OF COMMONS.

IN most parts of England and Wales there are to be found ranges of open land, which have never been subject to cultivation or agricultural improvement, and which have consequently remained in their original state of nature from the earliest times. Their permanence in this state has been due to the fact that the ownership of them is not absolute. They are burdened with the rights of numerous adjoining owners and occupiers to turn out cattle or sheep on them, and to dig turf or cut gorse, bracken, or heather thereon for fuel, litter, or thatching. The existence of such rights has prevented the nominal owners of the soil from exercising the full rights of inclosing and cultivating the land, and has indirectly been the means of securing to the public the unrestricted use and enjoyment of walking or riding over it in all directions, whatever may be their strict legal right. Such common lands are technically the wastes of the Manors in which they are situate, and must be distinguished from other lands, which, though open and uninclosed, are yet private property in the full

B

sense of the term, and which the owners could at any time inclose with fences.

These Commons are not to be found only in purely rural districts; many of them are near to London and other large towns. In such cases they form, as it were, oases of nature, in striking contrast to their surroundings. They have ceased, however, to be of any substantial profit to those who have rights of common over them. The growth of a large population in their neighbourhood has made it dangerous to turn out valuable cattle on them. Cheap coal has superseded the necessity of cutting turf or gorse for fuel. Bracken and heather are not wanted for litter or thatching. People have taken the place of cattle and sheep, and use the wastes for recreation, though it will be seen that the law has not recognised the change, or given full sanction to the new user. The common rights still subsist in law, though no longer of any practical value for the purposes which gave rise to them. They are valued by the adjoining owners of land only because they afford the means of preventing the owner of the soil, the Lord of the Manor, inclosing and appropriating the Common for building, and thus excluding the public.

Where such urban or suburban Commons exist it is difficult to exaggerate their value to the public. They are natural parks, over which every one may roam freely; for though the public may be trespassers in strict law, there are no practical means of preventing their going upon these waste lands for exercise and recreation. They are reservoirs of fresh air and health, whence fresh breezes blow into the adjoining town. They bring home to the poorest something of the sense and beauty of nature.

London has been exceptionally fortunate in this respect. Within fifteen miles of its centre there are no fewer than seventy-four such Commons, averaging 160 acres, and 120 smaller spaces, averaging 10 acres—making, with Epping Forest, a total of about 19,000 acres. Some of these, such as Hampstead Heath, Blackheath, Clapham Common, and the Hackney Commons, are bordered by a dense population. Others at a greater distance form almost a zone of open spaces, to which the suburban population is quickly tending. Thus to the West of London we find Wimbledon, Wandsworth, Barnes, Tooting, and Ham Commons, which, together with the Royal parks of Richmond, Bushey, Hampton, and Kew Gardens, make an almost continuous range of open land, which can never be built on. On the South are Mitcham, Streatham, Chislehurst, Hayes, Plumstead, and Bostall Commons, and the wide ranges of open land on the Surrey Downs, such as Epsom, Banstead, and Coulsdon Commons. To the East of London there is the great area of Epping Forest, of 6,000 acres, of which one-half has been rescued in recent years from those who had already inclosed and fenced it. The North of London is not so adequately provided with open spaces, and beyond Hampstead there is little but Stanmore and Tottenham Commons till we come to the Hertfordshire Commons, such as Berkhamsted,

B 2

beyond the fifteen mile limit. No other populous district is so much favoured as London in this respect. But there are not a few towns which owe a great part of their popularity as health resorts to the breezy Commons which adjoin them. What, for instance, would Tunbridge Wells be without its Common, or Harrogate without its "Stray," or Malvern without its wide range of open hills or chase, or Eastbourne without its downs on Beachy Head?

In rural England, though the Commons are not so essential for health and recreation, yet there are many districts which owe their residential charm and value to these wild and picturesque open spaces. This is specially the case with Surrey, Sussex, and Hampshire, which are greatly favoured by the number of their Commons still remaining uninclosed, by reason, probably, of the land being unprofitable for cultivation, and offering no temptation in past times to inclose them. In the more mountainous parts of England and Wales the common rights over wide ranges of land have been the means of securing to the public the unrestricted access to and enjoyment of the mountain tops, and have prevented the owners of the land from excluding the public, in the same manner as the Scottish landowners have done in the case of their forests and moors.

There is no accurate information as to the number and area of Commons which still remain uninclosed. So late as in 1871, the Inclosure Commissioners reported to Parliament that the Commons extended over an area of 8,000,000 acres, of which they said 3,000,000 were in the cultivated parts of England and Wales, and the residue in the mountain districts. Of this great extent they considered that one million acres might be cultivated with profit and advantage to the country, and that when this was effected there would still remain about one-sixth part of England and Wales open and uninclosed, and subject to common rights—an extent so great as to show how erroneous had been the apprehensions of the speedy inclosure of Commons.

Two years later, however, the same Commission presented a report to Parliament with a very different tale. They had, in the interval, made a detailed examination of the tithe commutation awards, which covered the whole country, and showed distinctly how much in 1834 was Common land. By this it appeared that there were at that time no more than 2,630,000 acres of Common or Commonable land, or five and a half millions less than their previous estimate. From this a deduction has to be made of land inclosed under private Acts between 1834 and 1845, and under the Commons Act of 1876, and also of land which has been filched from Commons under the Statute of Merton.* Making a rough estimate of these inclosures, it is probable that there remain from 2,000,000 to 2,250,000 acres of Commons still open. Of this, a very small proportion is believed to be suitable for cultivation as arable land. The remainder is either mountain land, which it would not be worth while to inclose with fences, or inferior land in cultivated districts or near to towns, which

* Deduction was made of inclosures under the Act of 1845.

might be of value for residential purposes, or for adding to parks and game preserves, but which is of far greater value to the public in its wild and uninclosed state, contributing so much to the amenities of the districts, and affording unrestricted enjoyment to the public.

Such Commons are confined to England and Wales; they do not exist in Ireland or Scotland. All the land in those countries, even where uncultivated and incapable of agricultural improvement, belongs to individual private owners, except so far as the recent Irish and Scotch Lands Acts have conceded rights of pasturage over adjoining mountain lands. There are no rights of common vested in adjoining owners, such as to forbid the inclosure and fencing of the land, and to prevent the owners of the soil excluding the public from it. Hence it arises that the Scotch landowners have been able to turn their moors into deer forests, and to prohibit the public from traversing them, or ascending the hills in search of the beauties of nature and fresh air. The reason is that Ireland and Scotland were not subjected to the Saxon and Norman Manorial systems, under which Manors, with their Lords and free and copyhold tenants, were created. The change from collective, tribal, or clan ownership of land to individual proprietorship was made without any transition, such as occurred in England under the feudal system. Had these countries passed through the same experience, it is almost certain that the occupiers would, at an early period, have been treated as the copyhold tenants were in England, and have had conceded to them fixity of tenure, with rights of pasturage and turbary over the adjoining mountains and moors; and the owners of such uncultivated lands would have had their ownership qualified by the rights of their neighbours, as was the case with Lords of Manors in England.

There has been much discussion of late years as to the origin of English Commons. Till lately, the views of the feudal lawyers of mediæval times were generally accepted, equally by antiquarians and historians, as by the Courts of Law. It was held that these open and uninclosed tracts were the uncultivated parts of areas of land, or Manors, granted originally by the Sovereign to individual owners, and that the rights of common over such wastes, enjoyed by the freehold and copyhold tenants of such Manors, had arisen from grants by their superior lords, or by custom, later recognised by law, in derogation of the lord's rights.

Owing, however, to the investigations of Professor Nasse, Von Maurer, Sir Henry Maine, and others, another theory is now more generally accepted : namely, that the common rights now existing are in most cases survivals of a system of collective ownership of land by the inhabitants of their several districts, the prevalence of which in the early stages of communities has been traced over the greater part of Europe. Under this system there was originally no individual ownership of land. It was owned in common by village communities. That portion of it only which was suitable and necessary for the production of corn and other crops was inclosed and cultivated; the remainder was open to the cattle of all; and all the members of the community were entitled to cut turf and bracken there for their fuel and litter. The inclosed part was generally divided into three great fields for a three-course system of husbandry, of which one field was in turn left in fallow. Each of these fields was divided into a certain number of equal parts, which were distributed annually by lot among the heads of families constituting the village community.

Very frequently the cultivated land was thrown open to the cattle of all, after the completion of the harvest, and until it was necessary to shut it off again, in the following year, for the next crop. Small portions of land were attached as gardens to the houses and homesteads of individual members, and acquired the status of private property. Other portions were inclosed from the open or common land, only as it became necessary to add to the cultivated part, in consequence of the increase of population.

By degrees the individual ownership of land was extended. The system of distributing the plots of the common fields by lot was given up; ownership in these parts became fixed in individuals, subject to the land being thrown open to the whole village after harvest. But the waste and uncultivated land still remained the common property of the community, and was called the " Folk-Land "—the People's Land.

It is certain that a very large portion of the inclosed part of England was in early times cultivated on this common field system, with its three great fields in each village or parish, and with its waste lands open to all. A large part of the inclosures complained of in Tudor times consisted not of inclosures of the waste lands, but in doing away with the system of common fields, and in converting them into individual property, freed from the obligation of throwing them open during a portion of the year. Such inclosures continued to be frequent, under the authority of private Acts, down to modern times, and not a few cases still exist of land called Common Fields, or Lammas Land, held on this system of tenure, and thrown open during a part of each year. Interesting examples of it will be referred to later in the cases of Tollard Farnham and the Hackney Commons.

The introduction of the feudal system gradually effected a great change in the relations of individuals to one another and to the waste lands. The new system had its origin in military necessity. The country was by degrees parcelled out into commands among military chiefs, who were at first appointed only for life, but who later acquired the right of inheritance for their eldest sons or heirs. The Chief assumed command, and later exercised the rights of property over the district assigned to him, which generally corresponded to the ancient village, and which became the "Manor." The Chief, thus appointed, had the right of summoning to arms the inferior landowners within his district or Manor, who thus became in a military sense his dependants, bound to render him military service. They held their land, however, on certain tenure, and

not at the mere will of the lord, and they had the
right of turning out their cattle on the waste land of
the Manor. An inferior class of persons, cultivating
small plots of land, fell into a much lower status, and
by a process of commendation or subjection, lost their
rights of property enjoyed under the Saxon system.
They were considered as having no rights independently
of the will of the lord. They held their land and
houses at his caprice. These people became the villeins
of the Manor. A yet inferior class of persons with no
holdings of land became the serfs or bondsmen of the
lord, without any rights whatever. The feudal Chief thus
became lord of the district or Manor. He came to be
regarded as owner of the Manor, subject to the admitted
rights of the larger landowners or free tenants; and
the Common or "Folk-land" was held by the lawyers
to be vested in him subject to the rights of pasture
of the free tenants.

The process by which this change from the Saxon
system to the feudal system was effected has been well
described by Monsieur de Laveleye. "The fief having
been granted by the Sovereign to the lord, the latter
assumed as a consequence that the whole land belonged
to him. He did not, on this account, suppose himself
able to despoil the peasants of the enjoyment of their
land or of their right of using the common Forest
or pasturage, but these rights were regarded as privileges exercised over the property of the lord."

Already before the Norman conquest this change
had begun in England, and was largely in force in

the time of Edward the Confessor. But as the result
of that event the feudal system was universally established. A vast proportion of the land was confiscated,
and was granted anew to the followers of the Conqueror,
to be held on military service; and they, on their part,
introduced the feudal system into the districts or
Manors so granted to them.

From this change, caused by the introduction of
the feudal system and the subordination of the rights
and customs of local communities to feudal lords, most
important results followed, which have made themselves
felt down to the present time, by creating a difference
between popular traditions and conceptions, and legal
theories.

An early result of the new position of the feudal
Chiefs or Lords of the Manors was their claim to treat
the common lands as their own property, subject only to
the admitted rights of the free tenants of their Manors,
and without regard to the users of their villeins and
serfs. There followed on this the further claim to
inclose portions of the waste for their own use, or
for the creation of small holdings, to be farmed by their
villeins. This claim was vigorously resisted by the
freehold tenants of the Manors who had rights of
pasture over the Commons. Ultimately it was decided
by Parliament (which then consisted only of Barons,
no popular representatives having yet been summoned)
in the well-known Statute of Merton (20 Henry III.,
c. 4, A.D. 1235) that the Lords of Manors should be allowed to inclose, or approve, as it was called, parts of

the waste lands of their Manors, provided it should
appear on complaint of the free tenants that there was
left a sufficiency of the Common to satisfy their rights,
with free access thereto.

The statute runs :—"As also because many great men in
England (who have enfeoffed knights and those who hold of them
in free tenure of small tenements in their great Manors) have
complained that they cannot make their profit of the residue of
their Manors, as of wastes, woods, and pastures, although the same
feoffees have sufficient pasture, as much as belongeth to their
tenements, it is provided and granted that whenever such feoffees
do bring an assize of novel disseisin for their common of pasture,
and it is acknowledged before the justices that they have as much
pasture as sufficeth for their tenements, and that they have free
ingress and egress from their tenement into the pasture, then let
them be contented therewith, and they of whom it was complained
shall go quit of as much as they have made their profit of their
lands, wastes, woods, and pastures. . . . If it be certified by the
assize that the plaintiffs have sufficient pasture with ingress and
egress, as before is said, let the others make their profit of the
residue, and go quit of the assize."

The measure thus passed was, in fact, the first Inclosure Act, but, unlike modern Acts of that kind, it had in
view the interests not of the community at large, but of
the great landowners.   Nevertheless, it threw the onus
of proof, whether sufficiency of Common was left for
the freehold tenants, on the Lord of the Manor.   But it
ignored altogether the use of the Commons by the
villeins in respect of their holdings of land, or by the
inhabitants generally, in respect of the cutting of turf
and firewood.   It enabled the lord, therefore, to inclose
without regard to these people.

As a large proportion, probably amounting to two-thirds of England, was at that time common or waste land of Manors, the right of approval thus conceded to the lords was of great value. It gave rise to frequent disputes between Lords of Manors and the free tenants of their Manors. The early law-books are full of such cases. Very often we find that inclosures were effected for the purpose of making parks for deer and other game. More frequent was the inclosure of a *pastura separabilis*, which it is often added *fuit quondam communis* and *quæ solebat esse communis totius villæ*, showing that the recollection of the folk-land of the vill had not been lost.

Later a much greater restriction was practically imposed on these inclosures, by the legal recognition of fixity of tenure, on the part of the villeins of the Manor, in the land which they occupied. This conversion of villeinage into fixed customary tenure, which was the origin of Copyholds, came about almost imperceptibly, without the intervention of Parliament, and by the gradual expansion of legal doctrines, borrowed by the judges from the Roman law. It cannot be traced earlier than the time of Henry IV. These Copyholders, when fixity of tenure was conceded to them, constituted the main class of yeomen. They had customary rights over the waste of the Manor, which were also recognised at the same time, and must have limited greatly the power of inclosing under the Statute of Merton.

About the same time, or perhaps somewhat earlier, the lowest class of dependants on the Manor—the serfs or bondsmen—became freemen. Some of them may have possessed houses and small plots of land inscribed on the rolls of the Manor, which entitled them to become Copyholders; but the greater number of them lived in cottages the property of the lord, or of the free tenants of the Manor, and on their emancipation from servitude continued as tenants, and did not acquire rights of property in their cottages as Copyholders. They were the ancestors of the agricultural labourers of the present day. It might be expected that, on the emancipation of this class, the law would have recognised as legal and valid the ancient customs of the village communities, by which they enjoyed, in fact, the privilege of cutting turf or wood, and of turning out their cattle on the waste of the Manor. The feudal lawyers, however, hesitated to recognise such customs.

It was not till the year 1603 that the claim of the inhabitants of a village or Manor to the legal recognition of that which they had always, in fact, enjoyed by custom was finally negatived by the Judges. A claim was made in that year by the inhabitants of the village of Stixwold, in Lincolnshire, to turn out cattle on the waste of the Manor according to ancient custom.* The Judges unanimously held that the custom pleaded was against the law, and could not be sustained; they assigned the pedantic and technical reasons that the inhabitants of a district are too vague a body to enjoy a right of a profitable

* Gateward's case, 6. Rep., 59.

nature; that such a right can only attach to property; and that, if conceded, there would be no person or persons in a position to extinguish or release the right. The case was of supreme importance, for it laid down the law for the first time, and has ever since been regarded as decisive. It finally extinguished the right of inhabitants, as such, and independently of any land they might own, to claim, by custom or prescription, the user of pasture, or of turbary upon the waste lands of a Manor. It will be seen later in this work how often this legal doctrine of the Courts that the inhabitants of a district are too vague a body to enjoy a custom or user of a profitable nature, or to prescribe for it, turns up to make difficulties and to defeat claims, which otherwise would appear to be just.

As often happens, however, when the Judges have laid down a broad proposition of a questionable character, their successors endeavour to whittle it down, or to set it aside by some ingenious quibble, so in this case it was later held by other Judges that the rule does not apply where the inhabitants of a district have been incorporated, for in such case there is existing a body, in whom the rights of common enjoyed by the inhabitants generally may be vested, and who can deal with them so as to satisfy the technical objections.

It was afterwards decided by other Judges, that a grant from the Crown to the inhabitants of a district, is a sufficient incorporation of them to satisfy the technical rule, and to enable them to claim the right so granted. Later still the Judges, in some cases, where the evidence

of user was very strong, have felt that they were bound
to find a legal origin for the custom or user, and have
gone so far as to presume that there must have been a
charter from the Crown in early times, though subsequently lost, and by this ingenious device have admitted
the rights of inhabitants in some instances. But these
cases have been few in number compared with the vast
number where, by virtue of the above decision, the
inhabitants of villages and Manors have been refused
legal recognition of customs and rights, which they
undoubtedly enjoyed from time immemorial, and
which were of the greatest importance to them. The
settlement of the law on this point enabled Lords of
Manors to inclose under the Statute of Merton, or
with the consent of the recognised tenants of their
Manors, without any consideration for the interests of
the inhabitants generally, no matter how much they
had actually benefited in the past from the practical
user of common rights.

So long, however, as a Common remained open and
uninclosed, the decision in Gateward's case did not
practically affect the position of the inhabitants, for as
residents in cottages belonging to the lord and other
persons, they continued to exercise the customary rights
of turbary or pasture. It was only when inclosure took
place that they suffered from the rule laid down, which
refused to them any legal claim to that which they had
practically always enjoyed.

The extent of Commons and open land in early
times was so great that it is probable they suffered

much shrinkage under the Statute of Merton—the ordinary form of inclosure—without seriously affecting the interests of the yeoman class or labourers. It was not till the sixteenth century that such proceedings began to cause discontent, and to affect the general condition of rural communities.

Throughout the reigns of Henry VII., Henry VIII., and Elizabeth there were grave complaints of the hardships inflicted upon the smaller yeomen and labourers by the inclosure of Commons. The copyholders, and smaller owners of land, were unable to resist the powerful and wealthy lords who inclosed, and the Judges appear to have lent their aid to those who were rich enough to pay for it. Frequent statutes were passed with the object of minimising the evil.

It appears that many of the complaints were directed not so much against the inclosure of Commons, in the ordinary sense of the term, as against the wrongful dealing with the lammas lands and common fields already alluded to. The tenants holding their lands in severalty during a part of the year were dispossessed of their holdings, and the land thus freed from common rights, affecting it during other parts of the year, was converted into private property and turned into sheep runs. The vast appropriations by Henry VIII. of the possessions of monasteries and other religious bodies, and the re-grant of them to courtiers and land speculators, led to the arbitrary exercise of power by the new owners, in striking contrast to the old-fashioned and sympathetic methods

c

of the ecclesiastical bodies. These new owners in many cases pushed their rights to the extreme, declared the rights of copyholders to be forfeited, and compelled them to give up their holdings or to accept leases for short periods.

Making every allowance for such acts, there still remains abundance of evidence that the inclosure of Commons, as we understand the term, was one of the main causes of discontent of the period. The Protector Somerset, in 1548, appointed a Royal Commission "for the redress of inclosures," and to inquire into the violations of law in ten counties where the main complaints had arisen. Among other things, the Commissioners were directed to inquire "whether any person hath taken from his tenants their Commons, whereby they be not able to breed and keep their cattle and maintain their husbandry as they were in past times." *

The Commission was a total failure. Witnesses were afraid to come before it, or if they came, and gave evidence against their landlords, they were made to suffer for it. Neither the Commission, nor the Courts of Law, were effectual in giving protection to the smaller Commoners.

The time arrived at last when the powers of inclosing under the Statute of Merton, leaving sufficiency for the Commoners, were practically exhausted, and when the Courts of Law gave greater protection against arbitrary inclosure under the Act, in defiance of existing rights. It was recognised that where, for the benefit of agri-

* Strype's Memorials, Vol. 2, p. 359.

culture, inclosure was expedient and necessary, and was desired in the interest of Commoners, as well as of the Lord of the Manor, some method should be devised under which legal partition might be effected, with due regard to the rights of all concerned.

In the reign of Queen Anne the practice began of applying to Parliament for private and local Acts, to facilitate the inclosure of commons with its sanction, and through the medium of independent commissioners, who were to allot the land thus dealt with among the persons entitled to share, in such a manner as to secure justice to all. From that time, till the contrary doctrine was revived a few years ago, it became the well-recognised opinion of lawyers that the Statute of Merton was practically obsolete, and that it was unsafe and unjust to attempt any considerable inclosure of a Common without the special sanction of Parliament. And although here and there small portions of Commons may have been filched under the Act, or under customs of certain Manors to inclose with the consent of the homage of Copyholders, yet in the main no serious attempt was made, for many generations, to inclose any substantial portions of Commons without obtaining the sanction of an Act of Parliament. The enormous number of private Acts for this purpose during the two hundred years from the commencement of such a course is the best testimony to the impossibility of proceedings under the Statute of Merton.

With the growth of population and the extension of manufactures, the inducement to make the most out of

the land, and for this purpose to inclose such Commons
and wastes of Manors as were suitable for cultivation,
greatly increased. It was recognised that it was a
matter of national importance and almost of safety
to add to the area of cultivated land. From the date
of the fall of the Stuarts, when England began to
intervene more actively in the affairs of the Continent,
and was seldom for many years without the luxury
of a foreign war, till the adoption of Free Trade in
1846, there was no hesitation or doubt as to the policy
of promoting inclosures. Under more than 4,000
separate Inclosure Acts, upwards of 7,175,000 acres
of Commons or common fields were inclosed.

The addition of so large an area to the cultivated
land of England and Wales, was doubtless of considerable advantage, by adding to its productive power, and
by affording additional employment for labourers in
rural districts. But it was not an unmixed benefit.
From the manner in which these inclosures were carried
out they had other and opposite effects. It is now
generally admitted that they were a large cause of the
extinction of the class of small yeomen, cultivating their
own land. The holdings of these men were of such a
size, that the rights attaching to them, of turning out
cattle on the waste lands, were of the greatest importance,
and indeed indispensably necessary, to their successful
cultivation. When these rights were detached from
the holdings, and were compensated for in money or by
allotments of land at some distance, the holdings could
no longer be cultivated at a profit. The owners were

eventually compelled to sell, and their land was bought up by the larger owners of the district. This effect may be illustrated by the fact that only in places where large Commons, or Forests, or waste lands still exist, are there to be found any considerable number of small ownerships and small holdings of land—as in Cumberland and Westmorland, in the mountainous parts of Wales, and on the borders of such Forests as Dartmoor and the New Forest.

The inclosures were also carried out without any regard to the interests of the agricultural labourers of the districts concerned. It has already been shown that the law did not recognise that these labourers had any rights whatever over the Commons, unless they were owners of land, however much they might have benefited from the usages which prevailed, so long as the wastes remained open and uninclosed. The In-closure Acts made no provision therefore in the nature of compensation to labourers, and no consideration was given to them. They had no *locus standi* to oppose such private Acts, even if they had the means. No local inquiries were held to ascertain what were the wishes and interests of these people. It has generally been admitted that great injustice was often done, and that inclosures were frequently authorised, where no public advantage accrued to the district, and where no attention was given to the change effected in the condition of the labourers.

The complaints became so frequent that at last Parliament was compelled to interfere, and the General

Inclosure Act of 1845 was passed for the purpose mainly of withdrawing the consideration of such schemes from Committees of Parliament, and substituting local inquiries held by independent Commissioners. It also introduced uniformity in the proceedings of inclosure. It provided that no application for this purpose should be made without the consent of one-third of the Commoners, and that no scheme should be finally sanctioned unless two-thirds of them gave their approval. It directed that all schemes for the inclosure of Commons, as distinguished from commonable land,* where approved by the Commissioners, were to come under the revision of Parliament in Annual Confirmation Bills. In respect of Commons within fifteen miles of London, or within five miles of towns of 10,000 inhabitants or upwards, it required that special reports should be made as to the expediency of inclosure. It gave power, within certain very narrow limits, to the Commissioners to require that allotments should be made for recreation and for field-gardens for the labouring people.

This Act was passed in 1845, just before the adoption of Free Trade, and the abandonment of the ᐧprotective system, and when it was still the general belief that inclosures were beneficial, and even necessary, by adding to the area of cultivated land and giving increased employment to labourers. The Act, though a vast improvement over the previous practice of inclosure under private Acts, was in its practical working almost

---

* This provision was afterwards extended to all inclosures.

as detrimental to the interests of the labouring people.
The Inclosure Commission proceeded on the principle
that its main function was to facilitate inclosures,
whether public interests were involved or not. Many
Commons were undoubtedly extinguished under its
authority, where no public interest whatever was concerned by the increase of cultivation or otherwise, and
where it would have been more to the advantage of the
public that they should remain open.

Between the years 1845 and 1869, 614,800 acres of
common land were inclosed under orders approved by
the Commission, and sanctioned by Parliament in the
annual Confirmation Acts. Of this great extent only
4,000 acres were set apart for public purposes—namely,
1,742 acres for recreation grounds, and 2,220 acres for
garden allotments for the labouring people. In great
numbers of cases the provision was miserably scanty
and inadequate. The plots selected for such purposes
were often the least suitable, and at a great distance
from the villages. No regard was had to public
interests. Commons were often inclosed in the neighbourhood of towns, where the land was not required or
suitable for cultivation, and where the interests of the
public were more concerned in leaving them open for
the recreation of the people.

Until, however, about the year 1864 little or no
public attention was directed to the subject. The annual
Acts confirming the schemes of the Inclosure Commissioners were passed as a matter of course, with very
rare discussion. The general drift of opinion was still

in favour of inclosure. So late as 1851 Parliament approved the disafforesting and inclosure of Hainault Forest, one of the most beautiful sylvan districts within reach of London. A Committee of the House of Commons recommended a similar scheme for Epping Forest, and its inclosure subject to a small allotment in favour of the public. The same utilitarian spirit threatened the New Forest and the Forest of Dean.

Between the years 1860 and 1870, however, there arose two very distinct movements with respect to Commons: the one of opposition altogether to their inclosure, when within reach of large towns, and especially of London, on the ground that they are of infinitely greater value to the public as open spaces for health and recreation than as cultivated land or for building sites: the other, from the point of view of the agricultural labourer, whose interests had been so shamefully neglected in past inclosures, claiming that in the future no inclosures should take place, even in rural districts, unless they should be distinctly proved to be for the public interest of the district, by adding to the production of the soil; and insisting that where inclosures might be thought advisable, there should be far greater regard for the interests of the labouring people and for the public interests of the district.

These movements were both promoted by the altered conditions brought about by Free Trade in corn. When so large a proportion of the food of the country was imported, it became a matter of little account whether a few more acres of indifferent land were added,

or not, to the cultivated area; and people began to see
that such open spaces in their natural state, adding
so much to the beauty of their districts and to the
general enjoyment of the public, had a value, which
would be lost if the land were inclosed and ploughed up.

Coincident with these movements, a change took
place in the condition of many Commons. The rights
of common, whether of turning out cattle or sheep on
them, or of cutting turf and bracken, were more and
more neglected and disused, where the Commons were
in populous places. The Manor Courts formed by the
freehold and copyhold tenants of the Manors, formerly
held with regularity, and attended with zeal, fell into
disuse. The Court rolls, which for centuries had been
kept up, were often discontinued. The Lords of
Manors, who in olden times acted in the position of
trustees or guardians for their tenants, maintaining
order on the wastes, and settling disputes between the
Commoners, abandoned this supervision, and allowed
the Commons to become subject to nuisances. Often
they complained that they were wholly without the
means of maintaining order in their Manors. The
enormous increase in the value of land in the neighbourhood of towns, and especially of London, offered a
great inducement to them to convert the land into building sites. When they found that public opinion was
setting against these inclosures through the processes
provided by Parliament, they advanced the claim through
their lawyers that the old and forgotten Statute of Merton
might be furbished up to empower them to realise the

great value of their Commons; and they maintained that the disuser of rights by the Commoners had operated as an abandonment of such rights, enabling them to put in force their powers under the Statute. In the succeeding chapters the development of the two movements, thus alluded to, will be described, and it will be shown how the new contentions of Lords of Manors and their attempts to appropriate the Commons have been met, and finally defeated, both in the Law Courts and in the Legislature.

CHAPTER II.

THE COMMITTEE OF 1865 ON METROPOLITAN COMMONS.

THE first movement for dealing with a Common in the interest of the public arose in respect of Wimbledon Common—one of the largest, most beautiful, and best valued of those in the neighbourhood of London—and at the instance of its lord.

In the autumn of 1864 Earl Spencer, the Lord of the Manor of Wimbledon, announced his intention to dedicate the greater part of this Common to the public. In bringing his proposal before the Commoners and Inhabitants of Wimbledon, he pointed out the very great changes which had occurred within recent years, by the growth of a large suburban population in the neighbourhood of the Common, and the grave responsibilities and difficulties entailed upon him as Lord of the Manor; he said that, however anxious he had been to fulfil these duties in an unselfish manner, and to consult the interests of the neighbourhood, he had found his powers as lord were inadequate to cope with the various cases in which complaint had been made to him, by the inhabitants and others, in relation to the want of drainage, to petty encroachments on the Common, to the gipsies and tramps who frequented it, and to the rubbish-heaps and other nuisances which disfigured it, and generally as to the want of power to improve it, and to manage it in the interest of the public.

The scheme which he propounded for remedying these evils, and which was in the next year embodied in a private Bill laid before Parliament, involved the sale of about one-third of the area of the Common, consisting of that portion of it known as Putney Heath, lying on the right hand of the London and Kingston road. The proceeds of this sale were to be expended in buying up and extinguishing any rights, which the Commoners might have over the Common, and in fencing, draining, and improving the remaining 680 acres. The public Park thus to be created, as distinguished from an open Common, was to be vested in trustees, one of whom was to be the Lord of the Manor. The trustees were to have powers to make bye-laws for the management and regulation of the Park. They were also to let the pasturage of it, and to lease or work the gravel-pits; the proceeds thus expected to be realised, were to be applied, first in payment of a rent-charge to the Lord of the Manor, equal to the average of his past receipts from gravel and otherwise, and secondly to the current expenses of management, and to the improvement of the Park. The Lord of the Manor was also to be allowed to erect a residence for himself in the centre of the Park, and he was to be responsible for any expense of maintaining it beyond the income derived as above.

This proposal was stated to be founded on the legal opinion that the Lord of the Manor was practically owner in fee of the Common; that the Commoners were so few in number that they might be disregarded, as they could oppose no obstacle to its inclosures under the Statute of Merton; and that practically the lord could do as he liked with it. In this view there would not be a doubt as to the very generous nature of the offer, or as to the intentions which actuated it. On the other hand, it soon became apparent that the Commoners of Wimbledon took a very different view of their legal rights, and of their relative position to the lord. They denied his right or power to inclose the waste; they did not desire to be bought out; still less did they wish that the area of the Common should be reduced by one-third; they did not approve of the proposal to turn what was to remain of the Common into an inclosed and fenced park. Those who lived in the neighbourhood of Rochampton and Putney objected most strongly to the sale of that portion of the Common which was nearest to them. A committee was consequently formed of the commoners and inhabitants of Wimbledon, with Mr. Peek (now Sir Henry Peek) as their chairman, which entered into an investigation as to the legal position of the Lord of the Manor and the commoners, and was prepared to contest that part of the scheme which proposed the sale of Putney Heath, or the impaling and fencing of the residue of the Common.

Meanwhile, the subject of the London Commons, their neglected condition, the threatened inclosures of them, and the inroads which had been made on them by various Railway Companies, had greatly roused public attention in London. In the session of 1865, Mr. Doulton, then

Member for Lambeth, moved in the House of Commons
for a Committee to inquire into the best means of
preserving for the use of the public the Forests,
Commons, and Open Spaces in the neighbourhood of
London. In the discussion which followed, much was
said about the scheme for Wimbledon Common,
and it was arranged that the Bill relating to it
should be included in the inquiry. The Committee,
consisting of twenty-one members, was presided over
by Mr. Locke, Member for Southwark. I had
myself taken part in the debate on the subject, and
was appointed a member of the Committee, my interest
having arisen from the fact that I had lived many
years with my father at Wimbledon, and was, therefore,
well acquainted with the Common.

Before this Committee, evidence was given by Lord
Spencer's legal advisers to the effect that he was practically owner of the Common; that the rights of the Commoners were so limited as to be unworthy of consideration, and as to offer no substantial check to his power;
that the public had no legal rights whatever to
the use or enjoyment of the waste; that in this
view the proposed scheme ought to be accepted by the
commoners and inhabitants without cavil. On the
other hand, the commoners asserted with equal confidence their rights over the Common; they denied the
claims of the Lord of the Manor; they claimed for
themselves rights over it sufficient to prevent all possibility of inclosure; they alleged a decided preference
for an open stretch of wild uncultivated land, such as

the Common was and is, as compared with a fenced park, however well drained and planted. They did not object to placing the Common under a scheme of regulation, but they claimed a large share in its management and control. They offered to raise funds in the district for any drainage that might be considered necessary; and they contended that, as their own rights of turning out cattle were in no way detrimental to the Common, but rather a safeguard against its inclosure, there was no necessity for selling any portion of it in order to compensate them.

It was obviously impossible for the Committee to decide on these disputed questions of law and fact as to the relative position of the Lord and the Commoners; nor did it seem necessary to solve them. They considered, however, that, apart from the question of taste between a free and open Common and an inclosed Park, there was much reason in the objections of the Commoners. If the land were allowed to remain open, there would be no expense in fencing it; there was also no object in compensating the Commoners for rights, which, if properly regulated, would be in no way prejudicial to the Common, or to the interests of the public.

The Committee, therefore, advised that while there was good reason for putting the Common under proper regulation, for the preservation of order and the prevention of nuisances, it was not expedient that it should be fenced or inclosed, or that the Commoners' rights should be extinguished, and that consequently it was not necessary that any part of it should be sold. After these recommendations, and upon the understanding that the scheme of fencing the Common should be dispensed with, the Wimbledon Bill was read a second time in the House of Commons, but was subsequently not further proceeded with.

Meanwhile, Mr. Doulton's Committee continued their inquiry into the other Commons round London. Evidence was laid before them as to the condition, physical and legal, of many of the most important of these open spaces, such as Hampstead, Blackheath, Barnes, Wandsworth, Tooting, Epsom, Banstead, Hackney, and Epping Forest.

In all these and other cases, the evidence showed that the difficulties, which had been described by Lord Spencer with regard to Wimbledon Common, existed in at least an equal degree. The surface of most of the Commons had been greatly deteriorated by excessive and careless digging of gravel-pits, by the collection of nuisances, the deposits of cinder and dust-heaps and manure, and by the firing of gorse or brushwood. Complaints were made that tramps and bad characters frequented the wastes without interference by the police. In some cases the Lords of the Manors admitted and deplored their inability to deal with these abuses. In other cases, it was apparent that there was neither the will nor the means to check them, as it was hoped that the want of order and the unchecked existence of nuisances would act as inducements to the commoners and residents to join in inclosure rather

than submit to unabated evils. It was found that some
of the Commons, such as Wandsworth, Mitcham, and
Barnes, had been intersected by railways, which greatly
interfered with their beauty and value. The Railway
Companies apparently had discovered that it was cheaper
to engineer their lines through such open spaces, than
through private property. There was no authority whose
duty it was to secure that, in the consideration of such
schemes, the interest of the public in the maintenance
of Commons should be properly regarded.

Confining themselves to the cases of Commons
within fifteen miles of London, the Committee reported
as to the supreme necessity of preserving all that still
remained open, for the health and recreation of the
people and for the training of volunteer corps. With
respect to the proper method of preserving these open
spaces, there was great difference of opinion. The
Lords of Manors, through their agents and lawyers,
contended that they were practically masters of the
position; that the rights of Commoners were so few in
number and so limited in value, that they might be
disregarded; that most of these rights had lapsed
through non-user; and that under the Statute of Merton or under customs of their Manors, they could
inclose without regard to the interests of the public, to
whom they denied any right, no matter how long or
how extensive and long-continued had been the user
for recreation.

On the other hand, it was contended with equal
confidence, on behalf of the commoners and residents

D

in the neighbourhood of Commons, and by able lawyers, that in every instance, there were rights of common subsisting at law, sufficient to prevent inclosure, as had been the case from the earliest times, if enforced by the holders in the Courts of Law.

A scheme was propounded by Sir John Thwaites, then Chairman of the Metropolitan Board of Works, on behalf of that body, for dealing with all the Commons within their district in a comprehensive manner. He proposed that the Board should be empowered to buy up the interests of the Lords of Manors and of the Commoners, and thus to become owners in fee of the Commons freed from such rights. It was admitted that such a scheme would involve an outlay of not less than £6,000,000, and that it would be impossible to provide for it by an increase of the rates. It was proposed, therefore, to meet the outlay by selling portions of the Commons for building purposes. In some respects the scheme was not dissimilar to that which had been propounded for Wimbledon Common.

The Report, agreed to by a majority of the Committee, was drawn up, in consultation with myself, by Mr. Philip Henry Lawrence, a solicitor of eminence in London, who, as a resident at Wimbledon, was greatly interested in the subject, and whose subsequent services to the cause of Commons cannot be over-estimated. This Report condemned the scheme of the Metropolitan Board as unwise and unnecessary, and as certain to result in a most serious diminution of the area of the London Commons. " There is no open space," it said,

" within fifteen miles of London which can be spared, or which should be reduced in area."

On the question of the existence of rights of common over the London Commons as against the rights of the Lords of Manors, the Report adopted the views of those who contended that the non-user of such rights of late years, had not operated as a legal abandonment of them; it expressed the confident opinion that rights of common subsisted over all the Commons sufficient, if enforced at law, to abate any attempted inclosure under the Statute of Merton; but it pointed out the very great hardship that the owners of such rights should be called to contest the arbitrary inclosures of Lords of Manors, in the expensive legal proceedings necessary for the vindication of their rights.

On the subject of the legal position of the public of London in respect of the use and enjoyment of their Commons, it said :—

" The rights of the public at large are vague and unsatisfactory, for while it is generally acknowledged that a right may exist to traverse any of these spaces at will in all directions, and that no action for trespass would lie for such traversing, and even that a ' servitus spaciandi' over open ground which has in some measure been devoted to public use is also intelligible and known to the law, yet the legal authorities appear most unwilling to admit any general public right to exercise and recreation upon any of these spaces, although such right may from time immemorial have been enjoyed, contending that it must be limited to some certain defined body of persons, as the inhabitants of a particular parish or the tenants of a particular manor.

D 2

"The opinions so expressed (as to the soundness of which, however, your Committee give no opinion) have proceeded from judicial decisions of ancient date; your Committee cannot help observing that, even if binding on legal tribunals, they appear to rest upon no very intelligible principle. Your Committee are at a loss to conceive why, upon general principles, a right of enjoyment which may be acquired by the inhabitants of a small hamlet should be denied to the inhabitants of the metropolis, or even to the general public. . . . It may deserve consideration whether some declaratory law should not be passed to remedy what appears to us to be a somewhat narrow doctrine of the Courts, hardly in accordance with the general principles of the law, having regard to the increased population of large towns in later times.

"The policy which dictated the earlier legislation in respect to Commons seems to have proceeded without regard to those particular interests of the public which we are now considering; but nevertheless, there is nothing to show that that legislation proceeded upon other than grounds of general public advantage.

"In early times the great extent of Commons and waste lands in England was regarded as prejudicial to the public, on whose behalf it may be fairly assumed that the Legislature acted in facilitating their inclosure, in order that agriculture might be promoted and the whole country benefited by an increase in the produce of the land."

The report then proceeded to discuss the Statute of Merton, and to show that it was passed in the interest of agriculture, and that in more modern times it had been superseded by Private and Public Inclosure Acts.

"It appears," the report added, "that even in agricultural districts any attempt at inclosure of lands under the alleged authority of the Statute of Merton would be entirely inconsistent with the more comprehensive legislation of the present day. With agricultural districts they have no concern in their present inquiry; but with regard to Commons near large towns, as these latter have rapidly increased in population, the necessity of providing open spaces for health and recreation has become paramount to the mere improvement of those lands in an agricultural sense; and seeing that the inevitable result of the inclosure by private individuals of lands in the populous suburbs of the metropolis would be not even agricultural improvement, but building, they have no hesitation in coming to the conclusion that it is time the Statute of Merton should be repealed. It may be that, owing to the very enjoyment by the public of the Commons in the neighbourhood of the metropolis, these spaces have become unproductive as pastures, and that much evidence of the rights formerly exercised by the Commoners has become lost. In such cases it might fairly be argued that the Commoners, by their acquiescence in the public enjoyment, had virtually transferred their rights to the public; and it might not be unjust that the Legislature should sanction and confirm such transfer rather than that the Lords should reap the benefit of the lapse of the Commoners' rights."

The Committee further recommended that no inclosures should be authorised within the Metropolitan Police area under the provisions of the Inclosure Act of 1845, and they condemned the scheme of purchase put forward by the Metropolitan Board.

"If," they said, "the Legislature should adopt the recommendation not to authorise any further inclosures within the Metropolitan area, we do not see the necessity for the immediate expenditure of so large a sum of public money as such purchase would require. We have already stated our reasons for thinking that the enjoyment which the public have hitherto had of these spaces may be allowed to continue, and will continue unless Parliament gives those facilities for inclosure, which we consider cannot be claimed by Lords of Manors or by Commoners as of right. The existence of these undefined rights is virtually the safeguard of the public in preventing inclosure. That being the case, we are unable to recommend a comprehensive scheme of purchase."

They recommended as an alternative that facilities should be given for putting the Commons under schemes of regulation for the protection of their surface from nuisances, and for relieving the Lords of Manors of the difficulties which they complained of, and for removing from them the temptation to inclose.

The Report was adopted in preference to that of Mr. Doulton, embodying the scheme of purchase and of sale of parts of the Commons, in order to secure the residue, by a majority of two to one. It will be seen later that the views of the Committee as to the existence of common rights sufficient to protect the Commons and to abate inclosures, where attempted, have been entirely confirmed by the long experience of subsequent litigation, and that their chief recommendation, for the repeal of the Statute of Merton, has at last, after nearly thirty years, been practically carried out by Parliament.

CHAPTER III.

The Commons Preservation Society.

The Report of the Committee of 1865 was followed almost immediately by most important consequences. The Lords of Manors of the London Commons, having failed to induce the Committee to adopt their contention that they were practically the owners of the Commons, and that the Commoners' rights had lapsed by non-use, took immediate steps to vindicate their claims. In all directions inclosures were commenced or threatened. In Epping Forest hundreds of acres were taken from the Forest, and were fenced. The Commons of Berkhamsted, Plumstead, and Tooting, and Bostall Heath were inclosed. Hampstead Heath and others were seriously menaced, and would doubtless soon have been lost to the public. If these inclosures had been allowed to remain unchallenged, the whole of the London Commons would have been undoubtedly lost to the public. The opponents to the pretensions of the Lords of Manors were equally determined to put in force their views, and to resist inclosures. In the autumn of 1865, on the suggestion of Mr. P. H. Lawrence, a Society was founded for the preservation of Commons in the neighbourhood of London, with the express purpose of offering resistance to these wholesale encroachments of the Commons.* Among its members were the late Mr. John Stuart Mill (who thenceforward, till his death, took a most prominent part in the Society, and rarely missed being present at its meetings), the late Mr. Charles Buxton, Mr. Cowper Temple (afterwards Lord Mount Temple), Sir T. Fowell Buxton, Mr. Thomas Hughes, Mr. Burrell, an eminent lawyer, Mr. Charles Pollock (now Baron Pollock), and others.

The Society, thus formed, elected me as its Chairman. I have acted in that capacity down to the present time, with the exception of the periods of 1870 to 1874, and 1880 to 1885, when Mr. Andrew Johnston, Sir Charles Dilke, and Mr. Bryce occupied the position; but even when unable to act as Chairman, on account of official work, I have always taken an active part in directing and maintaining its policy. Mr. Fawcett, to whom the cause owes so much, became a member of the Society in 1866, but did not attend its meetings until 1869, when, at his instance, its work was extended to other Commons than those in the neighbourhood of London. Thenceforward, till his death, in 1884, he was a most active and devoted member.

Mr. P. H. Lawrence acted as honorary Solicitor to the Society, and was professionally engaged in all the earlier suits till 1868, when he was appointed Solicitor to the Office of Works. He was succeeded by Mr. (now Sir Robert) Hunter, who, on being appointed in 1882, by

---

* As I have often occasion to refer to this Society, I have, for the sake of brevity, called it "The Commons Society."

Mr. Fawcett, Solicitor to the Post Office, was followed as legal adviser to the Society by Mr. Birkett, who has retained that position till the present time. These three gentlemen have all been enthusiasts for the cause of Commons; and to their legal knowledge and their skill in conducting the many suits against Lords of Manors, who had made inclosures, the success of the policy of the Society has been mainly due.

Among other prominent members—not, however, original members—have been Sir Charles Dilke, Mr. Bryce, Lord E. Fitzmaurice, Mr. E. N. Buxton, Mr. Burney, Mr. Briscoe Eyre, Miss Octavia Hill, Lord Thring, and Mr. Walter James (now Lord Northbourne). Many other prominent men have been subscribers and occasionally attended the meetings of the Society, such as the late Lord Granville, the late Mr. W. H. Smith, Sir William Harcourt, and others.

The Society soon had plenty of work on its hands. What the Committee of 1865 had anticipated came to pass. As each Common near London was inclosed or threatened, local opposition was aroused, which only needed the advice and assistance of the central Society to organise active resistance to the inclosure. In most cases the resident owners of villas adjoining the Commons formed committees, and raised funds to oppose the aggressors in the Law Courts, or public-spirited men took upon them the burden of resistance. Inquiry soon established the fact that common rights existed in every case sufficient to prevent inclosure, if enforced in the Courts. Although these rights had

not of late years been much used, they still subsisted
in law, and were effective as a weapon against the
Lords of Manors who were usurping the Commons.
It will be seen that Mr. Augustus Smith took up
the case of the Commoners of Berkhamsted against
Lord Brownlow; Sir Julian Goldsmid and Mr. Warrick
against Queen's College, Oxford, in the matter of Plumstead Common; Mr. Gurney Hoare on behalf of
Hampstead against Sir Thomas Maryon Wilson; Sir
Henry Peck against the Lord of the Manor of
Wimbledon; Mr. Hall against Mr. Byron in respect
of Coulsdon Common; Mr. Betts against Mr. Thompson
on behalf of Tooting Graveney; Mr. Minet against
Mr. Augustus Morgan of Dartford Heath; and ultimately the Corporation of London on behalf of Epping
Forest against the thirteen Lords of Manors who had
inclosed so large a part of it.

In many of these and other cases suits were commenced, within a few months, to vindicate the rights of
Commoners and to abate the inclosures. We had the
great advantage that, although these suits were promoted
locally by those immediately interested in the Commons
attacked, they were all under the direction and management of the Solicitor of the Central Society, Mr. P.
H. Lawrence, and had therefore the advantage of the
accumulated knowledge and experience of one inti-
mately acquainted with the somewhat obscure and
difficult subject of common rights. It was also, for
the same reason, possible to marshal the cases before
the Law Courts in the order which was most likely

to lead to successful results. It was found, on looking carefully at the legal decisions of the Judges for some time preceding, that their general tendency had been rather to favour inclosure than the reverse. It was determined to reverse this tendency by presenting the cases in the order best calculated to bring the Courts gradually to a different view of the subject, and to revive the older presumptions of the Law in favour of the Commoners, and against inclosure. We were assisted in this process through Mr. Lawrence finding it possible to revive an old and long disused form of suit, by a single Commoner, on behalf of the other tenants of a Manor, claiming a declaration of their common rights, and asking for an injunction to restrain the Lord of the Manor from inclosing the waste lands. This process enabled us to resort to the Equity Courts, whose Judges have taken a much broader and less technical view of the subject than the Common Law Judges. It was also possible at that time, within certain limits, to choose the Courts in which to proceed, and therefore the Judges by whom the suits should be tried and determined.

We had the benefit, therefore, of the enlightened views of such Judges as Lord Romilly and Sir George Jessel, to whose strong judgments the cause of Commons owes so much. It will be seen that this policy was eminently successful, and that a series of decisions were given by the Judges which completely justified the contention of the Report of the Committee of 1865, and established the fact that practically inclosures could no longer take place under the Statute of Merton, and that, if resisted by Commoners, such arbitrary attempts would certainly fail. The result, however, has only been arrived at after long years of anxious and costly litigation, in which the contest was a very unequal one ; for while, on the one hand, if the Lords of Manors had been successful in maintaining their pretensions to inclose, they would have secured land of enormous value for building purposes ; on the other hand, the Commoners were fighting only for the maintenance of the *status quo*, where their own pecuniary interests were not much involved, but where the public was mainly concerned in keeping the Commons open.

All this expensive litigation would have been unnecessary if Parliament had adopted the recommendation of the Committee of 1865, and had repealed the Statute of Merton, as practically obsolete, as working injustice whenever attempted to be put in force, and as mischievous to the public interest. Unfortunately, the Government of the day refused to adopt this suggestion; and although endeavours have been made at different times since to induce Parliament to take this course, they have till last year (1893) entirely failed.

In 1866, however, the Government carried a measure of great importance in furtherance of the other recommendations of the Committee of 1865—namely, the Metropolitan Commons Act. Under this Act, power was given to the Inclosure Commissioners, now the Board of Agriculture, in respect of any

Common within the Metropolitan Police district, on the application of the Commoners, or of any twelve Ratepayers, or of certain Local Authorities, to authorise a scheme for the regulation of a Common and its management by a Board of Conservators, elected by the ratepayers of the district. The consent of the Lord of the Manor is not necessary for such a scheme; but when he does not give his consent, his rights, whatever they may be, of inclosing or otherwise, are reserved, and are not affected by the scheme. These regulation schemes are subject to the approval of Parliament, in the same manner as schemes of inclosure. This measure, passed by Mr. Cowper Temple, then First Commissioner of Works, was prepared and recommended to him by the Commons Society. A very considerable number of the London Commons have since been brought under its protection, and schemes have been passed for their regulation.

The interest of the public in the subject of Commons was also greatly promoted in 1866–7 by the action of Mr. Peek, now Sir Henry Peek, who as a Commoner and resident was deeply interested in the preservation of Wimbledon Common, and in the application to it of a scheme of regulation under the Metropolitan Commons Act. Mr. Peek offered several valuable prizes, amounting in the aggregate to £400, for the best essays on the Preservation of Commons. These led to the legal and historical aspects of the question being studied by a number of able young lawyers. The first prize was won by the late Mr. Maidlow. The six best essays,

written by men, most of whom subsequently distinguished themselves in the legal professions, were
published at Mr. Peck's expense, in an interesting
volume, which forms a valuable repertory of the history and law of Commons.*

* Six Essays on Commons Preservation. (Sampson Low and
Marston. 1867.) One of these essays was written by Mr. Robert
Hunter, and led to his subsequent connection with the Commons
Society.

CHAPTER IV.

HAMPSTEAD HEATH.

THE first case of attempted inclosure which the Society
had to grapple with was that of Hampstead Heath:
perhaps the most important of all the London Commons, not by reason of its size, but from its position,
and its natural beauties, and salubrity, which make it
more popular and frequented than any other. On
Bank Holidays it is often visited by over 100,000
persons, and is most inconveniently crowded. It consisted in 1865, before the addition of Parliament Hill,
of not more than 240 acres, but these were so dispersed,
that the Heath appeared to be much larger. From its
great height above London, it enjoys healthy breezes, and
presents beautiful views over the surrounding country.

The Manor of Hampstead, of which the Heath is
the waste, is conterminous with the Parish. It is
mentioned in Domesday Book as having always
belonged to the Abbot and Convent of Westminster.
It remained in these hands till the dissolution of the
religious houses by Henry VIII., who granted it to
Sir Thomas North, from whom it passed through
various hands, by descent or purchase, till it became,
in 1743, the property of the Maryon family, the
ancestors of the present owner, Sir Spencer Maryon
Wilson, of Charlton. His predecessor in the title, Sir

Thomas, appears to have been advised that he was practically owner in fee of the Common. He denied that there were any Freehold tenants of the Manor. Of the numerous body of Copyholders of the Manor, he maintained that not more than three or four had any rights of common over the Heath. He claimed the right to inclose it without stint, under the Statute of Merton, and without regard to what he called the pretended rights of Commoners. He also asserted his unlimited right to dig and carry away sand from the Heath, to the extent of destroying its herbage and heather. This digging for sand was, in fact, being carried out to an extent that threatened to interfere with the natural features of Hampstead Hill. Dangerous pits appeared in all directions, and the surface of the Heath was injured to a degree that it has not yet recovered, after twenty-five years of cessation of digging. Sir Thomas was not only Lord of the Manor, but was also owner of a considerable demesne in the neighbourhood of the Common, 260 acres in extent. He was, however, only the tenant for life of this property, and as he had no son, he could not obtain the 'legal concurrence of the next in the settlement, that was then necessary to enable him to grant building leases, and to avail himself of the great demand which was growing up for houses near the Heath.

In 1829, he made application to Parliament, in a private Bill, for powers to grant building leases, not merely in respect of his demesne lands, but over all the lands mentioned in the Schedule, including "such part (if any) of the Heath, and other waste ground in Hampstead, whether occupied or not, which may be hereafter approved, and exonerated, or discharged from the customs of the Manor, and from all rights of common and other rights, for the sole use of and benefit of the lord for the time being."

The proposal caused the greatest alarm to those interested in the maintenance of the Heath. The Bill was opposed in the House of Lords by Lord Mansfield, the owner of a considerable property adjoining the Common, and was rejected by a large majority. From thenceforward repeated applications were made by Sir Thomas Wilson to Parliament in private Bills, for power to grant leases on his Hampstead property. The reference to the Heath was omitted in those subsequent to 1829, but as Sir Thomas refrained from giving an undertaking that he would not use his powers in leasing portions of the Common, Parliament refused to concede them to him. The Bills were invariably rejected by one or other of the two Houses. An exception was, therefore, made in respect of this single case from the general treatment of landowners, and Sir Thomas was refused the power of adding immensely to his income by giving leases for building purposes on his demesne lands.

This appears to have rankled in his mind, and before the Committee of 1865 he asserted his absolute interest in the Heath, free from any common or other rights, and his intention to make what use of it he could by leasing it for building purposes, to the limited

E

extent allowed by the general law to tenants for life.
"In 1829," he said, "I lost my Bill for building on
other parts of my property, and having always been
thwarted, I must now see what I can do to turn the
Heath to account, and get what I can.   By the outcry
that has been raised against me, I have been deprived of
£50,000 a year. . . . It never entered my head to
destroy Hampstead Heath at all, until I found that
I was thwarted in my Bill that I brought into
Parliament."   He added, however, that he had never
promised not to build on the Heath, if full powers
of leasing elsewhere were conferred upon him.   "I
am not disposed," he said, "to make any concession;
in fact, I will not do so."

The subject of the Heath had already engaged the
attention of the Metropolitan Board of Works, who,
alarmed as to the possibility of its inclosure, were prepared to negotiate for the purchase of the lord's rights;
but the price suggested on behalf of Sir Thomas—
£400,000, or £1,600 an acre—was so excessive that
nothing was possible in this direction.

Sir Thomas Wilson's lawyer supported his em-
ployer's evidence before the Committee, by asserting in
the strongest manner the right of the lord to treat the
Heath as his private property, denying the rights of
copyholders, and claiming the power of inclosing under
the Statute of Merton, or under the customs of his
Manor.   Very soon after the report of the Committee
of 1865, Sir Thomas Wilson began to put his claims to
a practical proof.   He commenced the erection of a

house on the highest part of the open Heath, and of other houses in another conspicuous part. It was a direct challenge to the Commoners of their rights, and if allowed to pass, would have resulted in the loss to the public of this most valuable health-space, or in its enforced purchase by the ratepayers at an exorbitant price.

Among the residents on the Common was the late Mr. Gurney Hoare. He was induced to put himself at the head of a local Committee for the protection of the Heath. Several meetings were held at Hampstead, which the writer and others attended, on behalf of the Commons Society, and explained the legal position of the Commoners, as they understood it, and the expediency of their asserting and maintaining their rights against the inclosures of the lord. A considerable fund was raised to support the necessary litigation, and a suit was commenced against Sir Thomas Wilson, in the name of Mr. Gurney Hoare, who was an undoubted Commoner. It was the first suit of the kind —that is, at the instance of a single Commoner, on behalf of all others of his class, asking for a declaration of their rights, and claiming an injunction to restrain the Lord of the Manor from inclosing.

The suit came on for hearing, after an interval of two years, before Lord Romilly, then Master of the Rolls. He overruled the objections taken to the form of the suit, and allowed it to be brought by a single Commoner on behalf of the other copyholders having rights over the Common. But unfortunately, he did that which was never again done either by himself, or

E 2

other judges, in subsequent and similar cases. He refused to decide himself on the issues of fact involved in the suit, as to the nature of the rights, and number of the Commoners, and directed that these issues, eleven in number, should be tried before a jury. This much disheartened the Commoners who had embarked in the suit, as they foresaw a long vista of further litigation.

The researches made into the Court Rolls, in the preparation of the Commoners' case in this suit, showed that from the date of 1684, previous to which the rolls had been burnt, there was undoubted evidence of the exercise of rights of common by the copyholders, and of the right to dig sand for the purpose of their holdings. No doubt whatever existed in the minds of the legal advisers of the Society, as to the sufficiency of these rights to maintain the case of the Commoners against the lord, and to justify a jury in finding the issues in their favour, and the Court in giving a permanent injunction against him. It was also of the utmost importance to all the Commoners' cases, in respect of other inclosures, that this case should be tried out, and should not be compromised.

In 1868, however, Sir Thomas Wilson died. His successor in the property evinced a different disposition. He announced his intention not to proceed with the buildings on Hampstead Heath. Negotiations were then opened for a compromise, by the purchase of the lord's interests and rights by the Metropolitan Board, who had always favoured the process of purchase of the Commons, and did not appreciate the importance of defeating the claims of the lords in these early cases. Mr. Gurney Hoare and the Commoners were glad to be relieved of their suit, which might have entailed costs on them. They were satisfied if their own Heath was preserved to them, and they were not disposed to think of the interests of other Commons. Finally, an arrangement was effected under which Sir Spencer Maryon Wilson transferred all his rights, as Lord of the Manor of Hampstead, to the Metropolitan Board for the sum of £45,000—an excessive sum, in proportion to their real value (especially when regarded by the light of subsequent experience in respect of other Commons, where the litigation was fought out), but very small in proportion to the freehold value of the land, if the Lord of the Manor should prove his right to inclose, or in comparison with the sum of £400,000 originally suggested by the lord before the commencement of the suit.

The result of the case, therefore, was a substantial victory for the views put forward by the Commons Society; though it would have been preferable, in the interest of all the other cases, that the suit should have been brought to issue, and a judgment given on the rights of the Commoners. The Heath has since the date of this compromise been under the charge and management of the Metropolitan Board and its successor, the London County Council.

The settlement of the Hampstead Heath suit, and the sense of security engendered by its being vested in a public authority, for the enjoyment of

the public, not unnaturally directed public attention
before long to the expediency of enlarging its area.
The immense growth of population at Hampstead, and
still more in the neighbouring London suburbs of St.
Pancras and Paddington, and the continually increasing popularity of the Heath as a place of recreation
on holidays to people from every part of London,
made it clear that the area of the Heath was quite
insufficient. The Common was a straggling one, intersected at more than one point by private property,
and was in danger of being seriously injured by the
extension of building on the fields adjoining it. It
owed much of its beauty and value to the fact that a
property to the north-east of it, known as Parliament
Hill and Ken Wood,* belonging to the Earl of Mansfield, and a small intervening property of Sir Spencer
Wilson, were still unbuilt on.

The Hampstead people, and to a less degree only,
the whole of London, looked with the greatest alarm
at the rapid approach of building operations to these
fields so necessary to their Common. Were these two
estates to be covered with houses, there could be no
doubt the value of the Heath would be seriously
diminished, and the beauty of the prospect in one
direction entirely destroyed.

---

* It was to Ken Wood that the poet Keats alluded in his
beautiful poem, "I stood tiptoe upon a little Hill." Keats spent
the two happiest years of his brief life at Hampstead, and wrote
there the greater part of "Endymion" and others of his best
works. It is said that these were inspired while wandering over
the Heath, which was then more secluded than now.

HAMPSTEAD HEATH & PARLIAMENT HILL

The Dark Green represents Hampstead Heath as it was
The Light Green represents the addition of Parliament Hill.
The Blue represents the remaining Ken Wood Estate

Sir Spencer Wilson had already advertised his property for building leases, and with a view to this, had converted it into an offensive and unsightly brick-field. It was understood that Lord Mansfield had no idea of selling his Ken Wood property or any part of it; but he was already of a great age, and his heir, the late Lord Stormont, made no secret of his intention to realise the building value of the land whenever he should come into possession of it.

Under these circumstances, a Committee of a representative character was formed early in January, 1884, for the purpose of effecting the enlargement of Hampstead Heath by the purchase of as much of the properties of Lord Mansfield and Sir Spencer Wilson as would be possible. The Duke of Westminster was President of this body, and the writer was Chairman of its executive Committee. Among other active members were Mr. Burdett Coutts, Mr. C. E. Maurice, Mr. Harben, Mr. F. E. Baines, C.B., Mr. Robert Hunter, and Miss Octavia Hill. The difficulty of the scheme consisted in effecting an arrangement at the same time with both landowners, and in providing the means for the purchase of a very large amount of land out of funds, more or less of a public character, not under the control of the Committee. Lord Mansfield's property consisted of 348 acres, and Sir Spencer Wilson's of 60 acres, immediately abutting on the Heath.

The whole of 1884 and the best part of 1885 were occupied in difficult and delicate negotiations with the two landowners. Sir Spencer Wilson agreed to hold his hand for a time. Lord Mansfield, after much discussion, consented to entertain a definite proposal for the purchase of a considerable part of his land, consisting of 200 acres, though he specially excluded Ken Wood and the land nearest to his residence. The Committee then entered into correspondence with the Metropolitan Board of Works. On July 17th, 1885, the writer introduced a deputation to the Board, and urged on their behalf that the Board should take up the negotiations with the two landowners, and effect the purchase of 260 acres.

The Board rejected the proposal of the Committee, alleging that the amount of money involved in the purchase was too large to justify it in imposing the burden on the ratepayers. It refused also to avail itself of the option to discuss the matter with the Committee, with a view to reducing the cost of the scheme by obtaining contributions from other sources. The Committee were not discouraged by this rebuff. Public opinion was strongly in their favour, and they determined to press their scheme. They carried a measure through Parliament, empowering, but not compelling, the Metropolitan Board to effect the purchase, and enabling other local authorities to contribute.

After long and difficult negotiations with the two landowners, the Metropolitan Board, and the Vestries of St. Pancras and Hampstead, they effected an arrangement for the purchase of the 260 acres for the sum of £300,000, and for the contribution towards this of

£150,000 from the Metropolitan Board, and £50,000 from the two parishes. Of the remaining £100,000, one-half was obtained through the Charity Commissioners from the funds of the City of London Charities, which had recently been under the review of Parliament, for the diversion of their income, from the useless and mischievous charities within the City, to the more manifold needs of the whole of London. The other half was raised by public subscription; and with this addition, the Metropolitan Board finally gave their assent to the scheme, and contributed out of their funds one-half of the purchase money.

Many minor difficulties were encountered and overcome, and finally, on March 6th, 1889, after rather more than five years of complicated negotiations, the contracts between the Metropolitan Board and the two landowners were signed. The 260 acres of Parliament Hill have since been thrown open and added to Hampstead Heath, and form the most important addition which has been made to the open spaces of London during the last forty years. It will remain at some future time to supplement this by the purchase of the remaining portion of Lord Mansfield's property, whenever he or his successors may be willing to part with it—for Ken Wood is almost indispensable to the full enjoyment of Hampstead Heath and Parliament Hill. With this addition, the whole will be the most beautiful and valuable of all the Parks or open spaces round London.

CHAPTER V.

BERKHAMSTED COMMON.

THE next case of Inclosure which came under the notice of the Commons Society—one of the most important, not merely as regards the interests of the public, but even more so in respect of the legal issues involved—was that of Berkhamsted. This Common, with an area of about 1,150 acres, is one of the finest tracts of open land in the South of England. It is distant from London about twenty-five miles, and is very accessible by railway. The town of Berkhamsted, of about 7,000 inhabitants, lies immediately to the south of it. The Common stretches thence to the north and west along an elevated ridge, for nearly three miles in length, by half a mile or a mile in breadth. Its green turf is interspersed with gorse, bracken, and furze bushes, and there are many clumps of fine beech-trees. It is, in fact, a natural park of great beauty. It is bounded on the east by the splendid domain of Ashridge, with its Deer Park, eight hundred acres in extent, the property of Lord Brownlow.

In very early times Berkhamsted Manor, with its Castle, its demesne lands, and Common, the latter originally consisting of 1,450 acres, was the property of the Crown. Edward the Third, in 1346, granted his interest in it to his son, Edward the Black Prince,

when creating him Duke of Cornwall, and from that
time, till a few years ago, the property was an appanage
of the Duchy of Cornwall, but for many years past it
was leased to the owners of Ashridge, with a special
reservation of the Commoners' rights.

The adjoining domain of Ashridge was from an
early date the property of the Earls of Bridgewater,
and on the death of the last of this line (the Duke of
Bridgewater), came into possession of Earl Brownlow,
the grandfather of the present owner. So long as the
Manor and its Common were vested in the Duchy of
Cornwall, there was little danger of inclosure. In an
evil time, however, and in pursuance of an unwise
policy, the Council of the Duchy of Cornwall, in 1862,
was induced to sell their estate to the Trustees of the
late Lord Brownlow, for the sum of £143,000. These
Trustees wanted the Common, not for the purpose
of turning it into cultivated land, but as an addition to
Ashridge Park. They had no sooner become possessed
of the manorial rights of Berkhamsted, than they commenced a series of proceedings, with the object of
getting rid of the Commoners and inclosing the Common. Their first act was to negotiate with the people
of Berkhamsted for the substitution of a metalled and
shorter road for the grass drive which traversed the
whole length of the Common from north to south, and
which formed the means of communication between
the town of Berkhamsted and the districts north of
the Common. The consent of the vestry of the parish
was obtained for this; but apparently they were left

under the impression that the grass drive would simply
be added to the Common, and were not informed that it
was the intention to inclose the whole waste and shut
out the public. Soon after this, ditches and banks were
made across the drive. A little later, gravel-pits were
dug with the object of diverting or stopping another
grass drive over the Common, called Broad Green
drive; and several small plots of land were at the
same time inclosed, with the intention of asserting a
paramount right on the part of the Lord of the Manor
to treat the Common as his absolute property.

Lord Brownlow's Trustees then set to work to purchase the rights of those Commoners who objected to
their proceedings, and thus to reduce the number of
those who could legally resist them. Besides the
numerous freehold and copyhold tenants of the Manor
who claimed the usual rights of turning out cattle
and sheep on the Common, and of cutting turf and
gorse and bracken for litter and thatching, the inhabitants of Berkhamsted had, from time immemorial,
claimed and enjoyed the user of cutting fern and gorse,
not in virtue of their ownership of land, but as inhabitants only. The Trustees appear to have been advised
by their lawyers that such an user by mere residents
could not be sustained as a legal right, inasmuch as
by the legal maxim already referred to, the inhabitants
of a district, when not incorporated, are too vague a
body to enable them to prescribe for a right of a
profitable nature. In order, however, to make some
concession to the public opinion of the district, in

respect of an immemorial user which they were about
to terminate, they offered to present to the people of
Berkhamsted a plot of land, of forty-three acres,
near to the town, as a recreation ground, conditionally
upon the Commoners, whose rights of common he
acknowledged, agreeing to surrender them. A deed
of gift of this land to Trustees, for the benefit of
the town, was prepared by Lord Brownlow, and deposited as an escrow, by which, if within six months,
a release of common rights should be so fully executed
that, in the opinion of his legal adviser, the Common
would be freed from all such rights, the deed would be
delivered to the Trustees therein named on behalf of
the town. Some of the Commoners interested were
induced to fall in with this arrangement, and thirty-
seven freehold tenants and seven copyhold tenants,
out of a much larger and undetermined number,
signed the deed releasing the Common from their
rights.

Before, however, the termination of the six months
provided for in the escrow, the Trustees, apparently
impatient of delay, proceeded to effect an inclosure on a
great scale. In February, 1866, the agent of the
estate erected iron fences five feet in height, with seven
horizontal rails, in two lines, across the centre of the
Common, inclosing 434 acres of it, and dividing the
residue into two completely detached portions. These
fences contained no openings; they were erected without regard to any public rights of way, and entirely
intercepted the public from access across the Common

to districts to the north and south. The inclosure
meant expropriation, immediate or prospective, of the
whole Common.

When remonstrances were made on the subject in
the columns of *The Times*, Lord Brownlow's solicitors
replied that "the public has no more right to pass
over the Common than a stranger has to pass through
a Commoner's private garden, and that even a copyhold
tenant of the Manor, entitled to common rights, can
only go upon the Common in order to place his sheep
there, and to look after them when there, and, therefore,
with that qualification, any person who drives, rides, or
walks across the Common out of the public highway is
a trespasser."*

It is fair to say that Lord Brownlow himself could
scarcely be held responsible for this inclosure. He was
at the time in very broken health, and left matters
almost completely in the hands of his Trustees and
agent. It often happens in such cases that the agent
and lawyer are more eager to aggrandise a great estate
than the owner himself is, and are mainly responsible
for such acts as the above. It was asserted by these
gentlemen that the object of the inclosure was to preserve the wild character of the place intact, and not to
exclude the public. It was claimed that three other
Commons in the neighbourhood—those of Hudnall, Pit-
stone, and Ivinghoe—had been inclosed in like fashion
within recent years, without detriment to their beauty.

However that may be, this arbitrary and high-

* *The Times*, February 16th, 1866.

BERKHAMSTED COMMON

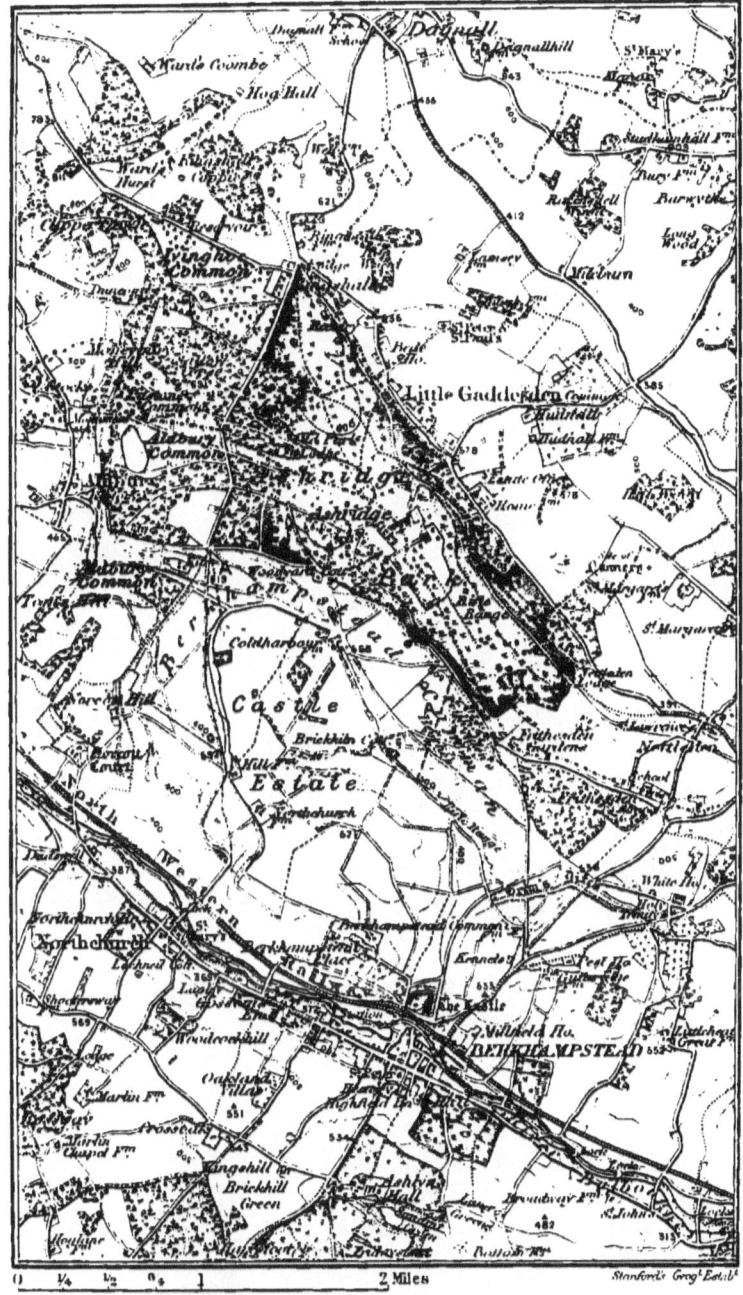

The part coloured light Green is Berkhamsted Common.
A.A. the site of the fences erected by Lord Brownlow.
The Castle Estate formed the demesne lands of the Manor of
Berkhamsted, & was bought by Lord Brownlow from
the Duchy of Cornwall.
The Commons coloured blue were enclosed before 1865.

handed proceeding aroused a very strong feeling throughout the district. There was, however, great fear and unwillingness to resist so powerful a magnate. Advice was sought of the Commons Society. Inquiry into the conditions of the Manor soon convinced them that the inclosure was as illegal and indefensible as it was arbitrary and without regard to public interests, and that it was a case where the rights of Commoners might certainly be vindicated, so as to defeat the particular inclosure, and to deter other Lords of Manors from similar acts in the future. The only difficulty was how to find a person possessed of rights over the Common, with a sufficiently long purse, and with independence and courage, to try conclusions at law with Lord Brownlow, who was so deeply interested in maintaining his inclosures, and in carrying them to the point of extinguishing the Common.

It was fortunately discovered that among the owners of land in the district, with undoubted rights of common, was just such a man as could be relied on for the purpose—the late Mr. Augustus Smith. This gentleman, better and more widely known as the Lord of Scilly, had taken a long lease from the Duchy of Cornwall of the Scilly Islands, the population of which he had found in a most neglected and miserable state. By the exercise of a wise paternal despotism, rendered possible by his position as landlord of all the houses in the islands, he had greatly improved the condition of the people, had waged successful war against public-houses and drink, had restored prosperity,

and had banished bad characters. He was also a
member for a Cornish borough, and in the House of
Commons had distinguished himself by annually asserting the rights of the public against the claims of the
Crown and the Duchy of Cornwall to the ownership
of the foreshore on the sea-coasts. His qualities of
courage and obstinacy marked him out as the man
of all others best suited to fight the cause of the
Commoners against an inclosure such as had been
effected of Berkhamsted Common.

Mr. Augustus Smith was, without difficulty, induced
to take up the cause, and to employ Mr. P. H. Lawrence,
the Solicitor of the Commons Society, in proceedings
to vindicate the Commoners' rights and interests.
After careful consultation between Mr. Smith, Mr.
Lawrence, and myself, it was decided to resort to the
old practice of abating the inclosure by the removal
bodily of the fences, in a manner which would be a
demonstration and an assertion of right, not less
conspicuous than their erection. For this purpose
it was thought necessary to employ such a force as
would not only speedily remove the fences, but render
any opposition on the part of the employés of Lord
Brownlow absolutely impossible.

With this object, it was arranged with a contractor
in London to send down at night to Berkhamsted
a force of 120 navvies, for the purpose of pulling down
the iron fences in as short a time as possible. On
March 6th, 1866, a special train left Euston, shortly
after midnight, with the requisite number of labourers,

skilled workmen, and gangers, armed with proper
implements and crowbars. The train reached Tring at
1.30 a.m. At this point the operation nearly miscarried.
The contractor, it appeared, had sub-let his contract to
another person. The two met together at a public-
house near Euston Station the evening before the
intended raid, and drank so freely that neither of them
was in a condition to lead the force into action, and the
navvies arrived at Tring without a leader, and with no
instructions. Fortunately, Mr. Lawrence had sent a
confidential clerk to watch the proceedings from a
distance, and this gentleman, perceiving the difficulty,
took the lead of the force.

A procession was formed at the station. A march
of three miles in the moonlight brought them to Berkhamsted Common, and the object of the expedition
was then first made known to the rank and file. The
men were told off in detachments of a dozen strong.
The substantial joints of the railings were then
loosened by hammers and chisels, and the crowbars
did the rest. Before six a.m. the whole of the fences,
two miles in length, were levelled to the ground, and
the railings were laid in a heap, with as little damage
as possible. It was seven o'clock before the alarm was
given, and when Lord Brownlow's agent appeared on
the scene, he found that Berkhamsted Common was
no longer inclosed. It was too late to do more than
make an energetic protest against the alleged trespass.

Meanwhile, the news spread, and the inhabitants
of the district flocked to the scene. Gentlemen came in

F

their carriages and dog-carts ; shopkeepers from Berkhamsted and farmers in their gigs; labourers on foot
tested the reality of what they saw by wandering over
the Common, and cutting morsels of the flowering gorse,
to prove, as they said, that the land was their own
again.   Thus were the 430 acres restored to the
Common, and two miles of iron fences removed. It
was said that the erection of these iron fences had cost
more than a·thousand pounds. Their removal entailed
a very heavy expenditure on Mr. Augustus Smith.
There could not have been a more direct and deliberate
challenge to Lord Brownlow, and it was to be expected
that, within three days of the demolition, he would
commence an action of trespass against Mr. Smith for
forcibly pulling down the fences. Later in the proceedings of the case, Lord Brownlow's counsel endeavoured
to raise prejudice against Mr. Smith by a vigorous
protest against what he called the lawless proceeding
of removing the whole of the fences, in lieu of raising
an issue by removing a single bar. The Judge who
tried the case—Lord Romilly—was not to be influenced
by any such argument. He intimated to the counsel
that the demolition of the fences was no more violent
or reprehensible an act than their erection, if Lord
Brownlow was not in his legal right, and that the issue
of the suit would determine which of the two acts was
unjustifiable. Subsequent events showed the wise and
sound policy of pulling down the whole of the fences, for
Lord Brownlow, who brought the action of trespass,
died before the case could be heard and determined, and

the action, from its nature, could not be revived, at
the instance of the defendant, against the brother who
had succeeded in the title and property. Mr. Smith,
therefore, found himself saddled with the costs already
incurred, without the means of recovering them, and
without a decision of the case; but at least the fences
no longer existed.

Meanwhile Mr. Smith had been advised to bring
a cross suit in the Court of Chancery against the
Brownlow Trustees, claiming on behalf of himself and
the Commoners that their rights should be ascertained,
and that the Lord of the Manor should be restrained
from interfering with them or from inclosing the Common. This suit did not terminate with the death of
the late Earl, but continued against his successor, who
had the misfortune to inherit this lawsuit together
with the family estate.

The case thus commenced led to a complete examination of the Court Rolls of the Manor, and of the history
of the Common from the earliest times. From these it
appeared that the rights of common had always been
esteemed of great value by the freehold and copyhold
tenants of the Manor. So far back as the death
of Edmund, Earl of Cornwall, in 1300, there was
an inquisition, in which the rights of the Commoners
were clearly defined. In 1607 there was another
survey of the Common by Mr. John Dodderidge. A
jury on this occasion presented—

"That the inhabitants and tenantes of this manor dwelling
in Berkhamsted and Northchurch have used by ancient
F 2

custom to have perceive and take in the Fryth (or Common) and other waste land, herbage and paunage, bushes, furze, stubbes, and ferne for their necessary use for their lands and tenements, and common of pasture for their cattle at all times of the year ' sans nombre', and that the Fryth and other waste lands cannot be estimated at anie yearely value, by reason that the tenantes and inhabitants aforesaid are manie, and that they perceive and take the benefit thereof. And the pannage likewise can be nothing worth to the Lord of the Manor, for that the tenantes have always had the benefit thereof.'

The freehold tenants at that time were stated to be 186 in number, and the copyhold tenants 57. The inhabitants of Berkhamsted also were even then numerous.

In spite of this survey, showing that the Common was no more than sufficient in area for the rights which existed over it, an effort was made within a few years to inclose the whole, or considerable parts, of it. In 1617, the Council of the Prince of Wales, afterwards Charles the First, took proceedings with this object. The tenants of Berkhamsted and Northchurch, the two parishes comprised in the Manor, were consulted on the subject. Those of Berkhamsted were willing to agree, on the terms that one-half of the Common should be assigned to them, in exchange for their rights; those of Northchurch held back, at the suggestion of a Mr. Edlyn, a landowner of the district, who exercised extensive rights over the Common. The people of Berkhamsted were propitiated by the promise of a charter of incorporation. The Northchurch tenants still refused; but after the exercise of pressure upon them, they finally consented to allow the Prince to take 300 out of the 1,480 acres, on the express condition that the remainder should remain open for the rights of the Commoners. They alleged that they had more beasts on the Common than the inhabitants of the town. The townsmen, on the other hand, wished to separate their portion of the Common to themselves for better government and order. It was finally agreed that the Prince should enclose 300 acres in the part " least offensive " to the Commoners, upon condition that the remainder should remain open. On February 20, 1619, 300 acres, forming what is now called Cold Harbour Farm, and a portion of which, within recent times, has been waste and uncultivated, were inclosed and separated from the Common. About the same time, and as part of the arrangement, James I. conferred a charter of incorporation on the people of Berkhamsted.

A few years later, in 1638, a further effort was made on behalf of the Council of the Duchy of Cornwall to appropriate another large slice of the Common. A Commission was issued for the purpose. The people of Berkhamsted were again not unfavourable, but demanded terms; the tenants of Northchurch were again strongly opposed. They were backed up by Lord Bridgewater and by Mr. Edlyn, son of the gentleman already referred to as being opposed to the previous inclosure. On February 12th, 1639, the tenants of Northchurch were heard before the Commission; they alleged that the Council of the Duchy had promised, when the previous inclosure had taken place, that there should be no further approvement. The Commissioners, however, in spite of this, advised that 400 acres should be inclosed by the Duchy, and that 100 acres should be given to the Corporation of Berkhamsted for the benefit of the poor. The Surveyor-General reported to this effect on October 22nd, but he added that the majority of the Northchurch tenants were refractory, and continued to oppose. In consequence of this report, Mr. Edlyn was taken into custody and imprisoned; but he was subsequently released by order of the Lord Treasurer. His arrest was, in fact, an arbitrary and illegal act, for the purpose of intimidating the Commoners of Northchurch into giving their consent to the inclosure.

In the hope that the imprisonment of Edlyn would have its effect, the Council of the Duchy proceeded to inclose 400 acres of the Common. The land selected for the purpose nearly coincided with the inclosure made by Lord Brownlow, 220 years later; and it is interesting to observe the close resemblance between the results. The land inclosed in 1639 was fenced, and was let on lease to a Mrs. Murray. In March, 1640, Edlyn, in spite of his previous imprisonment, decided to resist the inclosure. He employed 100 persons to pull down the hedges and stakes. This was effected in the presence of a vast number of people from Berkhamsted and the district. The Council of the Duchy thereupon petitioned the House of Lords that the Prince of Wales might be quieted in possession of the land during the privilege of Parliament, and that the delinquents, who had violated such privilege, might be punished.

On April 2nd, 1641, William and John Edlyn and Francis Fenn appeared before the House of Lords to answer the complaint of the Council of the Duchy; they were then committed to custody till the case should be heard. This appears to have been deferred till August 6th, when counsel were heard, and the House of Lords made an order for the quiet enjoyment of the inclosed land during the continuance of the then Parliament, but declined to give any decision as to the merits of the case. The following entry appears in the Lords' Journals :—

" Upon the Commissioners for the Prince his Highness's Revenue, shewing that of late and now sitting the Parliament, diverse disorderly persons have entered into certaine improved lands of the Prince his Highness, within the Manor of Berkhamsted and Meere, being parcell of the Dutchie of Cornwall, and have pulled down and carried away the fences of the said grounds: Whereupon William Edlyn, John Edlyn, and Francis Fenn, complained of by the said Commissioners, were convened as delinquents before their Lordships, and counsel being heard at large on both sides in open Courte at the bar, and after due consideration of the whole matter : It is ordered that the Prince His Highness (being a member of this House) shall quietly and peaceably hold and enjoy the said landes within the Manors aforesaid, for and during the continuance of the present Parliament, and the privileges of the same. And although this House was fully satisfied upon hearing the said matter that the Petitioners before complained of were delinquents, yet upon their submission this House was pleased to remit their offence, with this caution : that if they or any others whatsoever shall again, during the tyme aforesaid, offende in the like kinde, that then they shall be severely punished for the same. And nevertheless, it is not their Lordships' pleasure to determine anything in point of right to the title, but after the tyme of privilege of Parliament to leave to the determination of the lawe."

It would seem that the House of Lords was not very certain of its position in the matter. The delinquents who had suffered imprisonment at its instance, for four months, were released. They were not, however, intimidated by this, or by the threat of the House of Lords, for it appears from a complaint to the Council of the Duchy in February of the following year, that divers delinquents had again pulled down the inclosure of Berkhamsted, in spite of the order of the Lords for quieting the same during the time of Parliament. No further notice, however, was taken by the Lords, and no attempt was made by the Duchy of Cornwall to question as a trespass, in the Courts of Law, the act of pulling down the fences.

Under the Commonwealth, a few years later, the Manorial Rights and the demesne lands of Berkhamsted were sold by the direction of Parliament to Godfrey Ellis and Griffantius Phillips; and in 1653, Ellis offered for sale the 400 acres, approved in 1639, assuming that the inclosure, though no longer physically apparent, was valid in law. John Edlyn again came to the rescue. He presented a petition praying that Ellis might be compelled to make out his title of the land. It was ordered on this "that upon security being given by Ellis of all discharges which the Commonwealth or the parties concerned should be

at, in case he failed to make good his discovery, it
should be referred to the counsel for the Commonwealth
to peruse such evidence and proofs as might be produced by the petitioners touching their interests
claimed in the premises, and to state matters of fact
and certify the same." Ellis failed to give security,
and on April 27th, 1659, it was ordered "that inasmuch
as Ellis had not made out any title in the Commonwealth to the Common in question, the said cause
between the Commonwealth and John Edlyn should be
dismissed, and that the petitioner should be awarded
costs against Ellis." Edlyn, therefore, after his long
efforts and imprisonments, completely succeeded in
preventing the inclosure of the Common.

On the restoration of the Monarchy, the Duchy of
Cornwall resumed possession of the Manor and its
rights, and thenceforward no further encroachment or
inclosure was attempted, until Lord Brownlow, in 1866,
having bought the interest of the Prince of Wales in
the Manor, repeated the arbitrary act of the Council
of the Duchy in 1639, and inclosed the 434 acres in
the manner already described. Mr. Augustus Smith
proved an opponent not less determined to support
the rights of the Commoners and the interests of
the public than Edlyn, but not so unfortunate as
to be imprisoned as a delinquent by the House of
Lords, for violating their privileges by disorderly
conduct, in abating an inclosure by one of their
members.

The suit against Lord Brownlow, commenced in

1866, sped its intricate and dilatory course of proceedings for four long years, during which minute investigations were made, at great expense, into the past history of the Common, the origin and nature of the rights of the Commoners, and the number of persons so entitled. Every possible objection was raised by the Defendant. It was contended that the Manor was not a single one, but that Berkhamsted and Northchurch were two distinct manors : it was objected that Mr. Augustus Smith could not sue on behalf of the freehold tenants of the Manor; it was asserted that the rights of common were of a limited character; it was claimed that the inclosure was justified under the Statute of Merton. Only those, who are familiar with these Commons cases, can have an adequate notion of the elaborate nature of the documentary and oral evidence necessary for proof or disproof.

Finally, in January, 1870, Lord Romilly, then Master of the Rolls, decided the case in favour of Mr. Augustus Smith, on all the points raised by Lord Brownlow. "I am of opinion," he said, "that the objection that the Plaintiff cannot sue on behalf of the freeholders fails, and that though these rights of common may not be co-extensive, yet as the Plaintiff has proved, and indeed is admitted to be a copyholder, as well as freeholder, in the Manor, he is entitled to sue on behalf of both." He also affirmed that the rights of common of herbage, and pannage, of the cutting of turf and gorse, were established. "It remains," he added, "for the Lord of the Manor to show that he is entitled to

approve, and that sufficient is left for the commonable
rights. This he has failed to do; and, in fact,
the attempt made by the late Earl is only a renewal
of the attempts made, in 1638, and 1642, and which
did not end till 1659, to inclose exactly the same
land, and for which there appears to me to be as little
justification now, as there was in the seventeenth
century."*

There could not be a more complete vindication for
the action of Mr. Augustus Smith. After this it may
confidently be expected that the Common will remain
open and uninclosed for all time to come, and safe from
any further attacks by any future Lords of the Manor.
It is pleasant to be able to add that the relations
between Lord Brownlow and the people of the district
have not been disturbed by these events. Ashridge
Park has continued to be opened freely and generously to
the public, as in past times.

It will be seen that the suit did not raise the question whether the inhabitants of Berkhamsted have
rights over the Common, independent of the ownership
of land. The investigations, however, brought out the
fact that the town was incorporated by Charter in
1619, and it is probable that this was the renewal of an
earlier charter. It is true that the Corporation has ceased
to exist; but it is only dormant, and may be revived at
any time. The better opinion appears to be that the
inhabitants are sufficiently incorporated to satisfy the
rule of law as to prescription, and to enable them to

* Smith *v.* Brownlow.—L. R. 9 Eq., 241.

claim rights of Common. Apart from this, however, the other admitted rights are quite sufficient in number and importance to secure the Common, and to prevent a renewal of such arbitrary inclosures as those which have been described.

CHAPTER VI.

PLUMSTEAD AND TOOTING COMMONS.

IN the following year, 1871, decisions were arrived at in the Courts with respect to two other Commons, where inclosure had been effected shortly after the Committee of 1865. The Plumstead Commons, though little known as compared with Hampstead and others, are of great importance to London, by reason of their propinquity to the great working population of Woolwich and Deptford. They consist of three open spaces —Plumstead Common, of 110 acres; Bostall Heath, of 55 acres; and Shoulder of Mutton Green, of 5 acres. They are all parts of the waste of the Manor of Plumstead, and had existed in their present condition. little reduced in area, from the earliest times. Bostall Heath is a specially beautiful spot. It forms part of the brow of high table-land which overlooks the Thames Marshes below Plumstead. Its elevation gives it command of a very extensive prospect of the valley and shipping of the Thames, from Woolwich to Erith. The summit is a bare flat of dry gravelly soil, high and breezy. The surface soil had been nearly all carried off, and what remained was a pebbly gravel, covered with furze or stunted heath.

The Manor is mentioned in Domesday Book as belonging in part to the Monastery of St. Augustine, near Canterbury, and in part to the Bishop of Bayeux; but the latter portion appears to have been merged, at some subsequent period, in the former; and the united Manor remained in the hands of the Monastery till its dissolution by Henry VIII., when it passed into the possession of the King. In 1539, the King granted the Manor to Sir Edward Boughton, in whose family it remained till 1685, when it was sold to Mr. John Michel, who, dying, in 1756, left it by will to the Provost and Scholars of Queen's College, Oxford, in whose hands it has remained to the present day. There were no copyhold tenants of the Manor. The Manor consisted, therefore, wholly of freehold tenants, and of demesne lands. The Manorial Rolls, which existed in a perfect state from 1685, showed that the freehold tenants had exercised and enjoyed from the earliest times the right of common for cattle and for estovers, and the right to take turf, gravel, and loam in the waste of the Manor, and that all moneys derived from dealings with the waste, and from fines in the Manorial Court, were divided between the Lord of the Manor and the poor of the parish of Plumstead. The Courts ceased to be held in 1853.

From the year 1859, on the appointment of an eminent Solicitor of London as Steward of the Manor, a course of action was commenced and actively pursued, based on the denial of the existence of any rights over the Commons by the freeholders in the Manor, and on the assertion that the Fellows of the College were practically owners of the soil of the waste, with power to do as they liked with it. In pursuance of this policy, a series of aggressions and encroachments were carried out, by which Plumstead Common was reduced by about one-third of its area, and which culminated, in 1866, in the inclosure, on behalf of the College, of the whole of Bostall Heath and of the Shoulder of Mutton Green. These acts led to a crisis. There was general indignation in the district against the action of the College. The advice of the Commons Society was sought. Inquiries were made. A meeting of the inhabitants of East Wickham was held, and by the advice of the Society a Committee was formed by the Vestry, with Mr. John Warrick as Chairman; and under the authority of this body the fences round the Green were forcibly removed, in vindication of the claims of the inhabitants to use it for games and recreation as a Village Green.

It was ascertained that among the freeholders of the Manor was Mr. Frederick Goldsmid, then a member of the House of Commons. This gentleman was persuaded to put himself at the head of the movement to preserve the Common. He presided at a public meeting in Plumstead to enlist popular sympathy against the inclosure, and he put the matter into the hands of Mr. Lawrence. In the following month Mr. Goldsmid died suddenly; but his son, Mr. Julian Goldsmid (now Sir Julian), took up the matter with equal warmth, and in concert with Mr. John Warrick and another gentleman, undertook the litigation, which was necessary to vindicate the rights of the freeholders and of the public to the waste lands of the Manor. The College brought an action at law against Mr. John Warrick and others for trespass in respect of the removal of fences from the Green, but as they failed to proceed to trial with the case, a counter-suit was brought by Mr. Warrick and Mr. Goldsmid, on behalf of the freehold tenants of the Manor, asking for a declaration of their rights, and claiming an injunction against Queen's College to restrain its Fellows from inclosing the wastes of the Manor.

The College, in the meantime, had endeavoured to dispose of the Green, and of their encroachments on Bostall Heath and Plumstead Common. They refused an offer of £500 for the Green, and let it to a tenant at £9 a year. They also negotiated for the sale of Bostall Heath, but without coming to a conclusion. A portion of Plumstead Heath was bought by a building company, and was advertised for sale in building lots.

The suit on behalf of Messrs. Warrick, Goldsmid, and Jacobs was commenced on 4th August, 1866. The proceedings necessitated a careful examination into the history of the Manor, and the nature and extent of the rights claimed by the freeholders. The Fellows of Queen's College controverted every contention of the Plaintiffs in the case. They denied their right to sue on behalf of the freehold tenants; they traversed their claims of common rights; they contended that as there had been no admissions in recent years of freeholders as tenants of the Manor, and no payment of quit rents, their rights, whatever they might have been, were extinguished; they claimed the right to inclose the waste under the Statute of Merton, with or without the consent of the freeholders. On all these points Lord Romilly ultimately decided against the College.

On appeal, in 1871, Lord Hatherley—then Lord Chancellor—confirmed this decision in a luminous judgment. After defining the rights exercised over the Common, he said:—

"The question is whether these rights are vested in the Plaintiffs in such a manner that they can sustain a suit against the present Lords of the Manor—Queen's College—who have, since the year 1860, controverted and denied the existence of any such rights by issuing notices, and threatening with legal proceedings all persons attempting to exercise any of their rights, and who claim an absolute right to deal with the waste of the Manor as they please. . . . This is a very broad controversy, and it certainly would be very fatal to the interests of justice if, in the face of the evidence I have before me, such a claim on the part of the Lords of the Manor could be sustained. I have before me the Court Rolls of this Manor, extending over two hundred years, from which there appears most abundant evidence of some persons not only without interruption having exercised all these rights, but having laid down rules and regulations under which these rights might be exercised.

"It cannot be disputed that the Court is entitled—nay, bound by authority—when it finds rights which have been exercised in the manner I have described, to find the origin for them in some way if it can. . . . It so happens that the Manor has no copyholders; if they ever existed, they have disappeared. With regard to the condition of freeholders of customary Manors, there can be no doubt that they are in a different position from that of copyholders. I take it, however, that all persons having a common right which is invaded by a common enemy, although they may have different rights

G

inter se, are entitled to join in attacking the common enemy in
respect of their common right."

He repudiated the suggestion that the Plaintiffs had
lost their rights by neglecting to claim admission or to
pay quit rents.   He concluded his judgment by these
weighty words :—

> " The Defendants must pay the costs of the suit.   The
> litigation has been occasioned by a high-handed assertion of rights
> on the part of the College, who really seem to have said in effect
> to those who have been exercising these rights for two hundred
> years : ' You will be in a difficulty to prove how you have
> exercised them ; we will put you to that proof by inclosing and
> taking possession of your property.'   I think, therefore, that
> the whole expense ought to fall upon those who have occasioned
> it : namely, those who have brought into question rights which
> have had so long a duration, and to which I am glad to be able
> to discover—because it is the duty of the Court to discover, if
> it can—a legal origin." *

It will be observed that this judgment decided
several points in advance of those in the Berkhamsted
case, and was of the utmost value in subsequent cases.
It laid down the following propositions :—

1. That one freehold tenant of a Manor (claiming
by prescription on a presumed grant) can sue on behalf
of himself and all the other freehold tenants.

2. Where rights of common have been exercised
for many years the Court will endeavour to find a legal
origin for them.

3. Where rights of common have been exercised

---

* Warrick *v.* Queen's College, Oxford, L.R. 10, Eq. 105, 7 Ch., 716.

for many years by the freehold tenants of a Manor, and also by the inhabitants, the Court will presume that the inhabitants claimed through the freehold tenants.

4. A freehold tenant of a Manor does not by ceasing to pay quit rents, and by neglecting to claim admission, lose his rights against the lord.

The result of the suit was an unqualified vindication of the views of those who had maintained that the rights of Commoners, though dormant and unused, would avail to prevent inclosures. One of the most determined of all the efforts to inclose under the Statute of Merton was completely defeated. It is worthy of note that one of the Fellows of Queen's College —the late Mr. Maidlow—won the first prize offered by Sir Henry Peek for an Essay on the Preservation of Commons, in which he maintained that the Statute was practically obsolete, and ought to be repealed. It would have been well for the interests of the College if its Fellows had followed his advice in preference to that of their lawyers.

Later, a scheme for the Regulation of Bostall Heath was applied for by the Commoners, but was strongly opposed by the College. The Metropolitan Board then stepped in, and bought the interest of the College for a moderate sum. Later still, in 1891, the London County Council, with a contribution from the Local Board, made an addition to this Common, by the purchase of 62 acres of a beautiful wood adjoining it, the property of Sir Julian Goldsmid, who completed his good work in connection with the Plumstead Commons

G 2

by asking a very moderate price for this most important addition.

The suit respecting Tooting Graveney Common was not dissimilar to that of Plumstead as regards its legal aspects and conclusion. The Common is a comparatively small but important open space, in the neighbourhood of Tooting, of 63 acres, and adjoining Tooting Bec Common. The Manor of Tooting Graveney is mentioned in Domesday Book as being held of the Crown by the Abbey of Chertsey. It remained in possession of the Monastery until the thirtieth year of Henry VIII. Some years later it was granted to Sir John Maynard, and then passed through numerous hands by purchase, till 1861, when it was sold to Mr. W. S. Thompson, a gentleman residing in the district, for the sum of £3,650. The purchase included seven Copyhold messuages, which were let at a rental of £100. The proportion, therefore, of the purchase money given for the Manorial rights and waste could not have been much over £1,000: a very small sum as compared with the value of the waste as a freehold, if it could be treated as such by the purchaser.

It was alleged in the course of the suit that, when the Manor was advertised for sale, there was a strong feeling among the residents in the neighbourhood of the Common, that it should be purchased in the public interests, in order to prevent any attempt at inclosure, and several gentlemen were prepared to subscribe with this object. When, however, it became known that Mr. Thompson was intending to purchase, it was generally understood that his object was to preserve the Common, and his neighbours, under this impression, refrained from bidding against him. It very soon turned out, however, that Mr. Thompson had very different objects in view. No sooner had he become the purchaser than he commenced proceedings before the Inclosure Commissioners for the inclosure of the Common, and at first his application included the whole of the waste. On finding them adverse to this proposal, he reduced his claim to 25 acres; but the Commissioners refused to entertain even this modified proposal. A committee of gentlemen in the district, who had opposed this attempt at inclosure, then made an offer to join in a scheme, under which the Common would be managed in the interest of the public. This was declined.

In 1865, Mr. Thompson inclosed twenty-five acres of the Common, in spite of repeated protests. His neighbours still hesitated to incur the dangers of a lawsuit, and the fence remained standing till 1868, when it was broken in several places by Mr. Miles and other Commoners. Several actions of trespass were then commenced by Mr. Thompson; and finally, on July 10th, Mr. Betts, and two Commoners, on the advice of the Commons Society,* filed a suit against the Lord

---

* This action was mainly conducted by Mr. G. F. Treherne, whose family had property in the neighbourhood of Tooting, but Mr. P. H. Lawrence advised in its earlier stages.

of the Manor, on behalf of the Commoners, claiming a determination of their rights, and an injunction against inclosure.

The Rolls of the Manor existed from 1557 in fair order, and from these it appeared that small inclosures of the waste had taken place, from time to time, in eighteen cases, and that in all of them the consent of the freeholders of the Manor had been given, and that in twelve of them the purchase money had been divided between the Lord of the Manor and the poor of the parish, the latter receiving in the aggregate no less a sum than £1,417.

The Defendant denied that there was any freehold land held of the Manor, or that the tenants had any rights over the waste; he argued that no one had for a long time exercised any rights of common, except in cases where trespasses had been committed in assertion of such rights; and he also contended that, as Lord of the Manor, he could inclose under the Statute of Merton, without the consent of the freehold tenants, and without regard to their alleged rights.

The case was argued for eleven days, in 1870, before Lord Romilly, who finally decided in favour of the Commoners. From this there was an appeal, which was decided by Lord Hatherley, after six more days of argument, in 1871. Lord Hatherley affirmed the decision, and gave an injunction to restrain Mr. Thompson from inclosing the waste. " Mr. Thompson, he said, " had purchased the Manor for a comparatively small sum, and if he had succeeded in depriving the freeholders of all rights, would have made a very handsome profit; and he seemed to have considered that being the Lord of the Manor his title could not, without difficulty, be displaced. In that speculation he has been disappointed."* In spite of these observations, the Court, in consequence of some inchoate negotiations for a compromise, refused to award costs to the Plaintiff, who, consequently, had to bear the heavy charge of proving his title, and of obtaining an injunction against an inclosure of a most arbitrary character, and one which was proved to be utterly illegal.

The decisions of the Court of Appeal in the Plumstead and Tooting cases were pronounced about the same time. The clear and unmistakable judgments of so learned and sober a judge as Lord Hatherley, satisfied the legal world, as well as the outside public, that the views advocated by the Commons Society were not the wild dream they had at one time been considered. These decisions, following upon that of Berkhamsted, mark the first stage in the work of the Society. All the suits advised by Mr. P. H. Lawrence, including those respecting Wimbledon and Wandsworth, referred to in the next chapter, had now been brought to a successful issue, except those relating to Loughton and Epping— to which reference will later be made—which were still pending, and were not destined to be tried out.

In all these early and critical cases the leading counsel employed was Sir Roundell Palmer (now Lord Selborne), and their success was due in no small

* Betts v. Thompson, L.R., 7 Ch., 732.

measure to his skilful advocacy. With him was associated Mr. Joshua Williams, Q.C., to whose great learning and clear judgment the Commoners and the public were deeply indebted; for his support of the views of the Commons Society, there is no doubt, did much to commend to the Courts, what might otherwise have been thought extreme doctrines. The junior counsel employed were Mr. E. R. Turner (now a County Court Judge), the late Mr. W. R. Fisher, and Mr. A. P. Whateley, all of them men of great ability. His judicious choice of advocates was not the least of the services rendered by Mr. Lawrence to the cause of Commons Preservation.

CHAPTER VII.

WIMBLEDON AND WANDSWORTH COMMONS.

In the same year, 1871, in which the Plumstead and Tooting cases were decided, final settlements were arrived at in respect of Wimbledon and Wandsworth Commons, about which litigation had unfortunately arisen. Of the Commons within easy reach of the Metropolis, none is better known or more appreciated by Londoners than that of Wimbledon, and none has a more interesting past history. It is believed by antiquarians to have been the battle-field described by early Saxon writers as "Wibbandun," where Ceaulin, King of the West Saxons, attacked and defeated Ethelbert, King of Kent, in the year 568, and where Oslac and Cnebba, two of Ethelbert's generals, were killed. This conjecture, says Mr. Manning, is supported by the name of an ancient circular camp in an adjoining field, which was formerly part of the Common, and which, Mr. Camden says, was in his time called Bensbury, a natural abbreviation of Cnebbensbury. This earth-work is, or rather was recently, known as Cæsar's Camp, for the vandal, who owned it, did his best, a few years ago, to obliterate all traces of it by levelling its banks. The Common was the scene in modern times of many encounters of a different character. The Duke of York here fought his duel with Colonel Lennox, and it was here also that Lord Cardigan killed Captain Tuckett in a similar affair of honour.

The Manor of Wimbledon, in early times, formed part of the much larger Manor of Mortlake, which also included the Manors of Putney and Barnes. The Manor of Mortlake appears to have been granted by Edward the Confessor to the See of Canterbury. It was one of the many Manors belonging to that See which Odo, the fighting Bishop of Bayeux and Earl of Kent, took from the Archbishop. It was, however, recovered by Archbishop Lanfranc, in 1071, in the assembly of Nobles at Pinenden Heath, near Maidstone. It remained in possession of the See of Canterbury until Archbishop Cranmer exchanged it with Henry VIII. for other estates. The King soon after granted the Manor, with its extensive and valuable demesne lands, to Sir Thomas Cromwell, Earl of Essex, who, from having been the son of a blacksmith at Putney, may be supposed to have highly valued this mark of Royal favour. On the attainder of Cromwell, in 1540, the King settled the Manor on Queen Catherine Parr for her life. Queen Mary gave it to Cardinal Pole, but it reverted again to the Crown; and Queen Elizabeth granted it to Sir Christopher Hatton, who sold the Manor House to Sir Thomas Cecil, the second son of Lord Burleigh. The Manor appears to have reverted to the Queen, who, in 1590, granted it to Sir Thomas Cecil. Cecil was created Earl of Exeter by James I. He settled the Manor of Wimbledon on his third son, Sir Edward Cecil, who was a distinguished soldier in the time of James I. and Charles I., and was created by the latter, in 1626, Baron of Putney and Viscount Wimbledon. He died in 1639, leaving only daughters, who sold the Manor to trustees for Queen Henrietta Maria, in whose possession it remained till the deposition of Charles I.

In the time of the Commonwealth, the Manor, like many other possessions of the Crown, was put up for sale, and was bought, in 1650, by Adam Baynes, for £7,000. This gentleman re-sold it two years later, at a good profit, for £17,000, to General Lambert, in whom it remained vested till the restoration of Charles II., when it reverted to the possession of his mother, who gave or sold it, in 1662, to the Earl of Bristol, with whom scandal had connected her name; later it went to Thomas Osborne, Marquis of Carmarthen, afterwards created Duke of Leeds. During the time the Manor was in the possession of the Duke, an attempt appears to have been made to inclose the Common, but it was resisted successfully by a gentleman named Russell. On the death of the Duke, the trustees of his will sold it, in 1717, to Sir Theodore Janssen, one of the South Sea directors. On the bursting of the South Sea bubble, Sir Theodore Janssen was ruined. The Manor was seized, with his other property, and was sold to Sarah, Duchess of Marlborough, wife of the great Duke, and she, dying in 1744, bequeathed it to her grandson, John Spencer, youngest son of the Earl of Sunderland, who had married, for his second wife, the younger of

the two daughters of the Duke of Marlborough.
Spencer's son was created Viscount Althorpe and Earl
Spencer, and from him the Manor descended in direct
line to the present owner.

The late Earl, who died in 1857, sold Wimbledon
Park, the demesne land of the Manor, consisting of
1,200 acres, together with the Manor House. He is said
also to have offered to sell the Manor itself for £6,000.
His son, the present Earl, inherited the Manor, with
its manorial wastes of Wimbledon Common, Putney
Heath, and two smaller open spaces, East Sheen
Common and Palewell Common, but without much
adjoining property. He was also the Lord of the
Manors of Battersea and Wandsworth, in which are
the Common of Wandsworth and part of that of
Clapham.

What we know generally as Wimbledon Common
consists of about 1,000 acres, of which 730 are,
strictly speaking, waste of the Manor of Wimbledon;
200 acres are in the Manor of Putney, separated by
the Kingston Road; and about seventy acres are waste
of the Manor of Battersea and Wandsworth.

The Rolls of the Manor date from the time of
Edward IV., and, with a few breaks, are tolerably perfect
till very recent times.* Till 1728 they were written in
Latin. They are replete with interesting facts, bearing
on the condition of the Manor and the rights of its free-

* Extracts from the Rolls of this Manor were printed by the
Committee of Wimbledon Commoners in 1886, and form a bulky
volume.

hold and copyhold tenants. Besides the Rolls, there is a record of the Customs of the Lordship of Wimbledon, taken from the Black Book of Canterbury—an early record of Archiepiscopal Manors, apparently made at a time when Wimbledon belonged to the See of Canterbury, and also a Parliamentary survey of the Manor made in 1649. The earlier Court Rolls abound with orders and regulations respecting the rights of cutting wood and furze. Till within the last seventy years, there were a great number of oak pollards on the Common, which afforded fuel for the inhabitants in the winter months. During the summer the wood was not allowed to be taken; but it was usual for the Parish Beadle to go round every year at Michaelmas with his bell, and " cry the Common open." He went round again at Lady Day to " cry it shut."

The pollards were cut down and sold, in 1812, by the grandfather of the present owner, and the only wood which remained upon the Common in 1864 was a little brushwood near the Warren Farm: and there were some picturesque groups of bushes and hollies. But within recent times the poor of the parish were allowed to cut furze in the winter. The free and copyhold tenants of the Manor had the usual rights of turning out cattle on the Common, and at one time there were gates on the roads leading to it, to prevent cattle from straying.

The Homage appear to have appointed surveyors of the woods, gravel-diggers, and Common keepers. They also made bye-laws, and prosecuted offenders for tres-

pass, nuisances, &c.   In 1823, all the existing bye-laws
were rescinded.   Later the Homage ceased to appoint
the Common Keeper, and the appointment fell into the
hands of the Lord of the Manor.   There are very frequent notices in the Rolls about gravel-digging and the
taking of loam and peat, and there appear to have
been many disputes on the subject between the lord
and the Commoners.   The lord claimed, and eventually
maintained, his right to sell gravel, loam, and peat,
without limit, from the Common; and for a few years
before 1865 the income which he derived from these
sources averaged over £1,000 a year.

It has already been shown what an important
part the proposals of Lord Spencer in 1864 had, at an
early stage of the movement, in favour of preserving
Commons.   There cannot be a doubt that these proposals were made in the full belief that they were for
the benefit of the neighbourhood and the public.   The
scheme, however, did not meet with the approval of
the Commoners, and it has been already shown that
the project to sell a third part of the Common in order
to fence the remainder, and to buy out the Commoners'
rights, was rejected by the Committee of 1865.   This
led to the withdrawal of the Bill.

There followed what was to be expected and feared.
The Lord of the Manor and the Commoners were left
in a hostile attitude to one another, with wholly different views as to their respective rights and interests
in the Common.   It may be taken as certain that Lord
Spencer had no intention of withdrawing from his offer

to the public, or of attempting to deprive them of the use and enjoyment of the Common; but he was disappointed by the action of the Commoners; he did not recognise their right to interfere with him in the mode in which he proposed to deal with the land. They, on their part, contended that their rights were such as to place them at least on a par with the lord, and to make their consent necessary to any dealings with the waste in the public interest. They complained that the action of Lord Spencer's steward was such as to ignore and set aside their rights, and if permitted to continue, would have destroyed their claim to a voice in the destiny of the Common.

It happened that among the residents near the Common were many able lawyers, such as Mr. Charles Pollock, Q.C. (now Baron Pollock), Mr. Joseph Burrell, an eminent conveyancer, Mr. William Williams, Mr. Richard Ducane, and, not the least able among them, Mr. P. H. Lawrence, who played so important a part in the early movement for the preservation of Commons. There was also a wealthy Commoner, Mr. Henry Peek (now Sir Henry), who was determined at all risks to assert his rights, and to claim a voice in the management of the Common.

As was to be expected, the differences between the Commoners and the Lord of the Manor, turning as they did upon legal points, gravitated to proceedings in the Law Courts. The Committee of Commoners determined to bring a suit in the name of Mr. Peek against Lord Spencer, asking for a declaration of their rights, and claiming an injunction against him from continuing such acts as were inconsistent with these rights. Negotiations having failed to bring about an amicable settlement, a suit was commenced on December 1st, 1866, and an application was made under the Metropolitan Commons Act for a scheme for regulating the Common, and for maintaining order upon it. Lord Spencer's answer to the Bill in Chancery was not filed until August, 1868 : a period of nearly two years. The delay was doubtless due to an exhaustive inquiry into the history of the Manor. The answer gave an elaborate and interesting account of this, and contended that Lord Spencer was practically owner of the Common, and could do as he liked with it, without regard to the few persons, whose rights he admitted.

The Commoners then occupied some time in obtaining fresh evidence of the customs of the Manor and in identifying properties in Wimbledon and Putney, to which Commoners' rights were undoubtedly attached. There was every indication that the suit would be very protracted and costly. In the first instance, the case of the Commoners did not seem to be very hopeful. Large numbers of rights of common had been bought up, and the remaining rights appeared at first to be few in number. But further investigation led to the discovery that in respect of a large extent of land, formerly part of the demesne lands of the Manor, the original conveyances had specially conceded rights of common over the waste. When this became known to the Defendant's lawyers, negotiations for a compromise

were renewed; and finally, in April, 1870, terms of
an arrangement were happily arrived at between
Lord Spencer and the Committee of Commoners, and
the Chancery proceedings were brought to an end. The
principle of the proposed arrangement was the conveyance by Lord Spencer, to Trustees for the public, of
the whole of his rights over Wimbledon and Putney
Commons, and that portion of Wandsworth Common
which forms practically a part of Wimbledon Common,
in consideration of the continuance to him, by means
of a fixed annual payment, of the income which he had,
on the average of the previous ten years, derived from
the Common. It became necessary to embody the
terms of this agreement in an Act of Parliament, and in
the Session of 1871, a Bill, called the Wimbledon and
Putney Bill, was introduced.

Some difficulty arose in consequence of the natural
desire of Lord Spencer that the National Rifle Association should be allowed to continue in the use of the
Common, for the purpose of their annual Volunteer
Camp, and also owing to the strenuous opposition of
the Metropolitan Board of Works, who desired to
have the management of the Common, even though
they would only obtain this by throwing the expenses
upon London at large, whereas the neighbourhood was
willing to bear them. The measure, however, passed
through all its difficulties with little amendment, and
finally received the Royal Assent.

Under this Act, Lord Spencer conveyed all his
interest in the Common to eight Conservators, five to

H

be elected by the ratepayers under the Act, and the other three by the Home Secretary, the Secretary of State for War, and the First Commissioner of Works. The consideration of the conveyance was a perpetual annuity to Lord Spencer and his heirs and assigns of £1,200, representing his average receipts from the Manor. This, together with other expenses, was to be levied by a rate on houses assessed at £35 a year and upwards, situated within three-quarters of a mile of Wimbledon Common and Putney Heath. The maximum rate for houses within one quarter of a mile was fixed at 6d. in the pound, within half a mile, 4d., and beyond half a mile at 2d. in the pound, the distances to be measured by the nearest available road or footpath. The rate-payers were to have votes in the election of Conservators in proportion to the value of their assessments, and the election was to be triennial. The expenses of obtaining the Act were to be borne on this rate. It will be seen that the principle on which the expense of providing the annuity and of maintaining the Common is based is that of "Betterment." The preservation of the Common was considered to be in the interest chiefly of those who lived near to it, and they were to be taxed in proportion to their distance from the Common in a series of zones.

The dispute between the Lord of the Manor and his Commoners was thus finally set at rest, and the Common was placed under the management of those who are primarily interested in its maintenance. Under the Act, the Conservators were bound to allow the National Rifle Association to fence off a large part of the Common annually for their Volunteer Camp, and to erect targets for rifle practice. This was continued for some years; but in consequence of the objections of the Duke of Cambridge, the owner of the adjoining estate at Coombe, owing to the increased range of rifles, and to other difficulties which had arisen, it was ultimately found necessary to discontinue these meetings, and they are now held at Bisley Common. Wimbledon Common has been left to the enjoyment of the neighbourhood and public at all times of the year, subject only to the reservation of certain rifle ranges in favour of a few Metropolitan Volunteer Corps. Nothing can work better or more smoothly, or more for the interest of the public, and of the Commoners and inhabitants of Wimbledon, than the scheme of management, thus generously conceded by Lord Spencer.

WANDSWORTH COMMON.

The settlement of the Wimbledon dispute had the fortunate effect of making a precedent for a similar settlement of a dispute between the Commoners of the adjoining Common of Wandsworth and Lord Spencer, who was also Lord of the Manor of Battersea and Wandsworth. This Manor was, we learn from Domesday Book, given by William the Conqueror to the Abbot of Westminster, in exchange for the Manor of Windsor. It remained in the possession of the Abbey till the Dissolution of the Religious Houses by Henry VIII. James I. settled it, on the death of his eldest

H 2

son, on Prince Charles. This Prince, on coming to the throne, granted it to Oliver St. John, afterwards created Viscount Grandison. His nephew inherited the estate, but not the title, and was himself created, in 1716, Viscount St. John. He had an only son, the well-known statesman, who was created Viscount Bolingbroke in the lifetime of his father. His successor, in 1762, sold the Manor to the trustees of Lord Spencer, from whom it descended to the present owner.

No Common in the neighbourhood of London has suffered more cruelly in past times from encroachments of all kinds. It now consists of 194 acres, but a glance at the map will show that formerly it must have had a considerably larger area. In 1782, the then Lord of the Manor obtained the consent of the Parish of Wandsworth to an inclosure of 92 acres for an addition to his Park, on payment of an annual sum of £50, to be expended in charity; and at the same time Sir William Fordyce obtained leave to inclose 23 acres on payment of £20 a year to the parish. The late Mr. Porter also inclosed a considerable part of the East Common, which he claimed as waste of the Manor of Alfarthing, of which he was Lord; and his claim, though unfounded, does not appear to have been disputed.

About forty years ago, two Railway Companies— the London and South-Western and the London and Brighton—obtained leave to take their lines through the Common, severing it into three distinct parts, and almost ruining it as an open space; and later, chiefly in consequence of this severance, the Royal Patriotic Society was

WANDSWORTH COMMON.

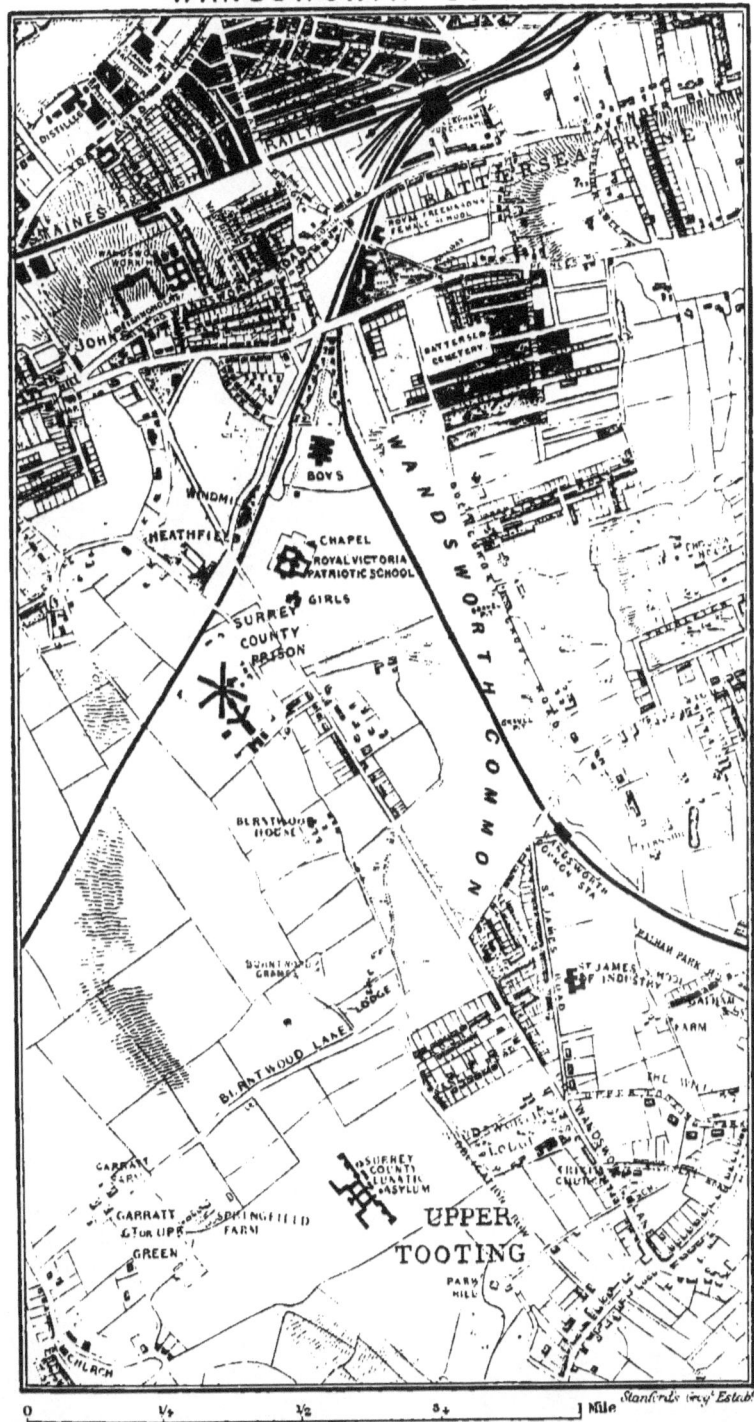

0   ¼   ½   ¾   1 Mile

allowed to take 60 acres for the purpose of an Asylum and its grounds. What remains of the Common, in its trisected and shorn condition, is still of considerable value to the residents in the neighbourhood. When the Committee was formed to contest the views of Lord Spencer's lawyers about Wimbledon, the attention of the Commoners of Wandsworth was directed to their legal position.

In 1870, a Committee for the protection of the Common was formed, at the instance of Sir Henry Peek, who offered £1,000 if the inhabitants would collect £4,000 for a suit against the Lord of the Manor to determine the rights of the Commoners. A great part of the money was collected, but when the Wimbledon dispute was arranged, it was ascertained that Lord Spencer was disposed to make a similar arrangement about Wandsworth, and an agreement was soon come to with him.

Under the Wandsworth Common Act, 1871, the Common was assigned to Conservators, elected by the Ratepayers of the Parish, in consideration of an annuity of £250, secured to Lord Spencer on the rates, based on his average income from the sale of gravel. The principle of Betterment referred to in the Wimbledon case was not adopted in the Wandsworth scheme. There arose, in consequence, an agitation among the ratepayers of that part of the parish which is remote from the Common, against the charge for its maintenance; and in 1887 the Metropolitan Board of Works obtained legislative powers for relieving the Parish of the charge, and vesting the Common in them, subject to the annuity to Lord Spencer.

Both these schemes of Wimbledon and Wandsworth may be regarded as Regulation schemes under special Acts, with the provision for the purchase of the lord's rights upon the basis of the average income from the sale of gravel or otherwise; they contrast favourably with the Act authorising the acquisition of Hampstead Heath, passed in the same Session. While Lord Spencer's interest was purchased at about £25 per acre, that of the Lord of the Manor of Hampstead was bought at the rate of about £200 per acre.

The Wimbledon and Wandsworth Acts were conducted through Parliament by Mr. Robert Hunter, the Solicitor to the Commons Society, and had the cordial approval and support of the Society, which looked upon them not only as important measures in themselves, but as valuable precedents for the permanent preservation and regulation of other Commons.

CHAPTER VIII.

Epping Forest.

THE next case, in order of date, which came up for decision in the Law Courts, and by far the most important, as affecting the public interests of London, was that of Epping Forest. It may be doubted, indeed, whether in the annals of litigation there has ever been a Common case of such magnitude, involving so many interests, or so wide-reaching in the effect of the issues determined. Epping Forest, as it now exists, after the abatement of the numerous inclosures which were effected in the twenty years before the commencement of the suit, and which had robbed it for a time of half its area, consists of a little over 6,000 acres of woodland, open to the public at all points, extending for a distance of nearly thirteen miles from Wanstead on the confines of London to the village of Epping, with an irregular breadth at its widest part of about one mile, and in its narrower parts of about half a mile. Some small portions of it are detached from the main Forest, the intervening land having been inclosed more than twenty years before the commencement of litigation. Apart from these, the Forest constitutes a continuous stretch of uncultivated land, very much in the condition in which it has been from the earliest times of our history. It is densely covered with timber, but here and there,

there are open spaces of heath or grass. The trees
are for the most part of hornbeam, beech, and oak,
which have from early times been pollarded, and
which were lopped for firewood during the winter
months, for the benefit either of the Commoners or
of the inhabitants of certain districts, in a manner
greatly interfering with their growth and beauty.
But there are several groves of fine beech trees to
which this process has fortunately not been applied,
and some well-grown oaks near to Queen Elizabeth's
Lodge.

The Forest was in olden times a part of the much
wider range of Waltham Forest, a district which extended over 60,000 acres in Essex, to which Manwood's
definition of a royal forest applied : "a territory of woody
grounds and fruitful pastures, privileged for wild beasts,
and fowls of forest chase and warren, to rest and abide
there in the safe protection of the King, for his delight
and pleasure." This wide district was not all uninclosed land or waste. Probably not more than one-
fourth or one-fifth of its area, even in very early times,
was in this condition. The remainder was either
cultivated land or inclosed woodlands, and was forest
only in the sense that the forest laws applied to the
whole of its area. These laws were framed with a view
to sustain the exclusive right of the Sovereign to sport
over a wide district. No fences within it could be
maintained high enough to keep out a doe with her
fawn; the farmers were not allowed to drive the deer
from their crops, on which they fattened ; no buildings

could be erected without the consent of the forest authorities, " because of the increase of men and dogs and other things which might frighten the deer from their food." Trees could not be cut down without the same permission.

Among other rights claimed by the Crown was that of entering into any private owner's woods within the range of the Forest, and cutting there the branches of trees as " broust " for the deer's winter food; this was exercised so late as the nineteenth century. Deer and other game were protected for the exclusive sport of the Sovereign by most severe laws, enforced in Courts peculiar to the Forest, by officers responsible to the Crown.

Dogs in the district were "expeditated," that is, three claws of their fore feet were cut close to the ball of the foot to prevent their chasing the deer. Mutilation and even death were the penalties in early times for killing a deer. These were mitigated by the Charta de Foresta extorted from King John at the same time as Magna Charta; but for centuries after, the forest laws were very harsh and were enforced with rigour.

The Forest Courts consisted of the Court of Attachment, presided over by four Verderers, elected by the freeholders of the County of Essex, who had summary jurisdiction in offences of a trivial character, where the damage was not more than fourpence ; and the Court of Swainemote, also presided over by the Verderers, assisted by a jury of freeholders, who tried for offences of a more serious kind; they could not, however, pronounce sentence; this was reserved for the highest Court of Justice Seat, held at somewhat long intervals, and generally presided over by one of the judges of the land, who for this purpose was called Chief Justice in Eyre. There were numerous minor officials, such as master keepers, foresters, agisters, and regarders, whose duty it was to preserve the game, and to prevent and report encroachments on the forest; woodwards, who were charged with looking after the timber ; and reeves, who marked the cattle of the Commoners. Over these officials was the Lord Warden, an hereditary officer, whose charge it was to maintain the Forest unimpaired for the King's pleasure.

No Court of Justice Seat has been held in Waltham Forest since 1670. The Court of Attachment survived to a much later period, and was occasionally held in the present century, but it gradually became obsolete. Verderers ceased to be elected, and in 1870 only a single Verderer survived, without power of enforcing any rights.

So long as the forestal rights of the Crown were enforced on the lands of private owners beyond the actual Forest, they were the cause of grave hardships. In a suit against Sir Bernard Whetstone, Lord of the Manor of Woodford, one of the Forest Manors, on the part of the Attorney-General, in the year 1700, for making illegal fences on his own land, a grievous picture is drawn by the defendant, of the losses caused by the deer to himself and his tenants. "They were forced," he

said, "to give over ploughing and sowing their arable
land, of which the greater part of the demesne of his
Manor consisted. He was still obliged to pay composition, in wheat and oats, for the King's household,
though not a foot of the demesne had been ploughed
for the last ten years, by reason of the number of deer,
which would utterly destroy the corn; and the cessation of ploughing caused the increase of deer, by reason
that the barren and dry fallows were converted into
sweet and fresh green pastures to layer and feed the
cattle." *

The uninclosed parts of Waltham Forest were
confined, even in early times, to two wide and distinct
districts: the one known as Epping Forest, which
consisted probably of 9,000 acres; the other, Hainault
Forest, of about 4,000 acres. It does not appear
that the ownership of the soil of Epping Forest, or
of any substantial part of it, was even in early days
vested in the Crown—at all events, from the time of
Henry II. at latest. The district had been granted
out in yet earlier times, in very numerous Manors,
and the waste land was vested in their Lords, subject
to the rights of Commoners. Epping Forest alone
was divided between no fewer than nineteen such
distinct Manors; Hainault Forest between seven
Manors.

Of the Manors in Epping Forest, thirteen were
granted at various times by successive Sovereigns, from

* Fisher's "Forest of Essex," p. 58.

Edward the Confessor and Harold* to Henry II., to
various religious bodies; six of them to the Abbey
of Waltham Holy Cross, three to the Monastery of
St. Mary, Stratford, and a single Manor to each of
the following bodies: the Cathedral Church of St.
Paul, the Priory of Bermondsey, the Abbey of Barking,
and the Priory of Christ Church, London. They remained in these hands till the dissolution of the
religious houses in the time of Henry VIII., when
they were appropriated by that Sovereign; but they
were subsequently granted by him or his successors
to private owners, from whom they descended
to the persons who held them at the time of the
great suit of the Corporation of London. The other
Manors, not granted to religious bodies, were at a very
early period in the hands of private owners, from whom
they descended by bequest or purchase to their late
possessors.

All these grants were subject to the right of the
Crown, under the Forest Laws, to forbid the inclosure of
the waste. The Manors included much land that was
not in the waste of the Forest, and where freehold and
copyhold tenants had properties, in respect of which
they had the right of turning out cattle on the waste,
and the right of pannage, that is, of turning pigs

---

* King Harold was a great benefactor to Waltham Abbey.
Tradition says that he came there to pray before going forth to
meet the Normans. After his defeat and death, at the battle of
Hastings, his body was brought to the Abbey for burial. His tomb-
stone in the chancel was inscribed with the words "Haroldus
Infelix."—"Epping Forest," by E. N. Buxton, p. 63.

into the Forest to feed upon acorns and beech-mast.
They had in many cases also the right of lopping
and pollarding the trees in the waste in the winter
months, for the supply of wood for fuel for their houses.
In some Manors these rights of cutting wood were
strictly regulated, and were called "assignments." In
the Manor of Loughton, it will be seen later that the
inhabitants generally claimed and exercised the custom
and right of lopping the trees for firewood. It is
probable that in early times similar customs had been
enjoyed by the inhabitants of other Manors, and that the
"assignments" were in some manner a substitute for
them. In most of these Manors there were also, till a
comparatively recent period, common fields, or commonable land, such as have already been described. But
these were all inclosed early in the present century.*

The origin of the Forest is lost in antiquity. It
was probably afforested long before the Norman
Conquest, for though no mention is made of it in
Domesday Book, yet the paucity of inhabitants in
these parts, as shown in that survey, tends to prove
that the district was uncultivated and covered with
timber. There are a few references to it in very early
charters, but the earliest description of it is the record
of a perambulation made immediately after the Charter
de Forestâ, in the ninth year of Henry III., by which

* Seven hundred acres were inclosed in Chigwell Manor; 340 in
Chingford; 534 in Epping; 360 in Leyton; 833 in Waltham and its
dependent Manors. These must all have been common fields, and
not wastes of Manors or Commons.

it was enacted that all lands added to the Royal Forests by Henry II., Richard, and John, should be thrown out again, and that they were to be viewed for that purpose by good and lawful men. A copy of this survey exists in the Bodleyan Library.

It appears from this and other documents that this perambulation substantially coincided with another in the reign of Edward I., the record of which also still exists. In spite of this, there appear to have been disputes from time to time with respect to the extent of the Forest, which were not definitely settled till the time of the Long Parliament.

The Forest was in these early periods, and for centuries later, the favourite resort of the sovereigns. It was described even so late as 1628 by Sir Robert Heath as being

"a very fertile and fruitful soyle; and being full of most pleasant and delightful playnes and lawnes, most useful and commodious for hunting and chasing of the game or redd and falowe deare . . .

"especiallie and above all their other fforests, prized and esteemed by the King's Majestie, and his said noble progenitors the Kings and Queenes of this realme of England, as well for his and their pleasure, disport, and recreation from those pressing cares for the publique weale and safetie, which are inseparablic incident to theire kinglie office, as for the interteyne-ment of forreigne Princes and Ambassadors, thereby to show unto them the honor and magnificence of the Kings and Queenes of this Realme."

In the reign of Edward VI. complaint was made that the forest laws had been neglected. The King consequently issued a proclamation setting forth that "yt hathe byne much brutyd and noysed" among diverse of his loving subjects that he intended to disafforest the Forest and to destroy the deer and game there, whereby many of them had been encouraged to destroy the rest and to hinder and disquiet the deer and game "sembleably to murdre and kyll a nombre of the said deere not a lyttle to our dyspleasure;" and informing the people that he intended to maintain the forest laws as his father or any other of his progenitors had done, under which every offender was liable to imprisonment for three years, and to pay a fine at the King's pleasure and to find sureties or abjure the realm.

Queen Elizabeth, before she came to the throne, is said to have hunted in the Forest, probably riding over from Hatfield, which was her permanent residence and which was at no great distance; she was also, when Queen, occasionally at Chingford, if we are to believe the local traditions.

James I. appears to have valued the right of sporting in the Forest. A short time after coming to the throne he violently scolded his subjects for their ill manners in interfering with the sport of himself and his family; and threatened not only to enforce the Forest laws against all stealers and hunters of deer, and to exempt them from his general pardon, but to debar any person of quality so offending from his presence, and to proceed against those who provoked his displeasure, by martial law ! *

* Fisher's "Forest of Essex," p. 197.

Charles I., more with the object of raising money than of enjoying sport, revived the claims of the Crown to the widest possible boundaries of the Forest. By his direction, extortionate demands were made on land-owners to buy off the dormant rights of forest, in respect of all the Royal Forests, and nowhere to a greater extent than in Essex. In this county alone the King is said to have raised by such means no less a sum than £300,000. These claims of forestal rights were reckoned, with the compelling of knighthood, with tonnage and poundage dues, and ship money, among the national grievances; they were no doubt planned and carried out, with the help of Sir John Finch, his Attorney-General,* and others, in order to raise money for the King, without the aid of Parliament. It was not till 1641 that the King found it necessary to retrace his steps. On March 16 in that year, just four months after the meeting of the Long Parliament, the Earl of Holland signified to the House of Lords that the King had commanded him to let them know " that, His Majesty understanding that the forest laws are grievous to the subjects of this Kingdom, His Majesty, out of his grace and goodness to his people, is willing to lay down all the new bounds of his Forests in

---

* Lord Falkland, in opening the impeachment of Finch, said of him, "He gave our goods to the King, our lands to the deer, our liberties to the sheriffs; so that there was no way by which we had not been oppressed and destroyed, if the power of this person had been equal to his will, or that the will of His Majesty had been equal to his power."

this Kingdom as they were before the late Justice's
seat held." An Act was passed in the same year,
declaring that thenceforth the limits and bounds of
all the Forests should be taken to extend no further
than those commonly reputed in the twentieth year of
James I.; and all subsequent acts, by which the
bounds of the Forests were further extended, were
declared void.

Almost immediately after the passing of this Act, a
perambulation of Waltham Forest was made by virtue of
a Commission under the Great Seal, directed to the Earl
of Warwick and forty-four other Commissioners. The
boundaries shown in the map attached to this survey
agree almost exactly with those laid down in 1301.
Thus ended a controversy about the bounds of the
Forest, which had lasted from the time of King
John.

That Charles I. was actuated mainly by the desire
to raise money, and cared little about the maintenance
of the Forest, is evident from the fact that he con-
templated a scheme for wholly disafforesting Waltham
Forest. There is extant a State paper in the Record
Office, giving a list of landowners of the district and
their claims under a scheme for this purpose. Had he
been able to carry it out, it would probably have resulted in large gains to him. For the disafforesting of
the comparatively small Forest of Gaultres, he received as
his share the sum of £20,000. For that of the Forest
of Dean, if it had been carried out, he was to receive
£106,000, and a fee farm rent of £1,600 a year for

I

ever. It will be seen later that he authorised the
disafforesting of Malvern Forest by Cornelius Vermuyden, and probably received a very large sum
for it.

The Forest of Waltham was in even greater danger
of extinction during the Commonwealth. On the 22nd
of November, 1653, the then Parliament passed an Act
vesting all Forests and all honours and lands within
their precincts and perambulations, belonging to the
late King, his relict or eldest son, and all royalties,
privileges, etc., belonging to them, in trustees, to be
sold for the benefit of the Commonwealth. But
Cromwell in the following year took the matter out of
the hands of the Parliament, and soon afterwards we
hear less of the Commonwealth and more of the Protector. In 1654 an ordinance was made by " His
Highness the Lord Protector, by and with the advice
and consent of his Council," that Commissioners should
be appointed by His Highness under the Great Seal to
survey all the late King's Forests, according to the
perambulations made in 17 Car. I., and to consider how
the same might, both for the present and the future, be
best improved and disposed for the benefit and advantage of the Commonwealth. They were directed to
make minute inquiries into the situation of the Forests,
and the public and private rights in them, including rights of wood and pasture; to hear and determine claims of rights and interests; to make allotments in satisfaction of them, and for highways, and
to treat for the disafforesting of all forest lands.

The Commissioners—Widdrington, Whitelocke, Sydenham, and Montagu — recommended that the forest rights of His Highness should be restored, and the Courts re-established. They reported to the Council that the forests being already by Act of Parliament vested in trustees to be sold for certain uses, there was a doubt as to the title, and a difficulty either in selling or leasing. It was therefore suggested that four forests should be sold by way of experiment, and as to the rest, that "Lawnes and Inclosures belonging to His Highness should be let from year to year at the best rates that could be got for them ; that fellable coppice woods should be preserved till fit for sale and then sold ; and that for finding out and restoring His Highness' rights in Forests, preservation of timber, punishments of wastes, spoiles, encroachments and other trespasses committed within the Forests, officers should be supplied."* They also recommended that the Forest Courts should be re-established for the enforcement of the forestal rights.

Nothing, however, was done in pursuance of these recommendations during the remaining years of the Commonwealth. On the restoration of the Monarchy the Forest Courts were re-constituted. Charles II. occasionally hunted in the district ; but after his time it does not appear that the Forest was ever again resorted to by Royalty for sport. It was probably due to this that, by degrees, the forestal rights of the Crown, over other lands than the waste of the Forest, were allowed

* Fisher's "Forest of Essex," p. 50.

I 2

to lapse, and were ultimately abandoned, and the Forest was practically limited to the two main districts of open land—those of Epping Forest and Hainault Forest.

In the Report of the Land Revenue Commissioners for 1793, it is stated that Epping Forest then consisted of 9,000 acres of open land. It appears that already the Forest was frequented by the public from London for recreation, for the Commissioners, in very strong terms, said that it was most important that nothing should be done to countenance its inclosure, and especially so because of its close proximity to the Metropolis.

From a report made by the Lord Warden, in 1813, as to the prevailing abuses, it appears that gravel and sand pits were open in all directions in the Forest, and that the materials were used without restraint; the turf was removed from large areas of ground; bushes and underwood were cut and taken away at pleasure; deer-stealers were so numerous that there was hardly a house for miles round the Forest which did not contain one or more; encroachments and inclosures were made in various parts; oak timber was shamefully destroyed; young trees were wasted, and pollards and underwood were lopped and carried away.*

From 1793 to 1848 an almost continuous series of small inclosures took place of the waste land in the Forest, but generally by arrangement between the Lords of Manors and their Commoners, and with a report of

* Fisher's "Forest of Essex," p. 336.

the verderers that no injury would be done to the rights of the Crown. In 1805, the Commissioners of Woods and Forests sold the Manor of West Ham with its wastes and forestal rights. The result of these inclosures was that the area of what was strictly forest or open land in Epping Forest was reduced, by the year 1848, from 9,000 to 7,000 acres.

This process was facilitated by the fact, that from the beginning of the present century, the Court of Attachment in the Forest, which was specially charged with the duty of preventing inclosures, gradually fell into desuetude. The growth of London also, and the proximity of a large population, made it difficult to maintain the forest laws.

The old use and value of the Forest for sporting purposes came to be disregarded, while its new value in relation to the health, recreation, and enjoyment of the great and constantly growing population of London, was not as yet recognised and appreciated. The general current of public opinion was still in favour of the inclosure of common lands. It was mindful of the vices and hardships of the forest laws, as enforced in olden times, and sympathised rather with the owners of land in the Forest, as against the claims of the Crown, and looked with utilitarian views to the greater return of produce or rent, which could be obtained from inclosed land, than from common or forest land.

In 1848 a Committee of the House of Commons, presided over by Lord Duncan, took this view both of

Epping and Hainault Forests. It recommended the inclosure of the latter, where the Crown was the Lord of the Manor, and with respect to Epping Forest advised that it should be disafforested, and that the Crown should sell its forestal rights to the Lords of Manors. It accompanied this, however, with a recommendation that something should be done to preserve a portion of the Forest for the enjoyment and recreation of the public. In the following year a Royal Commission on the subject of the Crown Lands, presided over by the late Lord Portman, took a different view from that of Lord Duncan's Committee. It emphatically recommended that the Crown rights over Epping Forest should be defended, observing that no injustice would result from such a course to private owners, inasmuch as they held their lands under original grants from the Crown, with the full knowledge of the existence of such rights.

Two years later the Legislature sanctioned a course in pursuance of the recommendations of Lord Duncan's Committee, and opposed to those of Lord Portman's Commission, by agreeing to a measure for the disafforesting of Hainault Forest. This Forest, like that of Epping, had been divided among several distinct Manors, some of which in very early times had been granted by the Crown to the Abbey of Barking. On the dissolution of the Abbey by Henry VIII., these Manors were retained by the Crown, and were not re-granted to private owners. A large part of Hainault Forest, therefore, was practically the property of the Crown, subject to the rights of the Commoners of the district, of turning out cattle in it.

In 1851 an Act was passed (14 and 15 Victoria c. 43) for the disafforesting of Hainault Forest and for its inclosure. The waste consisted of 4,000 acres, of which 2,842 were in the Manors belonging to the Crown ; and in this part was the beautiful King's Wood—a far finer woodland district than anything in Epping Forest. Of this, 1,917 acres were allotted to the Crown, and the remainder was given in compensation to the Commoners. The Lord Warden received £5,250 in compensation for the abolition of his hereditary office. The trees were grubbed on the Crown allotments, at a cost of £42,000, which was paid for by the sale of timber. The cleared land was laid out in farms. As a result, in 1863, the rent of the land was £4,000 a year as compared with an annual income from the Forest of £500. But it resulted that there was lost for ever one of the most beautiful of natural Forests in the south of England, within easy reach of London. Not a protest seems to have been raised against this course, either in Parliament, or on the part of the Press or the public.

In view of this proceeding of the Crown, it was perhaps to be expected that the owners of the Manors in Epping Forest should consider that they were only pursuing the same public policy, in endeavouring to follow its example, by inclosing the waste lands of the Forest within their several Manors, but with little regard for the rights of Commoners, and still less for the rights or interests of the inhabitants of their districts, or of the people of London. Their action was greatly facilitated and promoted by that of the Commissioners of Woods and Forests, who, in pursuance of the recommendations of Lord Duncan's Committee, and without any authority from Parliament, offered to sell to the Lords of Manors the forestal rights of the Crown over the waste lands of Epping Forest, at the rate of about £5 per acre. The effect of this was to extinguish these rights, and to leave the Lords of Manors, who bought them, free to deal with their Commoners, or to inclose in spite of them—a process which was practically impossible so long as the Crown rights were enforced.

The Lords of Manors of about a half of the Forest availed themselves of this offer, and bought up and extinguished the forestal rights of the Crown over their respective Manors. The more sales of this kind that were effected, the greater became the difficulty of maintaining the Crown rights, where they still subsisted in law. The Department further directed that the deer should be killed down; and, although the deer were never quite destroyed, the district ceased practically to be a forest in the legal sense of the term. The sale of the Crown rights over 3,513 acres produced £15,793.

The process of inclosure was further facilitated by the fact that, some years previously, the hereditary office of Lord Warden had, through his wife, the last representative of the Earls of Tylney, fallen to Mr. Wellesley Pole,[*] later Lord Mornington, a dissolute spendthrift,

---

[*] This person, whose memory still survives in the well-known line of " Rejected Addresses "—

" Long may Long Wellesley Tylney Long Pole live,"

who was also the Lord of four or five of the Manors within the Forest. He reduced the Verderers' Court to impotence by appointing his own solicitor to be its steward, and in lieu of maintaining the Forest as he was bound in duty to do, he led the way to its destruction by inclosing and appropriating a great part of its waste within his own Manors.

It was to be expected that his example would quickly be followed by others of the Lords of Manors. By the year 1851 the area of the Forest was reduced to 6,000 acres. In the years which ensued further large inclosures of the Forest were made by many of the Lords of Manors, some of them by arrangement with such of the Commoners as they were willing to recognise as having rights; others without any regard for the Commoners; some of them in respect of land where the Crown rights had been bought; others where the land was still subject by law to these forestal rights.

Meanwhile, the fate of Hainault Forest, and the increasing inclosures of Epping Forest, began to disturb the public mind, and to raise the question whether it was really for the interest of the people of

acquired through his wife a property with a rent roll of £70,000 a year. By reckless extravagance he dissipated the whole of it in a very few years. He fled the country to avoid his creditors, and became a pensioner on his brother, the Duke of Wellington. His wife died of a broken heart; his children were taken from him by the Court of Chancery. His mansion at Wanstead was pulled down.

London that they should be deprived altogether of such open spaces.

In 1863, Mr. Peacocke, one of the members for the County of Essex, induced the House of Commons to pass an address to the Crown, praying that thenceforward there should be no further sales of its forestal rights in Epping Forest.

In the same year a Committee of the House of Commons inquired into the subject of the Forest and reported upon the inclosures. It was of opinion that to employ the forestal rights of the Crown to obstruct the process of inclosure to which Lords of Manors and their Commoners were entitled, would be of doubtful justice, and would probably fail in effect. It recommended the sanction of Parliament for the inclosure of the residue of the Forest, and for the ascertainment of rights, and that partly by these means, and partly by purchase, an adequate portion of the waste should be secured for the purposes of health and recreation, for which the Forest had been from time immemorial enjoyed by the inhabitants of the Metropolis.

In the Committee on London Commons in 1865, Epping Forest again formed the subject of inquiry. In its report, already referred to, the recent inclosures of the waste were described, and the opinion was expressed that they would prove to be illegal if challenged in the Courts of Law. The report of this Committee was followed by still further and larger inclosures of the Forest, the Lords of Manors being

eager to challenge its conclusions as to their rights, and
to vindicate their claims to inclose. The Commoners,
a scattered and feeble folk, were little considered. The
nature of their rights being ignored, or not understood,
it was contended that they could only turn out their
cattle upon the wastes of the Manors in which their
lands were situate, and that the absence of boundary
fences alone was the foundation of the right or practice
of allowing their beasts to stray over the wastes of the
other Forest Manors. Many of these inclosures were
made by virtue of alleged customs of the Manors
to inclose with the consent of the homage-juries
of the copyhold tenants, summoned to the Manor
Courts. In some cases these Courts were held very
irregularly, and if anyone attended for the purpose
of objecting to grants of the waste, the Court at
which they were to be made was not opened till eight
or nine o'clock at night, when the wearied objectors
had departed. In one Manor the homage summoned
consisted of persons who were to receive grants of
waste; when it came to the turn of one of them to
receive a piece of land, he retired from the homage, and
another took his place; and when the grant had been
made to him, he returned to his post and assisted in
granting land to others. Thus the rights of the Commoners were overridden by collusive acts, which in
theory were done according to the custom of the
Manor. In other Manors the Commoners were left to
take any remedy which they could find. In the
Manor of Wanstead, between 1851 and 1869, there were

102 inclosures, containing over 286 acres. In that of Woodford, 146 inclosures of 205 acres. In Ruckholt Manor, 22 inclosures of 41 acres. In Higham Hills Manor 4 inclosures of 96 acres. The area of the open Forest was reduced by these and other inclosures, which were effected since 1851, from 6,000 acres to 3,000 acres.

The largest of these operations was that in the Manor of Loughton, the lord of which was Mr. Maitland, who was also rector of the parish. This gentleman inclosed in one swoop the whole of the waste of the Forest within his Manor, consisting of about 1,300 acres, with the exception of a trifling allotment of about nine acres, which he left for the recreation of the villagers. He attempted, in fact, a general inclosure without an Act of Parliament. He allotted portions of the land in extinguishment of the rights of those tenants of his Manor whom he admitted to be entitled. He bought up others of these rights for money. He compensated others of his copyholders by enfranchisement; and having, as he believed, settled with all of them, he held himself entitled to the bulk of the land inclosed. A stout fence was erected round the whole of the inclosures; the public was shut out; and a commencement was made of clearing the Forest by cutting down the trees.

The inhabitants of this Manor had, from time immemorial, enjoyed the right of lopping the trees, for firewood, during the winter months, from St. Martin's Day, November 11, to St. George's Day, April 23. It

EPPING FOREST (SOUTHERN PART)

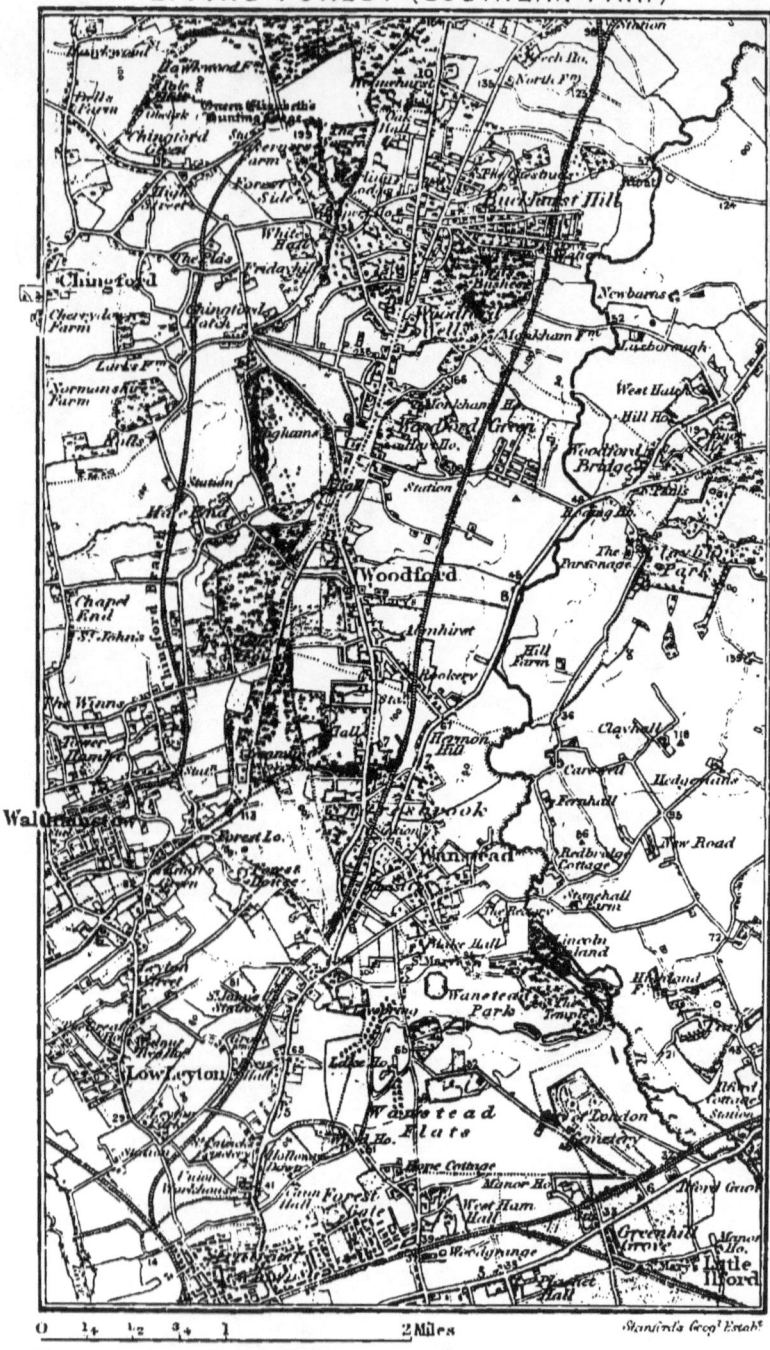

The parts coloured green, red & blue represent the present Forest
Those coloured red were enclosed & were restored to the Forest by Sir George
Jessels' judgment.
Those coloured blue have been purchased by the Corporation of London

EPPING FOREST (NORTHERN PART)

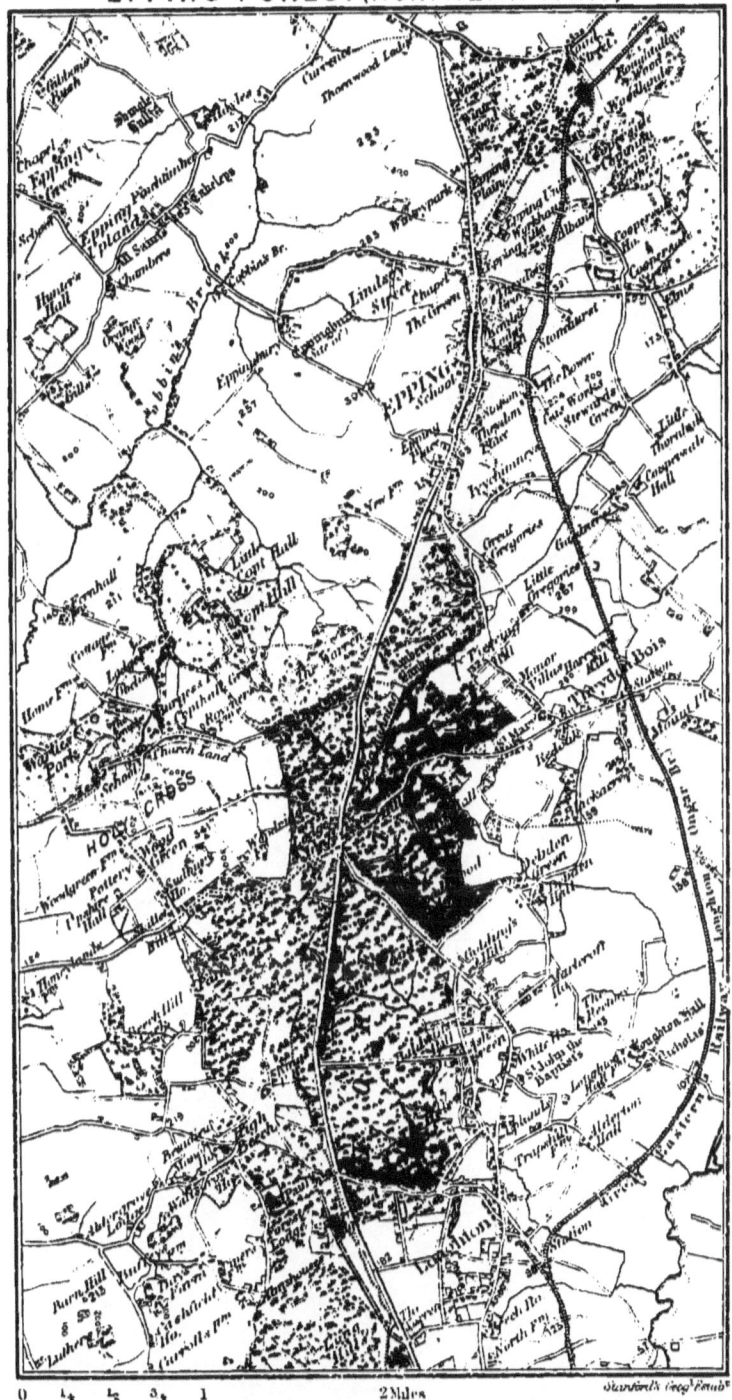

0   ¼   ½   ¾   1   2 Miles

Stanford's Geog.l Estab.t

was the tradition of the people that this custom had its origin in a grant from Queen Elizabeth, and that it was conditional on their beginning to lop the trees as the clock struck the hour of midnight on the preceding night. They were wont to meet for that purpose at Staples Hill within the Forest, where, after lighting a fire and celebrating the occasion by draughts of beer, they lopped from twelve till two o'clock, and then returned to their homes. The branches, according to the custom, could not be faggoted in the Forest, but were made into heaps six feet high, and were then drawn out of the Forest in sledges. In olden times the first load was drawn out by white horses. The wood could only be cut for the use of the inhabitants of the parish. Whatever the origin of this right may have been, it was certainly much older than the time of Queen Elizabeth ; for the rolls of the Manor in the early part of her reign mention the user as a custom. As there is generally some foundation for such traditions, it is possible the Queen may have confirmed this customary right by some document, which has since been lost. Whatever the origin of the custom, there cannot be a doubt that it had been persistently maintained by the inhabitants of Loughton for many centuries.

The story ran that about a century ago, the then Lord of the Manor, wishing to extinguish the custom, invited all his parishioners to a banquet on the eve of St. Martin's Day, and plied them plentifully with liquor, in the hope that midnight would find them in such a condition that they would be unable to perambulate the Forest, so as to maintain their rights. One man, however, kept his head clear of liquor, and stole from the feast at midnight, perambulated the Forest, and exercised his right by lopping some trees, and having done so returned to the feast, where he found his friends still being plied with drink; the lord, thereupon, angry at the failure of his scheme, bid them begone with many curses. Whether the story be true or not, the tradition as to the necessity for observing the midnight programme on St. Martin's Eve was firmly planted in the minds of the people.

After Mr. Maitland's great inclosure, when the day arrived, in 1866, for the annual assertion of the custom, a labouring man named Willingale, with his two sons, who had in past years made a living, during the winter months, by lopping wood for their neighbours, went out as usual at midnight, broke in upon the lord's fences, perambulated the Forest, and lopped the trees in accordance with the custom. For this act in vindication of their rights, the three Willingales were summoned a few days later by the Lord of the Manor before the local justices; and although they protested that they were only asserting their rights according to the custom, which should have ousted the jurisdiction of the magistrates, they were convicted of malicious trespass on property, and were sent to prison for two months with hard labour. It turned out that one at least of the magistrates had received an allotment of the inclosed lands in compensation for his rights. One of Willingale's sons was put into a damp cell in the prison, where he caught a severe cold, which developed into pneumonia, and resulted in his death.

These high-handed proceedings caused great indignation in the district and in the East of London. Meetings were held to protest against the inclosures of Loughton. When Willingale came out of prison, he was advised to seek the aid of the Commons Society. It appeared to the Society that the custom of the people of Loughton was such that, if supported by legal proceedings, it might result in defeating the inclosures, and in preserving this part of the Forest. A fund of £1,000 was raised among its leading members— the half of it from Sir T. Fowell Buxton, an owner and resident within the range of the Forest; and a suit was commenced in the name of Willingale, on behalf of the inhabitants of Loughton, claiming the right to lop the trees in that part of the Forest during the winter months, and asking for an injunction to restrain Mr. Maitland from cutting down the trees and inclosing the Forest. Another suit of the same kind was commenced in the name of a freehold tenant of the Manor named Castell, claiming the right of lopping the trees as a commonable right. An interim injunction was thereupon obtained to prevent Mr. Maitland cutting down the trees of the Forest, pending the hearing of Willingale's suit.

The case thus asserted, on behalf of the inhabitants of Loughton, was not free from difficulty, owing to the technical rule of law already alluded to, that the inhabitants of a place are too vague a body to enjoy a

custom or to prescribe for a right of a profitable kind. It
will be seen, however, that some years later the custom
received legal recognition, and that the inhabitants
were compensated for it on the final settlement of the
Forest.

Meanwhile, in the suit on their behalf, the claim
made was that, "by ancient charter from the Crown,
the right was granted to the labouring and poor people
inhabiting the parish to lop or cut boughs and branches,
above seven feet from the ground, for the proper use
and consumption of themselves, and for sale, for their
own relief, to all or any of the inhabitants for their
consumption within the parish as fuel; that the charter
which was formerly among the records of the Forest
Court, called the Verderers' Court, had, together with
other records, been long since lost or improperly disposed of; but that there were divers documents and
entries in the Court rolls relating to the Manor,
referring to and containing evidence of the charter."

To this the defendant made a preliminary legal
objection, or demurrer, on the grounds that the inhabitants of a parish are too vague a class of persons to
claim such a right by prescription, and that the right
itself could not exist at law, being a claim to take
profits in another man's land.

These objections were argued for three days in the
Rolls Court before Lord Romilly, who, in his judgment,
overruled the demurrer. In doing so he said—

"A passage has been cited from Shepherd's "Touchstone" to
the effect that a grant cannot be made to the inhabitants of a

village as such, but although they may be all capable of taking
individually as grantees, yet they cannot under that general
designation ; but that passage applies solely to grants by private
individuals. On the other hand, several authorities were cited
by Mr. Joshua Williams to establish the proposition that a
grant by the Crown to a class of persons is good. The distinction between a grant by a private individual and a grant
by the Crown is this : that as the Crown has the power to
create a Corporation, so, if it is necessary for the purpose of
establishing the validity of the grant, the grantees will be
treated as a corporation *quoad* the grant, which is not the case
with a grant by a private individual, because a private individual
has no power of erecting a corporation. . . . Another cir-
cumstance which is very strongly in favour of the suit is that
it is a grant by the Crown in derogation of its forestal rights.
The forestal rights were excessively oppressive upon the inhabitants, and accordingly the Crown frequently made to the inhabitants in the neighbourhood of a forest, certain grants in
derogation of those rights, which grants, though they might
not be good in every other respect, were good as far as they
were in derogation of the forestal rights." *

The legal objections being thus disposed of, there
remained the question of fact to be determined on the
main trial of the case—namely, whether there was
sufficient evidence to justify the presumption that a
grant had been made to the inhabitants in ancient times
of the right claimed by them, though the charter itself
had been lost. This was not decided in the Willingale
suit, for the old man died in 1870, before his case came
on for hearing, and his death abated the proceedings.
During the four years between the commencement of
the suit and his death, it had been difficult for him to

* Willingale *v.* Maitland, L.R. 3 Eq., 103.

J

find employment in Loughton, owing to the part he was taking in maintaining this suit against the chief owner of land in the parish ; it was necessary, therefore, to make him an allowance of a pound a week. Much difficulty, also, was experienced in finding a lodging for him in the village, without which he would have ceased to be an inhabitant. During this time he was more than once offered 'a large sum—as much, it was said, as £500—to abandon the suit. I had opportunities of seeing the old man, and always found him determined to stand by the case and to reject all such offers. His treatment by the magistrates and the death of his son aggravated the feeling of injustice, caused by the arbitrary inclosure of Mr. Maitland, in disregard of the rights of the Loughton people. Though Willingale's death abated the suit and prevented the issues being tried, there cannot be a doubt that the ultimate saving of the Forest was largely due to this case. It practically kept the Forest *in statu quo* for four years, until the commencement of the great Corporation suit. It prevented the destruction of the trees in the Manor of Loughton. It gave time and opportunity for a closer examination of the Rolls of the Manor and of the ancient Forest records. As the result of this examination, the opinion was formed that, without much greater funds than were then in hand, it would be difficult to impeach the general inclosures of the Forest; but that if some Commoner with ample means could be found willing to do so, there was every prospect of success.

It was not easy to find such a Commoner. The principal landowners in the district who were Commoners, and not Lords of Manors, were either indifferent to the inclosure of the Forest, or had already been bought off by allotments from it, or were afraid to incur the great hostility of their class, who were generally ranged on the side of the Lords of Manors. The case differed greatly from those of other suburban Commons, where the residents in villas around them were almost invariably opposed in interest and sympathy to inclosures, and could be relied upon to resist them. In Epping Forest the prize was great; the persons really interested against inclosure were few. It was not found possible therefore to enlist the larger Commoners in any sufficient number to fight the battle with the confederated Lords of Manors.

Fortunately, however, inquiry showed that among the owners of land within the precincts of the old Forest, having common rights, was the Corporation of London. They were possessors of an estate of 200 acres at Little Ilford, in the Manor of Wanstead. They had bought this property for the purpose of a cemetery; a portion of it had been devoted to this object, and the residue was let as a farm. Common rights were undoubtedly attached to this estate, in respect at least of that part of the Forest within the Manor in which it was situate. It was decided, therefore, to make every effort to induce the Corporation to undertake the great task of impeaching the inclosures of the

J 2

Forest, and of restoring it to its pristine extent, for the
benefit of the people of London.

I introduced to the Lord Mayor a deputation of
persons interested in the preservation of Epping Forest.
We insisted on the importance of the subject, and
represented that the Corporation would acquire great
and lasting honour by fighting the cause of London
generally. We pointed out the old connection of the
City of London with the Forest in respect of the annual
Easter hunt; we urged them to take up the cudgels
against the Lords of Manors on behalf of their
common rights at Ilford. The Lord Mayor gave a
friendly ear to our representatives. Mr. Scott, the
City Chamberlain, also took up the subject with great
ardour, and it was mainly at his instance that the Corporation was induced to move in the matter. This body,
with a keen eye to its advantage, perceived that great
popularity might be achieved by fighting for the interest
of the public in a case of such importance and magnitude,
and was the more inclined to embark on it at a time
when the separate exclusive rights of the Corporation
were threatened by the demands of London generally for
a single Municipal Government.

The Corporation having decided to take up the case
of Epping Forest, and to fight the cause of the
Commoners and the public, I felt that their proceedings could only be conducted to a successful
conclusion if piloted through the quicksands of the
Law Courts by a lawyer familiar with such cases, and
fully instructed in the intricate law of Commons. I

personally suggested to the Lord Mayor, in an interview on the subject, that the official City Solicitor, however able as a man of business, would probably be at sea on such a special subject, and that the wise course would be to associate with him the Solicitor of the Commons Society, Mr. Robert Hunter, who had been engaged in all the great Commons cases, who had brought so many of them to a successful conclusion, and who in the Willingale case had already made himself acquainted with much of the history and rights of the Forest. Fortunately, my advice was followed, and the great suit which was then initiated was practically conducted, on behalf of the City Solicitor, by Mr. Robert Hunter.

The effect of ample funds for the prosecution of the great cause of saving the Forest was soon visible. They enabled a much more searching and complete investigation of the records of the Forest to be made than had hitherto been possible; and this led to a discovery of the utmost importance, which was the keystone to the subsequent success of the Corporation suit.

It had long been the contention of the Lords of Manors that each of their Manors was entirely distinct from all others in the Forest, that the Commoners of each had rights of common only in the waste of their particular Manor, and not generally over the whole of the Forest. In this view, the process of inclosure by a Lord of the Manor of the forest waste within the boundaries of his own district was comparatively easy, for it was only necessary for him to come to terms with this limited number of Commoners; and after

he had once settled with the principal landowners
having rights of common therein, it would be difficult,
if not impossible, for any smaller Commoner to challenge
him in the Law Courts, and to incur the enormous costs
of a suit. The prize within the grasp of the Lords of
Manors was most valuable. The Forest land when inclosed would be worth in many parts from £1,000 and
upwards per acre. They reckoned upon gradually
buying up the rights of the important Commoners,
either in money or by allotments of the Forest, and
then approving under the Statute of Merton, and on
frightening the smaller Commoners, by arbitrary inclosure, against contesting their rights. For this purpose, then, it was all important for them to show that
the Commoners of a particular Manor were confined to
it alone, and had no rights over the whole of the Forest,
or over the wastes of other Manors.

The researches of Mr. Hunter into the ancient records
led to the discovery that this view of the Forest was
unsound, that instead of being a congeries of separate
Manors, the Forest was one great waste, over which the
Commoners of every one of the nineteen Manors had the
right of turning out their cattle, without the obligation
of confining them to their particular districts. The
importance of this discovery could not be over-rated.
It at once became clear that the arrangements, made for
inclosure by the several Lords of Manors with their
respective Commoners, were wholly invalid, and without
effect upon the rights not only of the other Commoners of
their own Manors, but of all the numerous Commoners in

every other part of the Forest. It became equally certain that any single Commoner in any part of the Forest, no matter what Manor he belonged to, could contest and upset the inclosures made by any one or all of the Lords of Manors in every other part of the Forest. It followed that the Corporation of London, by virtue of their property at Ilford, had rights of common over the whole Forest, and could in a single suit challenge and impeach every one of the inclosures, which had been made by all the Lords of Manors and others within recent years.

On this discovery—the importance and legal bearing of which was confirmed by the Counsel employed in the case—it was determined to initiate a single great suit in the name of the Commissioners of Sewers of the City of London, in whom the Ilford Estate was vested, on behalf of the Corporation, against sixteen out of the nineteen Lords of Manors, who had appropriated portions of the Forest by inclosures within recent years. In this suit the Corporation claimed on behalf of all the owners and occupiers of land, within the precincts of the ancient Forest of Waltham, without reference to their tenancy in any Manor, the right of common of pasture over the whole of the waste lands of the Forest, and asked for an injunction to abate existing inclosures, and to restrain the Lords of Manors and others from further encroachments.

With the object of providing themselves with funds for this great suit, and to enable them to undertake charge of the Forest and other Commons within reach of London, the Corporation induced Parliament to

prolong to them, for thirty years, a small fixed duty,
amounting to about £20,000 a year, on grain imported
into London, in lieu of a much wider charge, which
they had claimed, from time immemorial, for the metage
of grain. The Act authorising this provided that
the proceeds should be expended on the preservation of
Commons and open spaces within twenty-five miles of
the centre of London. But at the instance of the
Metropolitan Board, who were jealous of their own
jurisdiction, there were excepted from this provision
such Commons and open spaces as were within the
district of that Board. As Epping Forest lies beyond
this district, but within twenty-five miles of London,
the Corporation were able to use the funds provided by
this Act, for the maintenance of their suit and for the
ultimate settlement of the question.

The great suit was commenced in the month of July,
1871. The Lords of Manors at once replied to it by
demurring to the case set up by the Corporation,
alleging that such a claim to a right of common of
pasture over the whole of the Forest could not be valid
at law. The demurrer was overruled by the Master of
the Rolls, Lord Romilly, and his decision was maintained on appeal by the Lords Justices. It will be well
to quote from the judgment of Lord Justice Mellish:

"The right," he said, "alleged in the Bill is, in my opinion,
a right on the part of all the owners of lands in the Forest, for
themselves and their tenants occupiers of lands in the Forest, to
common over the wastes of the Forest. I can see no reason
why the right may not have a legal existence. I think it is
possible that the King, when the Forest was originally formed,

might have created that right. If, at the time when the Forest was originally formed, the land was the property of the Crown, I cannot see why the King, when he formed the Manors, might not have granted to the Lord of each Manor, for himself and his tenants, a right of common over all the wastes of the Forest. Or if the lands were not the lands of the Crown at the time when the Forest was formed, then the Forest might have been formed with the consent of the owners of the land over which the Forest was formed, because in point of law the King could not make a man's land into Forest without some agreement or consent from him. Then it may have been part of the arrangement by which the Forest was formed that all the owners of lands within the Forest were to have rights of common over the wastes of the Forest." *

This important preliminary legal point being determined, it remained to investigate and decide the issues of fact. Before, however, describing the result of the suit, it is necessary to point out other proceedings in Parliament on the subject of the Forest.

The continued inclosures in the various Manors of Epping Forest, and the consequent rapid shrinkage of its area, at last thoroughly aroused the attention of the public, and there were loud complaints against the Government for not enforcing the Crown rights, for the purpose of abating the inclosures and preserving the Forest. Especially had the action of a Mr. Hodgson excited indignation. This gentleman had within very recent years inclosed upwards of 300 acres of Forest in the Manor of Chingford, over which the Crown still retained its forestal rights, had cut down all the trees

* Glasse *v.* Commissioners of Sewers. L.R. 7, Ch. 456.

upon them, and had warned off the Crown officers from the land. He had done this with impunity.

In 1866, in consequence of the pressure of public opinion, and the reports of the several Committees which had dealt with the subject, a measure was passed transferring the management of the Crown rights in the Forest from the Commissioners of Woods and Forests—who regarded the property of the Crown only from the point of view of income and profits, and who had been the instruments of the sale of the Crown rights over more than a half of the Forest—to the Office of Works, presumably with the object of enforcing those rights, in the interest of the public, for the abatement of inclosures and for the preservation of the Forest.

In the same session, the Chancellor of the Exchequer —Mr. Gladstone—in answer to a question on the subject, stated that, with the entire sanction of the Queen, these rights would be enforced in accordance with the desire so often expressed by Parliament. Nothing, however, followed upon this, and the inclosures remained unabated, and continued to increase in number. In 1869, an influential deputation waited on the then Chancellor of the Exchequer—Mr. Lowe—with whom practically rested the question whether to risk the public money in vindication of these rights. They got little satisfaction, however, from him. He treated the whole subject with contempt and sarcasm, and declined to take any step in the Courts of Law for the enforcement of the Crown's rights.

In consequence of this rebuff, Mr. Fawcett, on February 14th, 1870, in a most able speech, brought the whole subject of the inclosures of Epping Forest before the House of Commons, and moved an address to the Crown, praying that Her Majesty would be graciously pleased to defend the rights of the Crown over the Forest, so that it might be preserved as an open space for the recreation of the people.

Mr. Fawcett was replied to by the Solicitor-General (now Lord Coleridge), who said he approached the subject with every sympathy for the object in view, namely, the preservation of Epping Forest, and without the smallest desire to throw any impediment in the way.

"If it were true," he said, "that any rights of the Crown had been interfered with, in which the subjects of the Crown shared, and if it could be shown that by a simple and cheap mode the Crown could maintain its own rights, and by maintaining its rights, maintain practically and effectively the rights of the subjects, he should decidedly approve the interference of the Crown. Indeed, he would go further and say that if the rights of the Crown were of such a character that they could be exchanged for something of a substantial value—as, for instance, if the Crown by parting with its rights over 3,000 acres could obtain 300 acres elsewhere of open space—it would be a sensible thing to do so."

He then proceeded to point out the grave difficulties in the way of enforcement of these rights.

"They were asked," he said, "not to maintain any rights of the Crown in which the subject was entitled to share, or in which he had the slightest interest, but they were asked to maintain certain rights of the Crown, at very great expense and with very doubtful issue, in which the subject had no share .

whatever; which would, if enforced at all, have to be enforced in opposition to the claims of the Lords of the Manors, of copyholders, and of others, claims which were perfectly defensible, which the proprietors had vested in them, and of which they could not be deprived except by the ordinary mode of passing an Act of Parliament, and by giving them compensation, or by adopting those friendly contracts following upon negotiations with which honourable members were familiar."*

He then pointed out the shadowy nature of the rights of the Crown in that portion of the Forest where they still subsisted; that the deer, for whose protection they were intended, had disappeared; and that in order to maintain and enforce these rights, it would be necessary to reinstate the special Courts in the Forest, by which alone the Forest laws could be enforced, and which had practically ceased to exist.

In spite of the difficulties thus urged by the Law Officer, the feeling of the House was so strongly in favour of something being done to preserve the Forest, that the Government was compelled to yield to it, and Mr. Gladstone assented to the motion, substituting, however, words in the proposed address, to the effect that measures should be taken for the preservation of the Forest, for the words aiming at the enforcement of the forestal rights of the Crown.

In consequence of this motion, a Bill was later in the same session introduced by the late Mr. Ayrton, then First Commissioner of Works, which proposed to deal with the Forest. It was the result of negotiations

* Parliamentary Debates, Vol. 199, p. 259.

with the Lords of Manors, and proceeded on the line of admitting their past inclosures, and allowing them to inclose the remainder of the Forest, on the condition of their consenting to set apart an allotment of it for the recreation of the public. It is difficult, with our subsequent experience, to believe that such a proposal could ever have been made to Parliament. It was, in fact, a measure for the inclosure of what remained of the Forest. Of the 3,000 acres still uninclosed, it provided that 2,000 should be given up to the Lords of Manors, free from the forestal rights of the Crown; that of the 1,000 remaining, 400 acres should be sold by Commissioners, to be appointed under the Act, for the purpose of compensating the Commoners for their rights over the whole, and that the residue of 600 acres only, or one-tenth of the present Forest, should be secured and appropriated for the recreation and enjoyment of the public.

This proposal caused great dissatisfaction amongst those who were chiefly interested in the preservation of the Forest and other open spaces. It is, however, fair to record the fact that, even among members of the Commons Society, there was difference of opinion as to whether this measure should be resisted and rejected *in toto*, or whether it should be accepted as the basis of a compromise with the Lords of Manors, with the hope of improving upon it at a later stage.

At a meeting of the Society held on July 23rd, 1870, within a few days after the introduction of the Bill by Mr. Ayrton, a long discussion took place upon it. Mr.

John Stuart Mill thereupon moved a resolution that
"the Society, considering the Bill introduced by the
Government as in direct opposition to the principles for
the assertion of which the Society was constituted, do
resist it to the utmost." An amendment on this was
moved by Mr. Andrew Johnston, then member for the
county of Essex, "that the principle of the Bill may be
held to be the assertion that some settlement is desirable, and that therefore it is not desirable to oppose the
Second Reading." On a division the amendment was
rejected by a single vote only. Mr. Fawcett accordingly
gave notice to move the rejection of the Bill on the
Second Reading. This determination of the Society to
refuse the proposed compromise, and to oppose the Bill,
led to its withdrawal by the Government. It was also
found to be against the Standing Orders of Parliament
to introduce such a Bill without notices.

In the following session another effort was made
to force the Government to take steps for the preservation of the Forest. Mr. Cowper Temple moved
that it was expedient that measures should be adopted,
in accordance with the address to the Crown of the
previous year, for keeping open those parts of Epping
Forest which had not been inclosed with the assent of the
Crown, or by legal authority. The motion was opposed
by the Chancellor of the Exchequer, Mr. Lowe, who
urged that the Government had fairly performed their
promises of the previous year by the proposals in Mr.
Ayrton's Bill. He contended that this measure was
one of conciliation, the result of negotiation with the

Lords of Manors, and that under it the public would secure 600 acres, where now they had no legal rights whatever. He also argued against the Government expending the general taxpayers' money for the benefit of a purely Metropolitan improvement. He enforced this argument by offering to allow the Metropolitan Board to make whatever use that body might think expedient of the Crown rights, and saying that he was at a loss to know in what other way the Government could respond to the motion. In spite of this speech, the Government was defeated in the division by a majority of more than two to one—197 to 96—showing how strong was the feeling in the House that steps should be taken to save the Forest.

In consequence of this hostile motion, Mr. Ayrton again tried his hand at legislation for Epping Forest. He now proposed a measure for the appointment of a Commission of enquiry into the condition of Epping Forest, and as to the respective rights of the Crown, of the Lords of Manors, and of the Commoners, with directions for the preparation of a scheme for the preservation of the open land of the Forest. This measure passed through Parliament without opposition. A week before it received the Royal assent, the Corporation of London commenced its great suit against the Lords of the Manors and other inclosers of the Forest.

In the following year an attempt was made to get rid of the Corporation suit. It was found necessary to amend the Epping Forest Act, and it was proposed in the Bill for this purpose to stay all the legal proceedings in the various suits affecting the Forest, pending the Report of the Commission. Strong objection, however, was taken to this, so far as the Corporation suit was concerned, and finally an exception was made of this suit, on the ground that it might materially assist the Commission, if the legal issues in the case were heard and determined by a competent legal tribunal. Thus it happened that two great inquiries as to Epping Forest were started and proceeded with at the same time— the one before the Courts of Law, in which the validity of the past inclosures was at issue, and the rights of the Commoners were to be decided; the other before a Royal Commission.

Being at the time a member of the then Government I was unable to take part in the above discussions in Parliament. I had ceased also for a time to be Chairman of the Commons Society, but I continued to attend its meetings, and took a part in guiding its general policy and action. In the discussions on Epping Forest I was not in favour of the attempt to urge the Government into proceedings for the enforcement of the Crown's forestal rights. I believed the legal difficulties opposed to such a course were very great, especially in view of the fact that the deer had been killed down, and that more than half the Forest had been already freed from the Crown's rights. I considered that by far the most promising line of action, for the abatement of inclosures and the preservation of the Forest, was through the medium of the Commoners and by enforcing their rights in the

Courts of law. I was personally much opposed to the course of bringing pressure upon the Government, until the issues in the great Corporation suit should be heard and determined by a judicial tribunal. I rather feared the effect of a compromise at an earlier stage. The sequel has shown that I was justified in my view of the position. It cannot now be doubted that the main, if not the sole, cause of success in saving the Forest was the decision of the Master of the Rolls defining the legal position of the Commoners, and giving an injunction against inclosure by the Lords of Manors. On the other hand, the Report of the Royal Commission was not without value in determining the scheme, which was ultimately applied to the Forest. Pending the report, the Forest Court of Attachments was revived, and verderers were appointed.

For nearly three years the two inquiries went on *pari passu*; witnesses were examined and cross-examined before the Royal Commission, and made affidavits in the Chancery suit. The composition of the Royal Commission was not such as to inspire much confidence in their conclusions, so far as the public interests were concerned. Strange to say, the Lords of Manors were equally animated with distrust of the Commission, and desired to have a legal decision as to their rights. The Corporation not very wisely, as it seemed, offered to suspend the proceedings in their suit, and to take the decision of the Commission. The Lords of Manors refused this offer with something approaching contempt, and insisted upon the suit being tried out in the Law

K

Courts. The Commission therefore withheld their report pending the decision in the Rolls Court.

Finally, on the 24th of July, 1874, exactly three years from the commencement of the suit, after a most protracted inquiry into the history of the Forest, and of the several Manors within it, and into the rights of the Commoners, involving a stupendous amount of evidence, the Master of the Rolls, Sir George Jessel, gave judgment. The arguments occupied twenty-three days, and the ablest men of the Bar were engaged on either side; but on the conclusion of the Defendants' case, Sir George Jessel, without calling upon the Corporation to reply, or taking time for consideration, and speaking without a note, summed up the case in a masterly manner,* and, in a most elaborate judgment, affirmed the case of the Corporation on all its main points of contention, and granted an injunction against the Lords of Manors, prohibiting them from inclosing in the future, and requiring them to remove all the fences erected within twenty years before the commencement of the suit.

The Lords of Manors had contended for two main

* Sir George Jessel, when at the Bar, had held a brief for some of the Defendants in the early stages of the proceedings, and had argued their case on the demurrer. But at the request of all the parties to the suit, he agreed to hear it. In the course of the trial he said : "I objected to hear this case because I had a prejudice against the Plaintiffs' case, and I told them so in Chambers. I had been Counsel for the Defendants, not on the merits. In the first instance I declined to hear it on that ground ; but it was very much pressed upon me, and I was told that it could not be heard at all unless I consented, and therefore I reluctantly consented."

propositions—the one that the Manors within the Forest
were independent of one another, and that there was no
general right on the part of the Commoners to turn
their cattle on to the whole of the waste of the Forest;
the other that the lords had, by custom or otherwise, the
right of inclosing. The evidence on either side in this
great case included all the documents connected with the
Forest and its Manors from the earliest of times, and an
immense amount of testimony showing the practice of
recent years. Sir George Jessel decided against the
lords on both points. On the question of costs he
said, " If I am right in the view I have taken of the
law, the Lords of Manors have taken other persons'
property without their consent and have appropriated it
to their own use. They will retain under the proposed
decree, of land covered with houses and of land inclosed
more than twenty years ago, considerable portions of the
property which they have illegally acquired. It does
not appear to me that litigants in this position are
entitled to any consideration as to costs. But I go
further; as regards the bulk of the Defendants, they
have been parties in a litigation, in which they have
endeavoured to support their title by a vast bulk of
false evidence. Considering that this evidence must be
wholly discredited, I cannot make them otherwise than
responsible for the acts of their agents who got up that
evidence without sufficient care, and, I think, should
have avoided raising the issues on which they fail, if
they had exercised more diligence and more discretion."*

* Glasse *v.* Commissioners of Sewers, L.R. 19 Eq., 137.

K 2

A few months later, in March, 1875, the Royal Commission on Epping Forest also made their first report, and having waited for the decision of Sir George Jessel, they came to the same conclusions as that great judge, as to the legal position of the Commoners and the illegality of the acts of the Lords of Manors. They had sat for 102 days, had examined 239 witnesses, and had collected together a vast number of documents bearing on the Forest. They found that the inclosures made within twenty years before the passing of the Epping Forest Act were unlawful against the Crown where the forestal rights had not been released, and were unlawful against the Commoners where the forestal rights had been released. They stated that the wastes of the Forest consisted of 6,021 acres, of which 3,006 acres had been unlawfully inclosed. They found that the inhabitants of Loughton had, from time immemorial, exercised the right of lopping the trees for firewood in that parish during the winter months, and they expressed their opinion that this right was valid at law. They also stated that although the public had been in the habit of using the Forest without objection on the part of the Crown or of the Lords of Manors, they were unable to say that a legal right had been acquired by such user.

In 1877 the Commission made their final report. In this they recommended the disafforesting of the Forest, and the preservation and management of the waste land, still uninclosed, as an open space for recreation. With regard to land which had already been wrongfully inclosed by the Lords of Manors, and had been sold or given to other persons, the Commission made the extraordinary proposal that these persons should be quieted in possession of the land thus stolen from the Forest, but that they should be required to pay certain rent-charges towards the fund for managing the remainder of the Forest, which was to be kept open. The effect of this proposal would have been to diminish the area of the Forest by 700 acres, dispersed about, and greatly to interfere with its general aspect and beauty.

This project gave general dissatisfaction, and as there was reason to fear that the Government, in framing their measure for dealing with the Forest, would act upon it, and would not insist upon the abatement of these inclosures, the Commons Society took early steps to prevent this objectionable part of the scheme being carried into effect. They organised a deputation to the First Commissioner of Works, introduced by the writer, which protested in the strongest manner against the proposal. They indicated their intention to oppose the whole scheme, if this arrangement should form part of it. They also urged the Corporation of London to resist it. Their view was further supported by the action of Mr. George Burney, an active member of the Society, who was also a landowner and Commoner in the Forest. He determined, without waiting for the decision of the Government, to take matters into his own hands. With the aid of a large body of men, he forcibly removed the fences from many of the inclosures.

The consequent litigation involved him in heavy law expenses, for it was held by Sir George Jessel that his action, in pulling down the fences, was a proceeding which was contrary to the terms of the Epping Forest Act of 1871, and therefore (for the time being) illegal, though it was quite clear that in other times he would have acted legally in removing the fences. A considerable part of these expenses, however, was ultimately repaid to Mr. Burney by the Corporation, on the ground that his action had an important influence in inducing the Government to disregard the recommendations of the Commission on this point. Certainly the Corporation was not averse to having the hands of Government forced.

In 1878, Sir H. Selwin-Ibbetson (now Lord Rookwood), on behalf of Lord Beaconsfield's Government, introduced and carried a measure for the final settlement of Epping Forest. The position had been somewhat simplified by the fact that the Corporation of London had, in the interval since the determination of their suit, bought up the interests of the Lords of Manors over a considerable part of the Forest—in all amounting to about 3,000 acres. They gave an average of about £20 per acre—a very small sum in proportion to the value of the land, if the Lords of Manors had been able to inclose, but a large sum in proportion to the interests of the lords on the assumption, now determined to be the case, that they could not inclose. In fact, the purchase of the lords' interests was scarcely necessary, though it facilitated somewhat the settlement of the question, and was probably justified in the view of the Corporation, mainly because it secured to them the management of the Forest.

The scheme, sanctioned by the Government measure, vested in the Corporation of London the future control and management of Epping Forest; it directed that the Forest should remain open and uninclosed, for all time to come, for the enjoyment and recreation of the people. It put an end to the Crown rights, to the Forest Courts and officers, and to any burthensome customs or Forest Laws. It directed that all the illegally inclosed land—that is, land inclosed within twenty years before the commencement of the Corporation suit—whether in the hands of the Lords of Manors or their grantees, should be restored to the Forest, except so much of it as, on the 14th of August, 1871, was already built upon, or was used as gardens and curtilages for such houses. The Corporation were required to purchase such of the wastes of the Forest as lay open, or would be thrown open, and which had not already been acquired by them. They were directed to keep the Forest unbuilt upon, and to protect and manage it. Queen Elizabeth's Lodge was made over to them, and any deer existing in the Forest were also transferred to them.

The Queen was empowered to appoint a Ranger, in whom certain formal duties were to be vested, such as the issue of bye-laws for the police of the Forest. An Arbitrator, Lord Hobhouse, was appointed, with power to decide many questions left unsettled by the Act. He was to determine what land should be thrown back

into the Forest, what land was to remain attached as
gardens and curtilages to houses erected before the
specified time, and what rent-charge should be paid by
the owners of such houses and curtilages towards the
funds of the Conservators, in acknowledgment of their
illegal inclosures. The Act provided that all rights of
lopping the trees for firewood were to cease in the future.
The Arbitrator was directed to assess the value of wood
assignments which was to be paid by the Conservators.
The Act preserved the other rights of the Commoners, but
gave power to the Conservators to regulate such rights.
It provided that in the future the four Verderers were
to be elected every seven years by the registered
Commoners, and that they were to be associated with
a Committee of the Corporation in the future management of the Forest.

With respect to the customary right of the inhabitants of Loughton to lop the trees in the Forest during
the winter months for firewood, the measure, as first
proposed, contained no power for awarding compensation. It simply declared such lopping to be illegal in
the future. I endeavoured to rectify this omission by
moving in Committee on the Bill, in the House of
Commons, a clause admitting the validity of the
custom, and directing the Arbitrator to assess the value
of it in compensation to the inhabitants of Loughton.

The Corporation of London—very unfairly, as I
thought—opposed this, and were most unwilling to
recognise the right or custom in any way, in spite of
the fact that so great an advantage had been derived

from the preliminary suit on behalf of this custom by Willingale. The utmost I succeeded in effecting for the Loughton people was the insertion of a clause directing the Arbitrator to inquire into the custom, and, if satisfied of its validity, to award compensation for it, in such manner as he might think fit.

Apart from this, the measure passed through Parliament with little or no amendment. The duties of the arbitrator, Lord Hobhouse, proved to be most laborious; they lasted over four years. On the 24th of July, 1882, he signed his final award, including a map of what was thenceforward to constitute Epping Forest. During the interval he held 114 public and many private meetings, and settled innumerable cases of dispute as to boundaries and compensation. He directed the payment of the sum of £13,000 for the fuel assignments in the Manors of Waltham and Sewardstone.

With reference to the Loughton lopping custom, the claims of the inhabitants were strongly resisted by the Corporation. Having regard to the past interest taken by the Commons Society in this right or user, and to the important effect of the litigation on behalf of Willingale, I was determined that every effort should be made to maintain it, and to defeat the Corporation in what I considered their unworthy attempts to defeat the claim.

When the 10th of November arrived, in the year 1879, the midnight of which by the Act was to be the last occasion on which the old custom of perambulating the Forest and lopping the trees would take place, I

went down to Loughton, with Mr. Burney, as representatives of the Society, and joined in the demonstration.
The whole population of the district turned out at
midnight to the number of 5,000 to 6,000. They
perambulated the Manor by torchlight, and then held
a meeting previous to commencing the lopping. I
addressed this midnight meeting in the Forest, and informed the people that it would be the last occasion on
which such lopping would be permissible by law. I
explained their position to them, and the effect of the
Epping Forest Act. I said that Counsel had been
instructed by the Commons Society to argue their claims
before the Arbitrator, and expressed the utmost confidence that the decision would be in their favour.

On the hearing of the case before Lord Hobhouse,
the Corporation appeared also by Counsel, and did their
best to resist the claim of the Loughton people, arguing,
as Mr. Maitland had done, that such a custom could
not be enjoyed by so uncertain a body as the inhabitants of a parish, and that they could not prescribe for
a right of a profitable character. Lord Hobhouse in his
decision brushed away these miserable technicalities.
He held that, in view of the evidence that the people
had in fact, from time immemorial, enjoyed and exercised
this right, he was justified in admitting it, and indeed
was bound to find a legal origin for it.

" The oral evidence," he said, " appears to me to establish the
following propositions :—That in point of fact the practice has
been for the inhabitants of houses to lop trees on the waste ;
that the lopping is limited to begin at a given instant of time,

and to end at a given instant of time ; that it is limited also in point of space, inasmuch as two portions of the waste—Monk's Wood and Loughton Rise—are not subject to it; that it is further limited by the obligation to leave uncut all branches within a certain height from the ground, so as to afford cover and browse for the deer, and also to leave the spears or maiden trees ; that persons occupying the positions of Head Keeper of the Forest, Purlieu Keeper, Woodward, and Bailiff of the Manors have attended and watched the operations ; that these operations have never been interfered with in any effectual way ; and that if attempts have been made by foresters or others to restrict it, they have been very few, and have been entirely set at naught. The evidence on these points, stating what the old witnesses say of their own knowledge, and what they must in their boyhood have heard their grandfathers say, must go back for at least 100 years. . . . Now it seems to me impossible to say that a well-defined, orderly, methodical, long-continued, recog- nised enjoyment, such as I have described, can have grown up at haphazard. It was calculated to injure both the Crown and the Lord of the Manor, and I cannot doubt that it would have been excluded from Loughton, as it was from Chigwell or Woodford, just over the borders, if it could have been rightfully excluded. . . . It must have had some foundation of a formal kind ; and it is the duty of the lawyer to find a legal origin for it, if such can be found. I might quote many authorities to this effect, but I can quote none stronger than the language used by the Master of the Rolls (Sir George Jessel), in the suit which established the right of forestal commonage. He says, ' Where user has been proved of a right for sixty years that is not con- tradicted by anything else, the law presumes a grant. . . . I am not at liberty to guess whether it is probable or improbable that there was such a grant. . . . I understand Lord Mans- field to say he would presume an Act of Parliament. I do not think I am at liberty to guess whether it is probable or improb- able there was a grant.' In plain English, this presumption of grants is a legal fiction resorted to for the purposes of justice."

After discussing at length the legal authorities on the subject, he said, "Epping Forest is one of the ancient forests whose origin is lost in obscurity. All we know is that it was a Royal Forest in the time of Edward the Confessor, when the Crown was also Lord of the Manor of Loughton. If, therefore, the grant we are seeking for was made by Edward the Confessor or by one of his predecessors, it would surely have antiquity enough to satisfy these authorities.

"If therefore the phenomena are such that they cannot be reasonably explained otherwise than by a long-standing belief and tradition among the inhabitants, I think that the strict rules of law warrant me in finding a legal origin for their practice by presuming either a grant of such antiquity as to be prior to the rule of law which requires incorporation, or a grant which effected corporation for the purpose of securing its due enjoyment."

Lord Hobhouse consequently awarded to the inhabitants of Loughton the sum of £7,000 in compensation for their rights. He was good enough to consult me as to how he should appropriate this fund, and at my suggestion he directed £1,000 to be paid to those of the cottagers who had actually exercised the right and derived profit from it, and the residue to be expended in building a village hall at Loughton, to be used as a reading-room and a place of meeting for the inhabitants, and to be called the Loppers' Hall.

It may be worth while to mention the sequel of this award. The day came, some two years later, when the foundation-stone of this village hall was to be laid, and it was made the occasion of a popular demonstration at Loughton. With singular infelicity, the local managers responsible for it invited the Lord Mayor of

London to perform this ceremony, unmindful of the fact that the Corporation of London had done their very utmost to defeat the claim of the inhabitants to any compensation for their rights. The Lord Mayor drove down in state to Loughton. The proceedings were there opened with a prayer by Mr. Maitland, the rector of the parish, and Lord of the Manor, who had also done his utmost to inclose the whole of the waste of his Manor, and to defeat the claim of the inhabitants of Loughton, and who had caused the imprisonment of Willingale and his sons for endeavouring to exercise them! There were those who were of opinion that a white sheet would have been the most appropriate garment for the rector on the occasion! The local managers had at least the good taste not to invite any members of the Commons Society to take part in the proceedings in such company. It was with some difficulty that the Corporation of London was later induced to give to the widow of old Willingale the paltry pension of five shillings a week. His son has kept up the tradition of the family, by maintaining the cause of the smaller occupiers of land to rights of common over the Forest, which the Corporation are now disposed to dispute and deny.

Apart from this, all questions affecting the Forest have been set at rest. The Forest was thrown open to the public by the Queen in person, at High Beech, in the presence of a great assemblage of persons, on May 6th, 1882. Restitution was thus in a sense made by the Sovereign, of land which in very ancient times had probably been taken from the folk-land for the purpose of a Royal Forest, and the Forest was dedicated for ever to the use and enjoyment of the public. It has been stated that the total cost of the proceedings of the Corporation, in vindication of their rights, in the purchase of the interests of the Lords of Manors, and in the extinction of the rights of lopping and other rights held to be detrimental to the Forest, was about £240,000. Of this, £33,000 was spent in litigation, and in the expenses incurred in Parliamentary Committees and before the Epping Forest Commission. There was recovered as costs from the Lords of Manors the sum of £4,000, which, it is understood, represented but a fraction of the real outlay. The amount thus paid for the purchase of the rights of the Lords of Manors was an unnecessary expenditure. There was no reason why those rights should not have been allowed to exist, subject to proper regulations.

The whole of the outlay was provided for out of the metage of grain duty, which was specially continued and appropriated by Parliament for such purposes, and not out of the general funds of the Corporation. Out of the same fund there was paid the sum of £8,000, the balance due on the purchase by the Corporation of Wanstead Park, formerly the residence of Lord Mornington, with 184 acres of land, a most valuable addition to the Forest. Some outlying portions of the Forest, of little importance to it, but of great value for building purposes, were given in exchange for the Park. This Park had in 1545 been inclosed from the Forest. It contains some beautiful lakes and a heronry. They also purchased, and added to the Forest, Highams Park, consisting of thirty acres, at a cost of £6,000, as well as a few small inclosures essential to the Forest.

Though I have had occasion to criticise the proceedings of the Corporation in some particulars, they cannot be too warmly commended for their spirited action in stepping forward as champions of the rights of the Commoners, and in freely spending the funds entrusted to them by conferring upon London a pleasure ground of exceptional size and beauty, and of rare historic interest. Their conduct stands in striking contrast to that of the late Metropolitan Board of Works, a body which never stirred a finger to fight the battle of the public, but, on the contrary, on many occasions embarrassed the efforts of those engaged in the contest, by offering money to Lords of Manors, and by indicating very plainly that its sympathy was rather with them, than with the Commoners and the public. Amongst those in the ranks of the Corporation who exerted themselves most actively to preserve the Forest for the public, should be mentioned Mr. Deputy Bedford, who was the first chairman of the Epping Forest Committee ; and the late Sir Thomas Nelson, the City Solicitor, who mainly guided the policy of the Corporation in its later stages.

It should also be mentioned that the late Mr. Justice Manisty, then at the Bar, powerfully contributed to the complete success of the Commoners in the proceedings before the Epping Forest Commission, and in the great suit, by the conspicuous tact and ability and untiring care with which, in the position throughout of leading Counsel, he conducted the case. The late Mr. W. R. Fisher acted also most ably throughout as Junior, and has left a valuable and exhaustive treatise on the Forest of Essex, as a lasting memorial of his connection with the case, and to which I have been largely indebted in my short account of the history of the Forest. None of the above, however, would have been able to achieve success if it had not been for the great experience in such cases of Mr. Robert Hunter, and the extraordinary care and ability with which he collected and sifted all the facts and evidence relating to the Commoners from the earliest times, by means of which their rights over the Forest were finally vindicated in so complete a manner, and the greatest of all the Commons suits was brought to a successful conclusion.

It may be confidently affirmed that never in the past experience of the Law Courts was there a decision by which upwards of 400 persons were compelled to disgorge 3,000 acres of land wrongfully inclosed, and by which there was secured for ever an area of double the size for the enjoyment for all time to come of the people of London.

CHAPTER IX.

Ashdown Forest and Malvern Hills.

ANOTHER very important case in the South of England, but beyond the limits of London, was that of Ashdown Forest in Sussex.

This ancient Chase is undoubtedly one of the remaining part of the great Forest of Anderida, which in very early times covered a large part of Kent, Sussex, Surrey, and Hampshire, extending from the Romney Marshes nearly to Portsmouth, and comprising the greater part of the district known as the Weald. In the time of Edward III., 1372, so much of it as then remained forest, consisting of about 14,000 acres, and lying between Tunbridge Wells and East Grinstead, was granted by the name of the Free Chase of Ashdown, together with the Castle of Pevensey, to John of Gaunt, Duke of Lancaster, and thenceforth, till after the Restoration, was attached to the Duchy of Lancaster.

In 1560, the Mastership of the Forest, together with the keepership of the "wild beasts" therein, was granted to Sir Richard Sackville, the ancestor, through the Dukes of Dorset, of the present Earl De la Warr, and the owner of several Manors in the neighbourhood of the Forest, including that of Buckhurst. This was the first connection of the family with the Forest.

Shortly after the accession of Charles I., the Earl of

L

Dorset and his son, Lord Buckhurst, were appointed Keepers of the Forest in succession for their lives. The Earl took the side of the King in his struggle with the Parliament, and his office of Keeper of the Chase, together with other privileges which he enjoyed in the Forest, were forfeited to the Commonwealth.

In 1650, a careful survey of the Forest, under the name of the Great Park of Lancaster, was made by order of the Commonwealth, on behalf of the trustees for the sale of the Crown rights. The surveyors on this occasion reported that, according to the usual rate of the pasturage, there was a surplus of forest, and that part should be allotted to the Commoners, and part appropriated by the State. This suggestion appears to have been adopted by the Commonwealth, for in 1658 a further survey was made, under which the Forest was allotted between the State and the Commoners, each parish extending into the Forest having a Common Allotment set apart for it, based upon the number of cattle turned out in respect of lands situated within it and conferring a right, the rate of allotment being one acre and a half for every head of cattle. The scheme of allotment, however, was not completed at the time of the restoration of the monarchy, when all the proceedings by the Commonwealth respecting the Forest were annulled.

After the Restoration, in 1660, a grant was again made by Charles II., under the Great Seal, of the Keepership of the Chase to the Earl of Dorset and his son, Lord Buckhurst, for their successive lives. The Earl was not satisfied with this, but desired to have an absolute grant of the Forest. The Earl of Bristol, however, had the greater influence at Court, and obtained a lease of it for ninety-nine years, together with the Manor of Duddleswell and the Honor of Aquila. In the lease then given, the King granted and declared the disafforesting of the Forest and Chase, and the disparking of the park and all woods, grounds, etc., within the limits thereof; and as a result of this the disafforesting of Ashdown took place. Leave was also given to the Earl of Bristol to plough up, divide, and inclose the Forest, and to allot to such persons as had rights of common and other rights, privileges and profits in it, parts of the soil in recompense and satisfaction of their rights, all such allotments to be confirmed by decree of the Court of the Duchy of Lancaster. There was also a grant of warren in the Forest to Lord Bristol, and a rent was reserved of £200 a year.

Lord Bristol thereupon began to inclose under this lease. The Commoners strenuously resisted, and litigation followed. A suit was commenced by Lord Bristol against the Commoners, but was not heard, probably owing to the forfeiture of the lease of the former. About the same time the dispute between Lord Dorset and Lord Bristol was settled by a renunciation by the former of his interest as Keeper of the Forest, on payment to him of £100 a year for ninety-nine years.

Shortly after this, Lord Bristol failed to pay his rent to the Duchy, and consequently his lease was forfeited; and in 1673 a fresh lease was granted to

L 2

trustees for the children of Colonel Washington. The
rent reserved was purely nominal, and we must presume
that a considerable sum of money was paid for the lease.
There was a covenant by the Duchy for the further and
more effectual division and allotment of the Forest
among the Commoners and the Grantees. The Trustees,
finding themselves unable to make a profit out of the
Forest, assigned their interest in the lease to Sir
Thomas Williams, a gentleman who was described as a
Doctor of Medicine, but who was probably one of the
class of speculators in Crown grants of waste lands, with
a view to inclosure, a speculation not uncommon in
those times. He further secured the reversion of the
Forest to hold in fee, at a fee-farm rent of £100 a year.
Having effected this, he inclosed 500 acres of the Forest
for the benefit apparently of Lord Dorset. Lord Dorset
also about this time obtained a grant from the Crown of
the fee-farm rent payable by Sir Thomas Williams.

Sir Thomas Williams then proceeded with his endeavours to inclose the Forest. Various proposals were
made, but the Commoners still objected; and in 1689 Sir
Thomas Williams commenced a suit, on behalf of himself and Lord Dorset, against the Commoners, 144 in
number, praying that he might be quieted in the
possession of the inclosures he had already made, and
protected in further inclosures of the Forest, and that
the Defendants, if they proved that they were entitled
to any common rights, might have a proportion of the
land allotted to them for the exercise of their rights,
so that the improvement of the Forest might be

proceeded with. The Commoners made a joint purse to defend themselves against this aggression. The suit came on for hearing, in 1691, in the Court of the Duchy of Lancaster before the Chancellor and the Council, assisted by Sir John Holt and Sir John Turton, Judges of the Court of Exchequer. The Court held that it was fully satisfied that there was sufficient common left uninclosed, of which parts might be approved, still leaving a sufficiency for the Commoners, and they directed that a Commission should issue to set out for the Defendants sufficient common, according to their respective rights, and in convenient places.

In 1693, the Commissioners made their return to the Duchy Court. They stated that they had agreed that 6,400 acres of the Forest would provide sufficient pasture and herbage for the Defendants, the Commoners, and others claiming common in the Forest, " so as they should enjoy the sole pasturage thereof, and the Plaintiffs, owners and proprietors of the soil, be excluded from all rights of pasturage either for sheep, horses, or cattle." They further stated that they had laid out the 6,400 acres in the most convenient places, contiguous and adjacent to all the several vills, towns, and farms, lying round the Forest, to which common rights attached. They had also left " the shares and proportions of the Crown grantees allotted for inclosure in several parts and parcels, and distinguished and divided them from the Defendants' and Commoners' parts set out for common, by metes, marks, and boundaries."

On this report, the Council of the Duchy, by the advice of Sir John Turton and Sir John Powell, made a decree in accordance with it. Under these arrangements about 7,600 acres of the Forest were inclosed, or if already inclosed, were quieted in possession; and the residue, 6,400 acres, was declared to be set apart for the rights of the Commoners. Soon after the decree of 1693, the interest of Sir Thomas Williams in what remained of the Forest was divided between three persons—Staples, Holland, and Lechmere—and passed from them through various hands, until Lord Dorset bought them out in 1730, and became possessed of whatever rights remained in the Crown grantees over the Forest. During the interval, the Forest appears to have been largely denuded of its trees, for when Lord Dorset purchased, the timber was valued at no more than £210.

The Dorset family having thus become possessed of the Crown rights and of the Manor of Duddleswell, commenced a series of acts, which have been continued down to very recent times, for the purpose of curtailing and getting rid of the rights of the Commoners. With this object persons were warned not to cut turf or to trespass on the Forest. In 1795, the then Duke of Dorset submitted a case to Mr. Serjeant Hill, in which it was stated—

"The farmers adjoining the Forest, many of whom are Copyholders of the Manor, and as such have right of Common-age, as well as many others who are not Copyholders and have no such right, have for many years past made a practice of

committing depredations upon the Forest by cutting and
carrying away the heath to the amount of many thousands of
loads in the course of a year, by means of which the herbage is
not only destroyed, and the tenants who have rights of
Commonage prejudiced, but the Lord of the Manor, who is
entitled to the timber in the Forest, is much injured, inasmuch
as the young oak trees, which may be coming up amongst the
heath, are cut down by the scythe, and consequently no timber
can ever grow where these cuttings take place. Independently
of this injury, the black game which used to abound in this
Forest, and which the Duke is extremely desirous of preserving,
are by this practice almost extirpated. His grace is therefore
determined to put a stop to it if it is possible to do so."

Mr. Serjeant Hill does not appear to have favoured
the Duke's view, for he gave as his opinion " that if
the Commoners had been accustomed to cut heath for
estovers as long as any living witnesses could remember,
they could not be restrained from doing so."

Later, in spite of this opinion, a notice was
issued forbidding altogether the cutting of litter within
the Forest. The taking of turf, peat, and stone was
also prohibited, with certain exceptions in favour of the
poor of the adjoining parishes. From thenceforward
these questions were perpetually in dispute between the
Dukes of Dorset and their successors in their property
—the Earls De la Warr—and the Commoners of
the Forest. These Commoners were not a class of small
owners and occupiers of land, as in many other cases,
little able to oppose a powerful and wealthy Lord of
the Manor. They contained in their ranks many of
the principal landowners of that part of Sussex—Lord

Sheffield, Lord Henniker, Sir John Shelley, Lord
Colchester, Sir Spencer Maryon Wilson,* Mr. Freshfield,
and others.   These gentlemen and others formed a Committee to resist the aggression, and finally, in 1867, the
dispute culminated in a suit by Lord De la Warr
against Mr. Bernard Hale, one of the Commoners, to
restrain them from cutting heath and brake in the
Forest for use as litter, and subsequently as manure
on their farms; and in a cross suit, by Mr. Hale
and others, on behalf of the Commoners, praying for
a declaration of their rights, and for an injunction
against Lord De la Warr to restrain him from interfering with their rights and inclosing any part of
the Forest.   The case turned mainly on the right to
cut litter from the Forest, and in support of this,
several ancient surveys were relied upon, and evidence
was given of user in the past by numerous witnesses
of great age.

The case came on before Vice-Chancellor Bacon in
1880, and was argued for the Plaintiff by Sir Henry
Jackson and Mr. Elton, and for the Defendants, the
Commoners, by Mr. Joshua Williams, Sir William
Harcourt, and Mr. (now Sir) R. E. Webster.   The
Vice-Chancellor ultimately decided in favour of Lord
De la Warr.   "At no period of the history of the
Forest," he said, "is there to be found a trace of

* It is to be observed that Sir Spencer Maryon Wilson, who was
so ready to inclose at Hampstead, where he was Lord of the Manor,
had in his time been a Commoner of Ashdown Forest, and his nephew
took an active part in preserving it.

the claims of right of the Commoners to cut and
carry away pasture or herbage, or brakes, heather, or
litter. On the contrary, there is more than negative
evidence that no such right was ever claimed or lawfully exercised. There is no ground on which I can
hold that at any time there existed within the Forest of
Ashdown a special custom conferring a right on the
Commoners to cut and carry any part of the growth of the
soil." Neither would he admit that the long-continued
user of cutting heather, by the Defendants, constituted
any right by prescription on their part.

The Commoners appealed against this decision, and
on February 5th, 1881, the Lords Justices Brett, James,
and Cotton overruled Sir James Bacon on the point of
the user by the Defendants of cutting heather for their
litter. "In my opinion," said Lord Justice James, "the
Defendants have proved that for a period of sixty years
they have claimed to take, and have taken, not by way
of permission, but as a right, the litter of the Forest for
their farms. That is clearly within the Prescription Act.
It appears to me that if we were to hold that it was not,
we should be repealing that Act." On the other hand,
the Court of Appeal held, upon the construction of the
decree of the Duchy Court in 1693, which they
regarded as in the nature of an approvement under the
Statute of Merton, that the Commoners were not to
have any new common nor any new rights in the
herbage or pasturage, but that they were to have
the enjoyment, as under the old right, of common
of pasture, exclusive of the Lord of the Manor, sole

as against the lord, but common as between themselves, and that the lord was to be excluded from having any right of common. "I am of opinion," said Lord Justice James, "that we cannot enlarge the words of their decree so as to include the right to take litter."

This victory, although on one line only of the defence, was decisive. Litter-cutting had been universal with the Commoners; and Lord De la Warr subsequently consented to a decree declaring the right to exist in all the Commoners entitled to ·pasturage. Subsequently the Commoners' Committee obtained a Provisional Order for the regulation of the Forest, under the Commons Act, 1876, and it is now managed and protected by a representative body of Commoners. If the judgment of the Court of Appeal had been in favour of Lord De la Warr, there can be little doubt that he would have been ultimately able to force the Commoners to inclose; as it is, the Commoners' rights have saved the Forest, which is an exceedingly beautiful and valuable open space.*

MALVERN HILLS.

A very similar case to Ashdown Forest was that of the Malvern Hills. This range of Hills, which adds so much to the attraction of Malvern, consists of about 6,000 acres of open land, subject to common rights. The Hills were originally subject to Forest Laws, and with the adjoining lands were known as the "Foreste de

---

* The litigation in this case, which was very heavy, was conducted by Mr. Hunter, in conjunction with Mr. Raper of Battle.

Malverne." The Forest was on the same footing as that of Epping, in the sense that the waste or common lands were claimed by the Lords of the thirteen Manors of the district, the Crown enjoying only forestal rights over them, and over the inclosed lands adjoining.

The earliest reference to the Forest in extant documents is a grant by Henry III., A.D. 1228, to the Monks of St. Mary of Malvern, of inclosures in the Forest. Edward I. granted the Forest to Gilbert de Clare, Earl of Gloucester, on marriage with his daughter Joan, whereupon the Forest became, technically speaking, a chase· The chase passed subsequently through the hands of the Despencer family and that of the Earl of Warwick. It afterwards reverted to the Crown, and so remained till the reign of Charles I.

Charles sold his interest in it to the Dutch engineer, Cornelius Vermuyden, with the understanding that it should be disafforested. The attempt to effect this gave rise to fierce disputes between the Grantee, the Commoners, and the Lords of Manors. For long the "countrie remained verie untractable," to use the language of one of the proceedings of the time. The outcome was that one-third of the waste lands was given to Vermuyden, in lieu of the forestal rights of the Crown, the other two-thirds being left to the Lords of the Manors and their Commoners, and to form the open Hills of the present day. It appears that the small holders of land, at the time of the disafforesting, attached great value to their rights over the Commons. In one of the many suits between the

Commoners and the Crown Surveyor, the order of the
Court of Exchequer contained the following passage :—

"Forasmuch as the Court is nowe informed that the
Comoninge in the said Chase concerneth tenne thousand poore
people, and that the not havinge and enjoyinge thereof maye
turne to their utter overthrowe and undoinge, therefore, it is
now ordered by the Court that the said inhabitants and
Commoners there shall be at libertie to take and receive such
reasonable comon within the said Chase as they have been
accustomed and of rights they ought to have."

An Act of Parliament was passed in 1664 confirming
the disafforesting. In recent years encroachments have
been made on the Commons in various parts, not only
by the Lords of Manors, but by outsiders and squatters ;
and actions were from time to time successfully instituted
against them.   These acts culminated about the year
1878 in the erection of a building on the summit of the
Worcestershire Beacon, the most prominent of the
Malvern Hills. This was followed by a number of
petty encroachments on other parts.   There appeared to
be danger of the permanent loss or disfigurement of the
magnificent open space which these Hills afford.   The
matter was taken up with spirit by the inhabitants of
Great Malvern.   The Commons Society was consulted,
and their solicitor was employed.   Fortunately litigation
was avoided, as the Messrs. Hornyold, who claimed as
Lords of the Manor of that part of the Hills, and had let
the summit to the person who had built on it, when
they became aware of the strong feeling of their neighbours, came forward and agreed to dedicate their rights

to the public, and to remove several fences and erections.

In 1882, an inclosure was attempted of one of the Commons, not part of the Hills, but adjoining them, and included in the limits of the old chase. An action was brought in the County Court of the district to abate this inclosure, by Mr. Henry Lakin, an old inhabitant of Malvern. The judge of the Court, Sir Rupert Kettle, an able lawyer, after long argument, recognised the old right of common over all the wastes of the ancient chase, without distinction of parish or manor boundaries, and ordered the fences to be removed. His judgment proceeded on the same lines as that of Sir George Jessel in the Epping case. The decision greatly facilitated a general arrangement.

The Malvern Committee, under the guidance of Mr. Edward Chance, and, after his untimely death, of Sir Edmund Lechmere, Bart., M.P., a large landowner in the neighbourhood, then negotiated with the Lords of Manors of the district, the Ecclesiastical Commissioners, and others. Ultimately the consent of all was obtained to a general settlement of the question, and to the regulation of all the Commons forming the Malvern Hills, under a special Act of Parliament passed in 1884.

The Act places the control and management of the Hills under a body of Conservators, partly elected by the vestries of surrounding parishes, and partly nominated by the Lords of Manors therein. This fine range therefore is safe from all future encroachments, and is free for the enjoyment of the public.

.

CHAPTER X.

COULSDON, DARTFORD, AND WIGLEY COMMONS.

COULSDON.

WHILE the Epping Forest case was wending its slow course in the Law Courts, two other cases arose in respect of Commons of great importance to London, namely, the Coulsdon Commons and Dartford Heath. The Parish of Coulsdon, conterminous with the Manor, and lying between the Parishes of Croydon and Caterham, within easy reach of London, consists of 4,815 acres, of which 400 acres are open downs on the Surrey Hills, at no great distance from Epsom and Banstead Commons. Two of the downs, Riddlesdown and Farthingdown, respectively of 77 and 126 acres, are in the north of the Parish; Kenley and Coulsdon Commons, of 77 and 88 acres, are in the southern part. There are also three village greens, parts of the waste of the Manor.

Domesday Book states that the Manor was then in the hands of the Abbey of Chertsey. It so continued till the dissolution of the Abbey, when Henry VIII. gave it to Sir Nicholas Carewe. It then passed through various hands, till it was sold, in 1783, to Mr. Thomas Byron, the ancestor of the Lord of the Manor, who, after the Report of the Committee of 1865, set to work to appropriate the Commons.

The Court Rolls are extant from the year 1359, and are in Latin, with the usual break for the Commonwealth, till 1732. There is an entry in these Rolls for the year 1359, showing the dependent state of the labouring people of the Manor. It records the payment of a fine, apparently by a free tenant, for marrying without leave the relict of Adam King, a born bondsman of the Lord of the Manor. Later, in 1363, there is an entry of an order given to seize a tenement into the lord's hands, because it had been acquired by a born bondsman of the lord, without his leave.

In 1762, a careful survey of the Manor showed that the waste lands then amounted to 551 acres. Since then, Hartley Down, consisting of 150 acres, appears to have been inclosed and appropriated by the Lord of the Manor. Mr. Byron, after failing to induce the Inclosure Commissioners to take proceedings for the inclosure of the remaining Commons, entered into communication with the principal landowners of the Manor, with the object of obtaining their concurrence to an inclosure without the sanction of Parliament. He encountered strong opposition to this course from some of the Commoners, including the Messrs. Hall, who subsequently undertook the suit against him. He found some willing confederates in other quarters. He then broached the idea that the Commons, instead of being all parts of the waste of the same Manor, where all the Commoners had the right of turning out cattle equally upon every part of them, were separate in

the sense that the Commoners could only exercise their
rights over the Commons nearest to them.

In this view he abandoned the intention of inclosing
all the Commons. He made arrangements with some
of the Commoners, by promising grants to them of
portions of the waste, in extinguishment of their
rights, and then began to inclose some parts of it.
He also commenced the sale of turf from Coulsdon
and Riddlesdown Commons on a very great scale, in
such manner as to ruin their surface.

It was in consequence of all these acts, which in
the aggregate amounted to an assertion of absolute
right over the Commons, that the Messrs. Hall commenced a suit against the Lord of the Manor, claiming
in the usual way, on behalf of the Commoners, a
determination of their rights, and asking for an
injunction to restrain the inclosures and the excessive
digging of gravel and loam. Mr. Byron replied, denying the rights of common, whether in the Messrs. Hall
or in the class of persons on whose behalf they claimed,
and asserting that no general right of common existed
over all the different Commons in the Manor, but that
each Commoner was restricted to a particular Common.

As in all the other Commons' cases, the investigation
of the history and customs of the Manor, and the
determination of the persons entitled to common rights,
gave rise to protracted, difficult, and expensive proceedings. After some years the case was ultimately
heard by Vice-Chancellor Hall in 1877, and occupied
eight consecutive days. In the end the Judge was

satisfied that one of the Messrs. Hall had proved his case. In the course of his judgment he said—*

"The law I take it to be that the Lord of the Manor may take gravel waste, loam, and the like, in the waste, so long as he does not infringe upon the Commoners' rights. His right to do so is quite independent of the right of approvement under the Statute of Merton or at common law, and exists by reason of his ownership of the soil, subject only to the interests of the Commoners. Judge Bayley, in 'Arlett v. Ellis,' said that the lord has rights of his own reserved upon the waste—I do not say subservient to, but concurrent with the rights of Commoners. And when it is ascertained that there is more Common than is necessary for the cattle of the Commoners, the lord, as it seems to me, is entitled to take that for his own use."

He went on to say that in the case of gravel digging, the "onus probandi" that it interfered with the right of common, rested with the Commoner, and not, as in the case of approvement, with the Lord of the Manor. He gave, however, an injunction to restrain Mr. Byron from making inclosures, and from carrying away or destroying the loam and gravel of the waste, or the pasture or herbage growing thereon, so as in any manner to prevent, disturb, or interfere with the exercise by Mr. Hall, or the other persons entitled, of these rights over the waste lands of the Manor.

The Judge also found against the attempted restriction of rights of common to particular Commons of the Manor, holding that the arrangements of this character

* Hall v. Byron, L.R. 4. Ch. Div., 667.

which had from time to time been made were only in the nature of temporary bye-laws, made by consent, and did not affect the rights of the Commoners.

The decree was a very substantial victory for the Messrs. Hall and the Commoners, and was the first of the more recent cases, which restrained the excessive digging of gravel and loam, which was being carried out in many other Commons. Unfortunately, the Judge refused to give the plaintiffs the costs of the suit as against Mr. Byron, and the result was that the Messrs. Hall had to bear the burthen of their own great costs in this expensive litigation—amounting to a very large sum. Ultimately, the Corporation of London was induced to purchase the rights of Mr. Byron over the Commons, and as a part of this arrangement, to relieve the Messrs. Hall of some of the burthen of their costs. The Coulsdon Commons are now under the safe custody of the Corporation, and are practically secured to the public.

DARTFORD HEATH.

The case of Dartford Heath was very similar to that of the Coulsdon Commons, and need not be described at length. The Heath, in the Manor of Dartford, consists of 334 acres. The Manor was originally in the hands of the Knights Templars, and later in those of the Knights Hospitallers of St. John of Jerusalem. On the dissolution of that Order, it vested in the Crown. It was subsequently re-granted, and ultimately came into the possession of Mr. Augustus Morgan. Mr.

Morgan, like many other Lords of Manors between 1865 and 1869, began to assume ownership over the Common, and with a view to that, commenced the digging of gravel on an extensive scale, so as to ruin and deface its surface.

The cudgels on behalf of the public were in this case taken up by Mr. Charles Minet, the owner of a considerable property, called Baldwyns, in the same Manor. This estate had formerly belonged to Cardinal Wolsey, who gave it to Cardinal College, Oxford; but on the attainder of Wolsey, it was seized by Henry VIII., who later granted it to Eton College. Subsequently it was exchanged for other property, and came into the possession of Mr. Minet, who, by the advice of the Solicitor of the Commons Society, Mr. Hunter, brought a suit against Mr. Augustus Morgan, in respect of his common rights, belonging to Baldwyns, to restrain the inclosure of the Heath and the excessive digging of gravel. Mr. Minet unfortunately died before the suit came to a hearing, leaving six daughters his co-heirs. Ultimately, one of these ladies undertook the task of saving the Heath, and was prepared to prosecute the suit. Mr. Morgan, however, thought it imprudent to contest the case any further.

On June 9th, 1874, a decree was made by consent, under which the Commoners were quieted in the possession of rights of common, and the Lord of the Manor was restrained from digging, in any one year, more than two roods of gravel, and two of peat, or more than two acres of turf. He was also restricted in all

M 2

excavations of loam and peat, and the cutting and
paring of turf to the supply for the inhabitants of the
parish. No inclosures were to be in future permitted,
save such as were temporarily necessary for the digging of
gravel. The Common was thus permanently saved from
inclosure and disfigurement.

WIGLEY COMMON.

In spite of the warnings which it was to be expected
would be drawn from the results of the many recent suits
respecting attempted inclosures of Commons, another
Lord of the Manor was found bold enough to encounter
the risk, and to inclose in one swoop the whole of
a Common in the neighbourhood of the New Forest.
There are two adjoining Manors there—those of
Cadnam and Winsor, and Wigley. The wastes of
these Manors also adjoin, that of Cadnam and Winsor
being no more than 95 acres, and that of Wigley
about 460 acres; they are separated only by a small
stream, which cattle can easily cross; and as the
pasturage of Wigley is far better than that of Cadnam,
the cattle turned out on the latter generally find their
way to the former, in search of a good nibble, and the
Commoners of Cadnam have always claimed this as
a matter of right.

These two Manors had in ancient times been in the
possession of the Prioress of Amesbury, a monastery
about twenty miles distant, and on the dissolution
of the religious houses, they were granted away by
Henry VIII., and passed through various hands,

till in 1587 they were bought by William Poulett, who, in 1647, sold Wigley Manor to William Stanley, the ancestor of the present owner, Mr. Hans Sloane Stanley. Successive members of this family had by degrees bought up all the land in the Manor of Wigley, and the Manor practically ceased to exist. A neighbouring landowner, Mr. Briscoe Eyre, had also bought the great majority of the holdings in Cadnam Manor, but his farm tenants and the remaining tenants of the Manor continued to turn out their cattle on Wigley and Cadnam Commons. The Manor of Cadnam and Winsor belonged to Sir Henry Poulett.

The grandfather of Mr. Sloane Stanley commenced the scheme of inclosure. Being an ardent sportsman, he inclosed, about thirty years ago, a part of Wigley called Black Hill, on account of its being the resort of black game; the fences, however, do not appear to have been sufficient to keep out the cattle. In 1880, the present owner proceeded to inclose the whole of Wigley Common with a stone fence. Mr. Briscoe Eyre, who was an active member of the Commons Society, was not the man to allow such a proceeding at his very gate without opposition. He addressed an earnest remonstrance to Mr. Stanley, backed by a memorial numerously signed, urging him to abstain from a step so ruinous to the district and with so little pecuniary advantage to himself. Mr. Stanley, however, positively declined to suspend his inclosure even until some friendly inquiry might be made into the precise legal position of the Common, and the accuracy of his own view of his legal rights. He claimed the Common absolutely as his private property, and his answer, in effect, to those who approached him, was that they should mind their own business, and leave him to do as he liked with his own. Mr. Briscoe Eyre, therefore, was compelled either to assert his legal rights or to acquiesce in the inclosure. He commenced a suit at once on behalf of the tenants of Cadnam and Winsor against Mr. Stanley, in the usual form.

A meeting of the tenants of Cadnam Manor was then held. At this meeting it was ascertained that it was reputed among them that their rights over Wigley Common had been declared by an "old paper," which was in possession of one of the tenants. No one knew the contents of the paper or what was its origin. The inquiry was pursued, and in the possession of one of the copyholders, John Wake, was found a heavy box with three locks. This box was known by the tenants as "the monster." All that Wake recollected of it was that his grandfather, soon after he was admitted as tenant of the Manor, brought it home and said: "See, I have brought home the monster!"

On opening the box there was found an exemplification, under the Great Seal, of a decree by Lord Chancellor Hatton, in the time of Queen Elizabeth, declaring that the tenants of the Manor of Cadnam were entitled to a right of pasture over the waste lands of Wigley. It appeared from this decree, dated April 26th, 1591, that the tenants of the Manor of Cadnam and Winsor had in those days brought a suit to determine their rights against the Lord of the Manor of Wigley, William Poulett; in this they graphically said, " that the said Complaynants were poore Coppieholders of the Manor of Cadnam and Winsor, and their whole estates and livynge depended upon the same, soo that yf they should be abridged of their ancyent customs it would be their utter undoinge." They claimed that—

"The Custom of the Manor of Wigley was, by all the tyme aforesaid begune, that the Coppeholde and customarie tenants of the Mannor of Cadnam had and ought to have comon of pasture for all their cattell that they doe reare and breade upon their Coppeholde and customarie landes and tenements within the said Manor, as well in and upon the Comon fieldes belonginge to the said Mannor, as in the waste ground of Wigley, and in those places that in ancyent time the tenants of the said Mannor have used to have Comon of pasture in as large and benefecyall manner as their ancestors tenants of the said Mannor have used to have and enjoye the same."

The suitors then alleged that Poulett, having bought the Manor, and seeking to make the best advantage thereof, had impugned the customs set forth, and among other things, " utterly refused to permit the said complainants to have any Common of pasture for their cattle in the waste lands and in the places where they had usually had Common."

The Defendant in his answer, after alleging his purchase of the Manor, traversed the customs alleged, and in particular, " that the said Coppieholders ought to have comon of pasture for their cattell in the ffeilds and Comons belongeing to the said Mannor, as in the said Bill was alleaged."

The decree then stated that a Commission was awarded by the consent of the parties for the examination of witnesses for the proof of the said customs, and was executed and returned and published, and that mention was made to the Court alleging that by such evidence—

"and by anncient coppies, customarye Rolles, and other evidence yt appeared that the said Complaynants had in substance proved the said customarye privileges, rightes and usages by theme set fourthe in their right."

The decree followed in these words :—

" It is therefore this p'sent tearme of Easter that ys to saye on Monday the six and twentieth daye of Aprylle in the three and thirteth yeare of the raigne of our Soveraigne Lady Elizabeth by the grace of God Queen of England France and Ireland Defender of the Ffaithe, etc., by the Right honorable Sir Christopher Hatton of the most noble Order of the Garter Knight Lord Chancellor of England and by the said heighe Courte of Chauncery ordered adjudjed and decreed by and with the consent of the said Complaynints and defendante their Counsellors and Attorneyes that the said customs privileges rights and usages bee ratefyed and confirmed by this Courte. And the said Complaynints their heires and assignes and all clayminge from by or under them or any of them shall frome hencefurthe for ever more have, hold, and enjoye all the customes privileges rightes and usages by them set fourythe in these tyll yealdinge payeinge and doeinge their yearelye rents and services as if right had been dewe and accustomed an such ffynes and heryotts as are before also sett fourthe and declared against the defendante his heires and assignes and all claymynge from by or

under hym or them or by his or there means consent command-
ment or hearement."

This exemplification of the decree under the Great
Seal was handed to the tenants of the Caduam Manor
as the charter of their rights. In the Court Rolls
of the Manor there is an entry dated December 9,
1783, to the effect that "At this Court Mr. Richard
Marsh, executor and trustee named in the last will and
testament of John Holloday deceased, one of the
customary tenants of this Manor, delivered the decree
of the Court of Chancery touching the rights and
privileges of this Manor, which was at the time of
the death of the said John Holloday lodged in his
hands, and by the unanimous consent of this Homage
the same is deposited for safe keeping in the hands
of Mr. Thomas Lovell one of the customary tenants of
the said Manor." Lovell on December 16, 1785,
produced a box prepared by him for the safe custody of
the decree touching the rights and privileges of this
Manor, with three locks and keys thereto. The Homage
directed that the box should be kept in the possession
of Thomas Lovell "with one of the keys thereof," one
other key was to be kept by Mr. Henry Hartley, the
third by Mr. John Comly.

The precautions taken by Lovell were fully justified.
But for the big box, which impressed itself on the
traditions of the tenants, as connected with their rights,
the deed might have been lost. It is singular that the
recollection of the decree should have so completely
faded away. Mr. Eyre had never heard of it. He

entered upon the suit without any knowledge of it, and simply upon the fact that the tenants of Cadnam had in practice turned out their cattle on Wigley Common. Wigley had in some way lost its name, and the waste was described in the Ordnance Maps as Half Moon Common.

On the same day that the box was discovered, the Solicitors of the Commons Society, employed by Mr. Eyre, after vainly searching in the records of the Court of Chancery under the title of Half Moon Common, discovered under the title of Cadnam and Winsor a reference which resulted in the finding of the original decree in the Public Record Office.

The decree was decisive on the point that the tenants of Cadnam had rights over Wigley Common. This could not be reopened. The only question in the new suit was whether the land which Mr. Stanley inclosed was part of the Wigley Common referred to in the decree. The Defendant expended much time and money in endeavouring to dispute this, but the decision of the Court was against him, and judgment was pronounced by Mr. Justice Field on August 8, 1882, in favour of Mr. Briscoe Eyre, and confirming the tenants of Cadnam in their rights of common over the waste of Wigley Manor.

The present conditions of the two Manors present some interesting features. The Manor of Cadnam consists of 493 acres of cultivated land in seventeen holdings of from three to sixty acres. Forty years ago there were as many separate owners, of whom the great majority

cultivated their own land. In the interval Mr. Briscoe
Eyre has himself, or through his father, acquired nine
of these holdings with 331 acres ; of the remainder, five
only are now owned by their occupiers. The holdings,
however, still remain small, and there cannot be a
doubt that the common rights attached to these small
holdings account largely for their continued existence.
If Mr. Sloane Stanley had succeeded in his inclosure,
these small holdings would have been rendered un-
profitable, and there would necessarily have followed a
consolidation of farms, and probably three or four large
farms would have superseded the small holdings. It is
quite certain, on the other hand, that but for Mr.
Briscoe Eyre and his fortuitous connection with the
Commons Society, the inclosures would not have been
abated, and Mr. Stanley would have succeeded in effecting his purpose. Not one of the smaller holders would
have ventured to cope with him in the law courts. The
aggregation of lands in a single owner has been carried
even further in Wigley Manor. In 1840 there were
eleven distinct owners of land, tenants of the Manor ;
they have now all been merged in a single owner—
Mr. Sloane Stanley. The two Manors well illustrate
the process of the gradual extinction of small owners
of land. That the small holdings have not been merged
in large farms has undoubtedly been owing to the
existence of the Commons.

CHAPTER XI.

Banstead Commons.

The last, but not the least important, of the great suits affecting Commons within reach of London, was that of the Banstead Commons. Indeed, no other suit has been more pertinaciously fought through long years of litigation, or was subject to more strange and unexpected vicissitudes. Commenced in the year 1877, it was not concluded till 1890, and only in the past year, 1893, has the future of the Commons been definitely provided for by a Regulation scheme, under the Metropolitan Commons Acts, in spite of the most determined opposition of those representing the Lord of the Manor before Select Committees of both Houses of Parliament. Seventeen years, therefore, have been spent in resisting the efforts to appropriate these Commons, and in securing to the Commoners and the public the enjoyment and management of them.

The Commons of Banstead consist of four distinct and separate areas, with an aggregate of about 1,300 acres. They lie on the summit of the North Surrey Downs, at an altitude of 500 to 600 feet above the sea, with splendid views, on the one side, of the Valley of the Thames, with its teeming population, on the other, of the Weald of Surrey and Sussex. Together with Epsom Downs, Walton Heath, and Coulsdon Commons,

BANSTEAD COMMONS

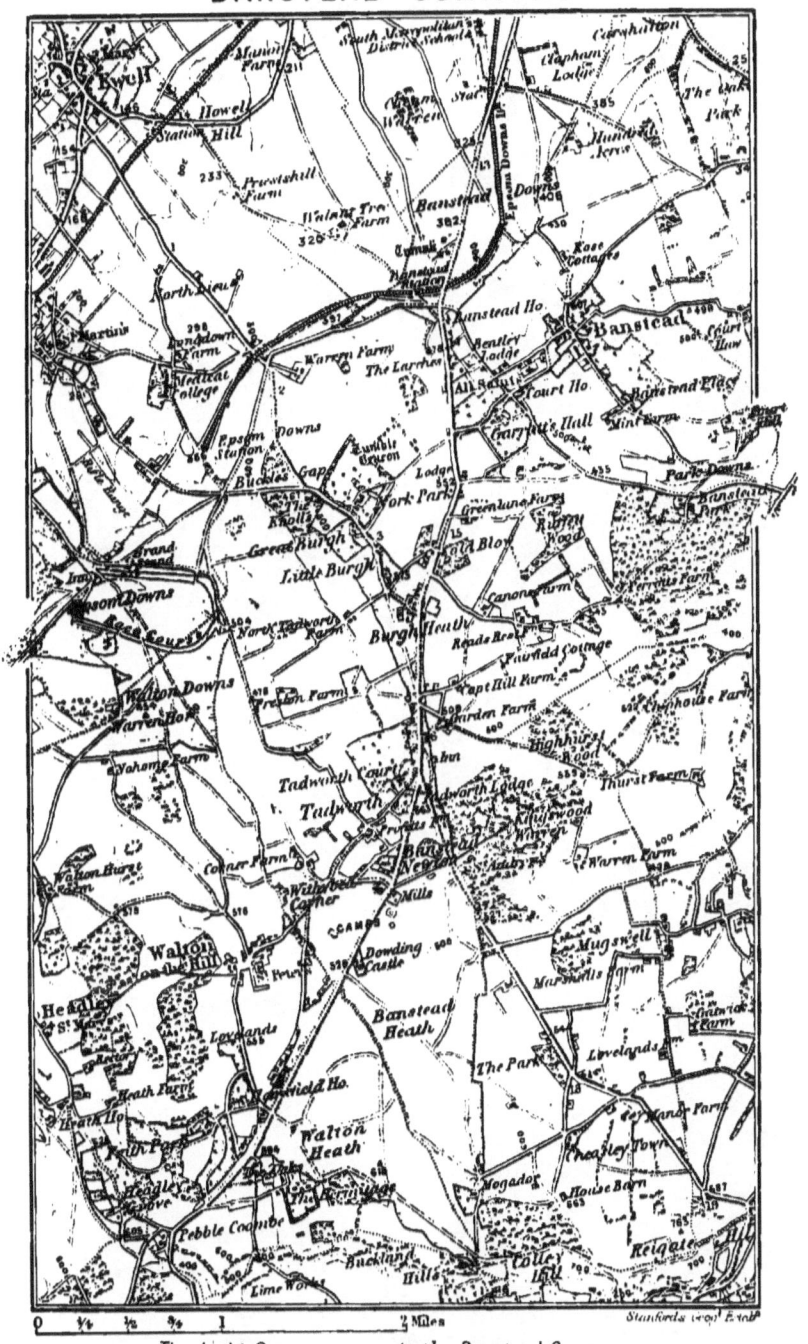

The Light Green represents the Banstead Commons
The Dark Green, Walton Heath & Epsom Downs.

they form a range of open land of the utmost value to London, the most bracing district within easy reach of it, from which salubrious breezes reach the crowded valley below, unaffected by any impurities.

Banstead Down, the second in size of these four Commons, lies immediately above the populous and growing suburb of Sutton. Banstead Heath, the largest, adjoins Walton Heath, which is in a separate parish and manor. Between them lie the Park Down and Burgh Heath—the one a range of open land near to the woods of Banstead Park, the other a small but picturesque area, nearly covered with gorse and bracken.

The Parish of Banstead consists of 5,528 acres, and is conterminous with the Manor of Banstead, and its dependent Manors of North and South Tadworth, Preston, Great Burgh, and Southmerfield. The earliest mention of the Manor of Banstead is in Domesday Book, which informs us that it was in the hands of the Bishop of Bayeux, and held of him by the Earl of Clare. It is probable that at some time in the reign of Edward the Confessor, the whole Parish was held by the King, and that subsequently it was divided into the several Manors above described.

The Manor of Banstead passed, in 119̃, into the hands of Mabel de Mowbray, wife of Nigel de Mowbray; and in 1223 into those of Hubert de Burgh, Earl of Kent, who secured a grant of Free Warren in Banstead from the King. In 1273 it reverted by exchange for other land to Edward I., and thenceforward remained in the possession of his successors

to the throne for 270 years till 1543, when Henry
VIII., having previously annexed it to the Honour
of Hampton Court, granted it to Sir Nicholas Carewe.
On Carewe's subsequent attainder it reverted to the
Crown, but Queen Mary regranted it to his son. In
1762 another Sir Nicholas Carewe sold it to Rowland
Frye, from whom it passed through other hands by
purchase, till in 1832 it was bought by Mr. Thomas
Alcock, whose representatives, in 1873, sold it to Sir
John Hartopp.

The first general survey of the Manor was in 1325.
It is still to be found in the charters of the British
Museum. There was another survey of the parish in
1598, in which the common lands are described as
extending over 1,300 acres. The Court Rolls commence in 1379, and continue in unbroken succession,
and in perfect order, till 1876. The history of the dependent Manors can be traced with equal precision
from the earliest times, and, indeed, they form an
interesting study from an historical and archæological
standpoint, as bearing upon the subject of the creation
of Manors. All the land in three of them was ultimately concentrated in the hands of the Earl of
Egmont, who held them at the time of the commencement of the suit hereafter described, with the exception
of Tadworth Park, which was the demesne land of the
Manor of South Tadworth, and which was bought, a
few years ago, by Sir Charles Russell, Q.C. There was
also another Manor, that of Chaldon, not in the Parish,
but dependent on the Manor of Banstead. This, at the

time of Domesday Book, was also held by the Bishop
of Bayeux, and passed through various hands till a few
years ago, when it was the property of Lord Hylton.

Much turned, in the suit, upon the relations of these
minor Manors to the principal one of Banstead, and upon
whether the owners of land within them had rights of
common over the waste lands of the Banstead Manor.
This was confirmed by the surveys already alluded to,
and by numerous extracts from the Rolls of the Manors.
Thus, in 1578, an order was made by the Court Leet
of Banstead Manor that none within Banstead or
Tadworth should keep in the Common of Banstead
more than two sheep per acre. This admitted a right
on the part of the owners of Tadworth to use the
Commons, subject, however, to the orders and regulations made by the homage of Banstead. It will be
seen later that the judges recognised that Sir Charles
Russell, as owner of the demesne lands of Tadworth,
was entitled to rights of common over the Commons
of Banstead.

In 1864, Mr. Alcock, then Lord of the Manor and
the owner of a property in the neighbourhood—the
demesne lands of the Manor—conceived the idea of
inclosing the four Commons of Banstead, and commenced proceedings with that view before the Inclosure Commissioners, but the proposal roused so
much opposition from his neighbours, the Commoners,
that he received no assistance from the Commissioners, and was compelled to abandon the attempt.
In the following year Mr. Alcock gave evidence

before the Committee of the House of Commons
on the London Commons. He pointed out the difficulties he had experienced, as Lord of the Manor,
in preserving order over the Banstead Commons,
and expressed his desire to dedicate his rights and
interest in them to the public, so that they might be
secure against inclosure, and that he might be relieved
of the burden of protecting them. The Committee
referred to his proposal in their Report, as an argument
in favour of their scheme for regulating Commons and
placing them under some protecting local authority or
governing body. In the same year Mr. Alcock joined
the Commons Society as one of its first members;
and when the Society propounded its scheme, which
ultimately developed into the Metropolitan Commons
Act, for regulating Commons within fifteen miles of
the Metropolis, he strongly supported it. Had he
lived, there can be no doubt that he would have placed
the Banstead Commons under the protection of the
Act, in such a manner that no future inclosure could
have been attempted.

Unhappily, Mr. Alcock died, in 1866, before any
proceedings could be initiated under the above Act, for
the regulation of the wastes of his Manor. His representatives showed no disposition to carry out his intentions. They renewed application to the Inclosure
Commissioners for the inclosure of the Commons, and
when their proposal was rejected, they sold, in 1873, their
interest in the Banstead Commons to Sir John Hartopp.
Unfortunately, the Manorial rights thus became separated

from the demesne lands, and the purchaser acquired only the soil of the waste of the Manor, subject to the rights of common over it, and the quit rents, heriots, and fines of the freehold and copyhold tenants of the Manor. Sir John Hartopp, having bought these manorial wastes and rights for a comparatively small sum, endeavoured to turn his purchase into a land building speculation, by getting rid of the Commoners and inclosing the Commons. In spite of the lessons which Lords of the Manors must or should have drawn from the experience of the recent litigation in respect of Berkhamsted, Plumstead, and Coulsdon Commons, and still more of Epping Forest, his legal advisers appear to have persuaded him that he could without difficulty convert the Commons into private property, free from common rights. The prize would have been a great one, for the land would have been most valuable for villa residences. The difficulty hitherto in such cases had been the uncertainty as to who were the owners of land within the Manor entitled to common rights, and whose assent it was necessary to obtain by agreement or purchase, before attempting inclosure under the Statute of Merton.

In the Banstead case, the course of approvement, under the Statute, had apparently been buoyed out by recent proceedings, under the authority of Parliament. In 1866, the London and Brighton Railway Company had obtained power to construct a branch to Epsom, and to carry this line through Banstead Down. Not only was this a great disfigurement and injury to the

N

Common by cutting it in two, but it was the cause of great danger to it, by affording the opportunity of ascertaining the exact limit of the persons entitled to common rights. Under the provisions of the Lands Clauses Act, the compensation payable in respect of the land, thus taken from the Common for the purposes of the railway, was paid into Court, and it was referred to the Inclosure Commissioners to apportion this sum between the Lord of the Manor and the persons who could maintain their claim to it as Commoners.

For this purpose an inquiry was held at Banstead by Mr. Wetherell, an Assistant Inclosure Commissioner, and an award was made by him specifying the persons who, in his opinion, had rights over the Common, and were entitled to compensation. This determination was not in law a final one, in the sense that it precluded any claim in future legal proceedings, on behalf of persons not recognised by him as Commoners; and, as the result showed, the conclusions of the Commissioner proved to be wholly untrustworthy. But such an inquiry by an independent official, with experience in such matters, confirmed to some extent by the rolls of the manor and by some old surveys, appeared doubtless to Sir John Hartopp's advisers to be of very high authority, and it was, perhaps, not to be wondered at that he should think it conclusive as to the rights affecting the Commons. He was, no doubt, advised that if he could, by purchase or otherwise, get rid of the rights of the persons thus designated as

Commoners, in the award of the Commissioners, he would be able to inclose under the Statute of Merton, or even to treat the Common as his freehold, discharged of any rights.

With this object, then, in view, Sir John Hartopp set to work to buy off the persons whose common rights were admitted in the award of Mr. Wetherell. One by one the Commoners were so dealt with. To some the temptation offered was the enfranchisement of their copyholds free of charge; to others, money payments. To two at least the promise was made of large allotments of the Common when inclosed. As he reduced in this manner the number of Commoners who could resist his scheme of inclosure, so the terms of the remainder rose, and it became necessary to expend very large sums in buying off those who held out the longest. In none of the other Commons cases had there been such an assiduous and well-devised effort to clear away the rights of Commoners, with the object of converting the wastes into private property. It is said that Sir John Hartopp expended in this manner not less than £18,000, and in so doing got rid of the rights of twenty-seven persons in respect of 1,400 acres of land.

The largest landowner in the Manor, having rights of common, was the late Earl of Egmont. His consent was obtained by a mixed process of threat and bribe. Lord Egmont was opposed in principle to the inclosure of the Common, but he was advised by his lawyers that Sir John Hartopp had already acquired

N 2

such a predominant interest in and power over it, that
he could inclose the greater part of it, under the Statute
of Merton; and threats were held out that the part
thus inclosed would be selected so as to be injurious to
Lord Egmont's property. Under this threat, Lord
Egmont consented to share in the appropriation of the
Commons, and to take in compensation for his rights
the whole of Burgh Heath. In the same manner
another large landowner in the district was induced to
consent to the inclosure, by the promise of the allotment
to him of Park Down.

By the year 1876, Sir John Hartopp had so far
progressed in his scheme of purchasing out the Commoners, that he thought he might safely commence
his proceedings for the inclosure of the Commons. He
began to show his hand by erecting a row of houses on
Banstead Downs, and by inclosing some parts of Banstead Heath. In spite, however, of his efforts to ward
off opposition, there remained many persons owning
property in the district, who strongly objected to his
schemes, who greatly valued the stretch of open land,
and who had been induced to reside there on account of
the Commons, and under the belief that they were
safe from inclosure. Some of these had rights of
common, and had rejected overtures of purchase;
others had no such rights, but were interested in
supporting any movement against inclosure.

By the advice of the Commons Society, a meeting
was held at Sutton in December, 1876, to protest against
Sir John Hartopp's inclosures; and a Committee was

formed, under the title of the Banstead Commons Protection Society, for the purpose of resisting them. Of this Committee Mr. Hamilton Fletcher was chairman, and Mr. James Nisbet Robertson and Mr. Garrett Morten were the most active members. Mr. Robertson was the owner of a house and twenty acres of land, and Mr. Morten of three acres of land, with undoubted rights of common attaching to them. These gentlemen undertook to challenge at law the proceedings of Sir John Hartopp. They were joined by two other copyholders named Bennett, who owned a small property on Burgh Heath, and who had for many years taken furze and sand from the Common. They also strengthened their position by purchasing a small property on Burgh Heath, in respect of which rights over the Commons undoubtedly existed. They formed a somewhat slender nucleus of opposition to Sir John Hartopp, and it was, perhaps, a great risk to commence a suit against a Lord of the Manor, who had shown such determination to spare no expenditure that was necessary to assert his right to inclose ; but there was no alternative but to see the Commons gradually filched away, and the Banstead Committee and their advisers rightly judged that when public opinion was so much roused on the subject of open spaces, it needed only a sturdy and judicious resistance to achieve success, though the precise means might not be altogether obvious.

These gentlemen, however, by the advice of Mr. Robert Hunter, who had been engaged in so many others of the Commons suits, undertook the risk, and commenced a suit against Sir John Hartopp on January 8th, 1877, on behalf of the Commoners, claiming the usual rights of common, and asking that the lord might be restrained from inclosure. They were supported to some extent by local contributions, and by promises of assistance from the Corporation of London. With a view to reinforce their legal position as Commoners, a deputation was introduced by the writer to the present Lord Egmont, who had lately succeeded his uncle in the title and property, and tried to persuade him to throw in his lot with the Commoners against the inclosure, and to withdraw from the arrangements with Sir John Hartopp. Lord Egmont replied that he was much averse to the inclosure, and would far sooner see the Commons left open as they were, but he felt precluded by his predecessor's agreement with Sir John Hartopp from joining in opposition to it.

Upon a motion for an interim injunction, Sir George Jessel put Sir John Hartopp under terms that, in the event of the suit being decided against him, he should pull down the buildings he had erected. Thenceforward for thirteen more years the suit dragged on its weary course through every form of litigious proceeding that could be devised. The originators of the suit could have little foreseen the maelstrom of litigation in which they were involved, but they never flinched from the task. Mr. Hamilton Fletcher and Mr. Nisbet Robertson died before the conclusion, but their places were filled by others.

The first brush in the courts of law arose upon the title of Mr. Robertson. This gentleman was only the lessee of the house and land, in respect of which he maintained the suit, but he had the right under his lease to purchase the freehold from his landlord before Michaelmas, 1878. His landlord, after giving this lease, but before the commencement of the suit, had sold the rights of common attached to his reversion to Sir John Hartopp. Mr. Robertson contended that this sale was void as far as he was concerned, and that he was entitled to claim the property, with the rights of common attached, in the condition in which it stood at the commencement of the lease. He gave notice to his landlord of his intention to exercise his option of purchase of the property, and demanded a grant of the rights, which had been attached to it. Sir John Hartopp refused to join in the conveyance, or to release the rights of common which he had purchased. It became necessary, therefore, for Mr. Robertson to join Sir John Hartopp in the suit against his landlord for a specific performance.

This preliminary suit was decided in favour of Mr. Robertson, and an order was made by Sir George Jessel, requiring Sir John Hartopp to join in a conveyance of the rights of common, together with the property, to him. This victory was of considerable importance, for it amounted to a legal recognition that Mr. Robertson was entitled to rights over all the Banstead Commons which could not be gainsaid. It was, perhaps, this defeat that abated the confidence of Sir John

Hartopp and his legal advisers in their ultimate success, and induced them to offer terms of compromise. They proposed to give up one-half of the Commons, and to secure it for the enjoyment of the public, provided they were allowed to inclose the other half.

The Banstead Committee consulted the Commons Society as to a compromise. As Chairman, I had strongly opposed, in every Commons case, proposals of this kind, as detrimental to the interests of the public in the particular cases, and as likely to offer inducements to Lords of Manors to attempt inclosures in other instances. But in the case of Banstead the obstacles in the'way of ultimate success were most formidable. There was great difficulty in obtaining funds for the proper conduct of the case; and the rights of common, at that time known to exist, were few in proportion to the extent of the Commons. A compromise therefore appeared to be expedient in this case. Fortunately, however, before any arrangement was come to, most unexpected events occurred, which completely changed the aspect of affairs, and made success almost certain to the Commoners.

In 1884, Sir John Hartopp's solicitors, who had been mainly responsible for the action which he had taken, and who were in some way partners in the speculation, became insolvent, and absconded, leaving their affairs and those of their client in the greatest confusion. Sir John Hartopp himself was involved in their ruin, and became bankrupt. The negotiations for a compromise came suddenly to an end for want

of parties to conduct them, and much to the relief
of those who desired to save the whole of the Commons.
Lord Egmont at this point, finding that Sir John
Hartopp was no longer in a position to carry out any
understanding with him, felt himself relieved of any
obligation under his uncle's agreement, and transferred
his interest to the side of the Commoners. As his
property within the Manor consisted of no less than
2,000 acres, and his rights of common were propor-
tionately extensive, this made a most important accession
of strength to the Plaintiffs. About the same time
also, Mr. Francis Baring purchased the Banstead Park
estate, and became greatly interested in maintaining
the Commons. He joined the Committee for their
preservation, and contributed largely to their funds.
Sir Charles Russell also bought the Tadworth Court
estate in the parish, which gave him interest in the
matter, and induced him to join the Committee.

Thus reinforced, the Committee found itself able
to push forward the litigation with energy, and was
supported with funds, which had before been greatly
wanting. Moreover, Lord Egmont's adherence to the
Commoners' cause altogether altered the proportion
between the acreage of land to which common rights
were attached, and that of the Common. Thenceforward it became absolutely certain that inclosure
could no longer be justified under the Statute of
Merton. It was hoped indeed that the bankruptcy of
Sir John Hartopp would lead to an abandonment of the
defence to the suit, and of further attempts at inclosure.

It turned out, however, that the interest of the Lord of the Manor in the soil of the Commons, subject to common rights, but with the possibility of inclosure, whatever it might be, had been mortgaged for the sum of £31,000 to two ladies, who were clients of the Messrs. Parker, and who had been, it is to be feared, fraudulently advised by them to embark their money upon what was, at best, a most shadowy and dangerous security, dependent wholly for its value on the success of the suit.

These mortgagees now took possession of the Commons under their mortgage deed. They at once endeavoured to realise an income for their unfortunate investment by excessive cutting of turf and digging of gravel, for sale, and refused to listen to any remonstrances of the Committee of Commoners. They stripped large areas of the Commons of their natural turf, and carted away the soil upon which the value of the land for pasturage depended. The Commoners, therefore, felt it necessary to revive the suit. They made the mortgagees parties to the action, and claimed an order to prevent the reckless destruction of the surface of the Commons to the detriment of their own rights. The point at issue was no longer directly the right of the lord to inclose ; the immediate question was the right to destroy the Commons by stripping them of turf and robbing them of loam. Indirectly this would have involved ultimately the fate of the Commons.

The new issue altered the onus of proof in the suit, and made the question far more difficult to the

Commoners. Where the right to the land of a Common is challenged by the Lord of the Manor, by inclosure under the Statute of Merton, it is well recognised by the Courts, upon the construction of the Statute, that the onus of proof that sufficiency of common is left for the remaining rights of other persons, rests with the Lord of the Manor who incloses. But when the question in dispute is the right to more or less digging of loam, or cutting of turf, it is equally well established by law that the onus of proof, that the acts of the lord constitute an injury to the Commoners' rights, is thrown upon the Commoners themselves. This was a much more difficult task for the Plaintiffs in the Banstead case, for it necessitated their proving exactly the number of persons entitled to rights, and showing that the paring of turf and digging of loam, as carried out by the Lord of the Manor, was such as to interfere substantially with their rights of common, and that the Commons in their impaired condition could not support cattle which might be kept on the land by the Commoners during the winter months.

Upon the Commoners of Banstead, therefore, the onus rested to establish in their suit against the mortgagees that there were still in existence rights, in respect of an acreage of land so large that the Commons, in their existing conditions with their surface injured by the cutting of turf and digging of loam, could not produce food enough for the cattle which might be kept upon such lands. For this purpose the rights pertaining to Lord Egmont's land, consisting of 2,000 acres, and to Sir Charles Russell's property, were of great importance, for if it could be shown that the whole of this land was entitled to common rights in addition to other lands, whose rights were no longer disputed, there could be little question as to the insufficiency of the Commons, as treated by the lord, to maintain the requisite number of cattle. The rolls of the manor and the evidence of living persons showed that, from time immemorial, rights had been claimed and exercised in respect of nearly every farm in the parish, and particularly by the occupiers of Lord Egmont's and Sir Charles Russell's properties. On the other hand, the defendants relied on an old survey of 1680, and on Mr. Wetherell's award of the money paid by the Railway Company in compensations to the Commoners, which limited greatly the extent of land in the district entitled to rights. Every effort also was made to narrow the rights of common, and to prove that sufficient pasture remained on the wastes for all the sheep that could be turned out. The issue involved most lengthy and costly investigations into the conditions and rights of every farm in the manor.

At length, in July, 1886, nine years after the commencement of the suit, the case was tried before Mr. Justice Stirling. The hearing lasted for several days. The result was not altogether satisfactory to the Commoners. Sir John Hartopp, who was not represented by counsel, was restrained from inclosing or destroying the pasturage of the Commons; and an order was made for the abatement of his inclosures. He was also ordered to pay the costs of the suit up to the hearing; but this was of no value to the plaintiffs, for Sir John was already a bankrupt. The Judge, however, declined to decide, as against the mortgagees, whether the destruction of the surface of the Commons was of such a character as to warrant an injunction. He directed a reference to Mr. Meadows White, Q.C., to inquire who were the persons entitled to rights of common, what their rights were, and whether there was sufficiency of common on the waste lands for the persons entitled to the rights. For the purposes of this inquiry, the right of common for sheep was directed by the Judge to be taken as limited to two sheep to every acre of land to which the right attached.

This was the first occasion on which, in the course of legal proceedings for the protection of Commons, an inquiry had been directed of this kind into the extent of the rights of common existing over the land. It was a course much to be deprecated, as it enormously increased the costs of the suit, without, as Lord Justice Fry, in giving judgment in the Court of Appeal, said, "lessening the intricacy of the arguments" used before the Court. It will be obvious that if the report of Mr. Meadows White had been adverse to the Commoners, it would have buoyed out the course for a future inclosure under the Statute of Merton.

The proceedings before the referee were most lengthy and costly; they occupied forty days. The mortgagees were represented at each sitting by two or three counsel; the Commoners on their part were represented by Mr. Percival Birkett, the solicitor in the suit, and legal adviser of the Commons Society, whose knowledge and experience on such subjects are very great. Mr. Meadows White was unable to make his report till March 11, 1888, nearly two years after the date of Mr. Justice Stirling's order. It was generally favourable to the contentions of the Commoners. Exceptions were taken to it on various legal points, which had to be argued at great length, and it was not till April 11, 1889, that Mr. Justice Stirling delivered his final judgment on this case, entirely favourable to the Commoners. The mortgagees appealed against this, and on December 21, 1889, nearly thirteen years from the commencement of this prolonged suit, Lord Justice Fry delivered the unanimous judgment of the Court of Appeal.*

This decision entirely vindicated the claims of the Commoners. The Court determined that there were rights of common in respect of 320 acres held as of the Manor—in other words, taking the agreed stint of two sheep to the acre, there were rights of common for 640 sheep. They also found that from three of Lord Egmont's farms 600 sheep had been turned out on the Common in such a manner as to maintain a right, and that from Sir Charles Russell's property of Tadworth 200 sheep had been turned out. Thus pasturage was needed for 1,440 sheep in all. The Court further

* Robertson *v.* Hartopp, 43 Ch. Div., 484.

held it to be proved that the Commons would not furnish pasture for more than 1,200 sheep, even if they were kept and turned out on the wastes according to the modern practice of sheep-farming; while if the sheep were turned out to get all their sustenance from the land during the summer months, according to the old practice, the Commons would not carry more than 600 sheep.

The Judges repudiated the doctrine contended for by the mortgagees that the measure of the rights of the Commoners was the average number of sheep which had actually of late years been turned out—a doctrine which involved the conclusion that because full use of their legal rights had not been made by the Commoners, they had therefore lost them.

They also declared that the Commoners were entitled to the several rights which they claimed over the wastes, that the mortgagees were not justified in continuing Sir John Hartopp's inclosures, and that the cutting of the pasture, herbage and turf, and the digging of loam by the mortgagees, were excessive, and constituted distinct injuries to the rights of the Commoners and should be restrained; and they directed that the costs of the whole proceedings from the time when the mortgagees were made parties to the action should be paid by them.

There could not have been a more triumphant victory for the Commoners. The judgment established all their claims. It is probable that, even without the accession of Lord Egmont and Sir Charles Russell, they would have succeeded. With these rights their case was complete, and indeed overwhelming. The case was also a thorough and final vindication of the principles laid down by the Committee of 1865, and always insisted upon by the Commons Society—namely, that practically it is not possible to inclose a Common under the Statute of Merton without the sanction of Parliament, and that if contested in the Courts of Law with adequate resources, such attempted inclosures would certainly prove to be invalid and would be abated.

In this case the policy of buying up and extinguishing rights with a view to such inclosure, was carried out with a pertinacity, and with a disregard of expense, exceeding that in any other attempted inclosure. Sir John Hartopp spared no exertions and no money. He expended many thousands of pounds, and gave up enfranchisement dues, valued at many more thousands. He thought he had left so few Commoners outstanding that they might be safely defied. The result showed that all this was to no purpose. The rights still subsisting proved, after full inquiry, to be far more than enough to prevent inclosure of a single rood of the Commons.

Sir John Hartopp, who had originally embarked on this policy, and the mortgagees, who advanced their thousands upon it, must have cursed the day when they acted upon the advice of their lawyers. The Commoners would gladly have compromised with the mortgagees after the failure of Sir John Hartopp, by paying a few thousand pounds, in order to secure

the Commons for ever, and to avoid further legal proceedings. Their overtures were disregarded, and the
mortgagees were induced to plunge further into this sea
of litigation, with the result only that they lost every-
thing, and were mulcted in enormous costs. The Commoners, in spite of their victory on every point, had
to pay their costs in the suit against Sir John Hartopp,
in consequence of his bankruptcy ; but they had at least
the satisfaction of knowing that their efforts had saved
the wastes, not only from immediate and prospective
inclosure, but from the destructive practices of the
lord, which were defacing the surface and destroying
the beauty of the Banstead Commons.

The battle, however, did not end with the litigation
in the Law Courts. The Commoners, having succeeded
there, were determined to strike further while the iron
was hot, and to put the Commons in such a position that
their interests would be no longer neglected. They
applied to the Agricultural Department for a scheme for
regulating Banstead Commons, under the Metropolitan
Commons Act. The Agricultural Department, hitherto,
·had generally been unwilling to pass regulation schemes
when the Lords of Manors opposed. In this case, however, the circumstances were so exceptional, the arguments arising from the action of the lord, in his long
efforts to inclose and to injure the surface of the Commons,
were so potent, that the Department after protracted proceedings gave way on the point, and made a scheme for
the regulation of the Banstead Commons in spite of the
vehement opposition of the mortgagees of the Manor.

o

This Order came under the review of Parliament in 1893 in a Confirmation Bill. It was bitterly and obstinately opposed by the mortgagees before Select Committees in both Houses of Parliament. Money was again poured out for lawyers' briefs before the most expensive tribunal in the world, but with the result only of again encountering defeat. Both Houses after long inquiries affirmed the Regulation Scheme. The Banstead Commons therefore are henceforward safe, not merely from any danger of inclosure, but from the bad treatment of their surface, and the neglect of the Lord of the Manor. Practically the Commons are taken out of the control and management of the lord. Conservators elected in the district have power to make bye-laws for the order and good government of the Commons, with a reservation, however, of any rights which the lord or his mortgagees may have. The case therefore forms an epoch in the history of Commons, and a striking example of the measures taken for their preservation.

The Committee of the Banstead Commons not only triumphed in frustrating the most systematic and determined effort ever made to get rid of rights of common, by purchase and private bargains, and to turn a Common into building land, but they have also asserted the principle that a Common may be taken out of the hands of the Lord of the Manor, against his will, and vested in those of a local committee, with powers to make bye-laws to preserve order and to prevent nuisances. The Court of Appeal has also laid down principles in this case, of the utmost value. It has reaffirmed the law, which had been almost forgotten, that the Courts will interfere on behalf of the Commoners, not merely to protect a Common from inclosure, but also to restrain the lord from destroying its utility and beauty by reckless defacement of its surface. The case ranks in importance with those of Berkhamsted Common and Epping Forest, and these three cases, together with the others referred to, have been a complete vindication of the policy of the Commons Society in resisting in every case, to the very end, and at all costs, the inclosure of a Common, otherwise than by the special sanction of Parliament.

CHAPTER XII.

TOLLARD FARNHAM COMMON AND ROWLEY GREEN.

TOLLARD FARNHAM.

FROM these numerous and splendid successes in vindication of the rights of Commoners, for the prevention of inclosure, it is now necessary to turn to the cases of two reverses, where there was failure to defeat aggression. In 1874 assistance was asked of the Commons Society to investigate the total inclosure of a Common at Tollard Farnham, a purely rural parish, about seven miles from Blandford, in the County of Dorset. Upon this Common the cottagers of the village had been in the habit, from time immemorial, of cutting furze and hazel tops, for the purpose of fuel, and for consumption in their own houses only. The hearths of all the cottages in the village were constructed for burning this kind of fuel, and were unsuitable for coal, which in former days it was impossible to procure, and which, in more recent years, could only be purchased in the village at a high price. The cessation of the supply of the customary fuel, it was alleged, had caused great inconvenience, and was the subject of serious complaint in the district.

While the Society was making inquiries into the inclosure, the Lord of the Manor, the late Lord Rivers, commenced actions against three villagers who had persisted in exercising what they considered their rights, according to ancient custom, and had continued to cut their wood in spite of the inclosure. The Society was unwilling that these poor men should lose, from want of means, and from lack of proper legal assistance, what they believed to be, and what there was strong *primá facie* evidence to believe was, their right, and therefore resolved to give its support to them.

Before the case came on for trial at the Assizes, an order was obtained from the Court, directing that the issues in the three actions should be ascertained by an arbitrator, in the form of a special case, for the opinion of the Court of Exchequer. Numerous meetings were held by the arbitrator, Sir A. E. Miller, Q.C., and eventually a case was drawn up by him, and laid before the Court.

It appeared that the Manor of Tollard Farnham was in very ancient times dependent on, or carved out of, the Manor of Cranbourne, which was part of the Chase of Cranbourne, extending over a yet wider district, and differing only from a Forest in that it was held by a private owner, and not by the Crown, and did not possess distinctive Courts. The Manor and Honour of Cranbourne are mentioned in Domesday Book as the property of the King. In the time of William Rufus the Manor and Chase appear to have been given to Fitz-Hamon, Lord of Corboile, in Normandy, together with numerous other Manors, constituting the Honour of Gloucester. They were escheated for want of heirs to Henry II. in 1175. They remained in the

hands of successive Sovereigns till they were granted
by Henry III. to the De Clares, Earls of Hertford
and Gloucester. On the death of the last male of this
family, they descended to his three sisters co-heiresses.
A partition was then made of De Clare's lands, and
Cranbourne Chase and Manor fell to the lot of Elizabeth,
wife of John De Burgh, and from her descended through
the De Mortimers, Earls of March, Plantagenet, Earl of
Cambridge, and Richard, Duke of York, till they vested
in King Edward IV. They remained in the possession
of the Crown till 1611, when James I. granted them to
the Earl of Salisbury, from whom the Manor, but not
the Chase, has come down to the present owner, the
Marquis of Salisbury. The Manor of Tollard Farnham,
we learn from an early survey, dated 6 Edward VI.,
was held of the Manor of Cranbourne by knight
service, by the Earl of Pembroke. Later it was purchased by Sir Thomas Arundel, in whose family it
remained till 1820, when it was sold by the then
Lord Arundel to Lord Rivers.

In 1828 the Chase of Cranbourne, which had been
separated from the Manor, and was vested in Lord
Rivers, was disfranchised, in the sense that all rights of
sporting were done away with. The Act effecting this
states in its preamble that Lord Rivers claimed to be
the owner of

"a certain Franchise or Chase called Cranbourne Chase, extending over divers Manors, and a large tract of land, situate in
the counties of Dorset and Wilts, and as such owner is possessed
of divers valuable and extensive rights and privileges over the

same, and whereas the said Lord Rivers, in right of the said
Chase, hath constantly exercised a privilege of feeding and
preserving the deer within the said Chase, and the number of
deer now fed and preserved therein, it is computed, amounts
to upwards of twelve thousand, but does not exceed twenty
thousand, and the deer range over the property of the different
proprietors of land, within the limits of the Chase, and whereas
the exercise of such privileges and of feeding and preserving
deer in right of Chase is extremely injurious to the owners of
lands within the limits of the Chase, and is a great hindrance
to the cultivation of such lands, and tends greatly to demoralise
the habits of the labouring classes and of the inhabitants
residing in and near the Chase; and whereas the said Lord
Rivers is willing to accept the clear yearly sum of eighteen
hundred pounds, as a compensation and satisfaction for the
extinguishing of his said rights; . . ."—

The Act proceeded to enact that "thenceforward all
right of feed and range of deer, and all privileges of
protecting them within the limits of the Chase, and
all franchises and privileges in respect of the Chase,
should cease, determine, and be for ever extinguished,
and the Chase should thenceforward be disfranchised."
In return for this a charge was imposed on the property
within the Chase for the yearly sum of eighteen hundred
pounds, in favour of Lord Rivers. The statute, however, expressly reserved all other rights.

Even to a late period, subsequent to this Act, deer
are said to have roamed over the district, and to have
found covert not unfrequently on Tollard Farnham
Common. The whole of the parish of Tollard Farnham
was in the Chase of Cranbourne. The Chase rolls are
extant from an early year of Edward III. They

contain many presentments of offences against the deer and wood. Many of them relate to Tollard Farnham. For several years a Chase officer, called a verderer, was sworn for it, and attended the Leet Courts.

There can be no doubt that, from time immemorial, the inhabitants of Tollard Farnham had in fact exercised the custom or right of cutting furze and hazel wood, called " haskets," on the waste lands of the Manor from Old Michaelmas Day till Old Lady Day, and that they derived from this source their only supply of fuel. The case, therefore, closely resembled that of the Loughton rights of lopping trees in Epping Forest, which have already been described, the only difference being that Cranbourne Chase was held by a private owner and not by the Crown. It had, however, often been in the possession of the Crown, and there was no more reason why a grant from the Crown should not have been presumed in the Tollard Farnham case than in that of Loughton.

Up to the year 1850 the parish of Tollard Farnham was a very interesting case of common-field cultivation. The parish consisted of 950 acres, of which 300 acres were held in severalty; 224 acres were in copses or woodlands in the hands of the Lord of the Manor; 159 acres were in Common, the waste lands of the Manor; and 267 acres were laid out in common fields, which were allotted amongst the tenants of the Manor, and held by them in severalty for purposes of tillage; these were farmed upon the three-course system : one part being in wheat, another in barley, and a third fallow or in clover. When the crops were carried, the common fields were thrown open for the benefit of all the tenants of the Manor. Cattle were first turned in, and subsequently sheep. The cattle appear to have been fed from the time of carrying the corn till November, and the sheep to have been folded on the fields during the winter. The fallow field was not to be broken up till Midsummer. The hedges round the common fields were repaired by the severalty holders, in proportion to their holdings in such fields. There were grass banks called lanchards in the common fields, which it was forbidden to plough up. The cattle were not pastured on these until the corn was carried. The ownership of land in each of these three common fields was minutely divided—each owner having three or four, and often more, detached lots in each of the fields. These lands were held by two kinds of customary tenure—(1) Copyholds held not absolutely, but during three lives, renewable upon the dropping of a life, on payment of a fine of considerable amount; (2) Leaseholds for a term of 99 years, if certain persons named in the lease should live so long. These leases were granted by the lord, on payment of a fine, at a small yearly reserved rent. They had probably been substituted for some more certain tenure, such as that which the copyholders enjoyed. There appear, in 1814, to have been thirty-five such customary tenants, of whom twenty-six were leaseholders. Up to the date of the sale by Lord Arundel to Lord Rivers, the tenancies of the Manor continued in much the same condition ; both copyholds and leases were renewed from time to time.

When Lord Rivers became owner, he took steps to extinguish this system of tenure. and to get the land into his hand, and by the year 1850 the greater number of holdings had, by non-renewal of leases and acquiescence by, or purchases from, the tenants, and otherwise, been in fact got rid of. There is no doubt that, previous to the extinction of such tenancies, the tenants, or owners, had rights of common over the waste land, and were rated for them, but after the change of tenure they lost their legal rights.

In 1850 the common fields were inclosed and allotted, under the Act for facilitating the inclosure of such commonable lands. Having got rid of customary tenancies and the common-field system, and having freed the Common of the rights pertaining to it, the late Lord Rivers began to inclose. In 1851 he took up twenty acres of the waste, and in 1854 sixty-four acres. In 1856 he inclosed the residue of the Common, of seventy-five acres. The main object of these operations appears to have been that of game preserving, as it was stated that the land quickly became covered with wood, and that paths were cut and the game preserved in the woodland. No one seems to have objected to these inclosures, on the ground of being entitled to rights of turning out cattle or sheep on the land, for practically no Commoners were left. The three villagers who, in 1867, committed the alleged trespass by entering the land thus inclosed, and cutting and carrying away underwood and furze, alleged that they and others had done so continuously ever since the inclosure, and without objection or remonstrance from the lord.

It was stated by the arbitrator that it had been proved before him

"That from the commencement of legal memory, down to the date of the inclosure, there had been 'user' on the Common by a very large number of persons in the cutting of furze and hazel wood for fuel. Such user was exercised continuously, openly, and as of right. . . There was no evidence to show that any person, living in any house in the parish of Tollard Farnham, had ever been prevented from exercising such user. Furze and haskets constituted the principal fuel in the village, and the construction of the houses prevented the use of coal. . . . The user has in every case been proved to be uninterrupted down to the time of the inclosure. No evidence has been adduced by Lord Rivers of any permission or licence given by him, under which the user took place, and there is no reference to any such permission or licence in the Court Rolls of the Manor, nor is such right made the subject of express devise in any lease which has been produced of any tenancy in respect of which user has been proved."

It was also shown clearly that the defendants' relatives in past times had exercised their user, and had often been presented at the Court Leet for cutting in an irregular manner.

The case stated by the arbitrator was argued before the late Chief Baron Kelly, and the Judges of the Exchequer Court, during several days, by Mr. Bowen (now Lord Bowen) for Lord Rivers, and Sir Edward Clarke for the villagers. On August 8th,

1878, Chief Baron Kelly delivered judgment, on behalf of the Court, in favour of Lord Rivers, and refused to admit the claim of the villagers.

"If," he said, "such a right could be claimed by custom there is evidence of user which, coupled with the evidence of reputation, might raise a question whether the custom did not exist. But the right claimed is 'a profit à prendre' in the soil of another, and the authorities are uniform, from Gateward's case in Coke's Reports, that such a custom is bad in law. . . Many sound reasons are given in the authorities for this conclusion.

"It might be added that where inhabitancy is capable of an increase almost indefinitely, and if the right existed in a body which might be increased to any number, it would necessarily lead to the destruction of the subject-matter of the Common. There cannot, therefore, be such a custom; and for the same reason and others there cannot be a prescription, and there could not be a valid grant to so fluctuating a body, or a body so incapable of succession, in any reasonable sense of the term, so as to confer a right upon each succeeding inhabitant.

"There was a considerable argument before us upon the effect of a grant by the Crown to the inhabitants of a parish or village. The question seems to have arisen in early times, and there are several decisions in the year books on the subject; and the effect of them appears to be that where there is a grant by the Crown to the inhabitants of a particular parish, if the grant is made for a specified purpose, it has the effect of incorporating them so as to carry that purpose into effect. . .

"In this case we are called upon to say that because there has been user in the inhabitants, there has been a grant in such a form as to make them into a body corporate, having perpetual successors. It appears to us that we ought not to make this presumption, not because it is impossible, but because it is inconsistent with the past and existing state of things. We are to presume that a corporation has been formed many hundred years ago, when there is no trace at any time of its having ever existed. If the inhabitants had held meetings in reference to this right, or appointed any person to look to the right, or done any act collectively of that description, the case would be different. We should then have the inhabitants acting in a corporate capacity in reference to their right, and from their doing so, and from their existence *de facto* as a corporation, we might according to the ordinary rule find a legal origin by a grant from the Crown; but to say that a corporation was created, which never existed, would be carrying the fiction of a grant further than has been ever done or than is consistent with reason." *

The decision may well be compared with that of Lord Hobhouse in the Loughton Lopping case. It may safely be said that if the one decision was right the other was wrong. In the one case we find a great Judge holding it to be his duty, if possible, to find a legal origin for a custom, which had undoubtedly existed from time immemorial. In the other we have the Court of Exchequer pushing legal technicalities to their extreme, in order to refuse recognition to a custom of at least equal age and equal certainty—a custom which was part of the very existence of the people in olden time.

It need not be said that those who supported the villagers were very dissatisfied with this judgment. They believed it might be upset by a higher tribunal on appeal; but they found themselves unable to incur the

---

* Rivers v. Adams. 3 Exch. Div. 361.

heavy cost of taking it there. The expenses of the investigation into the history of the Manor, and of the proceedings before the arbitrator and the Court, had been
already very serious. It was only by the forbearance of
the professional men engaged in the case that the cost
was able to be met, and it was found impossible to raise
funds for further litigation. Lord Rivers therefore
maintained his victory. He had whatever satisfaction
was to be derived from wresting from the labouring
people of one of his many parishes an user and custom
which had undoubtedly existed from time immemorial,
and the deprivation of which rankled in their minds,
and created grave discontent. This was part of his
scheme for concentrating in his own hands all the
property in the parish, and for turning the Common into
a game preserve.

How many other similar cases may there not have
been in rural districts where no one has been fortunate
enough to find assistance from outside to fight the
great owner of the district, and where ancient and
established customs have been arbitrarily set aside,
and the labouring people still further depressed by
their being deprived of the last vestige of a sense of
property in the land on which they were born and
bred! It cannot be doubted that such acts are to
some extent responsible for the exodus of population
from the country to the towns, which landowners (as
well as others) are at last beginning to deplore.

The case, thus described, was decided before the
judgment of Lord Hobhouse in the Loughton Lopping

case, which has already been dealt with, and it formed a main topic of the counsel employed by the Corporation of London to resist the claims of the inhabitants of Loughton.

Lord Hobhouse discussed the Tollard Farnham case in his judgment, and succeeded in drawing a distinction between the facts of that case and those before him.

" The Judges of the Exchequer," he said, " considered that the evidence of user was such as to raise a question whether a corresponding custom did not exist ; but they held there could not be such a custom.   On the question of prescription they gave their general conclusion upon an examination of the evidence which they do not give in detail.   That conclusion is that the evidence entirely fails to prove the user by the inhabitants generally, or as inhabitants, such as to justify the presumption of a grant by the Crown.   .   .   .   On the question of incorporation they felt great difficulty.   They held that it was necessary to enable the inhabitants to take an interest, and that they could not presume it in the absence of all evidence of corporate acts, and when there was another body legally existing—viz. the tenants of the Manor, who are exercising unrestricted rights and publicly asserting their entire control over the underwood on the Common."

It is difficult to grasp the distinction between the facts of the two cases.   Chief Baron Kelly and Lord Hobhouse arrived at different conclusions from the facts before them.   It appears almost certain that Lord Hobhouse, upon the principles he laid down, would have felt himself bound to find a legal origin for an user on the part of the inhabitants of Tollard Farnham, which was clear and definite, and went back to ancient times.   It is almost as certain that the Barons of the Exchequer would have decided the Loughton case against the inhabitants, for the reasons which they gave in the Tollard Farnham case.

The two cases are good illustrations of the old saying that "Where there is the will there is a way." The Loughton case had the good fortune to go before a great lawyer who had the will to find a legal origin for the custom. That of Tollard Farnham had the misfortune to go before a Bench of Judges who appear to have had no desire to find a legal origin for the user which had undoubtedly existed.

It cannot be denied that differences of this kind with reference to popular rights are to be found on the Bench, equally as on the political platform, and in the uncertainties of legal decisions of olden times there is ample excuse for Judges taking a course, in one direction or the other, as may be most conformable to their instincts.

ROWLEY GREEN.

The other case in which a reverse was experienced was that of a Common known as Rowley Green, in the Parish of Shenley, in Hertfordshire. The question involved was whether the Lord of the Manor had the right to inclose portions of the waste. with the consent of the homage of the copyholders, and making his own selection of the tenants to form such homage-jury for the occasion.

The Common is one of the few remaining attractive open spaces to the North of London. The Manor consists of 300 acres of land held by free tenants, 200 acres by enfranchised copyholders with rights of common, and 52 acres of waste land or Common. On April 5th, 1887, at a customary Court of the Manor, a piece of land—about half an acre—was granted by the lord, with the consent of the homage of copyholders, to Eleanor Ramsey. The land was part of the waste in a green lane communicating with the Common, and the inclosure almost blocked the public way to it. This proceeding aroused a strong feeling in the parish. It was considered an unwarrantable encroachment on the rights of the Commoners, and a hideous disfigurement of the Green. It was also regarded as a dangerous precedent for the whole Common. It was not, however, till May, 1891, that any action was taken, and that some of the inhabitants removed a part of the obstructive fence. Thereupon a suit for trespass commenced. The defendants justified their proceedings as Commoners. On the other hand, the Lord of the Manor defended his course on the ground of a custom of his Manor to inclose with the consent of the homage.

It appeared that the Steward summoned certain of the copyholders to be members of the homage for the occasion, and the proposed grant was submitted to these nominees of the lord, who gave their assent to it. The defendant in the case was an enfranchised copyholder, who had no longer any right to be summoned, but who retained his right of common under the Copyhold Act. He claimed that, whatever might be the validity of the alleged custom to inclose

P

with the consent of the homage, as against copyholders, it could not be valid as against a person who
had ceased to be a copyholder, but who still retained
his rights of common.

The case was tried before Mr. Justice Day and a
special Jury, in Middlesex, on October 27th, 1892.
The Judge held that the defendant was bound by the
custom of the Manor, after the enfranchisement equally
as before, when he was a copyholder; and as the Rolls
of the Manor showed that on several previous occasions
from 1700—the earliest date from which they existed—
small portions of the waste had been inclosed with
the consent of the homage, he directed a verdict for
the lord. The case was subsequently argued in the
Court of Appeal, which upheld the ruling of Mr.
Justice Day. The defendant was advised that there
was every prospect of success, if an appeal were made
to the House of Lords, on the two points: first, that
such a custom cannot be valid against others than
copyhold tenants of the Manor; and, secondly, that
the custom alleged—that the Lord of the Manor, with
the consent of his own nominees on the homage, might
inclose—was unreasonable, and one that could not be
sustained at law.

The question would have been one of the utmost
importance, for there are many Manors where customs
of this kind are alleged to exist, and it would be a most
serious matter if their lords could maintain their right
to inclose the waste, with the consent of a homage nominated by themselves, and without leaving a sufficiency

of Common for the other Commoners. Fortunately, however, within a few weeks after the inclosure which was the cause of this action, the Copyhold Act of 1887 was passed into law, a clause of which—as will be fully explained later—has practically made it impossible for Lords of Manors to avail themselves in the future of such customs, with any chance of success.

No similar inclosure is ever likely to take place hereafter, and Rowley Green, it may be confidently expected, will be safe from any further aggressions of this kind. Under these circumstances it did not seem to be worth while to incur the heavy costs of an appeal to the House of Lords, in respect of a matter which, important as it was before the Copyhold Act of 1887, was no longer a serious question, and which affected only the inclosure of a plot of land not exceeding half an acre in extent.

The two cases, however, of Tollard Farnham and Rowley Green, decided as they were by Common Law Judges, confirmed the view which the Commons Society formed at the commencement of their proceedings, that such cases are far better dealt with by the Equity Judges, who do not seem to be so closely bound by technicalities, and who have a wider range of knowledge of the older law relating to Commons and Customs.

CHAPTER XIII.

THE NEW FOREST AND THE FOREST OF DEAN.

THE NEW FOREST.

THE origin of Royal Forests in England (with two exceptions) is lost in antiquity. They certainly existed before the Norman Conquest, A.D. 1066. Whether they were created or reserved as such by the early Saxon kings, or even at some more distant time, we know not. The only two of whose origin we know anything are the New Forest, created by William the Conqueror, and that of Hampton Court, due to Henry VIII. There are said at one time, in England alone, to have been sixty-eight Forests in the possession of the Crown, and thirteen Chases, or Forests in private hands. All the sixty-eight Forests have long ago been disafforested, in the sense that the Sovereign has no longer the privilege of maintaining deer and other game in them for sport, protected by special laws and tribunals. A few only exist in the popular sense of the term, that the land is still uncultivated and covered wholly or partially by woods—such as the New Forest, the Forest of Dean, Epping Forest, Windsor Forest, Wolmer Forest, the Forest of Bere and Dartmoor. Some of these, such as Windsor Forest and Wolmer Forest, have been converted into the exclusive property of the Crown, free from any common rights.

We have it on the authority of some of the earliest historians, such as Walter Mapes, the Chaplain to Henry II., and Henry of Huntingdon, his contemporary, that William the Conqueror, in creating the New Forest, devastated a wide district of cultivated land, demolished thirty-six churches, exterminated the inhabitants, and converted the land to the use of wild animals ; and the late Mr. Freeman, the able historian of the Norman Conquest, gave to this legend the weight of his great authority, though admitting that there may have been some exaggeration. With all respect, however, to this eminent writer, it is difficult for anyone who knows the Forest to believe the story, to the extent that he has done.

That the Forest was established as such by this King admits of no doubt. He lived mainly at Winchester, when in England, and the district between the River Avon and Southampton Water was conveniently near; but the physical condition of this district and the miserable soil of the greater part of the Forest seem to negative the suggestion that it could ever have been thickly peopled, or have contained thirty-six churches, beyond what still exist there.

The Saxon Chronicle, written during the lifetime of William, by no means in a friendly tone to him, which gives in great detail the other important incidents of his reign, and which condemns in strong language the passion of the great monarch for the chase, makes no mention of the formation of the New Forest. Such an event as the devastation of a wide district and the

demolition of thirty-six churches could hardly have
escaped the notice of the Chronicler.

It is probable that the district in which the Forest
was created was wild and almost wholly uncultivated,
interspersed, perhaps, with a few hamlets in the more
fertile valleys. There are many indications in Domesday to this effect. We know, also, that many of the
Manors, of which the Forest consisted, were in the
hands of religious bodies before the Conquest. It
may be surmised that William took the wastes of these
Manors forcibly from these bodies, and converted them
into one great Forest subject to forestal law; and that he
may also in some cases have appropriated the land of
private owners for the purpose. There is a passage in
Domesday Book, quoted by Freeman, to show that the
King did take property, from one person at least, for
the purpose of adding it to the Forest. He may also
have extended the limits of his Forest over contiguous
private lands, in the sense already described in the case
of Epping Forest—namely, that while leaving the owners
in possession of them, he subjected them to the Forest
laws, and forbade the erection of fences above a certain
height, or the cutting-down of trees without his consent, or the exercising the right of sporting over such
private domains. The extension of a Forest in a legal
sense in this manner, and the enforcement in it of the
cruel game laws, must necessarily have caused great
indignation in the district, and the early detractors of
the Conqueror may have magnified the transaction into
the story told and repeated by others. The misfortunes

which fell upon William's family in connection with the Forest—the violent deaths of two of his sons and of a grandson when hunting there—may have acted as a motive to the monkish historians to find an adequate explanation for such calamities, which must have appeared to them to be of divine origin, as a retribution for some great crime connected with the Forest.*

That William, having constituted the Forest in this region, administered and enforced the Game laws in it with rigour and cruelty, cannot be doubted. The Chronicler of 1087 said of him, " He set mickle deer-frith and laid laws therewith, that he who slew hart or hind, that man should blind him. He forbade the harts, and so eke the boars; so sooth he loved the high deer, as though he were their father. Eke he set by the hares that they should fare free. His rich men moaned at it and the poor men bewailed it; but he was so stiff that he recked not of their hatred; but they must all follow the King's will, if they would live or have their land or their goods or well his peace."

The Forest thus created was extended by his immediate successors, and at one time it was thirty miles in length, embracing all the land between the Avon and Southampton Water. But these extensions were given up by Henry III. and Edward I., in deference to popular agitation, and from that time till the disafforesting took place in modern times the Forest

* The subject of the alleged devastation of villages by the Conqueror in order to form the Forest is fully discussed in Lewis's " History of the New Forest," and in the " History of Hampshire " by Woodward and Lockhart.

was about twenty miles from north to south, and fifteen from east to west, and embraced an area of 92,000 acres. Of this, however, nearly one-third, or 27,000 acres, was land in possession of private owners. Since the deer have been killed down, the Crown no longer attempts to en-force rights on enclosed lands. The Forest now prac-tically consists of 65,000 acres, of which a little over 2,000 are the demesne lands of the Crown, inclosed and cultivated, and the residue belongs to the Crown, but is, except so much of it as has been temporarily inclosed for the plantation of trees, open and unin-closed, and subject to the rights of common of a very large body of owners and occupiers of cultivated lands in the neighbourhood of the Forest—rights of turn-ing out cattle and horses, of turning out pigs to feed on the acorns and mast in the Forest, and rights of turbary and of digging loam, etc. A great part of this wide range is open heath and moor. Other portions of it are covered with groves or plantations of oak and fir. The trees belong to the Crown, and from an early time supplied oak timber to the dock-yards for the construction of vessels of war, so long as the days of wooden vessels existed. Large numbers of deer (for the most part fallow deer, but including some red deer) were formerly maintained in the Forest, and when they found food scarce in the uninclosed land, they ranged over the land of private owners, in such numbers as to make cultivation very un-profitable. My father, in the early part of this century, inherited a property in the Forest, known as Burley, of about 800 acres, one of the ancient reservations, completely surrounded by forest land. I have often heard him say that the deer came upon his land in such numbers, and so devastated the crops, that it was impossible to let the property, or to cultivate it to any advantage, and not being able to reside there, he was ultimately obliged to sell it at a very low price. This was at the time when the forestal laws were still maintained, and when it was not lawful for any owner, within the limits of the Forest, to erect fences, so as to exclude the deer.

Great abuses existed in the Forest from an early time, not merely as regards the timber, but also in respect of the deer. Poaching became a trade, and demoralised the people in the neighbourhood. It was proved before a Committee in 1848 that not more than 110 bucks were annually killed for the Crown on the average of years, and that each buck cost upwards of £100. The greater number of these were given to owners of land in the neighbourhood, in return for preserving the deer.

Of the wooded parts of the Forest, a portion consists of groves of ancient timber of natural growth and of very great beauty. In these the oaks and the beeches stand in groups separated by irregular patches of dwarf gorse and heather, or by glades fringed with ferns, or by broad lawns or moor. Many of the trees have been pollarded in past times to browse the deer. Bratley Old, Bramshaw Wood, Denny Wood, and Mark Ash, are among the noblest relics of the ancient Forest. In

Mark Ash especially an adequate idea can be formed
of a real Forest unspoilt by man. The trees stand
wide apart, and are all of great size ; at the edge of the
wood they are fully developed, and the boughs feather
to the ground, but within it the growth tends upwards.
Mixed with them are thickets of hollies and hawthorns
with a setting of fern, forming a sylvan scene of
unique beauty. Other portions of the Forest, in the
true sense of the term, consist of woods planted by the
Crown under legislative powers, which gave the right
to inclose land for the purpose, and to shut out the
Commoners until the trees should be grown to a size at
which the cattle could do no harm to them.

During the Civil Wars of Charles I. and the
Commonwealth the Forest was much wasted of its
timber. Later, the fear arose that there would not be a
continuous supply of timber for the Navy. Power was,
therefore, given by Parliament in 1698 to inclose 6,000
acres for planting. This was strictly limited to the
growth of timber for national purposes. The plantations were to be made gradually—2,000 acres were to
be inclosed at once, but the remainder at a rate not
exceeding 200 acres in any one year ; and the plantations were again to be thrown open to the Commoners
so soon as the trees were past damage by the cattle and
deer. When any part of the 6,000 acres had been thrown
open, a similar quantity might again be planted on the
same terms. Under these provisions about 10,000 acres
were inclosed and planted prior to 1851, but the whole
extent had been thrown open again, with the exception of

4,000 acres. The restriction as to oaks, and the selection of areas for planting, resulted in the general features of the Forest being little altered by these operations. There was no dull uniformity in the plantations, and most of those which still exist exhibit all the wild beauties of Nature. When thrown open, the cattle soon trod down the banks.

In 1851, in consequence of the abuses which were then made public, it was determined to do away with the deer in the Forest, and to disafforest it, in the sense of getting rid of all the exceptional laws respecting them. There were said to be 3,000 deer at that time. The Sovereigns no longer came to the Forest for sport, and there was no object in maintaining the deer. As the removal of them, it was thought, would add to the pasture for the Commoners' cattle, and would make it no longer important to prevent the turning out of cattle during the fence month, when the does were dropping their fawns, or during the winter heyning, when the Forest was reserved for deer, it was thought that the Crown ought to take some compensation for its forestal rights, in the shape of increased power to inclose parts of the Forest land for the planting of timber.

The Act of 1851, therefore, on this understanding, provided that the Crown should be empowered to inclose and plant an additional extent of 10,000 acres over and above the 6,000 acres already allowed under the Act of 1698. Under the joint provisions of the two Acts the Commissioners of Woods and Forests, in whom the later Act vested the control and management

of the Forest, claimed that they had the right to inclose
successively the whole of the open lands of the Forest,
whether timbered or not, on condition that, by successively
throwing down the fences of previous inclosures when
the trees were of a height to save them from destruction
by cattle, they should avoid keeping more than 16,000
acres at any one time within fences.   It is clear that,
from the year 1851, the Commissioners of Woods
assumed the position with reference to the Forest
that Lords of Manors have taken up of late years as
to Commons.   They asserted that the Crown was
practically owner of the Forest, that the Commoners'
rights were of little value and might be disregarded,
and that as officers of the Crown they were bound to
make the very utmost income out of the Forest, without regard to the interests of the Commoners or of
the public.

In 1854, under the authority of the Act of 1851,
a Commission, of which Mr. Coleridge, now Lord
Coleridge, was a member, sat for the purpose of deciding
upon the claims of persons entitled as Commoners; and
in spite of the fact that many persons neglected to put
in claims, and that the presumptions of the Commission
appear to have been rather against the extension of
rights, it was held that the owners and occupiers of no
less than 65,000 acres of land, not waste of the Forest,
situate in sixty-three parishes, were entitled to turn out
their cattle and horses, and to exercise other rights in the
Forest, and that the occupiers of 1,200 houses were
entitled to take turf in it for fuel.

There can be no doubt that these rights of common over the Forest had been, from time immemorial, of the greatest value to the small owners of land, copyholders, and tenants in the neighbourhood, and were the main cause that many small owners still existed, and had resisted the tendency elsewhere to aggregate land in few hands, and, still more, that small holdings of land prevailed, and had not been consolidated into large farms. They were also of equal value to the cottager with his half-acre of land attached, in respect of which he could turn out a cow or a pony, and could drive his pigs into the Forest to feed on the acorns. The neighbourhood of the Forest is the best place in England—one of the very few still remaining—for studying the condition of small owners, tenants, and cottagers under such circumstances, and for appreciating the effect, upon such classes in the agricultural community, of the great inclosures of past times.

The existence of these rights undoubtedly accounts for the large measure of prosperity among these people, and for the absence of pauperism. The Forest itself, on account of its varying conditions, its great variety of soil and water-supply, of shelter and exposure, is peculiarly suitable for the turning-out of hardy cattle and ponies. They can at all times, and in every kind of season, find fitting places for feed and shelter; any deficiency in one part is supplied by sufficiency or excess in another; and the animals travel long distances to find the most suitable conditions, whether for water and shade in dry seasons, or for dry land

when in wet seasons the lower ground is cold and
swampy.

The existence of these rights favours greatly the
smaller owners and tenants, and the cottagers. The
larger the farm. the less use is made by its tenant of the
Forest. The land of the large farm is of better quality,
and the proportion of meadow is sufficient ; the improved
breeds of cattle are too delicate to turn out in the Forest.
The wastes of the Forest are mainly for the benefit
of the smaller occupiers and cottagers. They make it
their business to turn out the proper kind of stock.
The right also of cutting turves for fuel is of the
utmost value to them. The rough turf formed of
roots of heather makes an excellent fuel in combination with wood bought from the Forest. This turf-
cutting does no injury to the surface, the rule being
to cut one and leave two turves. The old heath
being removed, a growth of new heath is insured,
and short grass often comes up in the pared spaces.
The turf renews itself in seven years; meanwhile the pasture is improved. The right of turning out pigs is also
of great importance. When the prospect of beech-mast
and acorns is good, the cottager buys his pigs as early and
cheaply as he can, and may rely upon a clear profit of ten
shillings on a pig. Cottagers have been known to make
twenty pounds in a year by their pigs. The turning-
out of a mare or a cow is likewise much valued by them.
The possession of an animal for this purpose is often
to a young labourer the first step on the ladder—the
inducement to him to save, with a view to becoming the

tenant of a larger holding; and many are the men who have risen in this way from the position of labourer to that of farmer. Thus it is that there has grown up round the Forest a class of small occupiers, thrifty and fairly prosperous even in these days of agricultural depression, independent and with the sense of property, and to the last degree tenacious of their rights.

As time went by, after the Act of 1851 it became more and more clear to the Commoners, and to those interested in the Forest from a public point of view, that the scheme of that Act, if carried out in the manner in which it was being put in force, would result in the destruction both of the beauties of the Forest, and of the value of the Commoners' rights over it. When an inclosure for planting was determined on, the whole of the ancient timber within the area was cleared away; the land was then drained by wide open drains, and was closely planted with Scotch firs and young oaks. These new plantations, owing to the preponderance of firs, were formal and gloomy in the extreme. All the former pasturage in the area was destroyed, and the growth of new feed in these closely-planted inclosures was impossible. It became apparent, from the disinclosed specimens of the much less mathematical and scientific method of planting under the Act of 1698 in the time of the early Georges, that the "nurseries" authorised by the Act of 1851 would replace the wild and picturesque woodlands with plantations of a most monotonous and artificial appearance, fatal to the natural beauty of the scenery, which they would destroy past all chance of restoration, whilst in themselves of little importance to the ship-builder and of no value to the Commoners.

The only defence of the Commissioners of Woods and Forests, who were responsible for the policy thus described, was that they were bound by their duty, as public servants, to look at the questions affecting the Forest from the point of view of the public revenue only, and to enforce their strict legal rights to the utmost. They did not pretend that their object was any longer to supply timber for the navy; it was notorious that, owing to the almost universal use of iron in shipbuilding, the demand for oak had almost disappeared. The timber of the New Forest had for many years been of no practical value to the navy.

The change of public opinion which occurred after 1865, on the subject of Commons, resulted in directing attention to the condition of the New Forest; and a movement grew up having the double motive of preserving to the Commoners the full enjoyment of their rights, and of securing to the public that the Forest, as far as possible, should be maintained in its state of Nature, as a kind of national park or recreation ground, and should not be regarded only from the utilitarian point of view of the greatest possible revenue it could produce, without respect to these other considerations.

In 1871 this movement had its result in a motion in the House of Commons, proposed by Mr. Fawcett, to the effect that, pending further legislation on the subject, no fresh inclosure or felling of timber should take place in the New Forest. The Government, under the pressure of opinion in the House, somewhat reluctantly assented to it. In 1875, when a change of Government had taken place, it was intimated to the residents in the Forest that this resolution of the House of Commons could not be considered as binding for an indefinite time, and that some steps must be taken to bring the subject to an issue. Thereupon Lord Henry Scott (now Lord Montagu, and then member for the division of Hampshire in which the Forest was situate) moved for a Select Committee "to inquire into and report upon the condition of the New Forest, into the operation of the Deer Removal Act of 1851, and particularly into the exercise and effect of the powers of inclosure given by that Act."

The case of the Commoners and of the public was presented before this Committee by Mr. Robert Hunter, on behalf of the New Forest Association, a body representative of the Commoners, and of the Commons Society; and among others Mr. Fawcett gave evidence as to the disastrous effect of the Act of 1851, if further enforced, in destroying the beauties of the Forest. Many also of the smaller Commoners appeared, and much impressed the Committee with the strength of their case, and with their conviction that the Act would result in their ultimate ruin and extirpation. Meanwhile, the attention of the public was aroused to the subject of the Forest by an exhibition of pictures and sketches of scenery in the district, projected by Mr. Briscoe Eyre and Mr. George Morrison, and the expression of opinion these evoked was

Q

embodied in several very influential petitions presented by Mr. Fawcett. The Committee was presided over by the late Mr. W. H. Smith, and among the members were Mr. Cowper Temple and Sir William Harcourt.

The result was eminently satisfactory. The report of the Committee consisted of a series of resolutions favourable to the Commoners, and to the maintenance of the Forest in its then state. The more important were as follows :—

1. That the New Forest should remain open and uninclosed except to the extent to which it was expedient
   to maintain the existing right of the Crown to plant
   trees.
2. That the ornamental woods and trees should be carefully preserved, and the character of the scenery
   maintained.
3. That the power of inclosure conferred by the statutes of
   1698 and 1851, should be exercised on that area
   which had till then been taken in at various times,
   and been either kept or thrown open. . . That
   the rolling power of inclosure over the open portion
   of the Forest, not then planted or inclosed under the
   two Acts, should cease.

In 1877, an Act was passed embodying these proposals. It also reorganised the ancient Court of Verderers on a popular basis of representation of the Commoners, so as to enable it to represent and protect their interests. This measure, which was strongly supported by the Commons Society, passed without

opposition, and became law under the title of the
"New Forest Act, 1877." The result was a victory
both for the Commoners and the public. Under the
Act of 1851, about 8,000 acres had been inclosed in
addition to the 10,000 under the Act of 1698, and
of these 18,000 acres 8,000 had been thrown open.
and 10,000 remained inclosed. The Act of 1877
provides that the power of inclosure enjoyed by the
Crown should be confined to these 18,000 acres, which
comprise the best land in the Forest, and which may
be thrown out and re-inclosed at will, provided that
not more than 16,000 acres are actually inclosed at
one time. The Commoners are thus secured in the
remainder of the 63,000 acres, or 45,000, of which about
6,000 are partially covered with old timber. It is laid
down by the Act as a matter of principle that the
natural beauties of the Forest are to be preserved, and
the right of the public to the enjoyment of it is fully
recognised and perpetuated.

At the first election of the Verderers, Mr. Briscoe
Eyre, who had done so much to preserve the Forest,
and to protect the interests of the Commoners, was
returned at the head of the poll. Owing to his exertions a serious blot in the Act was remedied in 1879.
A large number of owners and occupiers of land in
the neighbourhood of the Forest, but not on the
authorised Register of Commoners, through various
causes, had been allowed by the Verderers to turn
out cattle in the Forest; but on account of the fact
that registered Commoners were taxed under the Act of

Q 2

1877, for the maintenance of the Forest, it was held that those, who were not registered, would thenceforward be wholly excluded from the Forest. Such a course would have brought hundreds of families to the workhouse. Fortunately, the Government was induced to pass, in 1879, a short Act authorising the Verderers to allow persons not registered to turn out cattle in the Forest on payment of a small fee.

In 1891, another, and it is to be hoped a last, attack was made on the New Forest. At the fag end of the session, a clause was slipped into a Government measure called " the Ranges Act," empowering the War Department to appropriate any common land for rifle ranges, in spite of any prohibition or restriction contained in any local or personal Act, and notwithstanding any common or other rights or easements over such lands. This clause, though not mentioning the New Forest, virtually applied to it, and doubtless was intended to do so without alarming the Commoners.

Had any public explanation been given as to the effect that this clause would have in linking together various other Acts, such as the Volunteer Act of 1863, the Artillery and Ranges Act, 1885, and the Drill Grounds Act, 1886, there can be no doubt that the measure would have been most strongly opposed, for it placed every Common in the country at the mercy of the War Department, and would have enabled them to extinguish common rights over them, and afterwards to sell the land, when no longer wanted for ranges, as private property.

Later, in 1891, it came to the ears of the Verderers of the New Forest that the War Department proposed to establish a rifle range in the Forest under the recent Act, and to drive the Commoners off 500 acres, and to cut them off completely from a large part of the Forest. The Forest district was in arms directly the fact became public, and from all parts of the country the aid of the Commons Society was invoked to protect "the National Playground."

The Government was eventually compelled to promise a local inquiry in the Forest, as to the expediency of the proposed rifle range.

The Commissioner appointed for this purpose, Mr. Pelham, ultimately reported that the range would cause substantial interference with the Commoners' rights, and that it would be extremely difficult to ascertain who should be compensated; that the range as proposed would deprive the public of the enjoyment of a very beautiful part of the Forest; and that if another site could be found elsewhere, the proposed site should certainly not be taken.

In the meantime, the Secretary of State for War, in pursuance of a promise which he had given, introduced a Military Lands Consolidation Bill. This measure was referred to a Select Committee on which the writer of this book took an active part. After much discussion, a clause was inserted making it obligatory on the War Department to proceed by way of Provisional Order before acquiring any common land for the purpose of rifle ranges. By this measure, therefore, all Commons throughout the country were relieved from the danger of being appropriated for rifle ranges, without inquiry, or even the opportunity of objections being made to the proposals.

Later, the scheme for making a rifle range in the New Forest was abandoned. It has been alluded to for the purpose of showing that it is not Lords of Manors and Railway Companies, only, who are disposed to lay hands upon the Commons, and to convert them to their uses, but that public departments equally require watching, for they also have been under the impression that Commons may easily be expropriated for any purpose they have in view.

It would seem also that the Commissioners of Woods had not frankly acquiesced in the policy, with respect to the New Forest, directed by Parliament in 1877. They appeared to be constantly on the watch to obtain advantage at the expense of the Commoners. At one time their local officer encouraged a movement for establishing a training school in forestry for the purpose of experimenting with the open waste lands; at another he sanctioned and encouraged an encroachment on the open Forest by a water company. In the last session of Parliament, a Bill authorising various petty encroachments was introduced, the subsequent abandonment of which was due to the opposition evoked. Even at this moment litigation is pending between the Crown and the Verderers, with the view of establishing an alleged right of the Crown to cut up timber by steam saw mills, and to open glades in the Forest, and thus seriously to injure the Commoners' best pastures. In the meantime the Forest is more and more appreciated and frequented by the public, and there cannot be a doubt that any attempt to interfere with its general aspect, or to curtail the public enjoyment of it, will meet with the same fate as the scheme for a rifle range.

THE FOREST OF DEAN.

The Forest of Dean, of about 19,000 acres in extent, is another of the few remaining Royal Forests, which have come under the consideration of Parliament in recent years, and where the policy of maintenance has prevailed over that of inclosure.

This Forest lies in the Hundred of St. Briavel, between the estuary of the Severn, and the river Wye, about twelve miles from Gloucester. Its condition as regards the Crown, the Commoners, and the public, is very similar to that of the New Forest. The Crown is the owner of the soil and of all the timber growing upon it. It has also large powers of temporarily inclosing parts of the Forest for encouragement of the planting and growth of timber. Subject to such powers, the Commoners, who are the owners and occupiers of land in the Hundred, extending over many parishes beyond the Forest, have the right of turning out their cattle to graze in it, and their pigs to feed on the acorns. Of the Forest, about 4,000 acres consist of heath and open land; the residue is planted with oak trees of ages, varying up to ninety years, of which a

large proportion will be in their prime about thirty
years hence, and the remainder at later dates.

Unlike the New Forest, that of Dean is a very rich
mineral district, where coal and iron mines are worked.
A large population is engaged in these mines, residing
on inclosures of land, which have in past times been
taken from the Forest, dispersed about in very
irregular order. There is a very ancient and well-
recognised custom that the inhabitants of the Hundred
have the right to search for and to work the minerals
within the Forest, subject to certain customary
royalties to the Crown—a right not dissimilar to what
exists in many parts of Europe, notably Spain, but
not elsewhere known in England.

The iron mines were worked in very early times,
as far back as the Romans, and this was doubtless
facilitated by the Forest providing fuel for smelting
the ore. There existed till within recent years vast
heaps of partially smelted ore, called cinders, which
had been left by early workers, who had not sufficient
knowledge to extract the ore, and which it was worth
while to smelt again. These testified to the extent
of the industry in former times, and to the fact
that there must have been a large population residing
within the precincts of the Forest.* The town of

---

* Andrew Yarranton, in his work on the "Improvement of
England by Sea and Land," printed in 1677, says: "In the Forest
of Dean and thereabouts the iron is made at this day of cinders,
being the rough and offal thrown by in the Romans' time; they
then having only foot blasts to melt the ironstone; but now, by the

Cinderford, in the Forest, derives its name from these heaps.

As in the case of most of the Royal Forests, there is no record of the origin of that of Dean. It is first mentioned in Domesday Book as having been exempted from taxes by Edward the Confessor. William the Conqueror is known to have visited it occasionally for the purpose of hunting the deer. He was there in 1069, when he received tidings that the Danes had invaded Yorkshire, and had taken its capital. He is reported to have sworn a terrible oath by "the splendour of the Almighty," that "not one Northumbrian should escape his revenge," and he well kept his oath. *

The Forest, like others, was greatly enlarged by the Norman kings succeeding the Conqueror, in the sense that they applied the forest laws to a great area of land in private ownership, extending up to Gloucester and to the Severn and Wye. These boundaries were again reduced by Henry III. and Edward I., in consequence of the grave complaints of the people as to the

force of a great wheel that drives a pair of bellows twenty feet long, all that iron is extracted out of the cinders, which could not be forced from it by the Roman foot blast. And in the Forest of Dean and thereabouts and as high as Worcester, there are great and infinite quantities of these cinders, some in vast mounts above ground, some under ground, which will supply the iron works for hundreds of years, and these cinders are those which make the prime and best iron and will make less charcoal than doth the ironstone." —Nicholls, Forest of Dean, p. 223.

* *Ib.* p. 7.

extension of the Royal Forests. Thus diminished, it was confined to the Hundred of St. Briavel, a district about twice the size of the present waste.

King Stephen granted the Forest to the daughter of Fitz-Walter on her marriage with Herbert Fitz-Herbert; from her it passed through the families of the Bohuns and Newmarches, till it reverted to King John. This monarch was often in the district for sport. From his time to the present, the ownership of the soil appears to have been vested in the Crown; and there was a long succession of Wardens of the Forest, and Constables of St. Briavel's Castle, appointed for life by the Crown, till the duties of the Warden were vested, in 1834, in the Commissioners of Woods and Forests. The earliest perambulation of the Forest was in 1282; in 1333, Parliament confirmed the perambulation, and reduced it to the limits which existed up to 1834, when it was disafforested.

There are many interesting incidents connected with the Forest during this long period. It appears to have supplied timber for the construction of ships of war from an early time, and the oak grown there had the reputation of being exceptionally tough and well suited for war ships. So well was this reputation known that the destruction of the Forest was specially enjoined by the Spanish Government on the leaders of the Spanish Armada. Evelyn in his " Sylva " says on this point:—
" I have heard that in the great expedition of 1588 it was expressly enjoined the Spanish Armada that if, when landed, they should not be able to subdue our

nation and make good their conquest, they should yet be sure not to leave a tree standing in the Forest of Dean." Mr. Nicholls, the historian of the Forest, says on this, that Evelyn may have heard this story from Mr. Secretary Pepys, who might have been informed by his friend, Sir John Winter, the grandson of Sir William Winter, vice-Admiral of Elizabeth's fleet, and kinsman to Thomas Winter of Huddington, who was constantly aiding the Spanish Romanists in their intrigues.

In 1638, we first come across indications that there was fear of failure of the supply of timber from this Forest. A report was received by the Crown that the trees numbered 105,000, containing 62,000 tons of timber, of which only 14,000 loads were fit for shipbuilding, as the trees were generally decayed and past their full growth. By the authority of Sir Bayham Throgmorton 16,000 acres were ordered to be taken in. The Commoners after some discussion assented, in consideration of 4,000 acres being set apart for their own use, in different parts of the Forest. Before, however, anything could be done in this direction, Charles I., in his necessities, sold all the mineral rights in the Forest, and all the timber trees and underwood in it, to Sir John Winter, for £10,000 down, the yearly sum of £16,000 for six years, and a fee farm rent of £1,950 for ever.

This act was equivalent to a sale of the Forest, though the ownership of the soil was still retained in the Crown. The commoners and inhabitants of the Forest were greatly dissatisfied; they took advantage

of the disorders of the Civil War to throw down the
fences, which the grantee had already begun to make.
Sir John Winter was a prominent and devoted Royalist
during this period. He endeavoured to rouse the
population of the district in favour of the king ; but his
inclosures under the Royal grant had made him un-
popular, and the people sided in the main with the
Parliament. The supply of iron from the Forest for the
founding of cannon was an important consideration.
Finally Winter, after many conflicts, was forced to fly,
and his stronghold, Lydney House, was captured. His
property was assigned to his victor, General Massy,
together with his iron mills and woods, but with the
reservation of timber trees which were not to be felled.

During the Commonwealth, frequent orders were
made by Parliament with the object of preventing
the destruction of timber in the Forest by unauthorised
persons, and directing that any trees which had been
cut down should be reserved for the use of the
Navy.

In 1650, orders were given for the suppression
and destruction of the iron works,—partly with the
view of saving the timber of the Forest, which was
heavily drawn upon for fuel for the smelting. In
1656, an Act was passed for mitigating the rigour
of the forest laws, and for preserving the timber
in the Forest. An effort was consequently made to
carry out the arrangement of a few years previous,
under which 16,000 acres were to be inclosed and
planted. This was again resisted by the population of

the district. They broke in and destroyed the fences. On May 11th, 1659, Colonel White reported to the House of Commons that upon the 3rd of that month—

"divers rude people in a tumultuous way in the Forest of Dean did break down the fences, and cut and carry away the gates of certain coppices, inclosed for the preservation of timber, turned in their cattle, and set divers places of the Forest on fire to the great destruction of growing wood."

It appears that the popular feeling of the district had been aroused by the fact, that in pursuance of the policy of re-afforesting the 16,000 acres, 400 cottages of poor people living on the waste had been thrown down. This action of the Commonwealth created a reaction in the district in favour of the Royalist party, and it was reported that large numbers of people were ready to support the cause of the Stuarts.

On the restoration of Charles II., all the proceedings of the Commonwealth were nullified, and the grant in favour of Sir John Winter was revived. He proceeded to put his rights under it in force, by making inclosures. He was again strongly opposed by the inhabitants of the district. They petitioned the king for inquiry.

In December, 1661, a Commission was issued to inquire into the state of the Forest, and to advise in accordance with the prayers of the petitioners :—

"whether the Forest may be restored to his Majesty's demesne, and re-afforested and improved by inclosure for a future supply of wood for a constant support of the iron works there, producing

the best iron of Europe for many years, and other uses in time
to come which might be of great use for defence of the nation,
the old trees then standing being above 300 years growth, and
yet as good timbers as any in the world, and the ground so apt
to produce and so strong to preserve timber, especially oaks,
that within 100 years there may be sufficient provision there
found to maintain the Navy royal for ever."

The result of this inquiry was that the grant to
Winter was surrendered, and a new lease was given
to him for a term of years, after negotiations with
Pepys, which are duly mentioned in his Diary.

Acting under this new lease, Winter again began
to inclose the Forest, and again the popular feeling
of the district was aroused against him. Complaints
were made to the House of Commons, and a Committee
was appointed to consider the matter. It appears
that the freeholders, commoners, and inhabitants of the
district met together and made proposals to the Committee for the settlement of the Forest, in which they
offered very large concessions in the direction of inclosure
for the improvement of the growth of timber. The
Forest then consisted of 24,000 acres. They proposed
that 11,000 acres should be inclosed by the Crown, and
be discharged of rights of pasture, estover and pannage ;
and that the Crown, on throwing open any of these
inclosures, might take in as much, so that not more
than 11,000 acres should be inclosed at any one time ;
that the timber on the remaining 13,000 acres should
belong absolutely to His Majesty, discharged of estovers
for ever, and of pannage for twenty-one years ; that
the whole waste of the Forest should be re-afforested,

and be subjected to forestal law; but that this should not in future apply to the lands in private ownership, not waste of the Forest; that no more than 800 deer should be maintained by the Crown; and that all grants of the waste lands should be resumed and made void.

These proposals were agreed to by the Committee of the House of Commons, and were recommended to the Government. A Bill was introduced to carry them into effect, but Parliament was prorogued before it became law, and it was not till 1668, that an Act was passed substantially embodying these terms.

In the meantime Sir John Winter, under the powers of his lease, played havoc with the timber in the Forest. The Committee, in 1663, had already reported to the House "that Winter had 500 cutters of wood employed on the Forest, and that all the timber would be destroyed if care should not be speedily taken to prevent it." In vain the House of Commons made recommendations for the preservation of the timber. Winter still kept on his cutting; and in 1667, it was reported to the Government that of 30,233 trees sold to Winter, only about 200 remained standing, and that from 7,000 to 8,000 loads of timber suitable for the Navy were found wanting.

The Act of 1668 embodied the proposals of the people of the Forest, as approved by the Committee, with little variation. It maintained all the rights of miners of the district. Strangely enough, after all the complaints of Winter's conduct, the Act saved his rights under his lease. Whether it was that he had already exhausted all his power of cutting timber, or that he had influential friends at Court, in consequence of his efforts for the monarchy during the rebellion, it is clear that he was treated with great consideration.

The Act of 1668 has ever since been the charter of the Forest, and to the present time determines the relative rights of the Crown and the commoners. Immediately after it was passed, 8,400 acres of the waste were inclosed and planted, and the residue of the 11,000 were dealt with in the same manner a few years later. From that time till a comparatively recent date, there were constant complaints of encroachments on the Forest, and of illegal cutting of trees, mainly for the purpose of supplying timber to the miners.

Meanwhile the mining industry was continually increasing. Till relatively recent times, the iron mines were by far the most important, and for these the supply of wood from the Forest, for smelting, was most necessary. There is mention of coal so far back as the year 1300, but it was for long a subordinate industry. In 1610, a grant was made by James I. to the Earl of Pembroke of " liberty to dig for and take within any part of the Forest, or the precincts thereof, such and so much sea-coal as should be necessary for carrying on the iron works." This is the earliest notice of coal being used in the iron works. Coal was included in the grant by Charles I. to Winter, who, we learn from Pepys, was interested in a project for charring it so as to render it fit for the iron furnace—but apparently without success.

Cromwell also had been engaged in association with Major Wildman, Captain Birch, and other of his officers in an enterprise of the same kind; and large works were set up in the Forest for this purpose, but without any success. From the beginning of the eighteenth century the working of the coal mines rapidly increased, and they eventually became far more important and valuable than the iron mines. The timber of the Forest was essential to the working of these mines; and the coal was ultimately substituted for wood in the manufacture of iron.

The Crown had from an early date recognised the rights of the Free Miners, as they were called, to search for and work both iron and coal mines. It is very doubtful whether this custom would have been acknowledged as a legal right, if it had been questioned in the Law Courts, owing to the technical rule laid down in "Gateward's case" as to customs and prescriptions of the inhabitants of a district. In a case which turned indirectly upon the rights of miners,* Mr. Justice Byles laid down, that but for the Act of 1838, in which the rights of the Free Miners were confirmed, they could not have been sustained, on the ground that a custom could not be maintained to take profits out of another man's land.

"It seems to me," he said, "first, that the Free Miners themselves could, in point of law, have had no such right as the defendants' claim assumes them to have had. The claim of the Free Miners is to subvert the soil, and carry away the substratum of stone without stint or limit of any kind. This

* Attorney-General v. Mathias. 4 K. & J., 579.

R

alleged right, if it ever existed, must have reposed on one of three foundations: custom, prescription, or lost grant. The right of the Free Miners is incapable of being established by custom, however ancient, uniform, and clear the exercise of custom may be. The alleged custom is to enter the soil of another, and carry away portions of it. The benefit to be enjoyed is not a mere casement; it is a *profit à prendre*. Now, it is an elementary rule of law that a *profit à prendre* in another's soil cannot be claimed by custom, for this, among other reasons, that a man's soil might thus be subject to the most grievous burdens in favour of successive multitudes of people, like the inhabitants of a parish or other district, who could not release the right. The leading case on the subject is *Gateward's case*, which has been repeatedly followed and never overruled. . . .

" The next question is : Can such a right as this be claimed by prescription ? I will assume, against the fact, that there is no evidence to negative prescription. The present is a claim not only to carry away the soil of another, but to carry it away without stint or limit; it is a claim which tends to the destruction of the inheritance, and which excludes the owner. A prescription to be good must be both reasonable and certain (Comyn's Digest, " Prescription "); and this alleged prescription seems to me to be neither. . . .

" The only remaining question on this part of the case is this : Can the claim be sustained by evidence of a lost grant ? Prescription presupposes a grant ; and if you cannot presume a grant of an unreasonable claim before legal memory, *à fortiori* can you not presume one since. The defendants have relied on statutes of limitation ; but, as to that, a claim which is vicious and bad in itself cannot be substantiated by a user, however long."

Fortunately for the Free Miners, their rights were not in issue in this case. They had already been determined and legalised by the Act of 1838, which distinctly laid down that all the male persons born and abiding in the Hundred of St. Briavel, and of the age of twenty-one years and upwards, who should have worked a year and a day in coal or iron mines within the Hundred, should be entitled to be registered as Free Miners; and that only Free Miners should have the exclusive right of having gales or works granted to them by the officer, called the gaveller, to open mines within the Hundred. Such gales or grants confer an interest in the nature of real estate, and are perpetual, subject to conditions for the payment of certain rents and royalties to the Crown. These royalties are fixed on the assumption that, after the coal or iron has been reached, the Crown is entitled to one-fifth of the net profit of working the mine. In case of dispute the royalty is settled by arbitration, and then remains fixed for twenty-one years. The Free Miner can sell his gale, and a large part of the mines in the district are not now held by Free Miners, but by persons who have purchased up the interests in their gales. Nearly the whole of the coal field in the Forest is now included in existing gales.

Under this system the mining industry has grown up. The output of the coal mines now averages about 900,000 tons a year, and that of the iron mines about 160,000 tons. The royalties to the Crown produce annually about £12,000 for coal and £5,000 for iron. The existing gales of coal and iron are 260, of which not more than 80 are worked.

It would seem that the growth of population

u 2

caused by this great increase of mines, has long ago necessitated the appropriation of parts of the Forest for their accommodation. Of the 24,000 acres, of which the Forest consisted in the time of Charles II., only 18,500 acres are now forest or waste, 700 acres belong to the Crown, and 4,800 acres are the property of private individuals, as a result of encroachments from time to time on the waste, eventually recognised by the Crown. On this private land has grown up the town of Cinderford, and several other villages, in a very irregular manner, often without adequate drainage.

In 1874, in consequence of complaints of the want of sufficient accommodation for the population, and of the sanitary defects of the district, a select Committee was appointed by the House of Commons to inquire into the condition of the Forest. The inquiry escaped the notice of those interested in Commons, and the Committee, then appointed, contained no member who represented the views of the Commons Society.

The Committee reported that the rights of Free Miners tended to obstruct the advantageous development of the Forest mineral field, and were detrimental to the interests of the Crown, and of the public; that the rights were almost valueless to those not already holding gales; that the general feeling in the neighbourhood was in favour of the commutation of the legal rights of the Commoners; and that the convenience of the mining population, and of the mining works, required that the Crown should have power to sell portions of the Forest free from Common rights. They stated that the existing plantation was in a thriving condition, varying in age from ten to seventy years, and that in about fifty years a large proportion of them would reach maturity. The Committee did not consider that it would be expedient to destroy or alienate the existing oak plantations, or any large part of them; but that, as far as possible, the sales of land should be confined to the outskirts of the Forest, and to the vicinity of existing houses.

In the following year, 1875, a Bill was introduced by the late Mr. W. H. Smith, then Secretary to the Treasury, for the purpose of carrying these recommendations into effect. It was in fact an Inclosure Bill. It gave power to the Crown to ascertain and buy off the Commoners' rights, and to convert the Forest into its absolute property. As regards the Free Miners, it proposed that in future no fresh gales should be granted, and that the Crown should be empowered to buy up and extinguish existing gales.

It very soon appeared that the Committee of 1874 had been entirely misled as to the feeling of the people of the district, on the subject of their rights of common over the Forest, and as to the maintenance of the rights of Free Miners. Indignation meetings were held in the district to protest against the Bill. Numerous petitions were presented against it by the Free Miners and the Commoners, and the Commons Society was appealed to, to assist in defeating the measure. The Society, while not averse to giving power to the Crown to provide for the necessities of the district by selling sites for houses, gardens, and allotments, free from common rights, were of opinion that the conversion of the whole Forest into the absolute ownership of the Crown was unnecessary and unadvisable, and they lent their aid to defeat the scheme. The Bill was dropped for that year; but in the following autumn, notices were issued of the intention of the Government to introduce the Bill again in the ensuing Session. Thereupon, on behalf of the Commons Society, I entered into a correspondence with Mr. W. H. Smith, in which I pointed out the objections on principle to the inclosure of the Forest. I contended that there were precisely the same reasons against adopting this course, as had been asserted by the Committee of the House of Commons in 1875, of which Mr. W. H. Smith himself had been Chairman, against the inclosure of the New Forest; that the object and intention of that Committee was to preserve the New Forest open and uninclosed, for the benefit of the Commoners and the public enjoyment; that the Forest of Dean was not unworthy of the same treatment; and that, although there was less of ancient timber left in it, it had some natural advantages superior even to the New Forest.

I further informed him that we had reason to know that very strong opposition would be made by the Commoners and Free Miners of the Forest to the proposed Bill; but that I was authorised to say that these people would not object to the inclosure by the Crown, free from common rights, of portions of the open land of the Forest near to the towns and villages, to the extent of 1,000 or even 2,000 acres, sufficient to meet all the necessities of the district for increased accommodation of the population, for residences, gardens, and allotments. I also pointed out that there could be no reason why a different policy should be pursued in respect of the two Forests ; that both of them in their present condition were valuable legacies to the nation; that, if reduced into absolute ownership of the Crown, they could not be recovered ; while, so long as they were subject to Commoners' rights, they could from time to time be adapted to any necessary want, such as that now existing in the Forest of Dean for sites for miners' houses and for allotments, without depriving them of their value for public enjoyment and recreation.

The effect of this correspondence was that the Government announced that they did not intend to proceed further with their measure for inclosing the Forest ; and that they were advised by their Law Officers that they had, under an existing Act, power to sell limited parts of the waste, from time to time, for the necessities of the population. It resulted, therefore, that practically the same policy was laid down with respect both to the New Forest and the Forest of Dean. They are both to be preserved henceforth in the interest of the public and of the commoners, while the Crown is secured in its long established right of making large but temporary inclosures for the planting and growth of timber.

CHAPTER XIV.

BURNHAM BEECHES.

OF the Commons within twenty-five miles of London, easily accessible by railway, and every year becoming more and more the resort of Londoners, the most renowned for its beauty is that known as Burnham Beeches. It lies within three or four miles of Slough, at no great distance from Stoke Poges Church. It owes this reputation not so much to the lie of the land, as to its splendid groves of ancient beech trees. The poet Gray lived for some time within half a mile of it, and is supposed to have composed· his celebrated Elegy on a Country Churchyard when walking in it. Writing to a friend he said : " The Common is covered with most venerable beeches that, like most ancient people, are dreaming out their old stories to the winds—

> ' And as they bow their hoary tops relate
> In murmuring sounds the dark decrees of fate ;
> While visions, as poetic eyes avow,
> Cling to each leaf and swarm on every bough.' "

The beeches are of very great size ; each tree stands out by itself. They were evidently pollarded at some long distant date. Tradition says that this was done in Cromwell's time, in order to make stocks for muskets. They form a rare and unequalled picture of sylvan grandeur and beauty, quite unique of its kind.

The Common consists of 374 acres, of which about half is planted with these splendid beeches, and forms part of the Manor of Burnham.

This Manor was at the time of Domesday in possession of the Bishop of Lincoln; later it was escheated to the Crown. Henry III. granted it to the Abbess of the neighbouring Convent of Burnham. On the dissolution of the Abbey, the Manor was granted away by Henry VIII., and for generations remained in the possession of the Eyre family. The last representative of this ancient family was Captain Popple, who, in 1812, sold the reversion, after his death, of his property, including large demesne lands and the Manor, for a considerable sum, to Lord Grenville, the well-known statesman, the owner of the domain of Dropmore, within the same Manor. Dropmore itself is said to have been inclosed by Lord Grenville from a Common. Its park and pleasure grounds, consisting of 600 acres, are celebrated for their collection of trees. This and other purchases within the Manor, made Lord Grenville the owner of nearly the whole of it.

The acquisitions were in pursuance of the policy of the Grenville family to consolidate their political influence in the county. Captain Popple, contrary to all actuarial expectation, lived on till 1830, and Lord Grenville then at last came into possession of the Manor, to enjoy it only for a few months, to appreciate that he had made a very bad bargain, and to be conscious that the Reform Act, then imminent, would sweep away the political influence which he had so carefully built up. His widow survived for many long years to a very advanced age.

There is a most interesting account given of the parish of East Burnham, in her collected papers, by Mrs. Grote,* the widow of George Grote, the historian, and herself a woman of powerful intellect and independent judgment. The Grotes lived in the Manor for twenty years. Mrs. Grote gives a most graphic account of the neglected state of the parish, and of the evils brought about by the concentration of property in a single owner, when that owner is unwilling or unable to perform any of the duties pertaining to such a position.

The cottages were neglected and allowed to fall into dilapidation. Several of them were pulled down, to such an extent that the accommodation was insufficient, and great hardship was inflicted on some of the labourers, employed in the parish, by their having to walk long distances to their work. The highest rents were screwed out of the cottagers, increased by the fact that residents in the parish were entitled to the benefit of certain charities. The two public-houses were leased to brewers, who endeavoured to make up their high rents by selling deleterious mixtures to their customers. The Game Laws were enforced with the utmost severity. The owner never came near the hamlet. The agent lived in Cornwall and was seldom visible.

"The current impression in the place," says Mrs. Grote,

* "Collected Papers of Mrs. Grote," John Murray, 1862.

"was that Lady Grenville entertained a feeling akin to spite and aversion towards this portion of her estates; and certainly if such were the case, no one could wonder at it, after learning what I have narrated concerning the mistaken calculation which her husband fell into in purchasing the reversion to it at so high a rate. I never heard of her ladyship setting foot in any one of the cottages or farms on this estate during the twenty years of my connection with Burnham."

What, however, is more pertinent to the present narrative is that Lady Grenville, by the advice probably of her agent, began a series of arbitrary acts with reference to the Common, such as indicated a determination to assume absolute ownership over it, and to deny the rights of any others. The people of the district, whether Commoners by virtue of the ownership of land, or as tenants of the land of others, had been in the habit of cutting turf for fuel in the boggy parts of the Common, and firewood in its coppices. Mr. Grote, like others, had availed himself of this right for the benefit of the labourers he employed. Lady Grenville forbade the exercise of it, and when remonstrated with, her agent declared the Common not to be "a Common of turbary," and that Lady Grenville was entitled to the exclusive jurisdiction over it, to the entire abrogation of all rights or privileges on the part of any other persons. "If she granted leave," he said, "to anyone to take away any portion of the soil, such as turf, gravel, peat, and the like, it was as a matter of favour which might be annulled at pleasure."

Mrs. Grote says that she found but one feeling existing on the subject among the people of the parish—

that of extreme dissatisfaction, coupled with a sense of injustice. The cottagers asserted that carts belonging to persons living at a distance were continually sent to carry away from the Common, by permission of the steward, quantities of peat, sand, fallen leaves, and turf. They complained that these parties were allowed to benefit by the Common, although they contributed nothing to the rates, whilst not one of these very ratepayers could take a single barrow-load without going to Dropmore to ask leave. "They felt, in short, that Lady Grenville was seeking to establish an 'absolute' rather than a manorial property in the soil; giving away the same out of the parish in any quantity she thought fit, and preventing any one but herself from using the soil unless specially authorised by herself."

Mrs. Grote goes on to say that she felt a strong desire to probe the whole matter, and to contest Lady Grenville's rights, in the interest of the labouring people; and that she would willingly have taken steps to this end, but she found herself deterred by the fear of bringing down upon the heads of the labouring people the vengeance of the agent.

"He had lately, it seems, explicitly given them to understand that whoever moved in the matter or furnished information, tending to call in question Lady Grenville's supremacy, would be immediately turned out of their tenements. This menace had the effect of tying up the tongues of all her tenants, and of inducing them to wish that no further 'stir' should be made. The whole of the inhabitants, it may be said, rented cottages under Lady Grenville, with the exception of my gardener, Mr. Ludlam's three tenants, and one or two cottages on the Common;

so under these considerations, knowing how grievous a penalty the quitting a tenement would be to any East Burnham resident, I was obliged to lay aside whatever intention I had before cherished of seeking to aid my poor neighbours in this matter."

While tenacious to the last degree of her rights, or supposed rights, Lady Grenville took no pains to preserve order or even decency in the Manor. The roads were neglected. The gates which had formerly prevented cattle from straying from the Common were not maintained. Pigs, unrung, were allowed to tear up the surface of the Common.

Mrs. Grote attributed much of the evil to the fact that Lady Grenville, on account of her great age, delegated her power to an irresponsible and ignorant agent.

"The situation in which the large estate of Lady Grenville found itself at this period is one not unfrequently exhibited in England, but which is not only unfavourable to the interest of the inhabitants, and of those who are in any way dependent on the property, but is, in a minor degree, inconvenient to all residents in its vicinity. An aged landed proprietor delegates her authority over her lands and Manors to persons of an inferior station in life, who cannot take the same view either of public interests, or of the credit attaching to the condition of a gentleman, as the proprietor herself. . . . The whole system under which the district was administered revolved round Lady Grenville represented by a paid agent (living three hundred miles away in Cornwall), and he again by a young deputy instructed to keep down expenses and to maintain ' rights.' The poor were left without anybody to care for them, all trembling at the nod of ' the steward.' "

The annoyance, vexation, and sense of injustice

resulting from this state of things, at last induced the
Grotes to leave the district in which they had spent
twenty years. " The oft-recurring vexations incident to
the position I occupied," Mrs. Grote says, "namely that of
a lady residing in the centre of a population dominated
by a young servant, armed with the authority of the
owner of all the land, manorial privileges, and cottages
(nearly all) in my district, from whose arbitrary control
no appeal could be made on account of Lady Grenville's
advanced age; these oft-recurring vexations made me
feel very uncomfortable." She felt there was no redress.
Mr. Grote was not prepared apparently to take up
the cudgels against Lady Grenville in the Law Courts.
They left the district in consequence, in 1858, some
years before the revived interest in Commons, and
before the decisions in the Law Courts which might
have fortified their position against Lady Grenville.

The incident of Mrs. Grote's connection with
Burnham Common is the more important from the fact,
as she told me later, a short time before her death, that
she had been the cause of a change of opinion in John
Stuart Mill on the subject of Commons. Mill, like
the earlier economists, had been strongly in favour of
inclosing them, with a view to the greater production
of the soil; but she was able to point out to him, from
her personal experience, the importance of common
rights to the labouring people; her narrative of what
occurred in Burnham completely turned the current of
his views on the subject, and was the cause of the
active support which he gave to the preservation

of Commons as a member of the Society, from the year 1866 to the end of his life.

Nothing more was heard of Burnham Beeches till 1879, when on the death of Lady Grenville's successor to the property, the Manor with its Common and the beautiful beeches, together with 175 acres of freehold land adjoining, was offered for sale by public auction, separated from the great landed estate, of which it had for some years been a part, and which was possibly to some extent a security that the Common would not be inclosed.

In the particulars of sale, the common rights, existing over the Common, were represented to be few and unimportant, and expectations were held out that the purchaser would be able to inclose. At all events, there was danger that a wanton purchaser might do so, and might cut down the celebrated beeches, or otherwise interfere with the beauties of the place. The attention of the Commons Society and of the Kyrle Society was directed to the subject ; inquiries were made as to the common rights, and bearing in mind Mrs. Grote's account of the manner in which Lady Grenville had endeavoured to get rid of these rights, it was thought very desirable that all danger to the Common should be removed by the purchase of it by some local authority, in the interest of the public. Negotiations were entered into with the vendors, and a refusal was obtained for the property at an agreed price for a week.

The subject was then brought under the notice of the Corporation of London, which had recently obtained a private Act enabling them to deal with all Commons within twenty-five miles of London. A deputation consisting of members of the Society, and of the Kyrle Society, was introduced by the writer to the Committee of the Corporation having charge of the subject of open spaces. The only difficulty in the way of the Corporation was that their powers under their Act were limited to Commons, and did not extend to the purchase of adjoining freeholds. Sir Henry Peek, however, at the instance of Mr. Robert Hunter, who was at that time acting both for the Corporation in relation to open spaces and for Sir Henry, came forward most promptly to relieve the Corporation of this difficulty, and agreed to acquire the whole property as put up for sale, to retain himself the freehold, consisting of 175 acres, and to resell the Common to the Corporation at an agreed price. The Corporation, relieved of this difficulty, readily adopted the suggestion of purchasing the Common for the very moderate sum of £6,000, or less than £20 an acre, not a tenth part of the value of the land, on the assumption that it was free from common rights. This most interesting place, therefore, with its groves of noble beeches, presenting hundreds of pictures of sylvan grandeur, came under the protection of the Corporation of London, and has been secured for ever for the enjoyment of the public.

CHAPTER XV.

RURAL COMMONS.

THE movement for the preservation of Commons, which commenced in 1864, was for the first five years mainly directed to the saving of the Commons round London from arbitrary inclosure. In 1869, the late Mr. Fawcett became an active member of the Commons Society, and at his instance its operations were extended to rural Commons, in the interest mainly of agricultural labourers.

In the same year his attention was directed to the proposals then before the House of Commons, in the annual Bill of the Inclosure Commissioners, under which many rural Commons were scheduled for inclosure, with an aggregate area of 6,916 acres. Of this it was proposed by the schemes to appropriate the miserable pittance of three acres for the recreation of the people of the districts dealt with, and of six acres for allotments for labouring people, in lieu of their customary user of the common lands.

Among the Commons included in the Bill for inclosure was that of Wisley, an open space on the road from Kingston to Guildford, just beyond the pine woods of St. George's Hill, one of the beautiful Surrey Commons, which add so much to the beauty and residential charm of that county, and which are admitted to be of no value

s

for cultivation. It was very near to Fox Warren, the residence of the late Mr. Charles Buxton, and through him the inexpediency of the inclosure of this Common became generally known. Mr. Knatchbull-Hugessen, later Lord Brabourne, the Minister in charge of the Bill, agreed to treat Wisley separately, and to refer the question of the expediency of inclosing it to a Select Committee, but he pressed on the measure so far as it concerned the other Commons.

It was at this stage that Fawcett's attention was directed to the matter. He had already, in writing a few years before on the subject of the agricultural labourers, pointed out the injurious effect on their condition, of the inclosures of the past 200 years. He was now to deal with the subject in his quality of a practical statesman. The measure for confirming the inclosure of the Commons referred to had already reached its last stage. It was treated, as had been the custom since the Inclosure Act of 1845, as a mere matter of routine, not involving the responsibility of the Minister in charge of it. Fawcett gave notice of a motion for the recommittal of the Bill, upon the third reading, in order to extend the provisions in the schemes as to the allotments for labouring men. This was opposed by the Government, and night after night, until the early hours of the morning, Fawcett was in his place, with a dogged persistency, to prevent the measure being taken at a time when there would be no opportunity of discussing the matter, with any prospect of engaging public interest. At last, on April 9th, 1869, the Bill came on at a reasonable hour, and Fawcett made his motion. Aided by the late Mr. Locke, Q.C., and Mr. Thomas Hughes, he produced such an impression on the House that the Government was compelled to refer the subject to a Select Committee, and meanwhile to suspend further proceedings on the Bill. The Chairman of this Committee was Mr. Cowper Temple ; Sir William Harcourt and Fawcett were among its members. The Committee went fully into the question of inclosures, and the policy of the Inclosure Commissioners in giving their approval to them, and framing their orders. It became abundantly clear from the evidence, that the Commissioners acted on the principle that it was their duty, in carrying out the policy of Parliament, to facilitate and promote inclosures as far as possible.

The Committee came to the conclusion that the provision made for the public and the labouring people, where inclosures took place, was most inadequate. They recommended many amendments of the Inclosure Act of 1845, with the object of rectifying this great scandal. They insisted upon the necessity of local inquiries at hours, when the labourers would have the opportunity of presenting their views. They advised that no further schemes should be sanctioned until the Act of 1845 had been amended. They struck out the cases of Wisley Common, and Withypool Common, in Somersetshire, from the Bill before them—the one pending another inquiry as to the expediency of extending the Metropolitan Commons Act to twenty-five miles' distance from London, which would include

s 2

Wisley ; and the other, because the provision of a single acre for recreation, out of 1,800 proposed to be inclosed, appeared to them to be wholly inadequate. Subject to these exclusions, the Inclosure Bill was pushed on by the Government of the day, in spite of Fawcett's opposition, and was ultimately carried.

Owing to the recommendation of the Select Committee that inclosures should be suspended until the General Act had been amended, several schemes were stopped for the time. It was not till 1871 that the question again came on the *tapis* of Parliament. In that year I was for a short time Under Secretary for the Home Office, and in that capacity I had to deal with the subject of Commons. I accordingly introduced a Bill, founded on the recommendations of the Committee of 1869, and going much beyond them on several important points. It proposed that where inclosure of a Common was authorised, it should be only on the condition of an assignment to the public, either for recreation purposes, or for allotments, of one-tenth of the Common, where the acreage was 500 and under, and where above this, of not less than fifty acres, or more than one-tenth of it. It further proposed to prohibit altogether the inclosure of Commons within a certain distance of towns, varying between one mile for a town of 5,000 inhabitants, and six miles for one of 200,000 inhabitants. It extended, within these limits, the provisions of the Metropolitan Commons Act of 1866 for the regulation of Commons. It contained an important clause, enabling local authorities of London, and other towns, within such limits to purchase, or take by gift, rights of common, and to hold them in gross, with a view to the maintenance and improvement of Commons under regulating schemes.

I did not profess that the measure went so far as I personally desired, but proposed it as the maximum which was possible, under the then state of public opinion. It was referred to a Select Committee, of which Sir W. Harcourt, Fawcett, and myself were members, and by a large majority of which it was substantially approved; but it was not possible to carry the Bill further that year in consequence of the press of other business. In the following year it was introduced in the House of Lords, in the shape in which it had been settled by the Committee, and it formed the subject of long discussions in that House on several occasions. The clause requiring that one-tenth of the Common proposed to be inclosed, up to fifty acres, should be assigned for public purposes, for recreation or labourers' allotments, was specially singled out for hostile criticism. Lord Salisbury said of it :—

"The Lord of a Manor and his Commoners were entitled to ask from Parliament the means of obtaining a full enjoyment of their rights, and Parliament was now asked to interpose and levy blackmail upon them. . . . . It was certainly spoliation to enact that, when the Lord and the Commoners desired to inclose, they should be forced to concede to other persons rights which were perfectly new."*

* Hansard, vol. 212, p. 1507.

Finally, on the third reading of the Bill, the Duke of Northumberland moved its rejection, on the ground that it was an invasion of the rights of property. The motion was carried against the Government by a majority of sixty-five to fifty-three.

It was not till the year 1876, that the subject again came before Parliament. In the meantime no further inclosure orders were confirmed. Schemes for thus dealing with thirty-eight Commons, with a large acreage, had been approved by the Commission, and awaited confirmation by Parliament; but no new proceedings were initiated. In these thirty-eight schemes, in consequence of the views of the Select Committee of 1869, a considerable addition was proposed by the Commissioners to the public allotments for recreation and field gardens. Thus, in the case of Wisley, it was proposed to devote sixteen acres to this purpose, in lieu of the original two acres. In the case of Withypool, the one acre of 1869 was now increased to ten and a half acres. But in the view of the Commons Society even these allotments were insufficient in many cases, and several of the Commons, included in the list, were such as ought not to be inclosed, on the ground that no public advantage was to be expected from such a course.

In 1876, the Home Secretary, Mr. Cross, now Lord Cross, introduced a measure for amending the Inclosure Act of 1845. In many important respects it fell behind the Bill of 1871, especially in the requirement of allotments for public purposes. It left the question of the quantum of allotments to the discretion of the Commissioners. It did not extend the Metropolitan Commons Act to other Commons near to towns. It proposed, however, an alternative for inclosures of Rural Commons, in schemes for their regulation; but it provided that such schemes could only be adopted with the same consents as those for inclosure, namely on the approval of two-thirds, in value, of the Commoners, and also of the Lord of the Manor—while the essential feature of the Metropolitan Commons Act was that a scheme could be applied for by any one or more Commoners, and could be carried, not only without the approval of the Lord of the Manor, but in spite of his opposition.

Mr. Cross, in introducing the Bill, pointed out that the circumstances had greatly altered since the Inclosure Acts of 1801 and 1845.

"The feeling of the country," he said, "had changed, and the reason for it was not difficult to find. In the first place, the necessity for increasing the food supply of the people by the cultivation of Commons was not by any means so pressing as formerly. . . . Then the general increase of the population was so large that in discussing the expediency of inclosing lands, they had to consider not merely how to increase the food supply, but what was really best calculated to promote the health and material prosperity of the people. Whatever could be done in this way without interfering with private rights, it was their duty to do, and the question of Commons, viewed in this light, was perhaps of even greater importance now than it was in 1801 and 1845." *

The Commons Society did not consider that the Bill, as introduced, fulfilled these expectations or the

* Parliamentary Debates, vol. 227, p. 189.

promises made by the Home Secretary. They held that it was deficient in the following respects,—that it left too much to the discretion of the Inclosure Commissioners; that it did not forbid Parliamentary inclosure in the neighbourhood of towns; that it did nothing to put a stop to arbitrary appropriation of Commons without the sanction of Parliament, which had only been checked by the expensive and dilatory litigation of the previous few years; and that the regulation clauses would be little used owing to the veto of the Lord of the Manor. I moved a resolution to this effect, and was supported by Fawcett, who contended that the Bill would promote inclosures. Mr. Cross, in reply, denied that the Bill was intended to have this result. "The object of the Bill, he said, was as far as possible to prevent the inclosure of Commons, and to give facilities for keeping them open for the benefit of the people; so that not only those having rights of common should enjoy them, but that the public themselves might enjoy the use of these free spaces of land—improved, drained, and levelled." * After this assurance the motion was not pressed to a division.

On the Committee stage of the Bill, Fawcett returned to the charge, and moved a resolution to the effect that the Bill did not sufficiently protect agricultural labourers, nor provide adequate security against the inclosure of Commons required for recreation. He supported this with a vigorous speech, but was defeated on a division by 234 to 98. In Committee on the Bill, the representa-

* Parliamentary Debates, vol. 227, p. 543.

tives of the Commons Society, Mr. Fawcett, Lord E. Fitzmaurice, Sir Charles Dilke, Sir William Harcourt, Mr. Bryce, and myself, combined in a determined effort to improve the Bill. We succeeded in inducing the House to adopt a considerable number of amendments in the direction of strengthening the measure against inclosures, and also in the interests of agricultural labourers. We obtained the insertion of a provision of the utmost value, directing the Inclosure Commissioners not to proceed in any case, until they were satisfied that the inclosure would be for the benefit of the neighbourhood, as well as for private interests. The preamble was also altered in accordance with this direction to the Commissioners. Securities were taken for the adequate ascertainment of local opinion, by means of public meetings at a time when the labourers could attend; and amendments were made in the provisions with respect to recreation grounds and allotments. The Commissioners were also instructed to lay out paths and roads, so as to give access to the tops of hills or to picturesque parts of the lands inclosed. A *locus standi* was given to local authorities to object to the inclosures of Commons. Finally, the thirty-eight schemes which had originally been scheduled in the Bill for confirmation of inclosure, were taken out of it, and were relegated again to the Commissioners, to be dealt with, *ab initio*, on the principles laid down in the measure. As a result of this, the Commissioners eventually reported that they could not recommend inclosure in eighteen out of the thirty-eight cases, inasmuch as it was not proved to their satisfaction that such a course was for the benefit of the neighbourhood—a striking commentary on the previous proceedings, and on the new principle asserted by Parliament.

On the other hand, we failed altogether in Committee on the Bill to make the clauses with respect to the regulation of Commons more elastic and workable, either by reducing the required proportion of assents of Commoners, or by removing the veto of the Lord of the Manor. We failed also in numerous attempts to put an end to arbitrary inclosures of Commons otherwise than by the sanction of Parliament. The utmost we succeeded in obtaining was a clause directing persons, intending to inclose portions of Commons, to give three months' notice in a local newspaper of their intention to do so; and a further clause taken from the Bill of 1871, enabling local authorities to purchase land with rights of common attached to it, with the object of giving them a voice in the management of Commons and the right of objecting to inclosure.

After the passing of the Act, a Standing Committee of the House of Commons was appointed, to which all schemes for the inclosure or regulation of Commons under the Act were referred. On this Committee two members of the Commons Society have always sat. Mr. Fawcett and Sir William Harcourt were on the first Committee, and, later, were replaced by Mr. Bryce and myself. By their efforts, every scheme has been subjected to the strictest examination, before approval or rejection by the Committee. In several cases the Committee has insisted upon an increase of the appropriations of land for recreation or allotments. In others it has refused inclosure of parts of Commons, on the ground that no public benefit would result.

The case of Maltby Common, which came before this Committee in 1879, is a good illustration. This Common, of seventy-eight acres, is situate six miles from Rotherham and twelve from Sheffield. It is much frequented by visitors from both these towns, and there are no other Commons within the same distances. It was originally included in the list of thirty-eight schemes approved by the Inclosure Commissioners, under the Act of 1845, and it was then proposed to assign three acres for a recreation ground and three for allotments. The Commission now again sanctioned a scheme for its inclosure, but with the requirement that twenty-four acres should be set apart for recreation, and five for garden allotments. There was strong opposition to the inclosure from the people of Sheffield and Rotherham. There was no evidence that any public benefit whatever would result from it. It was represented indeed that part of the Common was damp; but this might have been remedied by a regulation scheme. It was threatened by the promoters of the scheme, that if Parliamentary sanction to the inclosure were refused, they would, by agreement with the Commoners, effect the desired object without such authority, and that in such case the public would lose the benefit even of the twenty-nine acres, proposed to be allotted to them. Under the influence of this fear the Committee, by a small majority, approved the scheme for the inclosure of Maltby Common. But on the motion of Lord Edmond Fitzmaurice, the following clause was inserted in the Report of the Committee, pointing out the anomalous state of the law in allowing inclosures otherwise than by the sanction of Parliament, and without the securities for the public interest which were in their opinion necessary.

" It was pointed out to the Committee that if the provisional order for inclosing Maltby Common were not accepted by Parliament, there was a possibility of the parties interested coming to terms and inclosing the whole Common, and that, if that were done, the intentions of Parliament for the protection of the rights of the poorer inhabitants, and the health, comfort, and convenience of the neighbourhood would be thereby frustrated, and that persons might arbitrarily inclose common land on the chance of nobody interfering. It is evident that this condition of the law might materially impair the free action of the Commissioners, and interfere with the intentions of Parliament, if the Commissioners were informed that, should they not accept the exact terms proposed by the majority of the parties interested, the inclosure would be carried out in another way without any reference to the Acts of Parliament bearing on the subject."

The opposition to the inclosure of Maltby Common did not end with the Committee. Mr. Mundella gave notice to move the rejection of the Bill in the House, and as the Government gave no assistance for the discussion of the Bill, at a time when it could be taken, it must be presumed that it was hostile to the scheme. In any case the scheme did not receive the sanction of Parliament; the inclosure was abandoned; and Maltby

Common still remains open to the public, though much in need of a regulating scheme.

A case of somewhat opposite character was that of Thurstaston Common, near Birkenhead. The Common, of about 150 acres, was one of great beauty, occupying the highest land on the peninsula between the Dee and the Mersey, and commanding fine views of the estuary of the Dee and the Welsh mountains. Its surface was also picturesquely diversified by masses of rock; and it contained one stone of much antiquarian interest called Thor's Stone, believed to have been a place of sacrifice in the time of the Danes. Unfortunately almost the whole of the parish was owned by two landowners, the Lord of the Manor and another wealthy proprietor, the remaining thirty acres being glebe. A threat was held out to the Inclosure Commissioners that if Parliament would not consent to the inclosure of the Common under the Act, the Lord of the Manor would by agreement with the other two persons interested, effect its appropriation. The Inclosure Commissioners in their report to Parliament, said that, considering the growing population of Birkenhead and the almost equal nearness of the great city of Liverpool, they would have declined the application for inclosure in order to keep the entire Common for public resort; but seeing that the owners might by agreement appropriate the whole Common for themselves to the exclusion of the public, they thought it better, by consenting to the scheme, to secure a part of it for the public. They agreed to the proposal, therefore, upon the terms that forty-five acres would be reserved for public enjoyment. The standing Committee took the same view, and approved the inclosure of the residue.

By the action of the Committee and by discussions in the House of Commons, an entirely new policy with respect to inclosures has been forced upon the Inclosure Commissioners. The very name of the Commission, which was misleading, as it seemed to point out to them the duty of inclosing, has disappeared. In 1887, it was changed to the Land Commission, which has since been merged in the Board of Agriculture. In the sixteen years which have elapsed since the Commons Act of 1876, twenty-four Commons only have been inclosed, with a total area of 26,500 acres, of which 498 acres have been devoted to recreation ground, and 289 acres to field gardens and allotments. Two-thirds of the applications for inclosure of Commons, which have come before the Inclosure Commissioners and their successors, the Board of Agriculture, have been rejected, on the ground that no advantage would accrue to the public from thus dealing with them. In many of the latest schemes for inclosures of mountain lands, a provision has been inserted, securing to the public a right of access over the land, so long as it should not be tilled or planted. Since 1886 there has been only one case of inclosure.

The change in public opinion marked by the Commons Act of 1876, and still more by the mode of administering it, can only be realised by those who have given close attention to the subject. To

Mr. Fawcett this change was most largely due. It was his dogged perseverance, in 1869, which forced the question into public notice, and which compelled legislation for amendment of the Inclosure Act of 1845 in a manner so beneficial to the labouring people and to the public.*

---

* For a more detailed account of Mr. Fawcett's personal share in the movement for the preservation of Commons, see Mr. Leslie Stephen's "Life of Henry Fawcett," chapter vii. (Smith, Elder, & Co., 1885). But for this I should have amplified this chapter.

CHAPTER XVI.

ROAD SIDE WASTES.

CLOSELY analogous to the question of Commons is that of the road-side wastes, so often to be found in rural parts of England, and not unfrequently even in the suburbs of our great towns. It need not be pointed out how valuable they are to the public. To horsemen they are welcome as affording soft turf, in lieu of the hard road, for a gallop. They are often the only playground for the children of labouring men. Where the fences are irregular, and the space between them and the road is interspersed with bushes and brambles, beneath which wild flowers find luxuriant growth, or with gorse or broom, the picturesqueness of the rural scene is greatly enhanced. Such strips of land are of far greater value in their present condition, than if added to the adjoining fields, even though the produce of the soil might be slightly increased; and no owner of land, who has any regard for public interests, would dream of advancing his fences so as to appropriate them. Yet such is the desire to add to their domains even a few yards of frontage, that many landowners—and especially small owners—seem to be unable to resist the temptation of inclosing these strips, when they can do so with impunity.

The soil of these road-side wastes is generally

vested in the owners of the adjoining land, as is the case
with the soil of the roads, subject to the rights of the
public over them ; but not unfrequently they are the
property of the Lords of Manors of their districts, as part
of the wastes of their Manors, and are therefore not subject to inclosure, without the consent of the Commoners.
It often happens, however, that the main part of the
waste has been inclosed, and that nothing remains of
it but the road-side strips ; and where this is the case,
but for the rights of the public, the lord may venture
to inclose without much fear of being called to account.

Fortunately, there is no doubt as to the law, or as
to the right of the public to the continued use and enjoyment of the road-side wastes. The law, however, is
apparently little known, even to those whose right it is
to put it in force, and to abate inclosures of these strips
of land ; for complaints are frequent, from all parts of
the country, that encroachments take place, and that
the highway authorities, so far from preventing them,
are too often aiders and abettors in them.

It has been well-settled law, for many years past,
that the public have the right of way over the road-side
wastes, no matter what the width of the metalled road
may be, and that any obstruction erected on them, in
the way of fences or otherwise, is a nuisance, for
which the author may be indicted in a Criminal Court.
The highway authorities have no power to consent
to such encroachments on the rights of the public,
and though the law has not cast upon them the same
obligations to protect the road-side waste as in

T

regard to the road itself, yet they are clearly justified in removing any obstructions upon it.

The principal case bearing on this subject, in which the law was clearly laid down, was that where a telegraph company, wishing to compete with another company, obtained the consent of the owners of the adjoining land to erect their poles on the road-side wastes, along the route where they desired to carry their wires. The obstruction caused by the poles was scarcely perceptible to the ordinary public. The rival company, however, acting ostensibly in the interests of the public, but really in their own interests only, with the object of preventing opposition, indicted the company, which had erected the poles, for obstructing the Queen's Highway.

In the trial which took place, Baron Martin directed the jury as follows:—

" In the case of an ordinary highway, although it may be of a varying and unequal width, running between fences, one on each side, the right of passage or way, *primâ facie*, and unless there be evidence to the contrary, extends to the whole space between the fences, and the public are entitled to the use of the entire of it as the highway, and are not confined to the part which may be metalled or kept in repair for the more convenient use of carriages or foot passengers. . . A permanent obstruction created on a highway, and placed there without lawful authority, while rendering the way less commodious than before to the public, is an unlawful act, and a public nuisance at common law, and if the jury believed that the defendants placed, for the purpose of profit to themselves, posts, with the object and intention of keeping them there, and the posts were of such a size and dimension and solidity as to obstruct and prevent the passage of carriages and horses or foot passengers upon the part of the highway where they stood, the jury ought to find the defendants guilty upon this indictment." *

The jury, upon this direction of the judge, found the defendants guilty of obstructing the highway. The summing-up of Baron Martin was subsequently approved by the Exchequer Judges.

The right of the public has been further vindicated by the advice of the Commons Society, during the last few years, in two cases, where, although there was no decision in the Courts of Law, it is certain that if any shred of law could have been found to sustain them, the inclosers of road-side wastes would have appealed to it.

In the first of these cases the late Marquis of Salisbury, in the year 1867, inclosed the roadside wastes over a wide district in the neighbourhood of Hatfield, where he was Lord of the Manor, and claimed as such the ownership of the soil of the wastes. For nearly two miles of road, where this was effected, the present Earl Cowper was owner of the adjoining land. He found the frontages of his land to the highways cut off by narrow strips of land thus inclosed. It would be difficult, therefore, to conceive a more glaring and obnoxious case of inclosure of roadside wastes.

Lord Cowper having in mind the then recent action of Mr. Augustus Smith, in removing the fences in the

* Reg. v. United Kingdom Electric Telegraph Co., 3, F & F, 73.

T 2

Berkhamsted case, took the advice of the Commons
Society and of its solicitor, Mr. P. H. Lawrence. He
was recommended to follow the example of Mr. Smith,
and to make an emphatic demonstration of the
illegality of the encroachments, by forcibly removing
the fences, and by employing for the purpose a body of
men so large, as to render any opposition on the part of
Lord Salisbury's employés impossible.

Lord Cowper, acting on this counsel, collected a large
body of tenants and labourers, who, under his personal
superintendence, removed the whole of the fences in
the night and early morning. Having effected this,
he sent a servant on horseback to Hatfield with a letter,
informing Lord Salisbury of what had been done, and
of his reasons for doing it. It was stated at the time
that the late Lord Cairns—then Lord Chancellor—
was a guest at Hatfield, when this missive arrived,
and it was surmised that his advice on the legal
aspects of the case restrained his host within prudent
bounds. However that may have been, Lord Salisbury
contented himself with issuing a writ for trespass
against Lord Cowper, but took no further action upon
it; he submitted to a defeat, and never attempted to
question the legality of Lord Cowper's action in removing the fences, or to assert his own right to erect
them.

A mutual friend of the two peers, it was said, endeavoured to induce Lord Cowper to tender an apology
to Lord Salisbury for so violent a course, upon the
understanding that no further attempt would be made

to inclose the roadside wastes; but Lord Cowper, with very proper spirit, replied that apology was due rather to himself by the author of the arbitrary and illegal fencings, than by himself for removing them. It is satisfactory to know that this encounter between the two Hertfordshire magnates did not permanently disturb the relations between Hatfield and Panshanger. In this case the public were fortunate in finding a great landowner, able and willing to vindicate its rights, as well as his own. But for that, it may be doubted whether any smaller fry in the district would have been willing to enter the lists against the Lord of Hatfield.

The other case was one in which I was personally concerned. In 1875, I was residing at Ascot, where I own a property adjoining the main road from Windsor to Reading. This road is a conspicuous illustration of the advantage of roadside wastes. On either side of it are broad strips, where horsemen are able to ride on soft turf, and which add much to the beauty of the district. Returning from the Continent in the autumn of that year, after some months of absence, I found that in the interval the numerous owners of land and houses, for nearly a mile on one side of this road near the church, had inclosed the roadside waste, by advancing their fences up to fifteen feet of the crown of the metalled road, and had planted the land, thus filched from the waste, with shrubs and trees. One of these owners had erected along this new line, for about 500 yards, a most solid and expensive wall. In common with the other encroachers, he had obtained the consent of the Surveyor of Highways of the district.

It was obvious that if these inclosures were to be recognised as lawful, the example would be followed by all the other landowners on either side for miles, and that the road would be reduced from its splendid width and beauty to a narrow one of thirty feet, with high fences on either side. It was essential, therefore, in the public interest, to upset these encroachments. I found, as is usual in such cases, that there was a general feeling of indignation on the subject, but that no one knew how to act, or whether these proceedings were legal or not.

I called together a Committee of neighbours—including the late Sir William Hayter, the late Mr. John Delane (then Editor of the *Times*), the late Mr. J. B. Smith, M.P., and others—and we determined to contest the legality of the inclosures. As the owners of adjoining land, who had inclosed the wastes, had been allowed to do so, without remonstrance pending the erection of their fences, and had obtained the consent of the Highway Board, it was felt that we should not be justified in forcibly abating the obstructions, and leaving the parties aggrieved to take action in the Law Courts, if so advised. We adopted the more moderate and conciliatory course of offering to remove all the fences, and to replace them, at the expense of the Committee, on their old and proper line, the cost being estimated at from £600 to £700.

The owners of the fences, when they found themselves confronted by a body able and willing to enforce its conclusions, with one exception gave way, and, while protesting they had not acted illegally, allowed us to replace their fences on the legal line. The one exception was the owner of the substantial wall already referred to. This gentleman refused our offer with contumely, informed us that he was advised by the best authority that he was legally justified in his encroachment, and threatened that he would resist us in the Law Courts, and fight his case up to the House of Lords.

Nothing daunted, we were equally sure of our position as members of the public, whose rights to the roadside waste we believed to be undoubted. We were advised by Mr. Robert Hunter, the solicitor to the Commons Society, that our best course was to apply to the Attorney-General for his consent to lay an information in his name against the encroaching land-owner, for interfering with the public right of way. The Attorney-General gave his consent, and an information was filed in the Court of Chancery on the relation of certain members of the Committee, asking that the author of the obstruction should be ordered to remove it. One of the members of the Committee—Mr. Ferard—was also Lord of the Manor of Wingfield, in which the strips lay, and a claim was in the same proceedings made on his behalf to the ownership of the soil of the strips.

When tackled in this way, our opponent felt himself unable to defend his encroachment. He submitted to a decree without contest in the Courts, and we had the satisfaction of seeing him remove his beautiful wall and re-erect it on its proper site, at his own cost, instead of at ours. So angry was he, however, that he subsequently ploughed up the strip of land which he was forced to throw out. Process was then taken before the magistrates at Maidenhead, and this foolish and ill-tempered attempt to annoy the public was visited with an appropriate sentence.

This vindication of the public rights put an end to the encroachments on roadside wastes in that district. We felt, however, that we had only performed a duty, which ought to have been undertaken by the local authority of the district, on behalf of the public. The difficulty consisted not in the law, but in the absence of a local authority interested, on behalf of the public, in enforcing it, in the ignorance of the law on the part of the highway authorities, and in the want of summary means for enforcing it. The law already gives a summary remedy by penalty, in the case of any obstruction within fifteen feet of the centre of the highway, and most highway boards are under the impression that this is a legal definition of the width of the road, and that adjoining owners are entitled to advance their fences up to this point, so as to inclose the roadside waste. This, however, is a distinct error, and although there is no summary remedy outside the limit of fifteen feet, yet it is clear that the public are entitled to the use of the land beyond, which is within the definition of a roadside waste, and that the Surveyor of Highways is justified in removing any obstruction.*

In 1878, I proposed a clause in the Highway Bill of that year for remedying the defect of the law, by extending the summary remedy for obstructing a highway to obstructions on the roadside waste, beyond the fifteen-feet limit; but the Government of the day refused their assent to it. It was not till some years later that there was another opportunity of advancing the question. In 1888, I proposed an amendment of the Local Government Bill, declaring it to be the duty of County Councils to protect the roadside wastes, in the case of main roads committed to their charge. The amendment was, in the first instance, opposed by the Minister who had charge of the Bill, but the feeling of the House was so strong in its favour that the Government found itself compelled to give way, and the amendment was adopted and became law.

The measure which has passed the House of Commons for the constitution of District Councils, contains a similar provision in respect of roadside wastes in the case of roads which will be under the control of these new local authorities. The question, therefore, is in a fair way for final settlement, and it is to be hoped that it will

---

* I hear on going to press that Mr. J. T. Brunner, M.P., a member of the Commons Society, has been successful in obtaining the removal of a mile and a half of fencing, which had reduced a fine Roman road, between Northwich and Middlewich, from a width of 60 feet to 30 feet, with the consent—nay, strong approval—of the Highway Board.

not in the future be necessary for private individuals
to take upon themselves the invidious, thankless, and
expensive task of protecting public rights over road-
side wastes, against the ignorant encroachments of their
neighbours.

CHAPTER XVII.

Village Greens.

It has already been pointed out that the law has not recognised the validity of any custom of the inhabitants of a district, manor, or parish, for the enjoyment of a right of a profitable nature ; and that so vague and uncertain a class of people, as the inhabitants of a place, cannot claim such a right by prescription. The judges, however, have admitted the possibility, subject to very narrow and strict limitations, of the inhabitants of a village claiming a right by custom to play games on the village Green, or even on land belonging to a private owner. The custom must be of a very definite character ; it does not extend to mere recreation, in the sense of roaming about an open space ; it must, apparently, be distinctly for games. It must also be alleged on behalf of the inhabitants of a parish, manor, or defined district, and not on behalf of all the world ; for it would seem that the older authorities have laid it down that a custom alleged on behalf of the public generally would be part of the general law of the land, and could not, therefore, be proved as existing only in a particular place. There must also be evidence of a continuous user without any commencement of the custom.

The right of villagers to play games on a village

Green appears to have been for the first time recognized by the judges in the time of Charles II., when, perhaps, there was a reaction in favour of such amusements, after the stricter notions and habits of puritanical times. In the seventeenth year of the Merry Monarch, the inhabitants of a parish in Oxfordshire, in an action for trespass on land belonging to the plaintiff in the case, pleaded "that all the inhabitants of the village, time out of memory, had been used to dance there at all times of the year for their recreation," and justified their entering on the land for this purpose. It was objected that such a claim "to dance on the freehold of another, *et spoil son grass*," was void, especially as it was laid at all times of the year, and not at seasonable times, and that it was also ill-laid in the inhabitants who "claim easements as in Gateward's case, yet there ought to be easements of necessity, as ways to a church, etc., and not for pleasure." The judges, however, held it was a good custom, and that it was "necessary for the inhabitants to have their recreation." *

This case was followed by another, in which the inhabitants of a parish claimed by custom, from time immemorial, to have enjoyed the liberty of playing at all kinds of lawful games, sports and pastimes, in a certain close, at all reasonable times of the year, at their free will and pleasure. The judges in this case acknowledged the validity of the previous decision. "It has been objected," they said, "that it is not alleged that

* Abbott *v.* Weekly.—Levinz, 176.

the pastimes were allowed for the necessary recreation of the inhabitants, but the case in Levinz decides that it is necessary for the inhabitants to have such recreation; if so it is matter of law." But this case, while it confirmed the previous decision, also laid down that a claim which was set up for a similar custom, averring the right to be in "all persons for the time being in the said parish," was as clearly bad as the other claim was good. " How that which may be claimed by all the inhabitants of England," said Mr. Justice Buller, "can be the subject of a custom, I cannot conceive. Customs must be in their nature confined to individuals of a particular description, and what is common to all mankind can never be claimed as a custom." *

The distinction between a class of persons, or the inhabitants of a district, and the public generally, was clearly brought out in two cases with regard to racecourses. In the one, a custom for all the freemen and citizens of the city of Carlisle to hold horse-races over the close of Kingsmoor on Ascension Day in every year was held good.† In the other, the trustees of Newmarket Heath had warned off the course a gentleman, who had made a violent attack on their conduct. He refused to leave, and an action at law was brought, to which he pleaded an immemorial custom on the part of the public to go and see the races held at Newmarket. The judges decided that the custom having been laid

* Fitch v. Rawlings.—2, H. Bl. 393.
† Mounsey v. Ismay.—1863, 34, L.J., Ex. 52.

in the Queen's subjects generally, was bad; that the
public had no right to be there; but they intimated
that if the defendant could have claimed as an inhabitant of Newmarket, he might possibly have maintained the custom.*

This distinction between the user by the public
generally, and that of the inhabitants of a parish, was
also brought out clearly in a later case, that relating to
Woodford Green, forming a part of Epping Forest. In
this case a claim was made on behalf of the inhabitants
of the village to the enjoyment of the Green, and to
prevent the inclosure of it by the Lord of the Manor.
It was maintained in the first place that there was
a right of way in all directions over the Green, and
secondly that the inhabitants were accustomed to
play at all lawful games on the Green. In sum-
ming up this case to the jury, Mr. Justice Wightman
said :—

"The question is, first, whether there was a right of way
over the spot where the hurdles were put up. In one sense
there was a way there, for it appears that the Green was part of
the ancient forest, and the effect of the evidence is that people
went wherever they liked, and so in that sense the whole forest
was one great way. . . But there was no distinct evidence of
any definite way in any particular direction, and though there
were tracks from time to time, which might last for a few
weeks or months, there was no beaten or enduring track in any
one direction which had lasted for years. Then, as to the
alleged custom, it is laid in the inhabitants; but the proof is
wider than the plea, for it appears that all the world went

* Coventry v. Willes.—12, Weekly Reporter, 127.

wherever they pleased. It may be a question whether that would be a good custom in law, and, of course, if in point of fact, it is proved as to all the world, it is proved as to the inhabitants. On the other hand, if the plea be taken to mean that the subject is only in the inhabitants, it is disproved, for the proof shows it to be, if it exists at all, in all the world."

Under this direction the jury found a verdict for the Lord of the Manor who had inclosed; and what was undoubtedly a village Green, where the inhabitants of Woodford had been in the habit of playing games, would, but for the action of the Corporation of London some years later, have been lost to them for ever, because the population of London had in recent years joined in the user of the Green, and it could no longer be proved that the custom was confined to the inhabitants of the place.

This unfortunate and, it would seem, most narrow and technical view of the case, was followed by an even greater lawyer, the late Sir George Jessel, in the case of Stockwell Green. Stockwell is, or rather was, until swallowed up by the ever-extending population of London, a hamlet in the parish of Lambeth. In the centre of it was a small open space, part of the waste of the Manor, of a little more than an acre, known as Stockwell Green, and so marked in all the old maps. It was till a comparatively recent date open to the public, and the evidence showed that the people of Stockwell had been accustomed to play games upon it. The growth of population, however, and the want of means for regulating it, made it a nuisance to the people living in the adjoining houses.

In 1813, a gentleman of large means, named Barrett,
living near the Green, took a lease of it from the Lord
of the Manor for sixty-one years, with the option of
purchase for £200. The lease contained a covenant to
inclose the Green, and to plant it with shrubs, and not
to erect any building without the lessor's assent. Barrett
did this for the purpose of preventing the place being
a nuisance to the neighbourhood. In the correspondence
with his neighbours, he expressly disclaimed having
taken the lease with a view to profit, and he offered to
let them join in the enterprise, bearing their share in
the expense. The Green was then fenced and planted,
but for some time the inhabitants made use of the
Green, breaking down the fence. In 1855 a Committee
was formed of the inhabitants, for the purpose of collecting subscriptions to erect a new fence round the Green,
and to restore it from its then disgraceful state. A sub-
lease was obtained from Barrett's successor, and a new
fence was erected. The Green was then drained and laid
down with turf. This was done with the object of
preventing nuisances and maintaining the decency and
appearance of the place ; but the public were excluded.
In 1874, the sub-lease came to an end, and a Mr.
Honey, who had obtained an assignment of Barrett's
lease from his representatives, and had exercised the
option of purchasing the fee from the Lord of the
Manor, commenced building operations on the Green,
and when remonstrated with by the inhabitants of the
adjoining houses, demanded £8,000, as the price for sur-
rendering his interest in this acre of land.

A Committee was then formed, who brought a suit against Mr. Honey, to restrain him from building on the Green, and claiming, on the part of the inhabitants, a right to the land as the village green of the hamlet of Stockwell. The question turned largely upon what was the use made of the Green before 1813, when it was fenced by Barrett. Sir George Jessel decided against the inhabitants, professedly on the ground that the evidence before 1813 showed that the Green was used as a place for games and recreation, not by the people of Stockwell only, but by people from all parts of London, though, no doubt, the fact of the inclosure (of a kind) since 1813 greatly influenced his decision.

"In the proof of usage," he said, "the usage must be not only constant to the custom, but not too wide. For instance, if you allege a custom to dance on a Green, and you prove in support of that alleged custom not only that some people danced, but that everybody else in the world who chose not only danced, but played cricket, you have got beyond the custom. Your custom is not confined to what you say it was ; if your evidence is good for anything, you will prove a great deal more. As I understand the evidence, before the time of inclosure by Barrett anybody who liked might recreate himself at his will and pleasure on the Green. There was no limit to the little boys, whether they were Stockwell boys or boys from Brixton, or anywhere else. I do not think many men played on the Green at any time, but I think occasionally girls played there, principally little girls, though some of them might be girls of a larger growth ; and I think occasionally young men played on the Green. It was hardly big enough for men's cricket, but I have no doubt that anybody who liked played on the Green. . . . The Green seems to have been open to everybody who wanted to go there, and whether there were or not constables of the vill, no-

U

body ever interfered, and there is no pretence of anybody interfering with the right of recreation, if it may be called a right,
or amusing themselves in any way they chose, by anybody
who went on this piece of land, without the slightest regard to
the fact whether he was or was not an inhabitant of the vill
or hamlet of Stockwell.   If that be so, the case is at an end."*

The effect of these decisions seems to be that as a
great town extends, and absorbs the smaller villages
surrounding it, and the village greens become places of
enjoyment for games and recreation to a wider class of
persons than the inhabitants of the village, and, therefore, are more valuable, the right to play games and to
prevent inclosure is lost, because it can no longer be
averred or proved that the custom of playing games
thereon is confined to the inhabitants of the village.
The same very technical distinction between the inhabitants of a village or parish, and those of a wider district
or great town, or the public generally, has operated
to prevent the judges drawing a legal analogy between
the village and its green, and London and its much-
frequented Commons, such as Hampstead, Hackney,
Blackheath, and others, however close the analogy may
be in fact.   It has resulted that, no matter how much
the people of London have in the past used and enjoyed
any one of these Commons for games, the law does
not recognise that any right has grown up.

On the other hand, so long as those Commons
remained open and uninclosed, there was no means
known to the law, by which persons roaming over them

* Hammerton *v.* Honey.—6, W.R., 603.

in all directions could be punished, provided they did no injury to the property of the Lords of the Manor or of the Manorial tenants. The public were at law trespassers, but they were dispunishable trespassers. They had no right to claim that the Common should remain *in statu quo*, or that inclosure should be prevented; their continued enjoyment of the Common therefore depended on the maintenance by the Commoners of their rights over the land. Where a great population has grown up round the Common, people have practically taken the place of cattle, but the law, which had originally recognised the user of copyholders to turn out their cattle on the Common, and had given it the sanction of right, has failed to adopt the same course with respect to the still more important user by people.

There are not wanting, however, signs that the judges are disposed to take a more popular view of the rights of the public to recreation, and not to be bound too closely by the doctrine of extinction of the local rights by the more general user by the public at large. Quite recently, in 1892, an important case was tried and determined at the Bristol Assizes, in which, though it was in the hands of a local solicitor, the advice of the Commons Society had been taken as to the right of inhabitants to a Common for recreation.

It arose in respect of Walton Common, which lies on the edge of the hills stretching along the coast-line of the Bristol Channel from Clevedon to Portishead. On the level ground at the top of this hill is a well-

U 2

marked circular camp, corresponding to that on Cadbury Hill, on the other side of the marshy valley which stretches from Clevedon to Portbury; and those who climb the hillside to reach the level ground are rewarded by a splendid view. The villagers of Walton-in-Gordano set great store on their Common Hill as their place of recreation. The turf is close and soft and springy, as it always is on the tops of these limestone hills, and the sheep and horses of the Commoners kept the grass always short. The Common is in the Manor of Walton, which is vested in the Trustees of Sir C. Miles, the owner of Leigh Court, who is also owner of most of the land in the parish.

The Lord of the Manor had from time to time bought up any land for sale in the parish, with the object of extinguishing the rights of common; and a series of aggressions took place, in the shape of inclosures of parts of the Common. The object apparently was to convert the Common into a game preserve. The villagers, tenants of the owner, who had been in the habit of turning out animals to graze on the hill, were warned not to do so, and so far as they were concerned, the warning was equivalent to a command, as they had but two alternatives, namely, to submit or to leave the parish. A considerable fringe of the Common was inclosed and planted. Barbed wire fences were erected across it. Thorns were planted in various parts of it. The footpaths over the hill were blocked up. A large portion of the Common was stocked with rabbits, and the shooting on it was let.

The Common Hill had been used from time immemorial for games by the villagers. They had played there football, rounders, and cricket. It was distinctly larger than an ordinary village Green, consisting of sixty-four acres, but the whole of it had been used by the people for recreation, and many parts of it for games. These were now prohibited. On the lord's agent being requested to explain the grounds on which the changes were made, and what justification there was for the keepers interfering with the use of the Common for games and recreation, he replied that the Lord of the Manor intended to prosecute any persons who in any way trespassed on the hill, over which he claimed absolute control; if the claim, he said, were persisted in, the question would have to be settled in a Court of Law. Mr. Virgo, a working gardener and florist, with land adjoining the Common, then took up the case of the Commoners and the public. He was informed that, in consequence of his action, the Lord of the Manor would stop him from using a cart-road across the Common, which afforded the only access in one direction. He was also told that the Lord of the Manor had ample means at his disposal, and that he must expect no quarter.

Undeterred by these threats, Mr. Virgo brought an action at law against the trustees for interference with the right of the inhabitants to play games on the Common, and claimed an injunction to restrain them from so doing. The case was tried at Bristol before a special jury by Mr. Justice Wills, in August, 1892.

There were numerous witnesses to prove that the inhabitants had been in the habit of going on the Common, from time immemorial, for recreation and games. The defendants relied mainly on evidence to negative this user and on the smallness of the population, which was only 147 at the beginning of the century; and they contended that there could not have been a custom for so small a body of inhabitants to play games on so large a Common, and that it was not confined to the people of the parish.

The judge submitted the case to the jury, who found their verdict for Mr. Virgo ; and an injunction was given to restrain the defendants from inclosing the Common, from erecting barbed fences on it, and from planting it with bushes. Sir A. Wills gave an important opinion in the course of this case, on the right of outsiders to contribute to the maintenance of such a suit. In answer to objections which were raised on this score, he said that it was perfectly lawful for anyone to subscribe to a suit, where it was believed that the public interest was at stake.

In the following year Mr. Virgo returned to the charge, and in his quality as a Commoner, claimed the restitution to the Common of a portion of it known as Common Hill Wood, which had been inclosed a few years previously. The defendants did not dispute the right of common, and the only question was whether the portion claimed was originally part of the Common. This was again tried before a jury at Bristol, who also gave their verdict in favour of Mr. Virgo. The case is another illustration that these attempts on the part of Lords of Manors, if resisted, will almost certainly fail. It was of the greatest importance, as showing the extent to which the judges will permit the claim for recreation to be maintained. If a small village population can maintain rights of recreation and of playing games on a Common of 64 acres, it is difficult to understand why the people of a large town should not be allowed to maintain similar rights over its adjoining Commons.

There are 79 open spaces within the Metropolitan Police district, described in the Ordnance Survey as village greens, and ranging in size from 2 roods to 25 acres. Of these 12 have been included in Regulation schemes of adjoining Commons under the Act of 1866. Many of the others, under the decisions referred to, appear to be endangered by the growth of London, and by the fact that it can no longer be proved that the customs to play games on them are restricted to the inhabitants of their districts. It is clear therefore that some remedy should be provided for the better security of these playgrounds.

CHAPTER XVIII.

The Regulation of Commons.

It has already been shown that there are two very distinct processes by which Commons may be placed under schemes of regulation; viz:—(1) Under the Metropolitan Commons Act of 1866, and (2) under the Commons Act of 1876. The first of these Acts, applying to Commons within the Metropolitan Police area, about fifteen miles from Charing Cross, provides that the Agricultural Department, on the application of any Commoners, of the Local Authority of the district, or of twelve inhabitants,* may approve of a scheme for the regulation of a Common, subject to its confirmation by Parliament. Under such a scheme the Common may be practically taken out of the hands of the Lord of the Manor, and placed under the charge and management of the Local Authority, or of a body of Conservators specially constituted, for the main-tenance of order, the prevention of nuisances, and the due regulation of the various rights over it, with power to make bye-laws for the purpose. If the Lord of the Manor gives his consent, the scheme is thence-forward binding upon him and his successors, and the Common can never be inclosed, wholly or partially, under the Statute of Merton, or otherwise. If he does

* See "Metropolitan Commons Amendment Act, 1869."

not give his consent, it is still in the power of the Board of Agriculture to approve the scheme, and it will be valid for all the purposes contained in it, save that the rights of the lord, whatever they may be, under the Statute of Merton or otherwise, are reserved, and, like other rights over the Common, cannot be materially interfered with without compensation. The lord may still put in force his rights of digging gravel and turf, and the Commoners may still exercise their rights of turning out cattle, subject to regulations made by the Conservators.

Under the Commons Act of 1876, which applies to all Commons beyond the Metropolitan Police area, schemes of the same nature may be made for the regulation of Commons, whether in urban or rural districts. There is, however, the important difference that a scheme can only be entertained by the Board on the application or consent of one-third of the Commoners, and it cannot be finally approved by the Department, unless two-thirds (in value) of the Commoners agree, and the Lord of the Manor consents. The lord, in fact, has an absolute veto on such a scheme. Schemes in respect of rural Commons are generally applied for, not in the interest of the public, but for the purpose of defining and regulating the rights of Commoners, in cases where inclosure is not likely to be approved, or where it is not worth while to inclose and fence the land—in fact, where the object is to turn them into stinted pastures, leaving them uninclosed and open to the public. In cases of this kind the Board of Agriculture almost invariably

inserts clauses, securing to the public the right of access
to and of walking and riding over the Commons.

As regards Commons within the Metropolitan Police
district, the Act of 1866 was brought into operation
very slowly, and a large number of them still
remain unregulated. This was due in part to the
unwillingness of the late Metropolitan Board to adopt
the Act, in part to the objections of the Inclosure
Commissioners to give their sanction, where Lords of
Manors objected to the schemes, and partly also to
the litigation in progress, with respect to so many of the
Commons round London, which deterred persons concerned from applying for schemes, until the Courts of
Law had determined on the validity of the claims of
the lords.

The Metropolitan Board would not readily abandon
their alternative plan for the purchase of the Commons
within their area, in spite of its rejection by the
Committee of 1865, and of the protests of the Commons
Society. They lost no opportunity of purchasing the
rights of Lords of Manors, often giving large sums for
them, wholly regardless of the fact that every such purchase tended to raise the hopes and demands of other
lords, and to encourage them in the view that they had a
valuable property or interest to dispose of. They took
advantage, however, of the decisions of the Judges
against the right of the lords to inclose, and in some
cases bought the interests of lords at very reduced
rates as compared with their original demands. Thus
they bought the lord's rights over Hampstead Heath

for £45,000 in lieu of £400,000, his original demand; in 1873 they bought the manorial rights over Tooting Bee Common for £10,200. Two years later, the Board purchased Mr. Thompson's interest in Tooting Graveney Common, which it has already been shown he had been restrained from inclosing, for £3,000. The acquisition appears to have been effected under compulsory powers.*

The first case of a scheme under the Act of 1866 was that relating to Hayes, a very beautiful Common near Bromley in Kent, and within the Metropolitan Police area. What is popularly known as Hayes Common, is in fact partly in the Manor of Baston, and partly in that of West Wickham; the waste in the former Manor being about 200 acres, and in the latter, till within recent years, about 100 acres. These Commons were not separated by any fence or defined boundary. The Lord of both Manors was Sir John Lennard. A short time before 1865 this gentleman inclosed about fifty acres of West Wickham Common, and disposed of them as sites for villas. There was great fear in the district that he intended to deal in the same way with the residue, consisting of a most picturesque open space, with a grove of the oldest and most beautiful oak trees to be found within twenty miles of London. He was owner of nearly the whole of the inclosed land in the Manor. *Prima facie* inquiries on behalf of the Commons Society failed to discover any

* The Metropolitan Board of Works (Various Powers Act), 1875.

Commoner with rights, on whose behalf proceedings could be taken against the lord, either to compel restitution of the fifty acres already abstracted, or to obtain a declaration of rights, so as to save what remained.

In the Manor of Baston, Sir John Lennard was not so predominant. There was a considerable body of Commoners, who, in 1868, applied to the Inclosure Commissioners for a scheme of regulation of their Common. The lord gave his consent to the scheme, and in the following year an Act was passed to confirm it. By this Act a Board of Conservators was constituted, of which the lord and representatives of the Vestry were members. This part of Hayes Common, therefore, was placed in a position of permanent security. West Wickham Common was not so fortunate. It was not included in the Baston scheme. From time to time public attention was called to the past inclosures of this Common, and to the danger which appeared to threaten what remained, but repeated inquiries by the Society failed to discover any Commoners.

Three or four years ago there were renewed indications of an intention to inclose the residue. Wire fences were erected, cutting it off from Hayes Common. When appealed to on the subject, Sir John Lennard denied that it was a Common, and claimed the land as his freehold, free from any Commoners' rights. About that time a local society was formed for the preservation of Commons and footways in the neighbourhood of Bromley. A discovery was made by this body of a property in West Wickham Manor, with undoubted rights of common over this waste, and whose owner was prepared, with adequate support, to contest Sir John Lennard's right to inclose. The time which had elapsed since the past inclosure was so long, that it was hopeless to contend for restitution, but at least what remained of the Common might be saved. Proceedings were commenced with this object, and a meeting was summoned at Bromley, to be presided over by the writer, with the view of raising funds and arousing public feeling on the subject. Fortunately, however, before the meeting took place it was ascertained that Sir John Lennard was willing to part with his interest in the fifty acres for £2,000, on condition that the Common should be kept open. As the litigation, even if successful, would have involved an expenditure not far short of this, it was thought advisable to compromise on these terms, and the meeting was turned into one for raising this money for the purchase of the lord's rights.*

The sum of £1,500 was obtained locally by subscription, and the residue was made up by the Corporation of London. The purchase was effected. The Common was vested in the Corporation as conservators, and is now safe from further encroachments. The case afforded yet another proof of the truth of the contention before the Committee of 1865, that no matter how hopeless the

---

* The feeling of the meeting was so strong against inclosure, that I had some difficulty in persuading it to adopt the compromise rather than to fight the Lord of the Manor in the Law Courts.

position of a Common might appear to be, there would always, on investigation, be found common rights sufficient to prevent inclosure. It is to be regretted that in this case the discovery of rights was not made in time to claim restitution of the fifty acres inclosed before 1865.

The example of the regulation of Hayes Common was followed in 1871 and 1872 by schemes for the regulation of Blackheath, Shepherd's Bush Common, and the Hackney Commons, under the conservancy of the late Metropolitan Board. Blackheath, consisting of 267 acres, is one of the most valued of the London Commons. It immediately adjoins Greenwich Park, and is the playground of the great population which has grown up near it. For many years the now popular game of golf was played on this heath, when it was quite unknown elsewhere in the south of England. The Blackheath Golf Club claims to date from the time of James I., and to be one of the oldest clubs in the United Kingdom. The Earl of Dartmouth, the owner of a large property in the neighbourhood, now nearly covered by houses, was the Lord of the Manor, and very readily gave his consent to the scheme, which has put the Common under the permanent protection and management of the authorities of London.

The case of the Hackney Commons differs in many respects from those of most of the London Commons. They consist of the Hackney Downs, of 40 acres, the London fields, of 27 acres, the Hackney Marshes, by the side of the river Lea, of 337 acres, and a few smaller areas. The first two of these open spaces are perhaps more important to the health and enjoyment of the people of their district than any others in London. They are in the centre of a dense population, very inadequately supplied with open spaces and breathing-places. They are worn almost bare by the constant use of the public for games. None of these spaces are Commons in the ordinary sense of the term. They are commonable lands, or common fields, survivals of the early system of communal tenure, referred to early in this work. They used to be inclosed during a part of the year, to be held in severalty by divers owners for the haying season, and to be thrown open to the cattle of all on Lammas day. This closing of the land in severalty had long fallen into disuse, in the case of Hackney Downs and London Fields, and no cattle were ever turned out there. The custom of shutting up for severalty was continued in the Hackney Marshes till recently. Mr. Tyssen Amherst, now Lord Amherst of Hackney, the owner of a great property in the district, which has of late years become most valuable for building purposes, is the Lord of the Manor of Hackney. His interest in these Commons, having regard to the rights in severalty of the tenants of his Manor, must have been very small.

In 1872, the Inclosure Commissioners approved of a scheme for the regulation of Hackney Downs and London Fields, not including the Marshes. The Lord of the Manor, in spite of his great interest in the district, and comparatively small interest in the Common Fields, did not consent to it, though he does not appear to have actively opposed. The scheme proposed to make the Metropolitan Board the Conservators of the Commons. It contained, however, no provision, as required by the Act of 1866, that really beneficial rights should not be substantially interfered with without compensation. This serious defect was in vain pointed out to the Board by the Commons Society.

It followed, after the confirmation of the scheme by Parliament, that the Lord of the Manor continued to dig gravel from the two Commons in a manner prejudicial to their user by the public, and contrary to the bye-laws made under the scheme. The Metropolitan Board thereupon brought a suit against him in 1879, to restrain him from doing this. The Master of the Rolls, Sir George Jessel, decided against the Board, on the ground that the Act of 1866 gave no power to the Board to restrain the gravel digging (if there was a right to dig antecedent to the scheme, a point which he did not decide and which was not raised by the Board) without compensation, and that the scheme contained no provision for compensation. In other respects the judgment was a complete vindication of the policy of the Metropolitan Commons Act, for it held that the scheme could properly restrain the lord in the exercise of mere acts of ownership, which were not of a beneficial character to himself; so that he could not keep people off the Common, and could not prevent the Board from appointing Common-keepers, or putting up seats, or draining, levelling,

and improving the surface, and preventing illegal encroachments; but that it could not substantially interfere with rights without compensating for them, though
it might regulate them.

The Board in fact had made a grave mistake in
tactics. It ought to have questioned the right of the
lord to dig gravel on Lammas Land, in the name of a
Commoner. The Board, when it discovered its mistake,
consulted, through its solicitor, the Commons Society,
and it was arranged that the Society should, in the
name of two Commoners, institute a suit against Mr.
Amherst, asking for a declaration of rights in the
Commons, and claiming an injunction against him for
excessive digging of gravel. Proceedings were accordingly commenced, and were conducted to a point when
there appeared to be certainty of success. At this
juncture the solicitor of the Metropolitan Board died;
his successor took a different view as to these proceedings; he advised the Board to withdraw its support
from the Commons Society and from the suit, and to
enter into negotiation for purchase. It resulted that
an arrangement was made with Mr. Tyssen Amherst
for the purchase of his interest for £33,000. This
rendered the further prosecution of the suit unnecessary, and the cost of the proceedings in it fell upon
the Society.

In the opinion of the Commons Society, the purchase
of Mr. Amherst's very shadowy rights for this considerable sum was wholly uncalled for, and would have been
avoided, if the suit had been allowed to proceed, and

v

had been properly supported. It was also a bad precedent for other cases. It followed, when some years later, in 1893, it became necessary to deal with Hackney Marshes, and to propound a scheme for placing this other important space under proper regulation, that Lord Amherst again put forward a claim for compensation on a scale commensurate with the precedent of 1872 ; and the London County Council, hampered doubtless by the bad policy of its predecessor, refused to give its support to the scheme, unless an arrangement were come to with the Lord of the Manor. Negotiations were entered into with him, and the other persons interested in the Common, and it was ultimately arranged that £75,000 should be paid for all the interests in the land, of which £50,000 was to be provided by the London Council, £15,000 by the Hackney Local Board, £5,000 by a private contribution from Lord Amherst, and the remaining £5,000 by public subscription.

The scheme thus matured was later confirmed by Parliament. It was, however, in the opinion of those who had conducted the movement, contrary to the spirit and intention of the Act of 1866, in so far as it provided for the payment of so great a sum to the owners of the soil and the Commoners. Fortunately it is the last transaction where the ratepayers' money in London will be drawn upon for such a purchase, as no other Common now remains undealt with within the district of the London Council.

Clapham, Plumstead, Streatham, Barnes, and

Tooting Graveney Commons, and Bostall Heath and others, which are within the area of the London Council, have been successively dealt with by regulating schemes. In the case of Barnes Common, consisting of 120 acres of most charming scenery, the Dean and Chapter of St. Paul's had been in the position of Lords of the Manor for upwards of 1,000 years under a grant made long before the Norman Conquest. They had always treated the neighbourhood with consideration, and had allowed the management of the Common to be in the hands of a local Committee, supported by voluntary contributions; and this Committee had appointed a Common keeper, and had expended money on improvements. In 1876 it was thought expedient to legalise this arrangement, by a scheme of regulation, placing the Common under the conservancy of the Vestry. The Ecclesiastical Commissioners, representing the Chapter of St. Paul's, without insisting upon any purchase of their rights, gave a ready assent to it.

The case of Clapham Common was very similar. The Manor of Clapham is mentioned in Domesday Book as being in the possession of De Manneville. In the time of King Stephen it was granted to Pharamus de Bolonia, nephew of his wife Maud. The daughter and heiress of Pharamus married De Fienes, who was slain at Ascalon in the Holy Land in 1190. King Richard restored the Manor to the widow of De Fienes, and empowered her to marry whom she liked. It then passed through various hands till it became the property of the Bowyer family. It appears that the Common,

v 2

consisting of about 200 acres, in about equal parts
in the Manor of Clapham and in that of Battersea
and Wandsworth, was, in the beginning of this century,
little better than a morass, till the late Mr. Christopher
Baldwin, a resident on the Common, used his influence
to form a committee of residents to manage it, and to
drain and plant it. In consequence of this, it became
one of the best ordered and most beautiful of the
London Commons. In 1877, on the application of this
committee, and with the consent of the Lords of the
two Manors, it was placed under a regulation scheme,
with the Metropolitan Board as conservators, £18,000
being very unnecessarily paid for the manorial rights.

Beyond the limits of the London County Council,
but within the Metropolitan Police area, the district to
which the Act of 1866 applied, there are very numerous
Commons, with an aggregate of more than 7,700 acres,
exclusive of Epping Forest. Of these, 17 Commons,
with an area of about 3,500 acres, have been placed under
regulation schemes, including Staines Common, 353
acres; Chislehurst, 116; Hayes, 200; Banstead, 1,300;
Mitcham, 570, and others. Of these it may be worth
while to mention the case of Mitcham, as an illustration
of the difficulties arising from the uncertainty as to the
persons entitled as Lords and Commoners.

The history of Mitcham Common, which formerly
contained nearly 900 acres, but which has been reduced
to 570 acres, is very remarkable, and the Common, it is
believed, stands in an unique position. The Common
originally lay in the parishes of Mitcham, Beddington,

and Wallington, and the Lords of no less than seven Manors—viz., Mitcham, Ravensbury, Biggin and Tamworth, Vauxhall, Beddington, and Wallington—claimed that parts of it were wastes of their Manors.

There have never been any boundaries between the various Manors, so far as the Common was concerned, and it had been left, therefore, for a long period of time in a most neglected and uncared-for state. Lords of Manors had wrought havoc on its surface by gravel-digging, and railway companies had done their best to destroy it by running lines in several directions over it. The Manors, in which the Common is supposed to lie, are all recorded in Domesday Book. The Prior of Merton, the Prior of St. Mary, Southwark, and the Prior of Canterbury acquired some of these Manors in very early times, and at the dissolution they were granted by Henry VIII. to Sir Nicholas Carewe and other persons.

This Common has been the subject of dispute, as regards the rights of the Commoners, from the earliest times to the present day. As long ago as the 24th year of Henry III., A.D. 1239, an action of trespass, then known as an assize of novel disseisin, was brought by the Prior of Merton, Lord of the Manor of Biggin and Tamworth, against the owners of land in Beddington, because the latter had driven off and impounded the Prior's cattle. The jury found that the owners of lands in all the parishes, or "vills," named above, had intercommoned on Mitcham Common as one waste. Later, disputes constantly arose between the Lords of the different Manors

of Mitcham and their Commoners, with respect to inclosures, but the great uncertainty as to the boundaries
of the Manors made it difficult to resist. In 1535,
a hundred acres were inclosed by the Lord of the
Manor of Beddington, and 200 acres were inclosed in
1820. In 1882 the Lord of the Manor of Wallington
commenced to assert his right to inclose a small portion
of the Common. The Commoners and inhabitants
determined to oppose. Mr. Bidder, Q.C., a resident in
the district, put himself at the head of the movement,
and brought a suit in the usual form to restrain the
inclosure, alleging his rights over Mitcham Common.
Owing, however, to the extraordinary conflict of evidence in the early and late records, it was impossible to
show conclusively that the piece inclosed was part of
this Common, and the Court held that the plaintiffs had
failed to establish their case.

Looking at all the documents dispassionately from
1086 to the present day, one is almost driven to the
conclusion that this fine tract of Common never formed
part of the possessions of any Manor. It appears that,
in very early times, the King held all of the Manors
interested, and granted them out without any specific
reference to the Common, and also granted out smaller
tracts of land in the same parishes as those in which the
Manors were situated. The consequence may have been
that the Common was retained as a Crown possession,
or, perhaps, was looked upon as public property, or
"folk-land," upon which all the neighbouring landowners might exercise common rights.

Happily the Common is now out of danger. By the advice of Mr. Birkett, the Solicitor to the Commons Society, an influential meeting of the inhabitants was held, in 1891, who decided to avail themselves of the provisions of the Metropolitan Commons Act. The usual steps were taken and inquiries held, and notwithstanding considerable opposition, the Common was placed under an elective body of Conservators. The small piece of waste, referred to as being inclosed by the Lord of Wallington, was unfortunately omitted from the scheme at the last moment, and litigation in respect to it has broken out afresh, and it has yet to be determined whether the lord can inclose against those who have rights of common in respect of that Manor. The waste of this Manor is, however, but a small fraction of Mitcham Common, and substantially the Common has been put into a position of safety under the guardianship of the ratepayers of the district.

There remain very numerous Commons with an aggregate area of about 4,600 acres, within the Metropolitan Police district, which might be brought under regulation schemes under the Act of 1866. Among them are the Epsom Commons, 870 acres; Tottenham Marshes, 180 acres; Hadley Common, 174 acres; Carshalton, 150 acres; Stanmore, 127 acres; Dartford, 360 acres; Ham Common, 126 acres; the Thames Ditton Commons, 300 acres, and others. Of these it may be well to refer to Epsom Common. In 1865 the Inclosure Commissioners approved and certified to Parliament a

scheme for the inclosure of Epsom Downs and Epsom
Common. The subject was carefully inquired into by
the Committee of 1865. The Steward of the Manor,
and the promoters of the inclosure, gave strong evidence
as to the expediency of this course, and as to the exclusive interest of the Lord of the Manor. On the other
hand, there was evidence of a powerful local feeling to
the contrary. The Committee reported against the inclosure, and the scheme was defeated. Since then, the
relations of the Lord of the Manor, the Commoners, and
the inhabitants of Epsom, have been in a state of tension,
aggravated by the position of the Grand Stand Association, who claim certain rights in respect of the
annual races held on the Downs, by virtue of a lease
from the Lord of the Manor.

A course of petty encroachments has been pursued
by the Lord of the Manor, intended to confirm his claim
to an absolute ownership of the land. In 1888 a Committee of Commoners, including Lord Rosebery, the
owner of an adjoining property, commenced a suit
against the Lord of the Manor and the Grand Stand
Association. This suit was stayed pending an application to the Agricultural Department for a scheme for
regulating the Common. On their part the Board of
Agriculture have declined to proceed with a regulating
scheme so long as the suit is undetermined. A deadlock
has consequently ensued. It is to be hoped that one
result of the Banstead scheme will be to remove the
difficulties respecting a scheme for Epsom Common.

Under the Act of 1876 there have been schemes

passed for regulating twenty-three Commons beyond the Metropolitan Police district, with an aggregate area of 31,300 acres. Most of these have been cases of mountain districts, where the object has been to define and regulate the Commoners' rights. Some of them, however, have been cases of Commons in populous parts, such as Red Hill Common, near Reigate, of 324 acres ; Totternhoe, in Hertfordshire, 234 acres, and Clent Common in Worcestershire. In these and other cases, special provisions have been inserted giving to the inhabitants of the districts the right of walking and playing games over the whole of the Commons. Ashdown Forest, of 6,000 acres, was also placed under a regulating scheme, after the long litigation to which it was subjected. Other Commons have been dealt with for special reasons under private Acts, based on the principle of regulation. Thus the beautiful range of open land in the Malvern Hills, near Malvern, of 6,000 acres, has been subjected to regulation under a special Act, and thus secured for public enjoyment. Torrington Common and Bournemouth Common have been similarly treated.

There can be no doubt that very numerous other Commons would be placed under regulating schemes, if it were not for the very rigid requirements of the Act of 1876, namely the consent of two-thirds in value of the Commoners and of the Lord of the Manor. There can be no possible reason why the same facilities which have been found expedient and necessary in the interest of the public in the case of Commons within fifteen miles of London, should not be extended to all other Commons in the country, or why the Lords of Manors should be allowed an absolute veto to schemes. After the decision of Parliament in the case of Banstead Common, in which, in spite of the most determined opposition in both Houses, it was approved that the Common should be practically taken out of the sole hands of the Lord of the Manor and placed under the control and management of a popularly elected body, it will be impossible to resist the extension of this policy to all other Commons in every part of the country. In cases near to towns, the municipal authorities would be the proper guardians and managers of their Commons. In regard to rural Commons, either the County Council or the District Council should be the Conservators, with certain duties delegated to Parish Councils.*

* In the Appendices will be found lists of Commons, which have been regulated under the Acts of 1866 and 1876 respectively.

CHAPTER XIX.

ATTACKS BY RAILWAY COMPANIES.

CHIEF among the dangers to which Commons were exposed before 1865, were the invasions of them by Railway Companies. Already several Commons had been seriously disfigured, if not irreparably injured, by railway companies having, in a very needless way as it appeared, intersected them with their lines, severing one part completely from another, interfering with their prospects, and destroying that charm, which results from rural solitude, and which constitutes, in the case of Commons near to towns, so much of their value. This was notably the case with Wandsworth, Banstead, Tooting, Mitcham, and Barnes Commons. It seemed that neither the local authorities of the district, if any, nor the inhabitants generally, nor even individual Commoners, were allowed a *locus standi* to appear before Select Committees of either House of Parliament for the purpose of objecting, in the interest of the public, to private Bills promoted by companies, or even of pointing out how the objectionable features of the schemes might be avoided or minimised. The Lords of Manors were generally not concerned in protecting their Commons from such invasions; it was rather their interest to invite them; for they realised their interest in the portions of Commons taken, and the award of the purchase money might necessitate

an ascertainment, by legal proofs, of those entitled to
Common rights, and might give important assistance in
any schemes for buying up the rights and inclosing
under the Statute of Merton.*

The promoters, so far from avoiding Commons, appear
to have intentionally laid their lines through them,
because they were certain of finding no opposition, and
because the purchase money payable for the land would
be less than for private and inclosed land. This arose
not only from the fact that the land was waste and
uncultivated, but from the mode in which compensation
was (and is still) ascertained and paid. The land in
such case is not valued as a whole, and the compensation
subsequently divided amongst the Lords and Commoners.
The Lords' interest in the soil is first purchased by
agreement or assessment; the Commoners are then called
upon to appoint a committee, and with this committee
the Company treats for the acquisition of the Common
rights. It is obvious that this method enables the
Company to cheapen the Lords' rights by reference to
the Commoners, and the Commoners' rights by the
Lords, and in this way to pay considerably less than
the full value of the land, taken as a whole, for the
amount would be less than for private and uninclosed
land. It was left to chance whether Parliamentary

---

* At Banstead, for example, as has been shown, the awards of the
Inclosure Commission distributing the money paid by the Brighton
Company for cutting through the downs, suggested to the Lord of the
Manor the idea of purchasing the rights of common and inclosing
the Commons.

Committees, to whom railway schemes were referred, had their attention directed to the injury done to public interests by the destruction of the value of Commons, or took any steps to protect them. To reject the whole of a scheme for a new line of railway, necessary for the advantage of the people at either end, because at one point it did injury to the public by intersecting a Common, would appear to most Committees a very serious responsibility.

The Commons Society determined, at the outset of its proceedings, to do its utmost to oppose and prevent such invasions in the future, and to make promoters of railways understand that it was their interest to avoid injury to Commons, if they hoped to carry their schemes. Railway companies were not the only offenders in this direction. Local authorities not unfrequently cast their eyes upon open spaces, with a view to convert them into sewage farms,* cemeteries, and water works, at a cost less than would have to be paid for inclosed lands. It was necessary to control these bodies, and to enlighten local opinion as to the importance of restraining the authorities from doing permanent injury to their Commons.

It was determined to attack such schemes in the

---

* On the eve of the transfer of Lord Spencer's rights in Wimbledon Common to the public, the Wimbledon Local Board (on which were some prominent members of the Local Commons Preservation Committee) proposed to acquire 300 acres of the Common for a sewage farm, and the proposal might probably have been carried, had not the Crown as a Commoner interfered by litigation to prevent it.

House of Commons, on the second reading of the Bills
containing them. Fortunately, the Society had within
its ranks several members of Parliament, who were
willing to undertake this task—one which in its in-
ception was invidious, as the course was a novel one,
and the House was unwilling to debate private Bills,
before referring them to Select Committees. It was
felt, however, that questions of public welfare were
far better dealt with in the full light of the whole
House, than in Committees where the railway companies were represented by the ablest counsel of the
day, and where public interests as a rule had been
disregarded or not protected.

In the first three years after the constitution of the
Society, it resisted and defeated three or four schemes
of railway companies for invading London Commons,
notably cases for intersecting Barnes Common, Hampstead Heath and Mitcham Common. It also defeated
a proposal of the Kingston Corporation to take 100
acres of Wimbledon Common for a sewage farm. It
was hoped that these cases had given a lesson to
promoters, and for some few years there was no serious
attack on the London Commons. By 1877 the lesson
appeared to have been forgotten, and several proposals
came before Parliament involving grave injury to Commons by railways and other schemes.

One difficulty which occurred arose from the fact that
it was by mere chance that information was obtained as
to whether, in any year, the multitudinous Private Bills
before Parliament, with schemes for every part of the

country, contained any objectionable proposals in this
direction. It was an impossible task to search through
the Books of Reference and deposited Bills, with a view
to discover whether any Commons were threatened. To
obviate this difficulty, I moved, in 1877, an amendment
to the Standing Orders of the House of Commons,
requiring promoters of private Bills to advertise, in the
London Gazette and in local papers, whether they
proposed to take any portions of Commons for their
works, and to state the extent which it was sought to
acquire, and also to deposit plans with the Home Office,
showing the details of the appropriation. The House of
Commons willingly assented to the Standing Order.
It had an immediate and important effect in disclosing
the nature and extent of the invasions by promoters of
all kinds on Commons, in every part of the country,
and in enabling the Commons Society to take measures
for opposing and preventing them.

In every succeeding year it appeared that there
were very large numbers of such schemes, more or less
interfering with and injuring Commons, amounting in
1880 and 1881 to forty and forty-one respectively, and in
other years to somewhat smaller numbers. These were
submitted to careful examination by the Society, and
formed the subject of local inquiry. Communications
were made with the local authorities and people of the
districts thus threatened, and negotiations were entered
into with the promoters.

There are very few Commons near London which
have not been menaced, during the last twenty years,

with expropriation of parts of their areas by railway companies or local authorities, but fortunately these attempts have almost always been defeated.

In 1877 a determined effort was made by the railway companies to prevent interference with their schemes in this respect. A proposal came before Parliament on behalf of the London and Brighton Railway, to make a branch line through the centre of Mitcham Common, severing it in two and taking eight and a half acres for the purpose of the line— a project which would have practically ruined the Common.

I moved the rejection of this Bill on its second reading. The railway companies gathered together all their force of directors in the House. They were supported by the Government whips, and by the Chairman of Committees. They defeated the motion by 143 to 100. The majority was mainly composed of railway directors. They only achieved this victory by agreeing to waive objection to the _locus standi_ of the inhabitants of Mitcham to be heard before the Select Committee. As a result of their evidence, the Committee rejected this part of the proposals of the Company, and the Common was saved.* In the same year the Croydon Local Board proposed in a Bill to

---

* It has frequently been the case, as in this instance, that a motion on second reading, though rejected by the House on a division, has saved the Common or open space threatened by the Bill, by leading to the subsequent rejection or amendment of the Bill by the Select Committee.

expropriate 100 acres of Mitcham Common for a
sewage farm. This was opposed by the Commons
Society and was ultimately withdrawn.

In the same year the London and South-Western
Railway introduced a Bill for taking a considerable
slice of Barnes Common, for a coal-siding. The Local
Board of Richmond also proposed to expropriate a part
of the same Common for a cemetery. Both of these
schemes were successfully opposed. Thenceforward
scarcely a year passed in which there were not several
schemes before Parliament for taking portions of Commons for railways, sewage farms, or cemeteries. They
were uniformly resisted by the Commons Society, and
were almost invariably defeated. Thus Wimbledon
Common was saved in 1880 from a serious invasion of
a railway company. Epping Forest was attacked in the
same way, in 1880 and 1883, and on each occasion the
proposals were defeated. In 1883 Mr. Bryce moved
an amendment on the second reading of a Bill for this
purpose, that "the House, while expressing no opinion
as to the propriety of making a railway to High
Beech in Epping Forest, disapproves of any scheme
which involves the taking of any part of the surface of
Epping Forest, which by the Epping Forest Act, 1878,
was directed to be kept 'at all times uninclosed and
unbuilt on, as an open space for the enjoyment of
the public.'" This was carried by a majority of 230 to
82, and the Bill was rejected. In the same year the
Didcot, Newbury, and Southampton Railway Company
proposed to construct a line through the very centre of the

w

most beautiful part of the New Forest; this also was successfully opposed, with the aid of Sir William Harcourt.

Numerous other cases of the same kind occurred. It came at last to be understood by railway companies that they had far better come to terms with the Commons Society, than attempt to fight it in the House of Commons. The Society in its negotiations with companies, has insisted that, where possible, new lines of railways should altogether avoid passing through Commons, especially when in the neighbourhood of towns; that where such a course was inevitable, the line should be constructed either in a tunnel or on the principle of "cut and cover," so as to avoid disfiguring the Common; and that where as was often the case small parts of Commons were required, the companies should undertake to add equivalent land in other directions so as to avoid reducing their areas.

The Society has also come into conflict with powerful Corporations. In 1878 the Corporation of Manchester proposed a scheme for taking Lake Thirlmere, in Cumberland, as a reservoir for the supply of water to their city, and it also proposed to expropriate a great area of Commons in the adjoining hills as a collecting ground for the water. The public had always enjoyed access to these open spaces, and it would have been possible for the Corporation, by acquiring these lands, to exclude them in the future. By threatening opposition, the Society induced the Corporation to insert a clause in their Bill to the effect "that the access heretofore enjoyed on the part of the public and tourists to the mountains and fells surrounding Lake Thirlmere shall not be in any manner restricted or interfered with by the Corporation."

In 1892 a similar proposal was made by the Corporation of Birmingham, on even a larger scale, in connection with the supply of water to their town. They introduced a Bill to enable them to purchase, in the mountain regions of South Wales, the sources of the rivers Elan and Clairwen, with a very great area of adjoining land, and with no less than fifty square miles of open and uninclosed land subject to common rights. It proposed to buy up all the rights over this immense district, and to convert it into the private property of the Corporation. The rights of common were enjoyed by a great number of small farmers to whose occupation they were essentially necessary as a means of existence; the public also had largely resorted to these hills for the sake of their fine air and scenery.

It appeared to the Commons Society that though it might be requisite that the Corporation, for the sake of securing the purity of its water supply, should have large powers over the collecting ground, yet it was quite unnecessary to deprive the small farmers of their rights of common, or to convert the land into private property. The scheme, in fact, was in this respect a great inclosure, without any of the securities afforded to the public, the commoners, and the labouring people of the district by an ordinary Inclosure award, which would have to be submitted to local inquiry, approved by the Agricultural Department, and confirmed by the Standing Committee of the House of Commons.

w 2

The Society determined to come to issue with the Corporation of Birmingham on this point. I moved on its behalf in the House of Commons, on the second reading of the Bill, that it should be an instruction to the Committee " to inquire and report whether it was necessary to extinguish the rights of common and the user of the Commons by farmers over so wide a district, and whether provisions should be inserted for securing to the public free access to the Commons proposed to be acquired." The instruction was at first vehemently opposed by Mr. Chamberlain, on behalf of the Birmingham Corporation, but the sense of the House was so strongly in favour of it that he withdrew his opposition, and the instruction was carried. As a result, the Committee to whom the Bill was referred, conceded all that we asked for. A clause was inserted, at the instance of Mr. Birkett, the solicitor of the Commons Society, saving the Commoners' rights over the district, and also securing to the public for ever the right of entering upon the land and walking freely over the range of hills. The clause went beyond that in the Thirlmere Act. That measure only secured to the public the same access to the hills as they had enjoyed in the past. The Birmingham Act gave to the public a *jus spatiandi*, or the right of roaming over the districts concerned.

It has not always been possible to induce Corporations to forego their schemes, framed in the interest of economy, to expropriate portions of Commons in their neighbourhood for the purpose of cemeteries. Two such cases have occurred in the last few years—those affecting Bulwell Common, near Nottingham, and the Bournemouth Commons. It is believed, however, that these are rare exceptions, and the view is now generally held that it is not wise to reduce the area of open land near towns for such purposes. In the case of the Corporation of Torrington, in Devonshire, a Bill came before Parliament in 1889, raising a kindred question. The Commons near this town are beautifully situated, lying on the crest of a lofty ridge rising abruptly from the river Torridge, and with an area of 300 acres. There had been disputes between the Commoners and the owners of the Rolle estate for many years, and the Bill was designed to put an end to them. It was proposed to vest these lands in the Corporation, giving them power to inclose and lay out for building purposes 100 acres, or one-third of them. The Commons Society gave notice of their intention to oppose the scheme, on the ground that it was not to the general welfare that these open spaces should be reduced by so large an amount. Public interest in Torrington was aroused on the subject; meetings were held to protest against the scheme, and ultimately, negotiations with the Corporation resulted in their abandoning this part of their measure. The Torrington Commons, therefore, will remain intact and secured for the public use and enjoyment.

These proceedings in Parliament, in opposition to Railway Companies and Corporations, had an indirect effect beyond their immediate object. They gradually educated public opinion to a full perception of the great importance of preserving such open spaces, and they strengthened continually the idea that the Commons are in a sense public property. For what end should attacks by Railway Companies be resisted, if later the Lords of Manors were to be allowed, under the Statute of Merton, or otherwise, to inclose and appropriate them for purely private purposes? These discussions therefore contributed, in no small degree, in combination with the great suits, which have been described in this work, to lead public opinion to the point, when it was possible at last to deal with the Statute of Merton in the manner which will be indicated in the next and last chapter.

CHAPTER XX.

The Repeal of the Statute of Merton.

It was shown in an early chapter that the Committee of the House of Commons, on London Commons, in 1865, advised by a large majority, as the first and most important step for securing them to the public, that the Statute of Merton should be repealed. They contended that the Statute, originally passed in the interest of agriculture, had long ago ceased to have this justification; that for centuries it had been recognised by most, if not all lawyers, that inclosures could not safely or justly, with regard to all the interests concerned, be made under it, or without the special sanction of Parliament; that the proposition urged on behalf of the Lords that the non-user of rights of pasture over Commons, near London or elsewhere, had amounted to an abandonment of them, and that the Lords had practically become owners in fee of the land, free from any rights, was unsound and would not be maintained, if inclosure was resisted in the Law Courts; that the temptation to revive the obsolete Statute for the purpose of converting the London Commons into building land should be removed; and that Lords of Manors should not be allowed arbitrarily to inclose portions of Commons under the Statute, trusting to the Commoners being unwilling or unable to bear the heavy cost of resisting them by legal proceedings.

The Government of the day unfortunately refused to adopt this advice and to repeal the Statute of Merton. There followed the long series of aggressions on Commons which have been described in this work. The Lords of Manors did their utmost to put in force their doctrines, and, by inclosing, to realise the great difference between the value of the Commons, as waste land, and as building sites. There resulted that which the Committee of 1865 expected and predicted. In every case of attempted inclosure, some public-spirited persons were found to undertake the cause of the Commoners, and indirectly of the public, and to contest the legality of the inclosures. Years passed by while this protracted and expensive litigation was proceeding, and as one by one the cases came to issue in the Courts, the contentions of the Committee were confirmed, and the pretensions of the Lords of Manors were condemned and frustrated.

Out of the seventeen cases which have been tried in the Courts, in proceedings for the purpose of preventing inclosure of Commons, by the advice of the Commons Society, and generally with the assistance of their able lawyers, there was not one in which the Lord of a Manor was able to justify his proceedings under the Statute of Merton. The cases of Berkhamsted, Plumstead, Tooting, Coulsdon, Epping Forest, Ashdown Forest, Dartford, Banstead, Wigley, Malvern and Walton formed an unbroken series of victories. In four other cases there was practical surrender by the Lords of Manors without coming to a decision in the Courts. This was doubtless due to successes which had been achieved in the other and principal cases.

The only two cases in which the results were unsatisfactory, those of Tollard Farnham and Rowley Green, were not inclosures under the Statute of Merton. The Tollard Farnham case turned upon the right of the inhabitants to provide themselves with fuel under a local custom. In the Rowley Green case, the inclosure was justified under a special custom of the Manor, not under the Statute of Merton.

Although these decisions in the Courts of Law completely bore out the contentions of the Committee of 1865, that the Statute of Merton was practically obsolete, and that inclosures under it, if resisted, would be defeated, yet there remained a constant danger of the Act being used for arbitrary inclosures, owing to the unwillingness or inability of the Commoners to oppose them in the Law Courts. The spirit of encroachment may slumber for a time, but is always on the watch for opportunities. The fear of resistance may deter the inclosure of open spaces in populous districts, but it is not of much avail to prevent the filching of bits of rural Commons. It was scarcely less important a year ago, as a measure of precaution, than it was thirty years ago, to repeal the Statute, or to deprive it of its danger.

As the Commons suits were decided in the Law Courts, it appeared that the arguments in favour of the repeal of this Statute, under which such wrongs

were attempted to be perpetrated, were greatly
strengthened; and from time to time the question was
raised in the House of Commons, at the instance of
the Commons Society. Thus, in the year 1871, in
the Select Committee on the Commons Bill which I
had introduced, Mr. Cowper Temple moved an amendment for the repeal of the Statute of Merton. He
was defeated by a majority of ten to four, in spite of
the fact that a majority of the members of the Committee were Liberals. Again, in the discussions in
Committee on Lord Cross's measure in 1876, the
same question was raised in various forms. I proposed
myself a new clause to secure that no Commons
should thenceforward be inclosed without the sanction
of Parliament. The Minister in charge of the Bill had
said on this that "he hoped no British Parliament would
ever consent to a scheme of pure confiscation, such as
was involved in the proposal." The clause, at his
instance, was rejected by a majority of 206 to 82.
Lord Edmund Fitzmaurice, at a later stage, renewed
the proposal by moving a new clause for the repeal
of the Statute of Merton. It was negatived by a
majority of 79 to 28. Lastly, Sir William Harcourt
proposed a clause providing that the "unlawful inclosure of any Common, or part of a Common, should
be deemed to be a public nuisance." This would
have made it possible for any outsider to raise a question as to the legality of an inclosure, quite irrespective
of whether he had any right of common or not, and
would have enabled the local authorities of a district

to undertake the cause of the Commoners, and to fight their battle against an inclosing Lord of the Manor. The clause was rejected by 64 to 30.

One definite advantage, however, resulted from these discussions. The Government at length consented, at the instance of Lord Henry Scott (now Lord Montagu), to insert a clause providing that any person proposing to inclose Common land otherwise than under the Inclosure Acts, should advertise his intention in the local papers, three months in advance. It will be seen that, combined with recent legislation, this provision may become of considerable value.

Later, between the years 1880 and 1890, the Commons Society, in every recurring Session, endeavoured through its members to obtain a discussion on a Bill for the repeal of the Statute of Merton, but never succeeded in doing so. Lord Meath, in a Bill dealing with Commons, introduced in the Lords in 1890, proposed a clause with this object. It was discussed in the Grand Committee of the Lords, and was strongly supported by Lord Herschell, on the ground that the Statute was obsolete, and that the long course of litigation of late years had proved that it was only put in force in the hopes that Commoners would be unwilling to incur the heavy expense of resisting inclosure. The clause was rejected by a large majority of their Lordships. It seemed, therefore, hopeless to expect that any measure would ever pass both Houses of the Legislature for effecting our purpose, and for repealing an Act which had been 600 years on the Statute Book.

Most unexpectedly, however, a remedy was found at last, which had its origin not in the representative House, but in the House of Lords. It came about in this manner. It has been already pointed out that in many Manors the practice had obtained of inclosing small portions of the waste, under the authority of a custom to make new copyhold grants, with the consent of the homage of Copyholders. Probably the practice originated in the desire to legalize encroachments. Some labouring man squatted on a Common, and took in a piece of the waste for a garden, pig-sty, or cart-shed to his adjoining cottage. Neither the Lord of the Manor nor any one else wanted to throw out such a petty encroachment. If, however, it was suffered to remain without condition of any kind, both Lord and Commoners were prejudiced. Again, if the Lord simply levied a rent, the Commoners were damnified. Under these circumstances, the idea occurred to some one, probably to an ingenious steward, of a copyhold grant. The encroacher was made to petition the lord at a Common Court for a grant of the piece of land in question. The tenants present on the homage-jury were consulted, and if they approved, the land was granted, with their consent and on such conditions as they might impose, to be held by copy of Court Roll. After a time the legality of this practice was challenged. It was argued that, as copyhold tenure depends absolutely on ancient custom, all copyhold land must be deemed to have been such from time immemorial, and the creation of a new copyhold was inconsistent with the very nature of the tenure. Under these circumstances the Law Courts did what they have so often done; they invented a theory to justify arrangements, which were considered to be convenient. They upheld the custom on the ground that the whole waste, of which portions were from time to time granted, must be deemed to have been demisable by copy of Court Roll time out of mind, and might, therefore, be actually so demised or granted in portions from time to time. This decision was given in 1803.* Under its authority grants of waste multiplied, and the practice was probably introduced in many Manors where it had not previously obtained.

The custom was carried in the case of Rowley Green, as has been shown, to the point of allowing the Lord of the Manor to select himself three or four copyholders to form the Homage, and with their consent to inclose not only as against other copyholders not present and not summoned, but against other persons with rights over the Common, quite independent of the copyholders.†

This creation of new copyholds did little harm, while the practice was confined to its original object, that of legalizing small encroachments, made in the interests of the labouring class, or of effecting some trifling inclosure for a public purpose. But as land increased in value in the neighbourhood of London and large towns, advantage was taken of the custom to make money for the Lord. Either valuable inclosures

---

* Lord Northwick *v.* Hanway : B. and P., 346.
† *Supra* pp. 225-7.

were granted for considerable sums of money, or arrangements were made by which the lord himself obtained
the benefit of the grant, and consequent inclosure.

In Epping Forest, to quote a striking case, no less
than 1,883 acres were inclosed under the assumed
sanction of customs to create copyholds out of the waste;
and part of this area was granted to trustees for the
Lords, and thus passed into the Lords' hands. At the
same time the consent of the tenants was reduced to a
mere form. The homage-jury of tenants attending at the
Court was selected by the Steward; no public notice of
any proposal to grant such was given; and in many
cases the grant became a simple matter of arrangement
between the grantee and the Steward, confirmed by the
verdict of two or three copyholders, who had themselves
obtained land on easy terms by the same means, or
hoped to do so in the future.

These facts had long been known to the advisers of
the Commons Society, and the usage of creating new
Copyholds, at the expense of Commoners, was looked
upon as one of the most dangerous weapons of inclosure
which the Society had to encounter. But it was not
easy to devise a means to protect Commons from a
danger to which the general public were hardly alive.
In 1887, however, a Bill was introduced to bring about
the speedy enfranchisement of Copyholds and the total
abolition of the tenure. It occurred to Mr. Robert
Hunter, who had seen the dangers attending the course
of the custom, in prosecuting the litigation relating to
Epping Forest and other Commons, that this Bill

afforded an opportunity of checking a pernicious practice. The Bill was introduced by Lord Hobhouse in the House of Lords, and referred to a strong Committee, of which the noble Lord was Chairman, and on which the late Lord Bramwell, Lord Kimberley, and other prominent Peers sat as members. Lord Hobhouse had acted as arbitrator in the Epping Forest Case, and had seen something of the working of the custom. Mr. Hunter suggested to him that provision should be made by the Bill to prevent the creation of new Copyholds, and was invited to give evidence before the Committee. He explained the nature of the custom of granting waste as copyhold, the extent to which it prevailed, and the abuses which had been grafted upon it; and he urged that it was inconsistent to pass a measure designed to effect a speedy and general enfranchisement of existing Copyholds, without some provision which should prevent the creation of new tenures. Mr. Hunter also pointed out that all the objections to the continuance of existing Copyholds, such as the complication of titles from the intermixture of freehold and copyhold lands, would be perpetuated if it were allowed to bring new Copyholds into existence. He further urged that a practice which had originated in a claim to meet public requirements, had been converted into a new means of aggrandizing Lords of Manors, while at the same time the safeguards which had formerly held the practice in check had disappeared. He repudiated the suggestion that compensation should be paid to the Lord if the custom were abolished, and proposed that, if it was thought necessary to provide any substitute, it should take the form of the grant of small farms as freehold, with the consent of the Vestry of the Parish, after due public notice.

The Committee, in the result, substantially accepted the views thus placed before them, substituting the consent of the Land Commission for that of the Vestry, and inserted in the Bill (which afterwards became law under the title of the Copyhold Act, 1887) a clause in the following words :—

"After the passing of this Act, it shall not be lawful for the Lord of any Manor to make grants of land not previously of Copyhold tenure to any person to hold by copy of Court Roll, or by any tenure of a customary nature, without the previous consent of the Land Commissioners, who, in giving or withholding their consent, shall have regard to the same considerations as are to be taken into account by them on giving or withholding their consent to any inclosure of Common lands ; and whenever any such grant has been lawfully made, the land therein comprised shall cease to be of Copyhold tenure, and shall be vested in the grantee thereof to hold for the interest granted as in free and common socage." *

The exact legal effect of this clause may in some respects be open to doubt. While it absolutely negatives the creation of new Copyholders, it assumes that the power of grant previously used will be maintained, and it does not in terms release any land, which a Lord may grant with the consent required by the Act, from the common rights previously existing over the land. But the important point in the interests of open spaces is, that no grant of any part of a Common, under any

* 50 and 51 Vic. c. 73, sec. 6.

alleged custom, can in future be made without the consent of the Board of Agriculture, who are directed, in effect, not to sanction the grant unless they are convinced that it is for the public benefit. Thus all inclosures under such alleged customs are brought under public control. The principle of the clause is far-reaching, and, as we shall see, has paved the way for a treatment of the Statute of Merton, which will render that Act also harmless in the future. It was not, however, till some time after the enactment of this clause, and till experience had been obtained of its working, that the Commons Society perceived the use which might be made of it as a precedent for dealing with other inclosures.

During the four years after the passing of the Copyhold Act, six applications were made to the Agricultural Department for approval of inclosures under this clause relating to grants of the wastes of Manors. In two only of them was the consent of the Board given. These were cases of applications for two very small plots of land, sufficient only for wells, which were required for the supply of water to the public. The other cases were refused on the ground that no public benefit could be shown to result from the inclosures. The Department therefore have acted in full accord with the spirit of the clause, and with the principles laid down in the preamble of the Commons Act of 1876. Practically, therefore, it may be concluded that no further proceedings will be possible under these customs of Manors, unless it be proved that the public interest is distinctly concerned in them.

x

The consideration of these cases at the beginning of last year, 1893, first suggested to me that the principle of the clause in the Copyhold Act might be applied equally to inclosures under the Statute of Merton, and that the argument in favour of such a course might be used with great force, and with every prospect of success in the House of Lords, where the clause had originated. In this view a Bill was drawn in exact accord with the clause in the Copyhold Act, but applying to inclosures under the Statute of Merton. Lord Thring was induced to take charge of this measure on behalf of the Commons Society. It was hoped that, under the shadow of the precedent of 1887, it might pass the Lords without much notice. It was, however, detected by Lord Salisbury, who made a powerful speech against it on the second reading.

"This is a Bill," he said, "simply to take away from landowners or Lords of Manors a right which they have had under Statute for six centuries, and to take it without a whisper or shadow of compensation . . . I do not believe the Statute of Merton, as it at present acts, does any harm. On the contrary, I believe that in the past it has done a great deal of good, and that it is largely the cause of the extensive cultivation of the poorer land in this country. But be that as it may, this right has been in the Lords of Manors without contest for six centuries, and it is contrary to all the principles by which Parliament guarantees the sanctity of property in this country, that property should be taken without some compensation." *

In a later speech in the Grand Committee on the Bill, he spoke of the Bill as a measure of spoliation, and

* Parliamentary Debates, vol. xv., p. 604.

added—"Except in the neighbourhood of large towns, all this cry about Commons preservation has a very large element of bunkum in it."

The Bill was defended on the second reading by Lord Thring, Lord Hobhouse, Lord Ribblesdale, Lord Selborne, and the Lord Chancellor ; and to the surprise of everyone Lord Salisbury, who had moved its rejection and who was supported by Lord Cross, was defeated in the division. The measure was read a second time by 32 votes to 23, and was ultimately carried through the House of Lords without much further difficulty. In the House of Commons it also passed without opposition or even discussion.*

It is difficult to exaggerate the importance of this Act. It is most significant of the change of public opinion that it should have passed through the House of Lords, in spite of the opposition of the leader of the majority there, and through the House of Commons, without a single protest. It has practically achieved the object which those who have advocated the right of the public over the Commons have aimed at since the commencement of the movement thirty years ago, but always hitherto in vain. Although it does not in terms repeal the Statute of Merton, it completely takes the sting out of that measure, and renders it quite innocuous, and will prevent its being made use of in the future by Lords of Manors for arbitrary inclosures, in the manner so often described in this work.

Henceforth, any Lord of the Manor desiring to

* Commons Law Amendment Act, 56 & 57 Vict., c. 57.

x 2

inclose under these Statutes, must obtain in advance the consent of the Board of Agriculture. This alone will be a most valuable security, for it will entail publicity, and will give opportunity for inquiry, and for the raising of objections on the part of Commoners or the public. But the Act goes much further, for it directs that the Board, in giving or withholding their consent, are to take into consideration the same questions which they are bound to entertain before consenting to inclosure under the Commons Act of 1876. In other words, it must be proved to their satisfaction that the inclosure will be of benefit to the public. The public interest is therefore imported for the first time by the Act of 1893, as a necessary condition to future proceedings under the Statute of Merton.

Furthermore, the clause in Lord Cross's Act of 1876, requiring a Lord of the Manor to give notice of his intention to inclose a portion of a Common, by an advertisement in the local papers three months before effecting it, becomes, in combination with the recent Act, for the first time a provision of value and efficiency. The Board of Agriculture, as in the case of inclosures under the Copyhold Act, will in the first instance, before entertaining a proposal to inclose under the Statute of Merton, insist that this notice shall have been given; the notice will give rise to objections. The Board must then be satisfied by the lord that the inclosure will be of benefit to the public. There will further arise the question whether a sufficiency of Common will be left for the Commoners. The Board will not give their consent unless there be some strong proof of this. But their decision will not prevent any Commoner from appealing to the Law Courts.

The most important bar, however, to inclosures under the New Act, will be the necessity of proving that the public interest will be promoted by them. This introduces a new element, fatal to the general pretensions of Lords of Manors. Hitherto they have not been compelled to have regard for public interests in their transactions under the ancient Statute. Private gain and aggrandisement, the desire to convert the Common into building land, or to add it to their parks or game preserves, have been their main or only motives. It is only necessary to consider how this new principle would have operated in the proceedings, which have been described in this work, to appreciate what a protection to the public it would have been. It may be claimed, with the utmost confidence, that in no one of these cases could the Board of Agriculture have been satisfied that the public interest was concerned in inclosure. It is certain, then, that if this Act had been passed thirty years ago, not one of these inclosures, which have been resisted and abated at such enormous cost, could possibly have been attempted, nor would the Lords of Manors have ventured to ask the approval of the Board of Agriculture on the ground of public advantage. The Act must be taken in connection also with the recent decision of Parliament in the Banstead Commons case, in which, as has already been pointed out, the principle has been finally affirmed that a Common may

be taken out of the sole management and control of
the Lord of the Manor, and, in spite of his opposition,
placed under the management of a Board of Conservators elected by the ratepayers of the district.

The two measures taken together amount practically
to this—that Commons are no longer to be regarded
as the private property of the Lords of Manors (subject
only to the rights of a limited body of Commoners),
entirely under their control and management, and
liable to inclosure in respect of so much of them as
may not be wanted to satisfy existing rights; but
that, on the contrary, the public interest is to prevail
over that of the Lords of Manors; that, if the lords
neglect or are unable to protect them from nuisances and
disorder, or to maintain them in a proper condition, the
Commons may be taken out of their hands, and placed
under the control and management of local authorities,
with power to expend the ratepayers' money upon
their maintenance; that, subject to this, the lords'
rights—such as those of sporting, of gravel digging,
or of timber—will be preserved; but that the right of
inclosing under the Statute of Merton will practically
be reduced to *nil* by the requirement that such inclosures
shall not be permitted unless it be proved, to the satisfaction of the Board of Agriculture, that the public is
interested in their being carried out.

It has taken nearly thirty years of sustained efforts
to effect this revolution in the position of Lords of
Manors, and to obtain this recognition of public interests
in common lands. The result has only been reached

after prolonged and costly litigation, and after frequent discussions in Parliament and the Press.

It may be interesting to point out that what has in England taken thirty years to effect, through a combination of efforts in the Courts of Law, in Parliament, and in the Press, was accomplished more completely in France, at the time of the great Revolution, by a few speedy enactments. The position of common lands in that country, under the feudal system, was strictly analogous to that in England. There was the same conflict through many centuries between the Seigneurs and the Communes. Successive Sovereigns of France endeavoured, from time to time, to restrain the rights of the Feudal Lords within reasonable bounds in favour of the Communes, but with little success, for arbitrary inclosures of communal lands were the subject of frequent complaint. At the time of the Revolution, the National Assembly abolished all the feudal rights of the Seigneurs over such lands, and vested them in the Communes of their districts, without reservation of any kind.

In England there is no evidence that the Sovereigns in olden time ever sided with the people against the landowners. The landowners on their part were all-powerful in Parliament till within very recent years. The Judges also assisted them by pedantic fictions and devices under which the rights of the public of the district were set aside. As a result, the function of a Lord of a Manor, originally rather in the nature of a trust for the benefit of the people of the petty lordship committed to his charge, came to be regarded as a property, subject

only to the rights of pasture of a comparatively limited
number of persons—those owning land within the
Manor.

The result of the movement described in this
work has been to reverse this idea of absolute ownership of Lords of Manors in the waste lands of their
districts, and so far to restore to the Commons something of the attributes of the ancient Saxon Folk-
Land, and to establish the principle that they concern
the interests of the people of the district, and the public
generally, even more than of the Lords of the Manors
and their Commoners. Much has still to be done to
complete this change, and to carry it to its logical conclusion. All the remaining Commons should be placed
under the protection and management of local authorities, and subjected to schemes of regulation. For this
purpose the provisions of the Metropolitan Commons Act
should be extended throughout the country, and the requirement of the assent of two-thirds in value of the Commoners, and of the Lord of the Manor, to a regulating
scheme, should be dispensed with. Although the Statute
of Merton has been virtually repealed by the recent
Statute, there still remains the danger that a Lord of
the Manor may purchase up every single right of common, and by so doing practically extinguish the Manor
and convert the Common into private property, in which
case inclosure would be effected, not under the Statute of
Merton, but by Common Law, on the plea that the land
has ceased to be legally a Common and has become
private property. So long as a single right of common

subsists, this would be impossible. It is most important, therefore, that the powers now conferred on Urban Authorities, of acquiring rights over Commons within their area, should be extended to other Local Authorities in rural districts, and should be acted upon. The acquisition in this way of a single right over a Common, will suffice to prevent the extinction of the Manor.

It is also time that the pedantic and senseless doctrines that the inhabitants of a parish or district are too vague a body to enjoy a "*profit à prendre*," or to prescribe for such a right, and that a custom to be valid must be proved to be enjoyed by the inhabitants of a district only, and not by the public generally—doctrines which it has been shown have been used to defeat claims and customs of a just and necessary character—must be reviewed by the light of modern ideas and common sense. These matters, however, are easy and certain of accomplishment compared to what has been effected during the past thirty years.

The result achieved during this period has not been without prevision. It was deliberately devised and steadily pursued through a long course of years. It has already been pointed out that at the commencement of the movement, when it was found necessary to fight the battle of the Commons in the Courts of Law, it was determined to use every effort to reverse the current of previous decisions, and to bring back the Judges to the older view of the relations of the Lords of Manors to their Commoners, and to accustom them to the idea that public rights and interests might be supported and vindicated through the medium of the Commoners' rights. The success of this work was largely due to the progress of public opinion on the subject. It would be a mistake to suppose that the Judges are not within certain limits amenable to public opinion. It would be very unfortunate if it were otherwise. Public opinion is an environment or atmosphere in which all functionaries, equally with legislators, perform their duties. Even the highest Judges in the land have many opportunities of almost unconsciously deferring to it. If public opinion had been in the opposite direction on the subject of Commons, it would have been quite possible, and indeed easy, for the Courts to have opposed obstacles to the use which was made of the Commoners' rights on behalf of the public. The insistence on what were really technical, rather than substantial, rights of common, for the purpose of preventing inclosures, ostensibly in the interests of Commoners, but really for a wholly different object, namely to secure the land for use and enjoyment by the public, might at one time be considered as scarcely worthy of the aid of the Courts of Law; whereas at another time, and with an universal desire to save such open spaces for the public, they might be welcomed as perfectly justifiable and efficient weapons for the purpose. In this view it was essentially necessary to proceed cautiously, and in no way ahead of public opinion, while at the same time discussions in Parliament and elsewhere gradually educated that opinion. This change made itself felt in the Law Courts, and doubtless lent its aid to the suits which were in progress there. Thus it came about that the battle, which was fought so largely in the Law Courts, owed its success in no small degree to efforts in Parliament and in the Press.

The experience of the past thirty years has also abundantly vindicated the opinion of the Committee of 1865, that the Commons within fifteen miles of London are none too large for the health and enjoyment of the ever-growing population of the district, and that the policy of the Metropolitan Board of Works, to sell portions of them in order to obtain full possession of the remainder, was both unwise and unnecessary. Not an acre of Common land has successfully been inclosed during this period. Much that was previously filched from Epping Forest has been restored to the public. So far from selling portions of Commons, the London authorities have found it necessary to add to the areas of several of them. Hampstead Heath, it has been already shown, has been more than doubled in size by the purchase of Parliament Hill; Bostall Heath has been also doubled by the acquisition of Bostall Wood. By the combined action of the London County Council, the Camberwell Vestry, and private subscribers, an addition of 49 acres has been made to Peckham Rye Common at a cost of £50,900. Even that portion of Epping Forest which is nearest to London, namely Wanstead Flats, has been increased by the purchase by the Corporation of London of Wanstead Park, consisting of 184 acres, and of Higham Park, of 30 acres. West Ham Park, of 80 acres, has also been purchased by the

Corporation for £25,000. Within the same period numerous additions have been made to the London Parks. Clissold Park, one of the most beautifully laid out and planted parks within the Metropolitan area, and with an area of 53 acres, was bought by the joint action and contributions of the Metropolitan Board, the Local Board, and private subscribers, at a cost of £95,000. The same method was adopted for the purchase of Brockwell Park, in the parish of Southwark, consisting of 78 acres, at a cost of £122,000; of the Hilly Fields, 42 acres, for £42,000; of Ravenscourt Park, in 1888, of 32 acres, at a cost of £61,600. Sir Sydney Waterlow, in 1891, made the generous gift of 26 acres at Highgate, now known as Waterlow Park. The Dulwich College Trustees made a similar gift of 72 acres for the formation of a public park at Dulwich. These are striking evidences of the strength of feeling which has grown up of late years, as to the necessity of ample open spaces for the recreation and enjoyment of the teeming multitudes of our great city.

In looking back on this long contest of thirty years, extending over more than an average generation, it is sad to recall what breaches have been made in the ranks of those engaged in it. Of the early coadjutors in the movement, John Stuart Mill, Henry Fawcett, Charles Buxton, Lord Mount Temple, and many other true friends, have not lived to see the success of the cause. The great Judges to whose decisions the victory was so largely due—Lord Romilly, Lord Hatherley, Sir George Jessel, Sir Charles Hall, and Sir W. M. James—are no longer in their places on the Bench. Of the eminent counsel, by whose advocacy and learning the cases were successively presented in their most favourable light, and the Courts were brought back to the almost forgotten view of the importance of common rights, Mr. Manisty (afterwards Mr. Justice Manisty), Mr. Joshua Williams, Mr. W. R. Fisher, and Mr. McClymont have passed away.* Of the public-spirited men who took upon themselves the burden of fighting against the inclosures, Mr. Augustus Smith, Mr. Gurney Hoare, Mr. Frederick Goldsmid, Mr. Hall of Coulsdon, Mr. Hamilton Fletcher and Mr. Nisbet Robertson of Banstead, Mr. William Minet of Dartford, and old Willingale of Loughton, are no longer alive to celebrate the final success. Enough, however, remain of the earlier and later friends of the cause, to recollect the perilous position of Commons at the commencement of the movement, to appreciate the revolution which has been effected in the relations of Lords of Manors to their Commoners and to the public, and to rejoice in the conclusion that never again in the future will it be said with truth—

"Our fenceless fields the sons of wealth divide,
And e'en the bare-worn common is denied."
—*Goldsmith's "Deserted Village."*

* Lord Selborne, who rendered such great services in the earlier cases, still happily survives, as does also Mr. P. H. Lawrence, to whom the initiation of the movement was largely due, and who, when called to the Bar, in 1876, was employed as Counsel in several of the later cases.

APPENDIX.

—◦◦◦—

APPENDIX I.

COMMONS WITHIN THE METROPOLITAN POLICE DISTRICT WHICH HAVE BEEN SUBJECTED TO REGULATION SCHEMES, UNDER THE METROPOLITAN COMMONS ACT, CONFIRMED BY PARLIAMENT.

Year in which Confirming Act passed.	Name of Common.	Managing Body.	Acreage of Common.
1869	Hayes Common.	Local Conservators.	200
1871	Blackheath.	London County Council.	267
,,	Shepherd's Bush Common.	,, ,,	8
1872	Hackney Commons (3).	,, ,,	166
1873	Tooting Bec Common.	,, ,,	144
1876	Barnes Common.	Local Conservators.	120
1877	Ealing Commons.	Ealing Local Board.	50
,,	Clapham Common.	London County Council.	200
,,	Bostall Heath (Plumstead).	,, ,,	55*
1880	Staines Moor (2).	Staines Local Board.	353
1881	Eelbrook Commons, Fulh'm.	London County Council.	27
1882	Acton Commons.	Acton Local Board.	12
,,	Chiswick Common and Turnham Green.	Chiswick Local Board.	21
,,	Tottenham Commons.	Tottenham Local Board.	48
1884	Streatham Common.	London County Council.	66
1886	Chislehurst Common (with St. Paul's Cray).	Local Conservators.	182
,,	Farnborough Common.	,, ,,	45
1891	Mitcham Common.	,, ,,	570
1893	Banstead Commons (4).	,, ,,	1,300
		Total	3,834

* Without including Bostall Woods.

APPENDIX II.

COMMONS WITHIN THE METROPOLITAN POLICE DISTRICT WHICH HAVE BEEN SECURED TO THE PUBLIC AND REGULATED UNDER SPECIAL ACTS OR WHICH HAVE BEEN BOUGHT BY LOCAL AUTHORITIES.

Name of Common.	Managing Body.	Acreage.	Remarks.
Hampstead Heath.	London County Council.	240*	Lord's rights bought for £45,000
Wimbledon Common.	Local Board of Conservators.	1,000	Annuity of £1,200 secured to lord.
Wandsworth Common.	London County Council.	194	Annuity of £250 secured to lord.
Tooting Graveney Common.	"	63	Lord's rights bought for £3,000.
Plumstead Common.	"	100	
Woolwich and Charlton Commons.	The War Office.	187	
Hounslow Heath.	"	270	
Wormwood Scrubbs.	London County Council.	193	
Peckham Rye.	"	64	
Epping Forest.	Corporation of London.	6,027	Lords of Manors' right bought at £20 per acre.
Coulsdon Commons (4).		400	Lord's rights bought by Corporation.
West Wickham Common.	"	50	Lord's rights bought for £2,000.
Hackney Marshes.	London County Council.	337	
	Total	9,125	

* Without including Parliament Hill.

APPENDIX III.

COMMONS OF OVER TWENTY ACRES EACH, WITHIN THE
METROPOLITAN POLICE DISTRICT, NOT YET PROTECTED
BY REGULATION SCHEMES UNDER THE METROPOLITAN
COMMONS ACT, 1866.

Name of Common.	County in which Situate.	Acreage.
Dartford Common.	Kent.	360
Dartford Brimp.	Kent.	60
Eltham Common.	Kent.	42
Keston Common.	Kent.	55
Carshalton Common.	Surrey.	150
Chelsham Common.	Surrey.	30
Epsom Common.	Surrey.	443
Epsom Downs.	Surrey.	430
Esher Commons (2).	Surrey.	315
West End Common.	Surrey.	134
Farley Commons (2).	Surrey.	40
Ham Common.	Surrey.	126
Palewell Common.	Surrey.	20
Petersham Common.	Surrey.	20
Piggs Marsh, Mitcham.	Surrey.	53
Rushet Common.	Surrey.	20
Sheen Common.	Surrey.	83
Thames Ditton Commons (4).	Surrey.	309
Walton Commons (2).	Surrey.	500
Walton-on-Thames Heath	Surrey.	150
Wocham's Heath, Chelsham.	Surrey.	90
Golders Green, Hendon.	Middlesex.	27
Hadley Common.	Middlesex.	174
Harrow Weald Common.	Middlesex.	44
Ruislip Common.	Middlesex.	60
Stanmore Commons (2).	Middlesex.	147
Tottenham Lammas Lands.	Middlesex.	250
Rowley Green (Shenley).	Hertfordshire.	119
Totteridge.	Hertfordshire.	52
Waltham Marshes, Cheshunt.	Hertfordshire.	154
Walthamstow Marshes.	Essex.	140
	Total	4,597

APPENDIX IV.

ROYAL AND PUBLIC PARKS WITHIN THE METROPOLITAN POLICE DISTRICT.

Name of Park.	Year in which opened to the Public.	By whom opened.	In whom vested	Acreage
Hyde Park			The Crown	350
Kensington Gardens			,,	270
The Green Park	These parks were opened by degrees by the public by successive sovereigns from Charles I. to George IV.		,,	53
St. James's Park			,,	91
Greenwich Park			,,	148
Richmond Park			,,	2050
Bushy Park			,,	680
Hampton Court Gardens	1838	Queen Victoria	,,	36
Regent's Park	Various dates	{ William IV. (Queen Victoria }	,,	275
Kew Gardens	1841	Queen Victoria	,,	243
Primrose Hill	1843	,,	,,	62
Hampton Court Park	1893	,,	,,	630
Victoria Park	1842	The State	The County Council	244
Kennington Park	1854	The Duchy of Cornwall	,,	20
Battersea Park	1858	The State	,,	198
Finsbury Park	1869	The Metropolitan Board of Works	,,	115
Southwark Park	1869	,,	,,	63
West Ham Park	1854	TheCorporation of London	The Corporation	80
Highbury Fields	1885	The Metropolitan Board of Works	TheCounty Council	27
Ravenscourt Park	1887	,,	,,	32
Clissold Park	1889	The County Council	,,	53
Dulwich Park	1890	Dulwich College	,,	72
Waterlow Park	1891	Sir Sydney Waterlow	,,	26
Brockwell Park	1892	The County Council	,,	78
Hilly Fields, Brockley	1893	,,	,,	42
Fulham Park	1893	The Ecclesiastical Commissioners	,,	19
			Total	5,957

N.B.—In the cases of Ravenscourt, Clissold, and Brockwell Parks, and of the Hilly Fields, the Vestries, the Charity Commissioners, and others, contributed to the cost of purchase.

Y

APPENDIX V.

COMMONS REGULATED OR ENCLOSED UNDER THE COMMONS ACT, 1876.

I.—SUBJECT TO PROVISIONAL ORDERS FOR REGULATION.

Year in which Act passed.	Name of Common.	County.	Acreage.	Allotments for Recreation.	Allotments for Field Gardens.
1879	East Stainmore (part of)	Westmoreland	6,383	—	
	Matterdale Common (part of)	Cumberland	2,665	Privilege of playing games on 30 acres, and right to walk over 420 acres.	
1880	Abbotside	York	9,700	Privilege of recreation over Staggs Fell Plain, about 80 acres.	
	Clent	Worcester	172	Privilege of recreation over the whole.	
	Lizard Common (part of)	Cornwall	70	Privilege of recreation over regulated parts.	
1881	Beamsley Moor	York	699	Privilege of recreation on certain portions.	
	Langbar Moor	York	668	Do. do.	
	Shenfield	Essex	88	Privilege of recreation over whole common.	
1882	Stivichall	Warwick	4	Privilege of recreation over whole common, and 11 acres to be added by a citizen.	
	Crosby Garrett	Westmoreland	1,806	Privilege of walking over the whole and playing games on a part.	
1884	Redhill and Earlswood	Surrey	324	Privilege of walking and playing games over the whole.	
1885	Drumburgh Common and Moss	Cumberland	275	Do. do.	
	Ashdown Forest	Sussex	6,000	—	
	Carried forward		28,804		

APPENDIX V. (*continued*).

Year in which Act passed.	Name of Common.	County.	Acre-age.	Allotments for Recreation.	Allotments for Field Gardens.
	Brought	forward -	28,804		
1886	Totternhoo -	Herts -	234	Privilege of walking and playing games over the whole, with a small exception.	
	Stoke -	Warwick	66	Privilege of walking and playing games over the whole.	
1887	Ewer -	Hants -	28	Do. do.	
	Laindon -	Essex -	26	Do. do.	
1888	Thirfield -	Herts -	431	Do. do.	
1889	Amberswood -	Lancashire	32	Do. do.	
1890	Cleve -	Gloucester	1,100	Do. do.	
1893	West Tilbury -	Essex -	105	Do. do.	
	Middleham -	York -	363	Do. do.	
	Henfield -	Sussex -	75	Do. do.	
	Total		31,264		

II.—SUBJECT TO PROVISIONAL ORDERS FOR ENCLOSURE.

Year in which Act passed.	Name of Common.	County.	Acre-age.	Allotments for Recreation.			Allotments for Field Gardens.		
				A.	R.	P.	A.	R.	P.
1878	Orford -	Suffolk -	46	6	0	0	—		
	Riccall -	York -	1,297	6	0	0	20	0	0
	Barrowden -	Rutland -	1,925	9	0	0	20	0	0
	North Luffen-ham -	Rutland -	1,636	7	1	8	20	0	0
	South Luffen-ham -	Rutland -	1,074	6	0	0	15	0	0
1879	Matterdale (part of) -	Cumber-land -	2,794	10	0	0	10	0	0
	East Stainmore (part of) -	Westmore-land -	4,075	40	0	0	10	0	0
	South Hill -	Cornwall	402	10	0	0	10	0	0
	Whittington -	Stafford -	53	8	0	0	10	0	0
1880	Lizard Common (part of) -	Cornwall	280	—			20	0	0
	Steventon -	Berks -	1,373	14	0	0	20	0	0
	Carried	forward -	14,955	116	1	8	155	0	0

Y 2

APPENDIX V. (*continued*).

Year in which Act passed.	Name of Common.	County.	Acre-age.	Allotments for Recreation.	Allotments for Field Gardens.
				A. R. P.	A. R. P.
	Brought	forward -	14,955	116 1 8	155 0 0
	Hondy Bank -	Radnor -	131	} Privilege of recreation over parts {	—
	Llandegley Rhos	Radnor -	322	{ uncultivated or } unplanted.	
	Llanfair Hills -	Salop -	1,634	10 0 0	15 0 0
				and Offa's Dyke.	
1881	Wibsey Slack and Low Moor	York -	400	67 2 9	—
	Scotton and Ferry - -	Lincoln -	1,605	10 0 0	48 0 0
	Thurstaston -	Chester -	210	45 0 0	5 0 0
1882	Arkleside - -	York -	450	Privilege of walking on all unplanted or uncultivated parts	20 0 0
	Bettws Disserth	Radnor -	656	Do. do.	—
	Cefn Drawen -	Radnor -	893	Do. do.	—
1883	Hildersham -	Cambridge	1,175	8 0 0	15 0 0
1885	Llanybyther -	Carmarthen -	1,891	Privilege of walking on all unplanted or uncultivated parts.	—
1886	Totternhoe Common Fields -	Herts -	1,717	No allotment from these common fields, but the Commons, consisting of 234 acres, are dedicated to the public.	25 0 0
1891	Mungrisdale -	Cumberland -	500	4 2 0	6 0 0
		Total -	26,539	498 0 0	289 0 0

APPENDIX VI.

ACREAGE OF COMMONS AND COMMON FIELD LANDS IN EACH
COUNTY IN ENGLAND AND WALES, COMPILED FROM THE
TITHE COMMUTATION MAPS OF 1834, SO FAR AS THEY
EXIST, WITH ESTIMATE BASED ON SAME AVERAGE FOR
PARISHES WHERE MAPS DO NOT EXIST.—*Parliamentary
Return*, 1874 (85).

ENGLAND.

County.	Total Area.	Area of Commons.	Area of Common Fields.
	Acres.	Acres.	Acres.
Bedford - - - -	295,516	4,630	19,981
Berks - - -	455,035	7,663	15,932
Bucks - - - -	468,574	10,438	4,680
Cambridge - - - -	547,427	5,919	7,476
Cheshire - - -	715,835	17,633	715
Cornwall - - - -	857,608	68,260	901
Cumberland - - -	973,510	187,718	2,045
Derby - - -	642,794	21,139	1,757
Devon - - - -	1,657,749	165,007	1,157
Dorset - - - -	628,225	38,713	7,603
Durham - - - -	699,626	51,461	1,207
Essex - - - -	994,608	12,974	4,909
Gloucester - - - -	810,995	15,069	7,313
Hereford - - - -	540,539	10,203	2,498
Hertford - - -	390,828	5,345	11,096
Huntingdon - - -	230,486	597	3,672
Kent - - - -	1,002,972	8,176	4,309
Lancaster - - - -	1,205,037	68,875	3,298
Leicester - - - -	511,428	676	135
Lincoln - - - -	1,725,641	13,432	17,081
Middlesex - - - -	178,466	4,316	1,567
Monmouth - - - -	345,722	27,802	67
Norfolk - - - -	1,352,291	16,510	3,954
Northampton - - -	633,286	2,947	17,549
Northumberland - - -	1,236,655	53,214	51
Nottingham - - -	529,281	1,513	10,899

APPENDIX VI. (*continued*).

County.	Total Area.	Area of Commons.	Area of Common Fields.
Oxford - - - -	467,306	3,834	8,959
Rutland - - - -	92,696	2,268	9,656
Salop - - - - -	852,493	33,814	525
Somerset - - - -	1,043,879	32,828	8,522
Southampton - - -	1,027,673	41,502*	6,388
Stafford - - - -	729,248	12,281	1,540
Suffolk - - - -	943,166	7,534	2,579
Surrey - - - -	479,921	42,936	4,009
Sussex - - - -	925,076	21,222	3,091
Warwick - - - -	565,448	1,216	2,440
Westmoreland - - -	508,115	172,344	784
Wilts - - - -	869,233	9,286	22,670
Worcester - - - -	463,730	4,519	4,253
Yorkshire, North Riding -	1,336,268	253,772	787
Yorkshire, East Riding -	742,701	11,039	11,405
Yorkshire, West Riding -	1,727,176	225,823	10,849
York, City of - - -	52,479	601	559
Total	32,456,742	1,700,049	250,868
Wales - - - -	4,700,431	668,416	13,439
Total	37,157,173	2,368,465	264,307

Total, subject to Common Rights, 2,632,772.

From this has to be deducted inclosures under private Acts between 1834 and 1845; inclosures made under the Commons Act of 1876; and inclosures since 1834 under the Statute of Merton, or under customs of Manors.

* This does not appear to be accurate, as the New Forest alone consists of 63,000 acres.

INDEX.

Z

Cloth, 10s. 6d.

AGRARIAN TENURES:

A SURVEY

OF THE LAWS AND CUSTOMS RELATING TO THE HOLDING OF LAND

IN ENGLAND, IRELAND, AND SCOTLAND,

AND OF

THE REFORMS THEREIN DURING RECENT YEARS.

BY

THE RT. HON. G. SHAW LEFEVRE, M.P.

SUMMARY OF CONTENTS.

" This book is of the highest practical value. It is the most valuable single contribution we remember to have seen to the literature bearing on present-day agrarian problems. Every page contains valuable information, and will repay careful study."—*Speaker*.

"Mr. Shaw Lefevre has produced a sober and statesmanlike account of the existing land-systems of England, Ireland, and the Highlands of Scotland, and the reforms he advocates are in a high degree reasonable and practical."—*Spectator*.

" We must be content with commending Mr. Lefevre's volume to our readers as the best existing work on its subject." —*Field*.

CASSELL & COMPANY, Limited: *London, Paris & Melbourne.*

A SELECTED LIST

OF

CASSELL & COMPANY'S

PUBLICATIONS.

7 G—10.93

Illustrated, Fine Art, and other Volumes.

Abbeys and Churches of England and Wales, The: Descriptive, Historical, Pictorial. Series II. 21s.

A Blot of Ink. Translated by Q and PAUL FRANCKE. 5s.

Adventure, The World of. Fully Illustrated. Complete in Three Vols. 9s. each.

Africa and its Explorers, The Story of. By Dr. ROBERT BROWN, M.A., F.L.S., F.R.G.S., &c. With numerous Original Illustrations. Vols. I. and II. 7s. 6d. each.

Agrarian Tenures. By the Rt. Hon. G. SHAW LEFEVRE, M.P. 10s. 6d.

American Life. By PAUL DE ROUSIERS. 12s. 6d.

Animal Painting in Water Colours. With Coloured Plates. 5s.

Anthea. By CÉCILE CASSAVETTI (a Russian). A Story of the Greek War of Independence. *Cheap Edition,* 5s.

Arabian Nights Entertainments (Cassell's). With about 400 Illustrations. 10s. 6d.

Architectural Drawing. By R. PHENÉ SPIERS. Illustrated. 10s. 6d.

Army, Our Home. Being a Reprint of Letters published in the *Times* in November and December, 1891. By H. O. ARNOLD-FORSTER, M.P. 1s.

Art, The Magazine of. Yearly Volume. With about 400 Illustrations, and Twelve Etchings, Photogravures, &c. 16s.

Artistic Anatomy. By Prof. M. DUVAL. *Cheap Edition,* 3s. 6d.

Astronomy, The Dawn of. A Study of the Astronomy and Temple Worship of the Ancient Egyptians. By J. NORMAN LOCKYER, F.R.S., F.R.A.S., &c. Illustrated. 21s.

Atlas, The Universal. A New and Complete General Atlas of the World, with 117 Pages of Maps, handsomely produced in Colours, and a Complete Index to about 125,000 Names. Complete in One Volume, cloth, 30s. net; or half-morocco, 35s. net.

Awkward Squads, The; and other Ulster Stories. By SHAN F. BULLOCK. 5s.

Bashkirtseff, Marie, The Journal of. Translated by MATHILDE BLIND. 7s. 6d.

Bashkirtseff, Marie, The Letters of. Translated by MARY J. SERRANO. 7s. 6d.

Beetles, Butterflies, Moths, and other Insects. By A. W. KAPPEL, F.L.S., F.E.S., and W. EGMONT KIRBY. With 12 Coloured Plates. 3s. 6d.

Beyond the Blue Mountains. By L. T. MEADE. Illustrated. 5s.

Biographical Dictionary, Cassell's New. Containing Memoirs of the Most Eminent Men and Women of all Ages and Countries. 7s. 6d.

Birds' Nests, Eggs, and Egg-Collecting. By R. KEARTON. Illustrated with 16 Coloured Plates of Eggs. 5s.

Breechloader, The, and How to Use It. By W. W. GREENER. 2s.

British Ballads. 275 Original Illustrations. Two Vols. Cloth, 15s.

British Battles on Land and Sea. By JAMES GRANT. With about 600 Illustrations. Three Vols. 4to, £1 7s.; *Library Edition,* £1 10s.

British Battles, Recent. Illustrated. 9s. *Library Edition,* 10s.

Browning, An Introduction to the Study of. By ARTHUR SYMONS. 2s. 6d.

Butterflies and Moths, European. By W. F. KIRBY. With 61 Coloured Plates. 35s.

Canaries and Cage-Birds, The Illustrated Book of. By W. A. BLAKSTON, W. SWAYSLAND, and A. F. WIENER. With 56 Fac-simile Coloured Plates. 35s.

Capture of the "Estrella," The. A Tale of the Slave Trade. By COMMANDER CLAUD HARDING, R.N. 5s.

Carnation Manual, The. Edited and Issued by The National Carnation and Picotee Society (Southern Section). 3s. 6d.

Cassell's Family Magazine. Yearly Volume. Illustrated. 9s.

Cathedrals, Abbeys, and Churches of England and Wales. Descriptive, Historical, Pictorial. *Popular Edition.* Two Vols. 25s.

Catriona. A Sequel to "Kidnapped." By ROBERT LOUIS STEVENSON. 6s.

Celebrities of the Century. Being a Dictionary of the Men and Women of the Nineteenth Century. *Cheap Edition,* 10s. 6d.

China Painting. By FLORENCE LEWIS. With Sixteen Coloured Plates, &c. 5s.

Chips by an Old Chum; or, Australia in the Fifties. 1s.

Choice Dishes at Small Cost. By A. G. PAYNE. *Cheap Edition,* 1s.

Christianity and Socialism, Lectures on. By BISHOP BARRY. 3s. 6d.

Chums. The Illustrated Paper for Boys. Yearly Volume. 7s. 6d.

Cities of the World. Four Vols. Illustrated. 7s. 6d. each.

Civil Service, Guide to Employment in the. *New and Enlarged Edition,* 3s. 6d.

Climate and Health Resorts. By Dr. BURNEY YEO. 7s. 6d.

Clinical Manuals for Practitioners and Students of Medicine. (*A List of Volumes forwarded post free on application to the Publishers.*)

Cobden Club, Works published for the. (*A Complete List on application.*)

Colonist's Medical Handbook, The. By E. ALFRED BARTON, M.R.C.S. 2s. 6d.

Colour. By Prof. A. H. CHURCH. *New and Enlarged Edition,* 3s. 6d.

Columbus, The Career of. By CHARLES ELTON, F.S.A. 10s. 6d.

Combe, George, The Select Works of. Issued by Authority of the Combe Trustees. *Popular Edition,* 1s. each, net.

The Constitution of Man.	Science and Religion.
Moral Philosophy.	Discussions on Education.
American Notes.	

Commercial Botany of the Nineteenth Century. By J. R. JACKSON, A.L.S. Cloth gilt, 3s. 6d.

Conning Tower, In a. By H. O. ARNOLD-FORSTER, M.P., Author of "The Citizen Reader," &c. With Original Illustrations by W. H. OVEREND. 1s.

Conquests of the Cross. Edited by EDWIN HODDER. With numerous Original Illustrations. Complete in Three Vols. 9s. each.

Cookery, A Year's. By PHYLLIS BROWNE. *New and Enlarged Edition,* 3s. 6d.

Cookery, Cassell's Popular. With Four Coloured Plates. Cloth gilt, 2s.

Cookery, Cassell's Shilling. 95*th Thousand.* 1s.

Cookery, Vegetarian. By A. G. PAYNE. 1s. 6d.

Cooking by Gas, The Art of. By MARIE J. SUGG. Illustrated. Cloth, 3s. 6d.

Cottage Gardening, Poultry, Bees, Allotments, Food, House, Window and Town Gardens. Edited by W. ROBINSON, F.L.S., Author of "The English Flower Garden." Fully Illustrated. Half-yearly Volumes, I. and II., 2s.

Countries of the World, The. By ROBERT BROWN, M.A., Ph.D., &c. Complete in Six Vols., with about 750 Illustrations. 4to, 7s. 6d. each.

Cyclopædia, Cassell's Concise. Brought down to the latest date. With about 600 Illustrations. *New and Cheap Edition,* 7s. 6d.

Cyclopædia, Cassell's Miniature. Containing 30,000 Subjects. Cloth, 2s. 6d.; half-roxburgh, 4s.

Delectable Duchy, The. Some Tales of East Cornwall. By Q. 6s.

Dickens, Character Sketches from. FIRST, SECOND, and THIRD SERIES. With Six Original Drawings in each, by FREDERICK BARNARD. In Portfolio. 21s. each.

Dick Whittington, A Modern. By JAMES PAYN. *Cheap Edition in one Vol.,* 6s.

Dictionaries. (For description see alphabetical letter.) Religion, Biographical Celebrities, Encyclopædic, Mechanical, Phrase and Fable, English, English History, English Literature, Domestic. (French, German, and Latin, see with *Educational Works.*)

Dog, Illustrated Book of the. By VERO SHAW, B.A. With 28 Coloured Plates. Cloth bevelled, 35s.; half-morocco, 45s.

Domestic Dictionary, The. An Encyclopædia for the Household. Cloth, 7s. 6d.

Doré Don Quixote, The. With about 400 Illustrations by GUSTAVE DORÉ. *Cheap Edition,* bevelled boards, gilt edges, 10s. 6d.

Doré Gallery, The. With 250 Illustrations by GUSTAVE DORÉ. 4to, 42s.

Doré's Dante's Inferno. Illustrated by GUSTAVE DORÉ. *Popular Edition.* With Preface by A. J. BUTLER. Cloth gilt or buckram, 7s. 6d.

Doré's Dante's Purgatory and Paradise. Illustrated by GUSTAVE DORÉ. *Cheap Edition.* 7s. 6d.

Doré's Milton's Paradise Lost. Illustrated by GUSTAVE DORÉ. 4to, 21s.

Dr. Dumány's Wife. A Novel. By MAURUS JÓKAI. *Cheap Edition,* 6s.

Earth, Our, and its Story. Edited by Dr. ROBERT BROWN, F.L.S. With 36 Coloured Plates and 740 Wood Engravings. Complete in Three Vols 9s. each.

Edinburgh, Old and New, Cassell's. With 600 Illustrations. Three Vols. 9s. each; library binding, £1 10s. the set.

Egypt: Descriptive, Historical, and Picturesque. By Prof. G. EBERS. Translated by CLARA BELL, with Notes by SAMUEL BIRCH, LL.D., &c. Two Vols. 42s.

Electricity, Practical. By Prof. W. E. AYRTON. Illustrated. Cloth, 7s. 6d.

Electricity in the Service of Man. A Popular and Practical Treatise. With nearly 850 Illustrations. *New and Revised Edition,* 10s. 6d.

Employment for Boys on Leaving School, Guide to. By W. S. BEARD, F.R.G.S. 1s. 6d.

Encyclopædic Dictionary, The. Complete in Fourteen Divisional Vols., 10s. 6d. each; or Seven Vols., half-morocco, 21s. each; half-russia, 25s. each.
England, Cassell's Illustrated History of. With 2,000 Illustrations. Ten Vols., 4to, 9s. each. *New and Revised Edition.* Vols. I. to VI., 9s. each.
English Dictionary, Cassell's. Containing Definitions of upwards of 100,000 Words and Phrases. *Cheap Edition.* 3s. 6d.
English History, The Dictionary of. *Cheap Edition,* 10s. 6d.; roxburgh, 15s.
English Literature, Library of. By Prof. H. MORLEY. In 5 Vols., 7s. 6d. each.
English Literature, Morley's First Sketch of. *Revised Edition,* 7s. 6d.
English Literature, The Dictionary of. By W. DAVENPORT ADAMS. *Cheap Edition,* 7s. 6d.; roxburgh, 10s. 6d.
English Literature, The Story of. By ANNA BUCKLAND. 3s. 6d.
English Writers. By HENRY MORLEY. Vols. I. to X. 5s. each.
Æsop's Fables. Illustrated by ERNEST GRISET. *Cheap Edition.* Cloth, 3s. 6d.; bevelled boards, gilt edges, 5s.
Etiquette of Good Society. *New Edition.* Edited and Revised by LADY COLIN CAMPBELL. 1s.; cloth, 2s.
Europe, Cassell's Pocket Guide to. *Edition for* 1893. Leather, 6s.
Fairway Island. By HORACE HUTCHINSON. With Four Full-page Plates. *Cheap Edition.* 3s. 6d.
Faith Doctor, The. A Novel. By Dr. EDWARD EGGLESTON. *Cheap Edition,* 6s.
Family Physician. By Eminent PHYSICIANS and SURGEONS. *New and Revised Edition.* Cloth, 21s.; roxburgh, 25s.
Father Mathew: His Life and Times. By FRANK J. MATHEW. 2s. 6d.
Father Stafford. A Novel. By ANTHONY HOPE, Author of "A Man of Mark." 6s.
Fenn, G. Manville, Works by. Boards, 2s. each; or cloth, 2s. 6d.

| Poverty Corner. | The Parson o' Dumford. |
| My Patients. | The Vicar's People. |

In boards only.

Field Naturalist's Handbook, The. By Revs. J. G. WOOD and THEODORE WOOD. *Cheap Edition,* 2s. 6d.
Figuier's Popular Scientific Works. With Several Hundred Illustrations in each. 3s. 6d. each.

The Insect World.	Reptiles and Birds.	The Vegetable World.
The Human Race.	Mammalia.	Ocean World.
	The World before the Deluge.	

Figure Painting in Water Colours. With 16 Coloured Plates. 7s. 6d.
Flora's Feast. A Masque of Flowers. Penned and Pictured by WALTER CRANE. With 40 pages in Colours. 5s.
Flower Painting, Elementary. With Eight Coloured Plates. 3s.
Flowers, and How to Paint Them. By MAUD NAFTEL. With Coloured Plates. 5s.
Football: the Rugby Union Game. Edited by Rev. F. MARSHALL. Illustrated. 7s. 6d.
Fossil Reptiles, A History of British. By Sir RICHARD OWEN, F.R.S., &c. With 268 Plates. In Four Vols. £12 12s.
Fraser, John Drummond. By PHILALETHES. A Story of Jesuit Intrigue in the Church of England. 5s.
Garden Flowers, Familiar. By SHIRLEY HIBBERD. With Coloured Plates by F. E. HULME, F.L.S. Complete in Five Series. Cloth gilt, 12s. 6d. each.
Gardening, Cassell's Popular. Illustrated. Complete in Four Vols. 5s. each.
Geometrical Drawing for Army Candidates. By H. T. LILLEY, M.A. 2s. 6d.
Geometry, First Elements of Experimental. By PAUL BERT. 1s. 6d.
Geometry, Practical Solid. By Major ROSS. 2s.
George Saxon, The Reputation of. By MORLEY ROBERTS. 5s.
Gilbert, Elizabeth, and her Work for the Blind. By FRANCES MARTIN. 2s. 6d.
Gleanings from Popular Authors. Two Vols. With Original Illustrations. 4to, 9s. each. Two Vols. in One, 15s.
Gulliver's Travels. With 88 Engravings. Cloth, 3s. 6d.; cloth gilt, 5s.
Gun and its Development, The. By W. W. GREENER. Illustrated. 10s. 6d.
Guns, Modern Shot. By W. W. GREENER. Illustrated. 5s.
Health, The Book of. By Eminent Physicians and Surgeons. Cloth, 21s.
Heavens, The Story of the. By Sir ROBERT STAWELL BALL, LL.D., F.R.S. With Coloured Plates and Wood Engravings. *Popular Edition,* 12s. 6d.

Heroes of Britain in Peace and War. With 300 Original Illustrations. *Cheap Edition.* Two Vols. 3s. 6d. each, or two vols, in one, cloth gilt, 7s. 6d.

Hiram Golf's Religion; or, the Shoemaker by the Grace of God. 2s.

Historic Houses of the United Kingdom. With Contributions by the Rev. Professor HONNEV, F.R.S., and others. Profusely Illustrated. 10s. 6d.

History, A Footnote to. Eight Years of Trouble in Samoa. By ROBERT LOUIS STEVENSON. 6s.

Home Life of the Ancient Greeks, The. Translated by ALICE ZIMMERN. Illustrated. 7s. 6d.

Hors de Combat; or, Three Weeks in a Hospital. Founded on Facts. By GERTRUDE and ETHEL ARMITAGE SOUTHAM. Illustrated, crown 4to, 5s.

Horse, The Book of the. By SAMUEL SIDNEY. Thoroughly Revised and brought up to date by JAMES SINCLAIR and W. C. A. BLEW. With 17 Full-page Collotype Plates of Celebrated Horses of the Day, and numerous other Illustrations. Cloth, 15s.

Houghton, Lord: The Life, Letters, and Friendships of Richard Monckton Milnes, First Lord Houghton. By T. WEMYSS REID. Two Vols. 32s.

Household, Cassell's Book of the. Illustrated. Complete in Four Vols. 5s. each; or Four Vols. in two, half-morocco, 25s.

Hygiene and Public Health. By B. ARTHUR WHITELEGGE, M.D. Illustrated. *New and Revised Edition.* 7s. 6d.

India, Cassell's History of. By JAMES GRANT. With 400 Illustrations. Two Vols., 9s. each, or One Vol., 15s.

In-door Amusements, Card Games, and Fireside Fun, Cassell's Book of. With numerous Illustrations. *Cheap Edition.* Cloth, 2s.

Into the Unknown: a Romance of South Africa. By LAWRENCE FLETCHER. 4s.

Iron Pirate, The. A Plain Tale of Strange Happenings on the Sea. By MAX PEMBERTON. Illustrated. 5s.

Island Nights' Entertainments. By R. L. STEVENSON. Illustrated, 6s.

Italy from the Fall of Napoleon I. in 1815 to 1890. By J. W. PROBYN. 3s. 6d.

"Japanese" Library, Cassell's. Consisting of 12 Popular Works bound in Japanese style. Covers in water-colour pictures. 1s. 3d. each, net.

Handy Andy. Oliver Twist. Ivanhoe. Ingoldsby Legends. The Last of the Mohicans. The Last Days of Pompeii. The Yellowplush Papers. The Last Days of Palmyra. Jack Hinton the Guardsman. Selections from the Works of Thomas Hood. American Humour. Tower of London.

Joy and Health. By MARTELLIUS. Illustrated, cloth, 3s. 6d. (*Édition de Luxe*, 7s. 6d.)

Kennel Guide, Practical. By Dr. GORDON STABLES. Illustrated. *Cheap Edition*, 1s.

"La Bella," and Others. By EGERTON CASTLE. Buckram, 6s.

Ladies' Physician, The. By a London Physician. 6s.

Lady's Dressing Room, The. Translated by LADY COLIN CAMPBELL. 3s. 6d.

Lake Dwellings of Europe. By ROBERT MUNRO, M.D., M.A. Cloth, 31s. 6d.

Leona. By Mrs. MOLESWORTH. 6s.

Letters, The Highway of; and its Echoes of Famous Footsteps. By THOMAS ARCHER. Illustrated, 10s. 6d.

Letts's Diaries and other Time-saving Publications are now published exclusively by CASSELL & COMPANY. (*A List sent post free on application.*)

List, ye Landsmen! A Romance of Incident. By W. CLARK RUSSELL. Three Vols. 31s. 6d.

Little Minister, The. By J. M. BARRIE. *Illustrated Edition*, 6s.

Locomotive Engine, The Biography of a. By HENRY FRITH. 5s.

Loftus, Lord Augustus, P.C., G.C.B., The Diplomatic Reminiscences of. First Series. With Portrait. Two Vols. 32s. Second Series. Two Vols. 32s.

London, Greater. By EDWARD WALFORD. Two Vols. With about 400 Illustrations. 9s. each. *Library Edition.* Two Vols. £1 the set.

London, Old and New. By WALTER THORNBURY and EDWARD WALFORD. Six Vols., with about 1,200 Illustrations. Cloth, 9s. each. *Library Edition*, £3.

London Street Arabs. By Mrs. H. M. STANLEY. Illustrated. 5s.

Medical Handbook of Life Assurance. By JAMES EDWARD POLLOCK, M.D., F.R.C.P., and JAMES CHISHOLM, Fellow of the Institute of Actuaries, London. 7s. 6d.

Medicine Lady, The. By L. T. MEADE. *Cheap Edition*, One Vol., 6s.

Medicine, Manuals for Students of. (*A List forwarded post free on application.*)

Modern Europe, A History of. By C. A. FYFFE, M.A. Complete in Three Vols., with full-page Illustrations. 7s. 6d. each.

Mount Desolation. An Australian Romance. By W. CARLTON DAWE. 5s.

Musical and Dramatic Copyright, The Law of. By EDWARD CUTLER, THOMAS EUSTACE SMITH, and FREDRIC E. WEATHERLY. 3s. 6d.

Music, Illustrated History of. By EMIL NAUMANN. Edited by the Rev. Sir F. A. GORE OUSELEY, Bart. Illustrated. Two Vols. 31s. 6d.

Napier, The Life and Letters of the Rt. Hon. Sir Joseph, Bart., LL.D., D.C.L. M.R.I.A. By ALEX. C. EWALD, F.S.A. *New and Revised Edition,* 7s. 6d.

National Library, Cassell's. In Volumes. Paper covers, 3d. ; cloth, 6d. (*A Complete List of the Volumes post free on application.*)

Natural History, Cassell's Concise. By E. PERCEVAL WRIGHT, M.A., M.D., F.L.S. With several Hundred Illustrations. 7s. 6d. ; also kept half-bound.

Natural History, Cassell's New. Edited by P. MARTIN DUNCAN, M.B., F.R.S., F.G.S. Complete in Six Vols. With about 2,000 Illustrations. Cloth, 9s. each.

Nature's Wonder Workers. By KATE R. LOVELL. Illustrated. 3s. 6d.

Nelson, The Life of. By ROBERT SOUTHEY. Illustrated with Eight Plates. 3s. 6d.

New England Boyhood, A. By EDWARD E. HALE. 3s. 6d.

Nursing for the Home and for the Hospital, A Handbook of. By CATHE- RINE J. WOOD. *Cheap Edition,* 1s. 6d. ; cloth, 2s.

Nursing of Sick Children, A Handbook for the. By CATHERINE J. WOOD. 2s. 6d.

O'Driscoll's Weird, and Other Stories. By A. WERNER. Cloth, 5s.

Odyssey, The Modern. By WYNDHAM F. TUFNELL. Illustrated. 10s. 6d.

Ohio, The New. A Story of East and West. By EDWARD EVERETT HALE. 6s.

Old Dorset. Chapters in the History of the County. By H. J. MOULE, M.A. 10s.6d.

Our Own Country. Six Vols. With 1,200 Illustrations. Cloth, 7s. 6d. each.

Out of the Jaws of Death. By FRANK BARRETT. *Cheap Edition,* One Vol., 6s.

Painting, The English School of. By ERNEST CHESNEAU. *Cheap Edition,* 3s. 6d.

Paris, Old and New. A Narrative of its History, its People, and its Places. By H. SUTHERLAND EDWARDS. Profusely Illustrated. Vol. I., 9s., or gilt edges, 10s. 6d.

Peoples of the World, The. By Dr. ROBERT BROWN. Complete in Six Volumes. With Illustrations. 7s. 6d. each.

Perfect Gentleman, The. By the Rev. A. SMYTHE-PALMER, D.D. 3s. 6d.

Phillips, Watts. Artist and Playwright. By Miss E. WATTS PHILLIPS. With 32 Plates. 10s. 6d.

Photography for Amateurs. By T. C. HEPWORTH. *Enlarged and Revised Edition.* Illustrated, 1s. ; or cloth, 1s. 6d.

Phrase and Fable, Dictionary of. By the Rev. Dr. BREWER. *Cheap Edition,* *Enlarged,* cloth, 3s. 6d. ; or with leather back, 4s. 6d.

Physiology for Students, Elementary. By ALFRED T. SCHOFIELD, M.D., M.R.C.S. With Two Coloured Plates and numerous Illustrations. 7s. 6d.

Picturesque America. Complete in Four Vols., with 48 Exquisite Steel Plates, and about 800 Original Wood Engravings. £2 2s. each.

Picturesque Canada. With about 600 Original Illustrations. Two Vols. £6 6s. the set.

Picturesque Europe. Complete in Five Vols. Each containing 13 Exquisite Steel Plates, from Original Drawings, and nearly 200 Original Illustrations. £21 ; half- morocco, £31 10s. ; morocco gilt, £52 10s. *Popular Edition.* In Five Vols. 18s. each.

Picturesque Mediterranean, The. With a Series of Magnificent Illustrations from Original Designs by leading Artists of the day. Two Vols. Cloth, £2 2s. each.

Pigeon Keeper, The Practical. By LEWIS WRIGHT. Illustrated. 3s. 6d.

Pigeons, The Book of. By ROBERT FULTON. Edited by LEWIS WRIGHT. With 50 Coloured Plates and numerous Wood Engravings. 31s. 6d. ; half-morocco, £2 2s.

Pity and of Death, The Book of. By PIERRE LOTI, Member of the French Academy. Translated by T. P. O'CONNOR, M.P. Antique paper, cloth gilt, 5s.

Planet, The Story of Our. By the Rev. Prof. BONNEY, F.R.S., &c. With Six Coloured Plates and Maps and about 100 Illustrations. 31s. 6d.

Playthings and Parodies. Short Stories, Sketches, &c., by BARRY PAIN. 5s.

Poetry, The Nature and Elements of. By E. C. STEDMAN. 6s.

Poets, Cassell's Miniature Library of the. Price 1s. each Vol.

Polytechnic Series, The. Practical Illustrated Manuals specially prepared for Students of the Polytechnic Institute, and suitable for the Use of all Students. (*A List will be sent on application.*)

Portrait Gallery, The Cabinet. *Series I. to IV.,* each containing 36 Cabinet Photographs of Eminent Men and Women of the day. With Biographical Sketches. 15s. each.

Poultry Keeper, The Practical. By LEWIS WRIGHT. Illustrated. 3s. 6d.

Poultry, The Book of. By LEWIS WRIGHT. *Popular Edition.* Illustrated. 10s. 6d.

Poultry, The Illustrated Book of. By LEWIS WRIGHT. With Fifty Exquisite
Coloured Plates, and numerous Wood Engravings. *Revised Edition.* Cloth, 31s. 6d.
Prison Princess, A. A Romance of Millbank Penitentiary. By MAJOR ARTHUR
GRIFFITHS. 6s.
Q's Works, Uniform Edition of. 5s. each.
Dead Man's Rock.
The Splendid Spur.
The Blue Pavilions.
The Astonishing History of Troy Town.
"I Saw Three Ships," and other Winter's Tales.
Noughts and Crosses.
Queen Summer; or, The Tourney of the Lily and the Rose. Penned and
Portrayed by WALTER CRANE. With 40 pages in Colours. 6s.
Queen Victoria, The Life and Times of. By ROBERT WILSON. Complete in
2 Vols. With numerous Illustrations. 9s. each.
Quickening of Caliban, The. A Modern Story of Evolution. By J. COMPTON
RICKETT. 5s.
Rabbit-Keeper, The Practical. By CUNICULUS. Illustrated. 3s. 6d.
Raffles Haw, The Doings of. By A. CONAN DOYLE. *New Edition.* 5s.
Railways, British. Their Passenger Services, Rolling Stock, Locomotives,
Gradients, and Express Speeds. By J. PEARSON PATTINSON. With numerous
Plates. 12s. 6d.
Railways, National. An Argument for State Purchase. By JAMES HOLE. 4s. net.
Railways, Our. Their Development, Enterprise, Incident, and Romance. By
JOHN PENDLETON. Illustrated. 2 Vols., demy 8vo. 24s.
Railway Guides, Official Illustrated. With Illustrations on nearly every page.
Maps, &c. Paper covers, 1s.; cloth, 2s.
Great Eastern Railway.
Great Northern Railway.
Great Western Railway.
London, Brighton, and South Coast Railway.
London and North Western Railway.
London and South Western Railway.
Midland Railway.
South Eastern Railway.
Railway Library, Cassell's. Crown 8vo, boards, 2s. each.
Metzerott, Shoemaker. By Katharine P.
Woods.
David Todd. By David Maclure.
The Admirable Lady Biddy Fane. By
Frank Barrett.
Commodore Junk. By G. Manville Fenn.
St. Cuthbert's Tower. By Florence War-
den.
The Man with a Thumb. By W. C. Hud-
son (Barclay North).
By Right Not Law. By R. Sherard.
Within Sound of the Weir. By Thomas
St. E. Hake.
Under a Strange Mask. By Frank Barrett.
The Coombsberrow Mystery. By J. Colwall.
A Queer Race. By W. Westall.
Captain Trafalgar. By Westall and Laurie.
The Phantom City. By W. Westall.
Jack Gordon, Knight Errant. By W. C.
Hudson (Barclay North).
The Diamond Button: Whose Was It?
By W. C. Hudson (Barclay North).
Another's Crime. By Sidney
The Yoke of the Thorah. By Sidney
Luska.
Who is John Noman? By C. Henry Beckett.
The Tragedy of Brinkwater. By Martha
L. Moodey.
An American Penman. By Julian Haw-
thorne.
Section 558; or, The Fatal Letter. By
Julian Hawthorne.
The Brown Stone Boy. By W. H. Bishop.
A Tragic Mystery. By Julian Hawthorne.
The Great Bank Robbery. By Julian
Hawthorne.
Rivers of Great Britain: Descriptive, Historical, Pictorial.
The Royal River: The Thames from Source to Sea. *Popular Edition,* 16s.
Rivers of the East Coast. With highly-finished Engravings. *Popular Edition,* 16s.
Robinson Crusoe. *Cassell's New Fine-Art Edition.* With upwards of 100
Original Illustrations. 7s. 6d.
Romance, The World of. Illustrated. One Volume, cloth, 9s.
Ronner, Henriette, The Painter of Cat Life and Cat Character. Containing
a Series of beautiful Phototype Illustrations. *Popular Edition,* 4to, 12s.
Rovings of a Restless Boy, The. By KATHARINE B. FOOT. Illustrated. 5s.
Russo-Turkish War, Cassell's History of. With about 500 Illustrations. Two
Vols., 9s. each; library binding, One Vol., 15s.
Salisbury Parliament, A Diary of the. By H. W. LUCY. Illustrated by
HARRY FURNISS. Cloth, 21s.
Saturday Journal, Cassell's. Illustrated throughout. Yearly Volume, 7s. 6d.
Scarabæus. The Story of an African Beetle. By THE MARQUISE CLARA
LANZA and JAMES CLARENCE HARVEY. *Cheap Edition.* 3s. 6d.
Science for All. Edited by Dr. ROBERT BROWN, M.A., F.L.S., &c. *Revised
Edition.* With 1,500 Illustrations. Five Vols. 9s. each.
Shadow of a Song, The. A Novel. By CECIL HARLEY. 5s.
Shaftesbury, The Seventh Earl of, K.G., The Life and Work of. By EDWIN
HODDER. Illustrated. *Cheap Edition,* 3s. 6d.
Shakespeare, Cassell' Quarto Edition. Edited by CHARLES and MARY COWDEN
CLARKE, and containing about 600 Illustrations by H. C. SELOUS. Complete in
Three Vols., cloth gilt, £3 3s.—Also published in Three separate Volumes, in cloth,
viz.:—The COMEDIES, 21s.; The HISTORICAL PLAYS, 18s. 6d.; The TRAGEDIES, 25s.

Shakespeare, Miniature. Illustrated. In Twelve Vols., in box, 12s.; or in Red Paste Grain (box to match), with spring catch, lettered in gold, 21s.

Shakespeare, The Plays of. Edited by Prof. HENRY MORLEY. Complete in Thirteen Vols. Cloth, in box, 21s.; half-morocco, cloth sides, 42s.

Shakspere, The International. *Édition de luxe.*
"King Henry VIII." By Sir JAMES LINTON, P.R.I. *(Price on application.)*
"Othello." Illustrated by FRANK DICKSEE, R.A. £3 10s.
"King Henry IV." Illustrated by Herr EDUARD GRÜTZNER. £3 10s.
"As You Like It." Illustrated by the late Mons. ÉMILE BAYARD. £3 10s.
"Romeo and Juliet." Illustrated by FRANK DICKSEE, R.A. Is now out of print.

Shakspere, The Leopold. With 400 Illustrations, and an Introduction by F. J. FURNIVALL. *Cheap Edition*, 3s. 6d. Cloth gilt, gilt edges, 5s.; roxburgh, 7s. 6d.

Shakspere, The Royal. With Exquisite Steel Plates and Wood Engravings. Three Vols. 15s. each.

Sketches, The Art of Making and Using. From the French of G. FRAIPONT. By CLARA BELL. With Fifty Illustrations. 2s. 6d.

Smuggling Days and Smuggling Ways; or, The Story of a Lost Art. By Commander the Hon. HENRY N. SHORE, R.N. Illustrated. Cloth, 7s. 6d.

Snare of the Fowler, The. By Mrs. ALEXANDER. *Cheap Edition in one Vol.*, 6s.

Social England. A Record of the Progress of the people in Religion, Laws, Learning, Arts, Science, Literature, and Manners, from the Earliest Times to the Present Day. By various writers. Edited by H. D. TRAILL, D.C.L. Vol. I.— From the Earliest Times to the Accession of Edward the First. 15s.

Social Welfare, Subjects of. By LORD PLAYFAIR, K.C.B., &c. 7s. 6d.

Sports and Pastimes, Cassell's Complete Book of. With more than 900 Illustrations. *Cheap Edition*, 3s. 6d.

Squire, The. By MRS. PARR. *Cheap Edition in one Vol.*, 6s.

Star-Land. By Sir ROBERT STAWELL BALL, LL.D., &c. Illustrated. 6s.

Storehouse of General Information, Cassell's. Illustrated. In Vols. 5s. each.

Story of Francis Cludde, The. A Novel. By STANLEY J. WEYMAN. 6s.

Successful Life, The. By AN ELDER BROTHER. 3s. 6d.

Sun, The Story of the. By Sir ROBERT STAWELL BALL, LL.D., F.R.S., F.R.A.S. Illustrated with Eight Coloured Plates. 21s.

Sunshine Series, Cassell's. Monthly Volumes. 1s. each.
The Temptation of Dulce Carruthers. By C. E. C. WEIGALL.
Lady Lorrimer's Scheme and The Story of a Glamour. By EDITH E. CUTHELL.
Womanlike. By FLORENCE M. KING.
On Stronger Wings. By EDITH LISTER.
You'll Love Me Yet. By FRANCES HASWELL; and That Little Woman. By IDA LEMON.

Sybil Knox; or, Home Again. A Story of To-day. By EDWARD E. HALE, Author of "East and West," &c. *Cheap Edition*, 6s.

Tenting on the Plains, or General Custer in Kansas and Texas. By ELIZABETH B. CUSTER, Author of "Boots and Saddles." With Numerous Illustrations. 5s.

Thackeray in America, With. By EYRE CROWE, A.R.A. Illustrated. 10s. 6d.

The "Belle Sauvage" Library. Cloth, 2s. each.

Shirley.	Adventures of Mr. Ledbury.	Old Mortality.
Coningsby.	Ivanhoe.	The Hour and the Man.
Mary Barton.	Oliver Twist.	Washington Irving's Sketch.
The Antiquary.	Selections from Hood's	Book.
Nicholas Nickleby. Two	Works.	Last Days of Palmyra.
Vols.	Longfellow's Prose Works.	Tales of the Borders.
Jane Eyre.	Sense and Sensibility.	Pride and Prejudice.
Wuthering Heights.	Lytton's Plays.	Last of the Mohicans.
The Prairie.	Tales, Poems, and Sketches	Heart of Midlothian.
Dombey and Son. Two Vols.	(Bret Harte).	Last Days of Pompeii.
Night and Morning.	The Prince of the House of	Yellowplush Papers.
Kenilworth.	David.	Handy Andy.
The Ingoldsby Legends.	Sheridan's Plays.	Selected Plays.
Tower of London.	Uncle Tom's Cabin.	American Humour.
The Pioneers.	Deerslayer.	Sketches by Boz.
Charles O'Malley.	Eugene Aram.	Macaulay's Lays and Se-
Barnaby Rudge.	Jack Hinton, the Guards-	lected Essays.
Cakes and Ale.	man.	Harry Lorrequer.
The King's Own.	Rome and the Early Chris-	Old Curiosity Shop.
People I have Met.	tians.	Rienzi.
The Pathfinder.	The Trials of Margaret	The Talisman.
Evelina.	Lyndsay.	Pickwick. Two Vols.
Scott's Poems.	Edgar Allan Poe. Prose and	Scarlet Letter.
Last of the Barons.	Poetry, Selections from.	Martin Chuzzlewit. Two Vols.

The Short Story Library. List of Vols. on application.

Tiny Luttrell. By E. W. HORNUNG. Cloth gilt, 2 Vols. 21s.

"Treasure Island" Series, The. *Cheap Illustrated Edition.* Cloth, 3s. 6d. each.
  "Kidnapp'd." By ROBERT LOUIS STEVENSON.
  Treasure Island. By ROBERT LOUIS STEVENSON.
  The Master of Ballantrae. By ROBERT LOUIS STEVENSON.
  The Black Arrow: A Tale of the Two Roses. By ROBERT LOUIS STEVENSON.
  King Solomon's Mines. By H. RIDER HAGGARD.
Treatment, The Year-Book of, for 1894. A Critical Review for Practitioners of Medicine and Surgery. Tenth Year of Issue. Greatly Enlarged. 500 pages. 7s. 6d.
Tree Painting in Water Colours. By W. H. J. BOOT. With Eighteen Coloured Plates, and valuable instructions by the Artist. 5s.
Trees, Familiar. By Prof. G. S. BOULGER, F.L.S., F.G.S. Two Series. With Forty full-page Coloured Plates by W. H. J. BOOT. 12s. 6d. each.
"Unicode": The Universal Telegraphic Phrase Book. Pocket or Desk Edition. 2s. 6d. each.
United States, Cassell's History of the. By EDMUND OLLIER. With 600 Illustrations. Three Vols. 9s. each.
Universal History, Cassell's Illustrated. With nearly ONE THOUSAND ILLUSTRATIONS. Vol. I. Early and Greek History.—Vol. II. The Roman Period.—Vol. III. The Middle Ages—Vol. IV. Modern History. 9s. each.
Vaccination Vindicated. By JOHN C. McVAIL, M.D., D.P.H. Camb. 5s.
Verses Grave and Gay. By ELLEN THORNEYCROFT FOWLER. 3s. 6d.
Vicar of Wakefield and other Works, by OLIVER GOLDSMITH. Illustrated. 3s. 6d. ; cloth, gilt edges. 5s.
Vision of Saints, A. By LEWIS MORRIS. *Édition de luxe.* With 20 Full-page Illustrations. Crown 4to, extra cloth, gilt edges. 21s.
Water-Colour Painting, A Course of. With Twenty-four Coloured Plates by R. P. LEITCH, and full Instructions to the Pupil. 5s.
Waterloo Letters. Edited by MAJOR-GENERAL H. T. SIBORNE, Late Colonel R E. With Numerous Maps and Plans of the Battlefield. 21s.
Wedlock, Lawful: or, How Shall I Make Sure of a Legal Marriage? By TWO BARRISTERS. 1s.
Wild Birds, Familiar. By W. SWAYSLAND. Four Series. With 40 Coloured Plates in each. 12s. 6d. each.
Wild Flowers, Familiar. By F. E. HULME, F.L.S., F.S.A. Five Series. With 40 Coloured Plates in each. 12s. 6d. each.
Won at the Last Hole. A Golfing Romance. By M. A. STOBART. Illustrated. 1s.6d.
Wood, The Life of the Rev. J. G. By his Son, the Rev. THEODORE WOOD. With Portrait. Extra crown 8vo, cloth. *Cheap Edition.* 5s.
Work. The Illustrated Journal for Mechanics. Vols. II. and III., 7s. 6d. each. Vol. IV., 6s. *New and Enlarged Series.* Vol. V., 4s.
World of Wit and Humour, The. With 400 Illustrations. Cloth, 7s. 6d.
World of Wonders, The. With 400 Illustrations. Two Vols. 7s. 6d. each.
Wrecker, The. By R. L. STEVENSON and LLOYD OSBOURNE. Illustrated. 6s.
Yule Tide. CASSELL'S CHRISTMAS ANNUAL. 1s.
Zero the Slaver. A Romance of Equatorial Africa. By LAWRENCE FLETCHER. 4s.

ILLUSTRATED MAGAZINES.

The Quiver, for Sunday and General Reading. Monthly, 6d.
Cassell's Family Magazine. Monthly, 7d.
"Little Folks" Magazine. Monthly, 6d.
The Magazine of Art. With Three Plates. Monthly, 1s. 4d.
Chums. The Illustrated Paper for Boys. Weekly, 1d.; Monthly, 6d.
Cassell's Saturday Journal. Weekly, 1d. ; Monthly, 6d.
Work. Illustrated Journal for Mechanics. Weekly, 1d.; Monthly, 6d.
Cottage Gardening. Illustrated. Weekly, ½d. ; Monthly, 3d.
⁎⁎ *Full particulars of* CASSELL & COMPANY'S **Monthly Serial Publications** *will be found in* CASSELL & COMPANY'S COMPLETE CATALOGUE.

Catalogues of CASSELL & COMPANY'S PUBLICATIONS, which may be had at all Booksellers', or will be sent post free on application to the Publishers :—
  CASSELL'S COMPLETE CATALOGUE, containing particulars of upwards of One Thousand Volumes.
  CASSELL'S CLASSIFIED CATALOGUE, in which their Works are arranged according to price, from *Threepence to Fifty Guineas.*
  CASSELL'S EDUCATIONAL CATALOGUE, containing particulars of CASSELL & COMPANY'S Educational Works and Students' Manuals.

CASSELL & COMPANY, LIMITED, *Ludgate Hill, London.*

Bibles and Religious Works.

Bible Biographies. Illustrated. 2s. 6d. each.

The Story of Joseph. Its Lessons for To-Day. By the Rev. GEORGE BAINTON.
The Story of Moses and Joshua. By the Rev. J. TELFORD.
The Story of Judges. By the Rev. J. WYCLIFFE GEDGE.
The Story of Samuel and Saul. By the Rev. D. C. TOVEY.
The Story of David. By the Rev. J. WILD.

The Story of Jesus. In Verse. By J. R. MACDUFF, D.D.

Bible, Cassell's Illustrated Family. With 900 Illustrations. Leather, gilt edges, £2 10s. ; full morocco, £3 10s.

Bible, The, and the Holy Land, New Light on. By B. T. A. EVETTS, M.A. Illustrated. Cloth, 21s.

Bible Educator, The. Edited by E. H. PLUMPTRE, D.D. With Illustrations, Maps, &c. Four Vols., cloth, 6s. each.

Bible Student in the British Museum, The. By the Rev. J. G. KITCHIN, M.A. *Entirely New and Revised Edition*, 1s. 4d.

Biblewomen and Nurses. Yearly Volume, 3s.

Bunyan's Pilgrim's Progress (Cassell's Illustrated). 4to. *Cheap Edition*, 3s. 6d.

Child's Bible, The. With 200 Illustrations. Demy 4to, 830 pp. *150th Thousand.* *Cheap Edition*, 7s. 6d. *Superior Edition*, with 6 Coloured Plates, gilt edges, 10s. 6d.

Child's Life of Christ, The. Complete in One Handsome Volume, with about 200 Original Illustrations. *Cheap Edition*, cloth, 7s. 6d. ; or with 6 Coloured Plates, cloth, gilt edges, 10s. 6d. Demy 4to, gilt edges, 21s.

"Come, ye Children." By the Rev. BENJAMIN WAUGH. Illustrated. 5s.

Commentary, The New Testament, for English Readers. Edited by the Rt. Rev. C. J. ELLICOTT, D.D., Lord Bishop of Gloucester and Bristol. In Three Volumes. 21s. each.

Vol. I.—The Four Gospels.
Vol. II.—The Acts. Romans. Corinthians, Galatians.
Vol. III.—The remaining Books of the New Testament.

Commentary, The Old Testament, for English Readers. Edited by the Rt. Rev. C. J. ELLICOTT, D.D., Lord Bishop of Gloucester and Bristol. Complete in 5 Vols. 21s. each.

Vol. I.—Genesis to Numbers.
Vol. II.—Deuteronomy to Samuel II.
Vol. V.—Jeremiah to Malachi.
Vol. III.—Kings I. to Esther.
Vol. IV.—Job to Isaiah.

Commentary, The New Testament. Edited by Bishop ELLICOTT. Handy Volume Edition. Suitable for School and General Use.

St. Matthew. 3s. 6d.	Romans. 2s. 6d.	Titus, Philemon, Hebrews,
St. Mark. 3s.	Corinthians I. and II. 3s.	and James. 3s.
St. Luke. 3s. 6d.	Galatians, Ephesians, and	Peter, Jude, and John. 3s.
St. John. 3s. 6d.	Philippians. 3s.	The Revelation. 3s.
The Acts of the Apostles. 3s. 6d.	Colossians, Thessalonians, and Timothy. 3s.	An Introduction to the New Testament. 2s. 6d.

Commentary, The Old Testament. Edited by Bishop ELLICOTT. Handy Volume Edition. Suitable for School and General Use.

Genesis. 3s. 6d.	Leviticus. 3s.	Deuteronomy. 2s. 6d.
Exodus. 3s.	Numbers. 2s. 6d.	

Dictionary of Religion, The. An Encyclopædia of Christian and other Religious Doctrines, Denominations, Sects, Heresies, Ecclesiastical Terms, History, Biography, &c. &c. By the Rev. WILLIAM BENHAM, B.D. *Cheap Edition*, 10s. 6d.

Doré Bible. With 230 Illustrations by GUSTAVE DORÉ. *Original Edition.* Two Vols., best morocco, gilt edges, £15. *Popular Edition.* With Full-page Illustrations. In One Vol. 15s. Also in leather binding. (*Price on application.*)

Early Days of Christianity, The. By the Ven. Archdeacon FARRAR, D.D., F.R.S. LIBRARY EDITION. Two Vols., 24s. ; morocco, £2 2s. POPULAR EDITION. Complete in One Volume, cloth, 6s. ; cloth, gilt edges, 7s. 6d. ; Persian morocco, 10s. 6d. ; tree-calf, 15s.

Family Prayer-Book, The. Edited by the Rev. Canon GARBETT, M.A., and the Rev. S. MARTIN. Extra crown 4to, cloth, 5s. ; morocco, 18s.

Gleanings after Harvest. Studies and Sketches. By the Rev. JOHN R. VERNON, M.A. Illustrated. 6s.

"Graven in the Rock ;" or, the Historical Accuracy of the Bible confirmed by reference to the Assyrian and Egyptian Sculptures in the British Museum and elsewhere. By the Rev. Dr. SAMUEL KINNS, F.R.A.S., &c. &c. Illustrated. 12s. 6d.

"Heart Chords." A Series of Works by Eminent Divines. Bound in cloth, red edges, 1s. each.

My Father. By the Right Rev. Ashton Oxenden, late Bishop of Montreal.
My Bible. By the Rt. Rev. W. Boyd Carpenter, Bishop of Ripon.
My Work for God. By the Right Rev. Bishop Cotterill.
My Object in Life. By the Ven. Archdeacon Farrar, D.D.
My Aspirations. By the Rev. G. Matheson, D.D.
My Emotional Life. By Preb. Chadwick, D.D.
My Body. By the Rev Prof. W. G. Blaikie, D.D.

My Soul. By the Rev. P. B. Power, M.A.
My Growth in Divine Life. By the Rev. Prebendary Reynolds, M.A.
My Hereafter. By the Very Rev. Dean Bickersteth.
My Walk with God. By the Very Rev. Dean Montgomery.
My Aids to the Divine Life. By the Very Rev. Dean Boyle.
My Sources of Strength. By the Rev. E. E. Jenkins, M.A.

Helps to Belief. A Series of Helpful Manuals on the Religious Difficulties of the Day. Edited by the Rev. Teignmouth Shore, M.A., Canon of Worcester, and Chaplain-in-Ordinary to the Queen. Cloth, 1s. each.

CREATION. By the late Lord Bishop of Carlisle.
MIRACLES. By the Rev. Brownlow Maitland, M.A.
PRAYER. By the Rev. T. Teignmouth Shore, M.A.

THE MORALITY OF THE OLD TESTAMENT. By the Rev. Newman Smyth, D.D.
THE DIVINITY OF OUR LORD. By the Lord Bishop of Derry.

THE ATONEMENT. By William Connor Magee, D.D., Late Archbishop of York.

Hid Treasure. By RICHARD HARRIS HILL. 1s.

Holy Land and the Bible, The. A Book of Scripture Illustrations gathered in Palestine. By the Rev. CUNNINGHAM GEIKIE, D.D., LL.D. (Edin.). With Map. Two Vols. 24s. *Illustrated Edition.* One Vol. 21s.

Life of Christ, The. By the Ven. Archdeacon FARRAR, D.D., F.R.S., Chaplain-in-Ordinary to the Queen.
CHEAP ILLUSTRATED EDITION. Large 4to, cloth, 7s. 6d. Cloth, full gilt, gilt edges, 10s. 6d.
LIBRARY EDITION. Two Vols. Cloth, 24s.; morocco, 42s.
POPULAR EDITION, in One Vol. 8vo, cloth, 6s.; cloth, gilt edges, 7s. 6d.; Persian morocco, gilt edges, 10s. 6d.; tree-calf, 15s.

Marriage Ring, The. By WILLIAM LANDELS, D.D. Bound in white leatherette. *New and Cheaper Edition.* 3s. 6d.

Morning and Evening Prayers for Workhouses and other Institutions. Selected by LOUISA TWINING. 2s.

Moses and Geology; or, the Harmony of the Bible with Science. By the Rev. SAMUEL KINNS, Ph.D., F.R.A.S. Illustrated. Demy 8vo, 8s. 6d.

My Comfort in Sorrow. By HUGH MACMILLAN, D.D., LL.D., &c., Author of "Bible Teachings in Nature," &c. Cloth, 1s.

New Light on the Bible and the Holy Land. By BASIL T. A. EVETTS, M.A. Illustrated. Cloth, 21s.

Old and New Testaments, Plain Introductions to the Books of the. Containing Contributions by many Eminent Divines. In Two Volumes, 3s. 6d. each.

Protestantism, The History of. By the Rev. J. A. WYLIE, LL.D. Containing upwards of 600 Original Illustrations. Three Vols. 27s.; *Library Edition,* 30s.

"Quiver" Yearly Volume, The. With about 600 Original Illustrations and Coloured Frontispiece. 7s. 6d. Also Monthly, 6d.

St. George for England; and other Sermons preached to Children. *Fifth Edition.* By the Rev. T. TEIGNMOUTH SHORE, M.A., Canon of Worcester. 5s.

St. Paul, The Life and Work of. By the Ven. Archdeacon FARRAR, D.D., F.R.S., Chaplain-in-Ordinary to the Queen.
LIBRARY EDITION. Two Vols., cloth, 24s.; calf, 42s.
ILLUSTRATED EDITION, complete in One Volume, with about 300 Illustrations, £1 1s.; morocco, £2 2s.
POPULAR EDITION. One Volume, 8vo, cloth, 6s.; cloth, gilt edges, 7s. 6d.; Persian morocco, 10s. 6d.; tree-calf, 15s.

Shall We Know One Another in Heaven? By the Rt. Rev. J. C. RYLE, D.D., Bishop of Liverpool. *New and Enlarged Edition.* Paper Covers, 6d.

Shortened Church Services and Hymns, suitable for use at Children's Services. Compiled by the Rev. T. TEIGNMOUTH SHORE, M.A., Canon of Worcester. *Enlarged Edition.* 1s.

Signa Christi: Evidences of Christianity set forth in the Person and Work of Christ. By the Rev. JAMES AITCHISON. 5s.

"Sunday:" Its Origin, History, and Present Obligation. By the Ven. Archdeacon HESSEY, D.C.L. *Fifth Edition,* 7s. 6d.

Twilight of Life, The: Words of Counsel and Comfort for the Aged. By JOHN ELLERTON, M.A. 1s. 6d.

Educational Works and Students' Manuals.

Agricultural Text-Books, Cassell's. (The " Downton " Series.) Fully Illustrated. Edited by JOHN WRIGHTSON, Professor of Agriculture. **Soils and Manures.** By J. M. H. Munro, D.Sc. (London), F.I.C., F.C.S. 2s. 6d. **Farm Crops.** By Professor Wrightson, 2s. 6d. **Live Stock.** By Professor Wrightson. 2s. 6d.

Alphabet, Cassell's Pictorial. Mounted on Linen, with rollers. 3s. 6d.

Arithmetic :—Howard's Anglo-American Art of Reckoning. By C. F. HOWARD. Paper, 1s.; cloth, 2s. *Enlarged Edition,* 5s.

Arithmetics, The Modern School. By GEORGE RICKS, B.Sc. Lond. With Test Cards. (*List on application.*)

Atlas, Cassell's Popular. Containing 24 Coloured Maps. 2s. 6d.

Book-Keeping. By THEODORE JONES. FOR SCHOOLS, 2s. ; or cloth, 3s. FOR THE MILLION, 2s. ; or cloth, 3s. Books for Jones's System, Ruled Sets of, 2s.

British Empire Map of the World. New Map for Schools and Institutes. By G. R. PARKIN and J. G. BARTHOLOMEW, F.R.G.S. Mounted on cloth, varnished, and with Rollers. 25s.

Broadacre Farm ; or, Lessons in Our Laws. By H. F. LESTER. Uniform with " Facts from the Furrows." Illustrated. 1s. 6d.

Chemistry, The Public School. By J. H. ANDERSON, M.A. 2s. 6d.

Cookery for Schools. By LIZZIE HERITAGE. 6d.

Dulce Domum. Rhymes and Songs for Children. Edited by JOHN FARMER, Editor of " Gaudeamus," &c. Old Notation and Words, 5s. N.B.—The Words of the Songs in " Dulce Domum " (with the Airs both in Tonic Sol-Fa and Old Notation) can be had in Two Parts, 6d. each.

Energy and Motion : A Text-Book of Elementary Mechanics. By WILLIAM PAICE, M.A. Illustrated. 1s. 6d.

English Literature, A First Sketch of, from the Earliest Period to the Present Time. By Prof. HENRY MORLEY. 7s. 6d.

Euclid, Cassell's. Edited by Prof. WALLACE, M.A. 1s.

Euclid, The First Four Books of. *New Edition.* In paper, 6d. ; cloth, 9d.

Facts from the Furrows, or More Talks at Broadacre Farm. Uniform with " Broadacre Farm." Illustrated. 1s. 6d.

French, Cassell's Lessons in. *New and Revised Edition,* Parts I. and II., each, 2s. 6d. ; complete, 4s. 6d. Key, 1s. 6d.

French-English and English-French Dictionary. *Entirely New and Enlarged Edition.* 1,150 pages, 8vo, cloth, 3s. 6d.

French Reader, Cassell's Public School. By GUILLAUME S. CONRAD. 2s. 6d.

Galbraith and Haughton's Scientific Manuals.

Plane Trigonometry. 2s. 6d. Euclid. Books I., II., III. 2s. 6d. Books IV., V., VI. 2s. 6d. Mathematical Tables. 3s. 6d. Mechanics. 3s. 6d. Natural Philosophy. 3s. 6d. Optics. 2s. 6d. Hydrostatics. 3s. 6d. Steam Engine. 3s. 6d. Algebra. Part I., cloth, 2s. 6d. Complete, 7s. 6d. Tides and Tidal Currents, with Tidal Cards, 3s.

Gaudeamus. Songs for Colleges and Schools. Edited by JOHN FARMER. 5s. Words only, paper, 6d. ; cloth, 9d.

Geometry, First Elements of Experimental. By PAUL BERT. Illustrated. 1s. 6d.

Geometry, Practical Solid. By Major ROSS, R.E. 2s.

German Dictionary, Cassell's New. German-English, English-German. *Cheap Edition,* cloth, 3s. 6d. ; half-roan, 4s. 6d.

German Reading, First Lessons in. By A. JÄGST. Illustrated. 1s.

Hand-and-Eye Training. By G. RICKS, B.Sc. Two Vols., with 16 Coloured Plates in each Vol. Crown 4to, 6s. each.

"Hand-and-Eye Training" Cards for Class Work. Five sets in case. 1s. each.

Historical Cartoons, Cassell's Coloured. Size 45 in. × 35 in. 2s. each. Mounted on canvas and varnished, with rollers, 5s. each. (Descriptive pamphlet, 16 pp., 1d.)

Historical Course for Schools, Cassell's. Illustrated throughout. I.—Stories from English History, 1s. II.—The Simple Outline of English History, 1s. 3d. III.—The Class History of England, 2s. 6d.

Italian Grammar, The Elements of, with Exercises. In One Volume. 3s. 6d.

Latin Dictionary, Cassell's New. (Latin-English and English-Latin.) Revised by J. R. V. MARCHANT, M.A., and J. F. CHARLES, B.A. 3s. 6d.

Latin Primer, The New. By Prof. J. P. POSTGATE. 2s. 6d.

Latin Primer, The First. By Prof. POSTGATE. 1s.

Latin Prose for Lower Forms. By M. A. BAYFIELD, M.A. 2s. 6d.

Laundry Work (How to Teach It). By Mrs. E. LORD. 6d.

Laws of Every-Day Life. For the Use of Schools. By H. O. ARNOLD-FORSTER, M.P. 1s. 6d. *Special Edition* on green paper for those with weak eyesight, 2s.

Little Folks' History of England. By ISA CRAIG-KNOX. Illustrated. 1s. 6d.

Making of the Home, The. By Mrs. SAMUEL A. BARNETT. 1s. 6d.

Marlborough Books:—Arithmetic Examples. 3s. French Exercises. 3s. 6d. French Grammar. 2s. 6d. German Grammar. 3s. 6d.

Mechanics for Young Beginners, A First Book of. By the Rev. J. G. EASTON, M.A. 4s. 6d.

Mechanics and Machine Design, Numerical Examples in Practical. By R. G. BLAINE, M.E. *New Edition, Revised and Enlarged.* With 79 Illustrations. Cloth, 2s. 6d.

Natural History Coloured Wall Sheets, Cassell's New. Consisting of 18 subjects. Size, 39 by 31 in. Mounted on rollers and varnished. 3s. each.

Object Lessons from Nature. By Prof. L. C. MIALL, F.L.S., F.G.S. Fully Illustrated. *New and Enlarged Edition.* Two Vols. 1s. 6d. each; or in One Volume, 3s.

Physiology for Schools. By ALFRED T. SCHOFIELD, M.D., M.R.C.S., &c. Illustrated. 1s. 9d. Three Parts, paper covers, 5d. each; or cloth limp, 6d. each.

Poetry Readers, Cassell's New. Illustrated. 12 Books. 1d. each. Cloth, 1s. 6d.

Popular Educator, Cassell's New. With Revised Text, New Maps, New Coloured Plates, New Type, &c. Complete in Eight Vols., 5s. each; or Eight Volumes in Four, half-morocco, 50s.

Reader, The Citizen. By H. O. ARNOLD-FORSTER, M.P. Cloth, 1s. 6d.; also a Scottish Edition, Cloth, 1s. 6d.

Reader, The Temperance. By Rev. J. DENNIS HIRD. 1s. 6d.

Readers, Cassell's "Higher Class." (*List on application.*)

Readers, Cassell's Readable. Illustrated. (*List on application.*)

Readers for Infant Schools, Coloured. Three Books. 4d. each.

Readers, The Modern Geographical. Illustrated throughout. (*List on application.*)

Readers, The Modern School. Illustrated. (*List on application.*)

Reading and Spelling Book, Cassell's Illustrated. 1s.

Round the Empire. By G. R. PARKIN. With a Preface by the Rt. Hon. the Earl of Rosebery, K.G. Fully Illustrated. 1s. 6d.

School Certificates, Cassell's. Three Colours, 6¼ × 4¾ in., 1d.; Five Colours, 11¾ × 9¼ in., 3d.; Seven Colours and Gold, 9¼ × 6⅞ in., 3d.

Science Applied to Work. By J. A. BOWER. Illustrated. 1s.

Science of Every-Day Life. By J. A. BOWER. Illustrated. 1s.

Sculpture, A Primer of. By E. ROSCOE MULLINS. Illustrated. 2s. 6d.

Shade from Models, Common Objects, and Casts of Ornament, How to. By W. E. SPARKES. With 25 Plates by the Author. 3s.

Shakspere's Plays for School Use. Illustrated. 9 Books. 6d. each.

Spelling, A Complete Manual of. By J. D. MORELL, LL.D. 1s.

Technical Educator, Cassell's New. An entirely New Cyclopædia of Technical Education, with Coloured Plates and Engravings. In Volumes, 5s. each.

Technical Manuals, Cassell's. Illustrated throughout. 16 Vols., from 2s. to 4s. 6d. (*List free on application.*)

Technology, Manuals of. Edited by Prof. AYRTON, F.R.S., and RICHARD WORMELL, D.Sc., M.A. Illustrated throughout.

The Dyeing of Textile Fabrics. By Prof. Hummel. 5s.	Design in Textile Fabrics. By T. R. Ashenhurst. 4s. 6d.
Watch and Clock Making. By D. Glasgow, Vice-President of the British Horological Institute. 4s. 6d.	Spinning Woollen and Worsted. By W. S. McLaren, M.P. 4s. 6d.
	Practical Mechanics. By Prof. Perry, M.E. 3s. 6d.
Steel and Iron. By Prof. W. H. Greenwood, F.C.S., M.I.C.E., &c. 5s.	Cutting Tools Worked by Hand and Machine. By Prof. Smith. 3s. 6d.

Things New and Old; or, Stories from English History. By H. O. ARNOLD-FORSTER, M.P. Fully Illustrated. Strongly bound in Cloth. Standards I. and II., 9d. each; Standard III., 1s.; Standard IV., 1s. 3d.; Standards V., VI., and VII., 1s. 6d. each.

World of Ours, This. By H. O. ARNOLD-FORSTER, M.P. Fully Illustrated. 3s. 6d.

Books for Young People.

"Little Folks" Half-Yearly Volume. Containing 432 pages of Letterpress, with Pictures on nearly every page, together with Two Full-page Plates printed in Colours and Four Tinted Plates. Coloured boards, 3s. 6d. or cloth gilt, gilt edges, 5s.

Bo-Peep. A Book for the Little Ones. With Original Stories and Verses. Illustrated with beautiful Pictures on nearly every page, and Coloured Frontispiece. Yearly Volume. Elegant picture boards, 2s. 6d. ; cloth, 3s. 6d.

The Peep of Day. Cassell's Illustrated Edition. 2s. 6d.

Maggie Steele's Diary. By E. A. DILLWYN. 2s. 6d.

A Sunday Story-Book. By MAGGIE BROWNE, SAM BROWNE, and AUNT ETHEL. Illustrated. 3s. 6d.

A Bundle of Tales. By MAGGIE BROWNE, SAM BROWNE, & AUNT ETHEL. 3s. 6d.

Story Poems for Young and Old. By E. DAVENPORT. 3s. 6d.

Pleasant Work for Busy Fingers. By MAGGIE BROWNE. Illustrated. 5s.

Born a King. By FRANCES and MARY ARNOLD-FORSTER. Illustrated. 1s.

Magic at Home. By Prof. HOFFMAN. Fully Illustrated. A Series of easy and startling Conjuring Tricks for Beginners. Cloth gilt, 5s.

Schoolroom and Home Theatricals. By ARTHUR WAUGH. With Illustrations by H. A. J. MILES. Cloth, 2s. 6d.

Little Mother Bunch. By Mrs. MOLESWORTH. Illustrated. Cloth, 3s. 6d.

Heroes of Every-Day Life. By LAURA LANE. With about 20 Full-page Illustrations. 256 pages, crown 8vo, cloth, 2s. 6d.

Ships, Sailors, and the Sea. By R. J. CORNEWALL-JONES. Illustrated throughout, and containing a Coloured Plate of Naval Flags. *Cheap Edition*, 2s. 6d.

Gift Books for Young People. By Popular Authors. With Four Original Illustrations in each. Cloth gilt, 1s. 6d. each.

The Boy Hunters of Kentucky. By Edward S. Ellis.	Jack Marston's Anchor.
Red Feather: a Tale of the American Frontier. By Edward S. Ellis.	Frank's Life-Battle.
Fritters; or, "It's a Long Lane that has no Turning."	Major Monk's Motto; or, "Look Before you Leap."
Trixy; or, "Those who Live in Glass Houses shouldn't throw Stones."	Tim Thomson's Trial; or, "All is not Gold that Glitters."
The Two Hardcastles.	Ursula's Stumbling-Block.
Seeking a City.	Ruth's Life-Work; or, "No Pains, no Gains."
Rhoda's Reward.	Rags and Rainbows.
	Uncle William's Charge.
	Pretty Pink's Purpose.

"Golden Mottoes" Series, The. Each Book containing 208 pages, with Four full-page Original Illustrations. Crown 8vo, cloth gilt, 2s. each.

"Nil Desperandum." By the Rev. F, Langbridge, M.A.	"Honour is my Guide." By Jeanie Hering (Mrs. Adams-Acton).
"Bear and Forbear." By Sarah Pitt.	"Aim at a Sure End." By Emily Searchfield.
"Foremost if I Can." By Helen Atteridge.	"He Conquers who Endures." By the Author of "May Cunningham's Trial," &c.

"Cross and Crown" Series, The. With Four Illustrations in each Book. Crown 8vo, 256 pages, 2s. 6d. each.

Heroes of the Indian Empire; or, Stories of Valour and Victory. By Ernest Foster.	By Fire and Sword; a Story of the Huguenots. By Thomas Archer.
Through Trial to Triumph; or, "The Royal Way." By Madeline Bonavia Hunt.	Adam Hepburn's Vow; A Tale of Kirk and Covenant. By Annie S. Swan.
In Letters of Flame; A Story of the Waldenses. By C. L. Matéaux.	No. XIII.; or, the Story of the Lost Vestal. A Tale of Early Christian Days. By Emma Marshall.
Strong to Suffer; A Story of the Jews. By E. Wynne.	Freedom's Sword; A Story of the Days of Wallace and Bruce. By Annie S. Swan.

Books for Young People. *Cheap Edition.* With Original Illustrations. Cloth gilt, 3s. 6d. each.

Under Bayard's Banner. By Henry Frith.	Bound by a Spell; or, the Hunted Witch of the Forest. By the Hon. Mrs. Greene.
The Champion of Odin; or, Viking Life in the Days of Old. By J. Fred. Hodgetts.	

Albums for Children. Price 3s. 6d. each.

The Chit-Chat Album. Illustrated.	My Own Album of Animals. Illustrated.
The Album for Home, School, and Play. Set in bold type, and illustrated throughout.	Picture Album of All Sorts. Illustrated.

"Wanted—a King" Series. *Cheap Edition.* Illustrated. 2s. 6d. each.

Robin's Ride. By Ellinor Davenport Adams.	Wanted—a King; or, How Merle set the Nursery Rhymes to Rights. By Maggie Browne.
Great-Grandmamma. By Georgina M. Synge.	
Fairy Tales in Other Lands. By Julia Goddard.	

Crown 8vo Library. *Cheap Editions.* 2s. 6d. each.

Rambles Round London. By C. L. Matéaux. Illustrated.
Around and About Old England. By C. L. Matéaux. Illustrated.
Paws and Claws. By one of the Authors of "Poems Written for a Child." Illustrated.
Decisive Events in History. By Thomas Archer. With Original Illustrations.
The True Robinson Crusoes. Cloth gilt.
Peeps Abroad for Folks at Home. Illustrated throughout.

Wild Adventures in Wild Places. By Dr. Gordon Stables, R.N. Illustrated.
Modern Explorers. By Thomas Frost. Illustrated. *New and Cheaper Edition.*
Early Explorers. By Thomas Frost.
Home Chat with our Young Folks. Illustrated throughout.
Jungle, Peak, and Plain. Illustrated throughout.
The England of Shakespeare. By E. Goadby. With Full-page Illustrations.

Three and Sixpenny Books for Young People. With Original Illustrations. Cloth gilt, 3s. 6d. each.

† Bashful Fifteen. By L. T. MEADE.
The King's Command. A Story for Girls. By Maggie Symington.
† A Sweet Girl Graduate. By L. T. Meade.
† The White House at Inch Gow. By Sarah Pitt.
Lost in Samoa. A Tale of Adventure in the Navigator Islands. By E. S. Ellis.

Tad; or, "Getting Even" with Him. By E. S. Ellis.
† Polly. By L. T. Meade.
† The Palace Beautiful. By L. T. Meade.
"Follow my Leader."
For Fortune and Glory.
† The Cost of a Mistake. By Sarah Pitt.
Lost among White Africans.
† A World of Girls. By L. T. Meade.

Books marked thus † can also be had in extra cloth gilt, gilt edges, 5s. each.

Books by Edward S. Ellis. Illustrated. Cloth, 2s. 6d. each.

The Hunters of the Ozark.
The Camp in the Mountains.
Ned in the Woods. A Tale of Early Days in the West.
Down the Mississippi.

The Last War Trail.
Ned on the River. A Tale of Indian River Warfare.
Footprints in the Forest.
Up the Tapajos.

Ned in the Block House. A Story of Pioneer Life in Kentucky.
The Lost Trail.
Camp-Fire and Wigwam.
Lost in the Wilds.

Sixpenny Story Books. By well-known Writers. All Illustrated.

The Smuggler's Cave.
Little Lizzie.
The Boat Club.
Luke Barnicott.

Little Bird.
Little Pickles.
The Elchester College Boys.

My First Cruise.
The Little Peacemaker.
The Delft Jug.

Cassell's Picture Story Books. Each containing 60 pages. 6d. each.

Little Talks.
Bright Stars.
Nursery Joys.
Pet's Posy.
Tiny Tales.

Daisy's Story Book.
Dot's Story Book.
A Nest of Stories.
Good Night Stories.
Chats for Small Chatterers.

Auntie's Stories.
Birdie's Story Book.
Little Chimes.
A Sheaf of Tales.
Dewdrop Stories.

Illustrated Books for the Little Ones. Containing interesting Stories. All Illustrated. 1s. each; or cloth gilt, 1s. 6d.

Tales Told for Sunday.
Sunday Stories for Small People.
Stories and Pictures for Sunday.
Bible Pictures for Boys and Girls.
Firelight Stories.
Sunlight and Shade.
Rub-a-dub Tales.

Fine Feathers and Fluffy Fur.
Scrambles and Scrapes.
Tittle Tattle Tales.
Dumb Friends.
Indoors and Out.
Some Farm Friends.
Those Golden Sands.
Little Mothers and their Children.

Our Pretty Pets.
Our Schoolday Hours.
Creatures Tame.
Creatures Wild.
Up and Down the Garden.
All Sorts of Adventures.
Our Sunday Stories.
Our Holiday Hours.
Wandering Ways.

Shilling Story Books. All Illustrated, and containing Interesting Stories.

Seventeen Cats.
Bunty and the Boys.
The Heir of Elmdale.
The Mystery at Shoncliff School.
Claimed at Last, and Roy's Reward.
Thorns and Tangles.

The Cuckoo in the Robin's Nest.
John's Mistake.
Diamonds in the Sand.
Surly Bob.
The History of Five Little Pitchers.
The Giant's Cradle.
Shag and Doll.

Aunt Lucia's Locket.
The Magic Mirror.
The Cost of Revenge.
Clever Frank.
Among the Redskins.
The Ferryman of Brill.
Harry Maxwell.
A Banished Monarch.

Eighteenpenny Story Books. All Illustrated throughout.

Wee Willie Winkie.
Ups and Downs of a Donkey's Life.
Three Wee Ulster Lassies.
Up the Ladder.
Dick's Hero; & other Stories.
The Chip Boy.

Raggles, Baggles, and the Emperor.
Roses from Thorns.
Faith's Father.
By Land and Sea.
The Young Berringtons.
Jeff and Leff.

Tom Morris's Error.
Worth more than Gold.
"Through Flood—Through Fire."
The Girl with the Golden Locks.
Stories of the Olden Time.

"Little Folks" Painting Books. With Text, and Outline Illustrations for Water-Colour Painting. 1s. each.

Fruits and Blossoms for "Little Folks" to Paint.
The "Little Folks" Illuminating Book.
The "Little Folks" Book. Cloth only, 2s.
The "Little Folks" Proverb Painting

Library of Wonders. Illustrated Gift-books for Boys. Cloth, 1s. 6d.

Wonderful Adventures.
Wonderful Escapes.
Wonders of Animal Instinct.
Wonderful Balloon Ascents.
Wonders of Bodily Strength and Skill.

The "World in Pictures" Series. Illustrated throughout. 2s. 6d. each.

A Ramble Round France.
All the Russias.
Chats about Germany.
The Land of the Pyramids (Egypt).
Peeps into China.
The Eastern Wonderland (Japan).
Glimpses of South America.
Round Africa.
The Land of Temples (India).
The Isles of the Pacific.

Cheap Editions of Popular Volumes for Young People. Illustrated. 2s. 6d. each.

In Quest of Gold; or, Under the Whanga Falls.
On Board the *Esmeralda*; or, Martin Leigh's Log.
The Romance of Invention: Vignettes from the Annals of Industry and Science.
Esther West.
Three Homes.
For Queen and King.
Working to Win.
Perils Afloat and Brigands Ashore.

Two-Shilling Story Books. All Illustrated.

Stories of the Tower.
Mr. Burke's Nieces.
May Cunningham's Trial.
The Top of the Ladder: How to Reach it.
Little Flotsam.
Madge and her Friends.
The Children of the Court.
Maid Marjory.
The Four Cats of the Tippertons.
Marion's Two Homes.
Little Folks' Sunday Book.
Two Fourpenny Bits.
Poor Nelly.
Tom Heriot.
Aunt Tabitha's Waifs.
In Mischief Again.
Through Peril to Fortune.
Peggy, and other Tales.

Half-Crown Story Books.

Margaret's Enemy.
Pen's Perplexities.
Notable Shipwrecks.
Wonders of Common Things.
At the South Pole.
Truth will Out.
Pictures of School Life and Boyhood.
The Young Man in the Battle of Life. By the Rev. Dr. Landels.
Soldier and Patriot (George Washington).

Cassell's Pictorial Scrap Book. In Six Sectional Volumes. Paper boards, cloth back, 3s. 6d. per Vol.

Our Scrap Book.
The Seaside Scrap Book.
The Little Folks' Scrap Book.
The Magpie Scrap Book.
The Lion Scrap Book.
The Elephant Scrap Book.

Books for the Little Ones. Fully Illustrated.

Rhymes for the Young Folk. By William Allingham. Beautifully Illustrated. 3s. 6d.
The Sunday Scrap Book. With Several Hundred Illustrations. Boards, 3s. 6d.; cloth, gilt edges, 5s.
The History Scrap Book. With nearly 1,000 Engravings. Cloth, 7s. 6d.
Cassell's Robinson Crusoe. With 100 Illustrations. Cloth, 3s. 6d.; gilt edges, 5s.
The Old Fairy Tales. With Original Illustrations. Boards, 1s.; cloth, 1s. 6d.
My Diary. With Twelve Coloured Plates and 366 Woodcuts. 1s.
Cassell's Swiss Family Robinson. Illustrated. Cloth, 3s. 6d.; gilt edges, 5s.

The World's Workers. A Series of New and Original Volumes by Popular Authors. With Portraits printed on a tint as Frontispiece. 1s. each.

John Cassell. By G. Holden Pike.
Charles Haddon Spurgeon. By G. Holden Pike.
Dr. Arnold of Rugby. By Rose E. Selfe.
The Earl of Shaftesbury.
Sarah Robinson, Agnes Weston, and Mrs. Meredith.
Thomas A. Edison and Samuel F. B. Morse.
Mrs. Somerville and Mary Carpenter.
General Gordon.
Charles Dickens.
Florence Nightingale, Catherine Marsh, Frances Ridley Havergal, Mrs. Ranyard ("L. N. R.").
Dr. Guthrie, Father Mathew, Elihu Burritt, Joseph Livesey.
Sir Henry Havelock and Colin Campbell Lord Clyde.
Abraham Lincoln.
David Livingstone.
George Muller and Andrew Reed.
Richard Cobden.
Benjamin Franklin.
Handel.
Turner the Artist.
George and Robert Stephenson.
Sir Titus Salt and George Moore.

⁂ The above Works can also be had Three in One Vol., cloth, gilt edges, 3s.

CASSELL & COMPANY, Limited, Ludgate Hill, London; Paris & Melbourne.

www.ingramcontent.com/pod-product-compliance
Lightning Source LLC
Chambersburg PA
CBHW030952110726
47900CB00004B/1233